(1)

THE PAST IS ANOTHER COUNTRY

Peter Wludyka

SIMON AND SCHUSTER

*New York   London   Toronto
Sydney   Tokyo*

cop. 1

SIMON AND SCHUSTER
Simon & Schuster Building
Rockefeller Center
1230 Avenue of the Americas
New York, New York 10020

Copyright © 1988 by Peter Wludyka

SIMON AND SCHUSTER and colophon are registered trademarks
of Simon & Schuster Inc.

Designed by Jeanne Joudry
Manufactured in the United States of America

10 9 8 7 6 5 4 3 2 1

Library of Congress Cataloging in Publication data

Wludyka, Peter.
  The past is another country.
  I. Title.
PS3573.L84P37 1988   813'.54   88-11382
ISBN 0-671-65253-2

For E & A, and Scott—whose support made this possible

It was a time of yearning for peace. Oh, there was exhaustion. A kind of fatigue that accumulates from decades of tension. But, more than anything, there was that yearning, that overwhelming yearning, that, like the yearning of a mother for a lost child, is so blind to truth or reason or prudence that nothing can prevent the release of the scream of recognition and joy the mother expels at sighting the child. No matter if the child is not really hers; no matter if it is all a mistake or deception. It was a scream that could be heard around the world.

—Gustavus Roman
The Plot to Kill Paul Creticos

Chapter

1

"Alexander Mikhailovich, are you still with us?"

That was one of Brownsky's most embarrassing affectations: being very formal and Russian. As if someone could mistake him for a true Russian.

"Yes, Mr. Brownsky."

Craning forward like a cantankerous young bird which has just spotted its first worm, "What is that in your notebook?"

Feigning innocence, Alex looked up over the binder that rose at a forty-five-degree angle from his diaphragm. Without releasing Brownsky's eyes, he slid The Book deep into the binder. Odd, he had from the beginning called it The Book. Even though on the first page, in pen, someone had written: *The Plot to Kill Paul Creticos.*

What a title. Right from the start you could tell it was a mystery. And they were very hard to find. The Party frowned upon mysteries. Oh, from time to time one appeared on television. But they weren't real mysteries. Not like the ones in books.

"Well?"

Trying to push The Book from his mind, "Nothing, sir." He let the large-ringed spiral binder down slowly until it rested flat on the desk.

"Nothing, Alexander Mikhailovich?"

Again. Wasn't once enough? Alex could feel his cheeks begin to sizzle. Why was Brownsky such an embarrassment? And only to him. Everyone else just laughed. Even Goodwin and Planov. After all, they were Americans. If anyone was going to find him an embarrassment it should be them.

"Stand, please."

He obeyed, making sure not to draw attention to the notebook by touching it.

Approaching, "Nothing?"

"Ah," he struggled. His embarrassment was quickly being devoured by fear. He tried to think.

"Nothing?"

"I was glancing over my calculus notes, sir," he blurted out.

"Calculus?" Brownsky mimicked, with pretended awe.

The open spiral notebook fluttered in the breeze. He wanted to restrain it, to reach down with his open hand and stop the pages from turning, but his hands were as heavy as bowling balls.

"Calculus. Such an . . . elegant subject."

Alex could feel his head inflating. He should have turned it over to the authorities. Yes. He should have done that immediately. Or left it where it was. That was exactly what he should have done. He should have left it right where he had found it.

"In here, Alexander Mikhailovich," he came one step closer, "we sacrifice elegance for truth. Real truth. We study history." With a curt, military turn Brownsky marched back to the lectern.

That was close. He would have to turn it over to his father that afternoon. But his father would want to know why he had kept it overnight. He would want to know if he had read any of it. It had only been a page or two. No more than that, really.

Quite formally, "Alexander Nurov."

The pages of the notebook had stopped fluttering. All along they had been singing away like a loony mockingbird, "Here's The Book! Here's The Book!" Now there was only silence. Alex tried to look down without lowering his eyes. Only a blur. Was it just sitting there exposed?

"Are you going to stand there all day?"

A murmur of laughter leaked from the class. Brownsky clamped it off with a single bony rap on his wooden perch.

"No, sir." Melting into the desk like licorice in a warm palm, "Thank you, sir."

"No need to thank me," he replied with exaggerated humility. "It is the State's time you have squandered. Perhaps you will be more appreciative after writing a paper on class oppression in America before the Glorious Uprising."

10

Alex slid his fingers across the bulge in his calculus notes before folding his hands on top of the invisible book.

"Five pages."

The fear had completely vanished. "Yes, sir," he replied automatically. Suddenly, in fact, he felt just fine. Not relaxed. No. There was a pleasant tinge of excitement. Not just from having escaped detection. There was more to it than mere relief. It was that it was there. A book. Right there under his calmly folded hands. Better yet, a mystery book. And not one of them had any idea it was there. That was a new and very nice feeling. Of course, you could spend a year in a reeducation center for possession of an unauthorized book. Not that that would happen to him. But he had heard of cases where that had been done. Or worse. People had gotten their heads opened up. No. That was too extreme. The authorities were fairer than that. That would only be done when someone was loony beyond any shadow of a doubt.

"Are we ready?" Mr. Brownsky cleared his throat. "Alexander Mikhailovich, are we ready?" He looked at Alex with a mixture of sadness and disbelief.

"Yes, sir." He flipped over to a blank sheet of paper and picked up his pen.

"This daydreaming is not the kind of behavior they are accustomed to at Moscow University," he offered gravely. "But then they are not accustomed to . . ." he began, before stopping himself. Brownsky squinted for a moment as if he were trying to overcome his near-sightedness long enough to study Alex's reaction.

Alex looked up noncommittally.

"The time of the Great Uprising, that's where we were, weren't we." Brownsky fumbled around with his notes for a second. Clearly his little slip, or near slip, had disturbed him. Alex surveyed the room: no one seemed to have noticed. "Yes. The Great and Glorious Uprising." Looking down at the lectern, "And when did that occur, Alexander Mikhailovich?"

He responded without a moment's thought. He had heard it all a thousand times.

Alex half listened, half remembered, while Brownsky droned on. At one point it seemed that something new—well, if not new, at least slightly different—had been added. In fact, he was sure of it.

That might be worth making note of, he decided.

As was his habit, a few seconds before the bell Brownsky closed his notes and said, "Enjoy your lunch, comrades." Apparently recovered from his earlier attack of uncertainty, he added, "Be prepared to read your paper in class tomorrow, Alexander Mikhailovich."

"Yes, Mr. Brownsky," he replied on his way by, intent only upon escaping.

Without making eye contact, "That's five pages."

"Yes, Mr. Brownsky. Five pages."

After a moment Brownsky looked up. There it was, that same inquisitive, slightly disdainful look that had accompanied his reference to Moscow University. Alex had seen it from the moment his acceptance had been announced. A kind of cautious disbelief. And not just Brownsky. Why, Gregorov still cocked his head to one side when Alex approached, tilting it as if to say, "I know I didn't hear that right. No. A Russamsky at Moscow University? No. I must have heard that wrong."

He waited, poised to burst through the door.

"Enjoy your lunch, Alexander Mikhailovich."

He stepped onto the black, smooth-as-fresh-ice hallway and took a deep breath. Damn. They were already going down the stairs. He skated after them, past the huge, toothy face of Patrice Lumumba. Don't run, he reminded himself. Serving as a bizarre street sign, Che's three-feet-across, defiant jaw pointed toward the stairwell. He skidded to a stop and, collecting three stairs at a time, descended into a cloud of cabbage soup.

Anna Kopenskaya was leaning against the cafeteria door, chummily face to face with Boris Karpov. What did they find to talk about? And always touching. Something was always touching.

"Really, Alex," she exclaimed, as he ducked under the arm which hung loosely against Boris's hip.

Without looking back, "I think your hand's taking root, Comrade Kopenskaya."

"Don't be disgusting, Alex."

His seat was still vacant. There had been no need to hurry. Almost everyone was seated and eating. All in their usual places away from the windows. The Americans, Goodwin and Planov (What had that been? Nothing came to mind) were the only ones within arm's reach

12

of sunlight. And that was an accident. They moved about like a pair of gypsies: first one table, then another. But the rest were as predictable as watches. He started to put his notebook on his tray. No. He walked back to the shelves near the door and wedged it into an unoccupied cubicle. No point in arousing interest. He tried to relax. He let his eyes roam over the food: cold sandwiches and soup. No fruit again. The woman behind the counter lifted a bowl and ladled the soup. Why were they so damned slow?

"I don't have all day," he blurted out in Russian.

She spilled a little of the soup, which trickled down the bowl onto her big, ruddy hand.

Accepting the soup, "Thank you."

She took forever to assemble the sandwich. It never paid to be impatient. They'd fuck you every time.

"Thank you." Making amends, "Looks good today. I could smell the soup halfway up the stairs."

She licked the back of her hand.

A narrow, irregular channel banked by back-to-back metal folding chairs led to the windows. He waded in, avoiding the furry, eating heads that popped up like water lilies. Midway he encountered Gregorov. Unlike the others his hair was neatly trimmed—and glistening with oil. Alex tried to squeeze quietly past the back of his chair, but Gregorov arrested him with, "Ah, Nurov. The mathematician. Looks like Brown," he carefully enunciated the name as he leaned forward and rotated his shiny black head, "was a little out of sorts today."

With the tray between them, "If you say so."

"Oh, I do. I do." He paused to stroke his cropped black hair with his fingertips. "But, in the future," he turned toward the others in his group, "let's not slight the queen of the sciences." There was subdued laughter.

Alex continued with his tray held up at his shoulders.

"The queen of the sciences. That would be," he paused, "history, wouldn't you agree, Comrade Nurov?"

"You're quite right." Gregorov was a block commander. It paid to be careful around him. "I'll remember that, Comrade Gregorov."

Light chuckles evaporated behind him.

Finally. He put down the tray and adjusted the blinds. Damn. He was too late: the field was empty. He picked up the sandwich before

13

returning his eyes to the playing field. First Brownsky. Then Gregorov. The little policeman. So he was a true Russian. So what. His father was only a naval officer. Not even an admiral.

Alex peered into the vacant, grassy field.

Suddenly he heard it whiz by. Or could he? The window was shut. Before he could decide, it was vibrating in the ground like a pounded-out spring. He watched her trot out and extract it. Sweat was running down the inside of her thigh, circling around the ridge of tendon that ran from just above her knee to an invisible conjunction in her bright red shorts. He watched the muscle vanish into the shadowy recesses of those red shorts as she bent to yank the javelin from the ground.

"Track and field. I thought basketball was your event, Alex." Myslov. Apparently he felt some sense of kinship. Didn't he know that Moscow University had fifty thousand students? This sudden attack of friendship seemed so damned forced. No, not forced; just . . . he couldn't make up his mind what it was.

"How about a quick game?"

"Ah, I don't know." She began to run, at first slowly, the javelin bouncing up and down with her.

"We have twenty minutes."

Then faster. When she hurled the javelin her entire body snapped, toe and fingertip at maximum separation. Again he could almost hear it whizzing by. For an instant, transfixed, it glistened in the sunlight like a wingless, metallic dragonfly before buzzing off to the far side of the field.

"What do you think?"

She vanished after it.

Distractedly, "No. I have some work to do."

Hesitating, "Well, if you'd rather not." Alex looked up. The chess set was tucked under Myslov's arm; he looked a little silly, waiting. And sad. But looking sad was Myslov's occupation. You never really wanted him there, but, on the other hand, it was hard to muster up the meanness to send him off.

"Go ahead and set them up."

Did Myslov almost smile? No, not really. There was that ever-present, meaningless half-smile that in someone else might have intended to please but in Myslov only helped sell the sadness. "Thank

14

you. We want to be as sharp as possible for next year. With the lack of competition it will take a lot of work." Unctuously, "Except for you, of course." After pausing to open the box, he remarked, in as convincing a way as he could, "It will be important for us to make a good showing."

He peered at the empty field while Myslov set up the pieces. That had probably been her last throw of the day.

After the game, in a voice as close to critical as one could expect from Myslov, he said, "You seemed a little distracted today, Alex. You seem to forget how important it will be for us to, well, make a good showing." With his head cocked to one side, "You don't seem to be concerned about that at all."

"Relax, Myslov." Ominously, while rising from his chair, "You'll probably get pneumonia and die this winter anyway."

Putting his hand to his throat as if there were a leak in his sweater, "That's not very humorous, Alex."

He strolled over to the shelves to retrieve his books.

"It wasn't, you know."

It was impossible to be relaxed about Moscow University around Myslov. He consumed worry as other people do beer and sandwiches. It was nearly a year away. If Myslov kept that up they would both be a wreck by then.

Calculus was devoted to Martina Antipova's red shorts. And that fine line of sweat perpetually racing down her leg. Every time Morgan turned to write on the board the line of sweat began its descent: Alex watched it caress the long guitar string of tendon that stretched the length of her inner thigh. But by late afternoon the image that had once been so powerful was as dead as an old photograph. Even the purr of the electric bus, which usually evoked drowsy images of her athletic thighs, failed to do its usual magic. In fact, the ride wasn't making him sleepy at all.

It was The Book. At first it had been only a question of what was in it. Now there was the question of what to do with it.

It would be absurd to try to keep it. Absurd. Even though mysteries were so damned hard to come by and the only ones he had were wrecks, the pages almost dissolved from use. And this one looked like a real mystery. *The Plot to Kill Paul Creticos.* That had a ring to it that just wasn't there in authorized works. At least, he assumed that

15

The Book was not authorized. It certainly didn't look like it. The paper was strange. Slippery. And the title had been added in long-hand. No. That didn't sound authorized at all. And that made it dangerous. In fact, just getting rid of it would be dangerous. And it seemed obvious that the longer he kept it the greater the danger would be.

That damned Brownsky (or Brown, as the true Russians called him behind his back, disdainfully enlarging the big, round o in his name to comic proportions) had made sure that he wouldn't have a moment to look at it today. Five pages. On that old dead stuff. The Great Uprising. Every schoolboy knew it by heart. It seemed to grow every year. The words got a little longer. But it was same. For that reason he would have to be careful to use only the most authoritative sources. That was the key. Especially if he was going to have to read it in class. Only the most authoritative sources would do.

That was the kind of thing his father would know about. But that might raise the awkward question "Why?" There was no point in getting into that.

The window framed the faded green marsh. Decayed, bird-covered pilings dotted the near bank of the inland waterway. Remnants of primitive stilt houses left by a vanished tribe. He used to navigate among them in his rubber raft, half hidden in the marsh grass, lip-stick lines drawn across his nose.

It was still summer really.

He tried to imagine what it would be like next year in Moscow. All he could see was sad, perpetually cold Myslov shivering on Nevsky Prospect. He rested his head against the window and let the sunlight shine into his face. He could feel it warming his air-conditioned skin. He laughed. Would he be the mirror image of the visiting Russians who secluded themselves in their air-conditioned Zlotnys fearful that the Charleston sun would scar their pink skin? No. He was, as his mother so often reminded him, "both Russian and American. Perhaps a little more Russian. But still both." Perhaps a lot more Russian, when he thought about it. And why not? There was no point in being anything else. But he was sure he would miss the beautiful Indian summers that lingered over the island through October.

And he would be coming back. At least for the summers. Unless his father was recalled. But could that really happen? After all this time? It had been years since he had allowed himself even to think that. But it could be that his being accepted was a sign that something like that was being considered. If that was the case it would be important to make just the right impression. Damn! He was starting to sound like Myslov!

The humming had stopped. With a nearly imperceptible nod to the bus's American driver he jumped onto the sandy roadside and, the binder pressed tightly to his chest so that The Book was in no danger of falling out, bounded up the road to the house.

As soon as he pushed open the door he knew there was no one there. Corinne would have been singing, at least until she heard the door shut. And his mother's afternoon scent was missing. Had she arrived early, a vivid gardenia trail would have led across the living room into the hallway leading to her room. Perhaps she was staying late at the clinic.

Partly to be sure, he strolled down the hall to his mother's door.

Rapping lightly, "Mother?"

It wasn't like her to leave the door ajar. Or Corinne either.

He eased it open.

In the soft, gauze-curtain-filtered light the four-poster bed seemed forever away from the windows. The only other objects, a dresser and chest, hugged the wall like faraway islands.

He advanced as far as the dresser and stopped. Its only ornament was a sterling-framed photograph of Sonia Ouspenskaya. He ran his finger along the smooth dresser top, back and forth, a few centimeters in front of the photograph.

He felt a little uncomfortable looking at it. Odd, it was the only likeness of her he had ever seen. There were pictures of the General Secretary everywhere. There was even one on the dining-room wall. But you didn't see pictures of his sister. Even though you heard her name from time to time.

And there were no others in the house. Not even in his father's room. Where you might expect one. Especially considering his father's parents—there were no pictures of them either. Perhaps the memory was too painful? —they had vanished in the Urals (the small plane they were in was just never seen again) twenty years ago, leaving Sonia Ouspenskaya as his father's closest living relative. Yes. You might expect—

He heard a noise. But when he got out to the living room he

17

realized that it had just been a Zlotny passing by. Or his imagination. He could still feel his heart pounding.

He was going to have to do something about The Book. Before he gave himself a heart attack.

He switched on the television and sat down on the carpet with the binder resting on his crossed legs. The only place to take it was the dune. And then only for a day or two.

Leaving the television blaring, he went back to his bedroom, exchanged his school jumpsuit for shorts, and, after a moment's deliberation, dropped The Book into a black plastic garbage bag he fetched from the pantry. The dune was the only place for it, he repeated to himself, as he raced across the back porch onto the wooden walkway that traversed the sticker-infested passes between the small dunes protecting the house from the surf. The only large dune on the island, old and avocado-topped, was clearly visible for several kilometers as it posed for the island's only other landmark, a long-abandoned, unblinking lighthouse that tilted toward it with gentlemanly deference from the southern tip of the island.

Squatting on the last slat of the walkway, Alex removed his sneakers, tied the laces together in a bow, and looped them over his neck. He could feel the shoes bounce against his chest as he walked, reminding him not to move too quickly. To be convincing, he stooped from time to time, examined a shell, and discarded it. There was no doubt that he looked exactly like any other afternoon shell gatherer.

"Well, Nurov, I expected you to—" Gregorov paused, as was his habit, in midsentence.

"Gregorov," he blurted. Or had he? Perhaps he had just sounded startled to himself. The damned bicycle hadn't made a sound.

Brushing into his hair the sweat that had accumulated on his forehead, "—be hard at work on your essay."

"I thought I might wait until my father gets home." While bending to examine and then discard a shell, "He has access to the most up-to-date and authoritative sources."

Clearly taken aback, "Yes, I'm sure he does."

"That is," already regretting lying, "if he gets back from the Ministry early enough."

"Well, I'm sure any advice Vice-Minister Nurov has to offer will be helpful." Gregorov had said that with what seemed to be genuine admiration. After a moment, he offered, "Found any good ones?"

"Oh," looking down intently, "no. Today hasn't been much of a day."

"Nothing exciting, then?"

"No."

"Too bad." Hot dew drops began to reassemble on Gregorov's forehead. "There are a lot more later in the year, wouldn't you say? When it's cooler."

"Yes, I think you're right."

"I think I've heard that somewhere." Sitting erect on the bicycle seat, "Well, good luck with your essay. I know things like that can be—" He paused characteristically. "Can be trying." Was there a note of real sympathy in Gregorov's voice? No matter. It paid to be careful. Especially with a block commander.

"Enjoy your ride, Comrade Gregorov."

"Thank you." He followed the contour of the waterline, where the sand was hard and wet, awkwardly adjusting the handlebars each meter or two so that the smooth water's edge was approximated by a series of short, straight lines. After fifty meters or so he stopped and reached down into the water to extract something. Still astride the bike, his right foot planted firmly on the pedal to avoid the water, he rinsed his find in the next wave before holding it up toward Alex. "This is a very nice one." Not as loudly, "Would it fit into your collection?" He waited for Alex to reach him. "See? It's a rather nice one, isn't it?"

"Yes."

Extending the shell, "For . . . your collection." After a moment, "It is rather nice, don't you think?"

Alex shifted the black garbage bag to his right hand.

"I'm," pausing, but a little differently than usual, perhaps with mild embarrassment, "not much of a nature buff. Oh, I'm fond enough of the outdoors. I mean, I love to get out in it, but I'm not much of a collector."

Reluctantly accepting the gift, "Thank you." Right away he continued, "It's very nice," before appending, "Anton."

"Yes." Positioning himself to pedal off, "I hope it fits nicely into your collection."

"It will." He looked down at Gregorov's find, hoping that he would take that opportunity to continue his excursion.

Convivially, "What do you call that?"

"It's a sand dollar," Alex replied without reflection.

Distantly, "Really? That must be an Old Name."

"I," regrouping, "guess you're right. Or perhaps," he stopped to think, "well, who knows." Alex smiled with as much unconcern as he could muster.

"Things like that are," Gregorov made him wait while he searched for just the right words, "sometimes hard to root out."

He could feel himself being examined. After bouncing it in his hand a couple of times, while offering conversationally, "It pays to be careful with shells like this. They're very delicate, you know," he inserted the sand dollar in the plastic bag on top of The Book.

"Yes, I imagine so, Comrade Nurov," was Gregorov's crisp reply before pedaling off.

"Old Name," Alex repeated to himself with a mixture of disdain and anger. That was sheer invention. Oh, from time to time it was mentioned by television commentators. There was something of a Party position on it, or at least there appeared to be. But nothing official. Gregorov had acted as if it were a crime to use an Old Name—and who's to say that he had used one at all? Had he ever heard them called anything else? Gregorov the policeman. It was maddening the way he always pretended to be so sure of himself. Especially about things like that. And he never, given the opportunity, failed to make some back-door allusion to Alex's mother: that was clearly what he was up to. Well, the way he'd handled it must have been a disappointment to Gregorov, he decided proudly before renewing his pretense of looking for shells.

About a hundred meters south of the dune, Alex sat down on a washed-up palmetto trunk. Why hadn't that damned Gregorov come back by yet? he wondered, massaging the bleached, crusty surface of the old log with his palm. He couldn't have gone much farther. After the beach disappeared around the point it abruptly turned into marsh. Since the road didn't go this far north, Gregorov would have to pedal right past the dune. Damn! He couldn't wait all day for Gregorov to jack off. That was certainly what the oily son of a bitch was doing: jacking off. Unless, of course, that was an Old Name.

He had been excavating the log for five minutes with his foot before realizing it. Funny, it had been there no more than a week and it was half covered; in another week it would be gone completely. Anybody who walked by would have no idea it was even there. Unless a big storm unearthed it. And they never seemed to hit here. Not really big ones. Still, every year, there was a mock evacuation of the island. The authorities always worried about things like that. Disasters that would probably never occur. Every year, he found himself almost hoping, in the back of his mind, that one would slam right into them. Not one that would injure anyone. Not seriously. Just a nice, exciting storm that would blow the tiles off the roofs and unearth a few old stumps.

Sometimes he thought he could remember wishing, years ago, that a fierce, unstoppable storm would blow all the Russians out to sea, leaving only himself and his mother free to roam the island as they pleased. But that, if he had ever wished it at all, had been a long time ago, when he hadn't known any better.

He stood and looked at the dune.

"Are you going to jack off all day, Gregorov?"

He picked up the plastic bag.

Loudly, "I said, are you going to jack off all day," before screaming, "Gregorov!"

He sat back down and stared at the bend in the beach. Well, if Gregorov couldn't hear he couldn't see, he concluded. Unless he was just watching. But there was no reason for him to do that. No reason at all. Alex had done nothing to arouse suspicion. Nothing at all. Of course, it was a block commander's job to be vigilant. And Gregorov was, if nothing else, conscientious.

He decided to wait five more minutes: one hundred and thirty-two waves sputtered up to the beach to die.

Gregorov must have jacked off to death.

He casually removed himself to the first row of small dunes, where he stretched out on his belly behind a clump of sea oats before counting another one hundred waves as they vanished into the beach. When Gregorov pedaled by he would just conclude that Alex had gone home for supper. There would be no reason to think anything else.

He rolled down into the gully that separated the dune he had been on from its neighbors and circled to the far side of the big one before ascending its western slope. At the crest he sat, pulled a sticker from

21

his foot, and slipped on his shoes. The twenty-meter white volcano lorded it over the barrier island like an ancient, extinct god. He walked along the inside of the soft rim, concealing himself in the cool green lava that proudly gushed out of the bowels of the huge sand dune.

The entire island was visible. As far south as the old lighthouse the oleander was alive with row after row of rooftop solar panels that glistened as brightly as one of his mother's necklaces. North, the beach transformed abruptly into marsh as it veered into the inland waterway.

Still no Gregorov.

He collapsed comfortably into the sand. The three water oaks, his ancient Greek wrestlers, were still going at it, arms and legs entwined, encircling one another, indistinguishable. Playing the plutocrat, he clapped his hands crisply before tilting his head back and aristocratically ordering, "To the death, slaves." He had watched them fight to the death a thousand times. Grimly, inflating his cheeks (all plutocrats were fat), he inverted his thumb before half sliding and half walking to the cool bottom of the dune.

Sitting, his back against one of the oaks, he opened the black bag and pulled out the sand dollar. The damned thing was still wet. He sailed it backhanded into the soft wall of the dune before removing The Book. The plain brown cover had a spot on it. He mopped it dry with his shirttail.

The Plot to Kill Paul Creticos was written in longhand at the top of the first page. Below the title, near a large, jagged black spot, "Gustavus Roman" had been penciled. What a strange name, he remarked to himself while experiencing a jolt of anticipation. The rest was typed on funny, slick paper which, if you examined it very carefully, had faint lines across it resembling those on notebook paper. But it wasn't notebook paper. It was too smooth. And the lines were too faint.

WHY?

Why did I do it? That's what you are asking, isn't it? Why did I shoot the most beloved, most universally adored man of my age? Ah, ask me if I am Starbuck and I will reply, "Yes. I think so." And was he Ahab? "Oh, yes. And more." But which Ahab?

Or was I Ahab and he the whale, white and beautiful?

Yes, beautiful. The most beautiful man I have ever seen.

And I . . .? Well, as two hundred million of you have seen, I am as ugly as hell.

And perhaps it was all one of hell's tricks to juxtapose us—the grotesque, the oh so beautiful.

But why this book? Not, of course, to plead innocence. Not with two hundred million witnesses!

The purpose behind this chronicle is to reveal the truth. "The truth?" you say. "The papers and television screens have been bursting with the truth." To that I respond that you have seen nothing, read nothing, but news. Here is an opportunity for you to see through my eyes. To feel what I felt. To touch what I touched. Just, as best I can reconstruct it, as it occurred.

So be prepared. My concern, common to all those who serve in the army of Jesus Christ, is the truth. And that, friend, is often as ugly as I am.

Alex turned back to the first page. *"The Plot to Kill Paul Creticos,"* he repeated softly. It didn't seem to make much sense at all. And right off the bat you knew who did it. What kind of mystery started off like that? And who was this Jesus Christ? A general?

THE BEGINNING

I was transferred from Poland, my mother church and home, because another period of reconciliation with the authorities was under way. And I was an embarrassment. Oh, nothing like that was ever said. After all, I was now Monsignor Piotr Babulieski. I was, as Cardinal Rudolfo put it, no longer just a foot soldier in the army of Christ.

But I rather preferred being plain Father Piotr, especially if it allowed me to be on the cutting edge of the great conflict of our times. But we all know how diplomats think: if we present a new face the tyrant will change his tune. Later, when that tired policy failed

23

again, they would want my kind. The ones who were willing to serve Christ in the cellar of the Gdansk police station. Funny how infrequently one runs into members of the diplomatic curia in places like that.

Suffice it to say that the sight of the hunchbacked priest would glaringly contradict the hopes of those who wished accommodation with the authorities. Better to let everyone dream. He could wake them up with his ugliness later. When they were again ready to face the truth the old hunchback would be trotted out. Of that I was confident.

Still, I argued as best I could against the change. But in the Church there is finally only obedience. And besides, I knew, in the depths of my heart, that God had great plans for me. Why else would He have made me the way he had? My time would come.

In the meantime I had a new if less exciting mission. I was to assist one Father Paul Creticos and "to report to the curia as I saw fit regarding the progress of his momentous mission." Momentous? Please understand, I, as much as anyone, wished to rid the world of the means of its own destruction. But the mission of Father Paul was, well, a bubble on the crest of a tiny wave pretending to be a fierce storm.

The first time I saw him he was in the lobby of the New York Hilton. A strange place for a servant of Christ to be ministering to his flock, I thought as I passed through the revolving door. Not that I am completely opposed to displays of wealth; after all, I had just spent two months in the majesty of the Vatican waiting for Cardinal Rudolfo to find just the right place for me. It was the shininess, I think, that offended me. The seductive, just-paid-for look that screamed of ongoing exploitation.

He was in the center of about twenty or thirty people, hidden by them, so that I approached only out of curiosity. This was, after all, my first trip to America; certainly my first encounter with New York City. I didn't know what to expect. It crossed my mind—I can clearly remember being struck by a moment of fear—that a mugging or rape or some other act of violence peculiar to America was being committed.

His back was to me. In fact, I knew only that the man was a priest. He was writing on a young girl's T-shirt, just above her breasts.

24

"NØ," it screamed out in bold, jagged red that resembled a sign forbidding smoking on an airplane. He half turned toward me to write the same thing on another girl's forehead. No more than seventeen, she was pressing her lips so tightly together you would think she was getting an inoculation.

This would have to be reported to the curia. It was the kind of thing one would expect from a rock-and-roll star. And his groupies. Not a representative of the Church. Did they know in Rome that this was going on? Probably not.

On the other hand, they might have been aware that something was amiss. Why else would they have sent me? Perhaps the benefit of my experience was what they had in mind. Perhaps just taking the young priest aside (I can remember when I was too impetuous) would be all it would take. After striking through the O in "NO," he kissed the top of her head. I remember being struck by the kiss: it was clearly the act of a priest ministering to his flock. I was almost envious. It was so natural, so simple. Opposition, righteousness—they were the hallmarks of my ministry. Oh, the foundation was love. Surely. I could feel it in my heart. But it didn't flow from my lips as effortlessly as rain from a spring cloud.

When he faced me I was nearly struck dumb. Paul Creticos was the most beautiful being I had ever seen. It was as if Jesus Christ had transformed himself into flesh, for, as blasphemous as it sounds, he was beauty incarnate.

I found myself staring at him for several seconds before being overcome by a rush of profound embarrassment. Without introducing myself, I escaped to my room. Out of breath, I leaned against the closed door wondering whether he had seen me. Surely he had. Another priest only five meters away. What must he be thinking?

I hadn't run away like that in years.

Qua-si-mo-do. Qua-si-mo-do.
Won't you come and play?
Qua-si-mo-do. Qua-si-mo-do.
Won't you go away!

Was he going to think I was some kind of fool? Perhaps he would interpret my quick departure as disapproval. And that was, after all, accurate enough. I would have to have a talk with him about things

25

like writing on live T-shirts, anyway. That was clearly not the way for a young priest to behave. As for why I had departed so suddenly, I would just let him draw his own inferences.

I reclined on the bed with my briefcase and examined the materials the curia had given me. The news photo stapled to the first page was a fraud. Oh, it looked something like him. The features were correct. The secret police would have been more than happy to use something like that to ferret out the remaining members of Solidarity. It told their version of the truth. But it in no way prepared you for the man himself.

There was also a seminary photograph. Out-of-focus enough to be anyone.

None of this stuff was going to be of value, I concluded, before sliding it back into the briefcase.

Escaping from the shiny new room, with its crisp carpet and gawking television set, I knelt on the concrete balcony just past the glass sliding door and let God wrap His arms around me.

I prayed until the sun sliced through the dawn haze, opening the sky as if it were the rind of a wet, ripe melon.

Oh, God. What an incredible sight!

Gradually the feeling returned to my knees.

Yes. What an incredible sight!

Did the streets go on forever? They stretched toward the horizon, each narrowing into a line, each line converging on its neighbor. I felt like a small boy peeking over the edge of a globe. Perhaps long ago I had done that myself?

After rinsing my eyes with water, I tucked Fodor's Guide to New York City *under my arm and, feeling more like a space traveler than a hotel guest, hurtled down to the city in the freshly buffed aluminum elevator. In spite of my excitement I cautiously surveyed the street from the revolving door: there were no thugs or rapists in sight. Or gangsters. Perhaps they were all in Chicago.*

One gulp of air and I was starving. How amazing, I thought. Suddenly, after months, I was hungry. Perhaps I had finally recovered. (They had inserted their riot sticks down my throat to make me vomit. After each meal. They just waited me out. And when I finally ate, in they came, with their hungry, cold sticks. Even now I involuntarily gag when I think of it.) For the first time since then I was not overwhelmed with nausea at the sight of food. First fresh-squeezed

26

orange juice (vendors sold it on the street!) and a cheese danish. Then a slice of pizza. And another. Why hadn't I been able to eat in Italy? Perhaps the inactivity? No. Not that. Not exactly. It was that I was back in the thick of things again, I decided. Yes. And that was a very healthy thing. For a person like me. So I celebrated my recovery with a hot dog with sauerkraut.

By the time I returned to the hotel it was noon. Dietra Christian was on the elevator. Oh, I didn't know her name then. I didn't know her at all. She was leaning against the wall near the elevator controls, obscenely snarling, a large, shiny safety pin fastened in the fleshy part of her cheek.

"Four, please," I requested, my eyes fixed on the safety pin.

She didn't budge.

"Thank, you," I said sarcastically while reaching for the button. Four was already lit. Embarrassed, I apologized.

In reply she first looked at—no, examined—me. As if I were some kind of specimen.

"Have you never seen a priest before?" I wanted to ask.

Her lip curled up slightly, perhaps from the safety pin. Small traces of dried blood and pus had accumulated around the entry and exit points of the pin.

I inadvertently jumped when the elevator door burst open. Sneering like an evil gunslinger in an old American movie, she strutted out into the hall to face herself in the large mirror that opposed the elevator. For the first time I noticed she was wearing tight leather pants. A kind of belt draped diagonally across her waist and then looped back around her thigh just below her crotch. Adorned with bright metal studs, it might as well have been a badman's gunless holster. Her reflection, masked in fist-sized aviators, looked contemptuously from the mirror before gliding down the hallway.

I had to lurch forward and grab the elevator door to keep it from slamming shut with me trapped inside.

"Now where is room four-twelve," I mumbled to myself, not so much a reminder as an attempt to bring myself back to the world of the ordinary. I followed the embossed arrows on the wall to room 412.

When I rounded the corner she was just entering what turned out to be room 412. She must have entered without knocking. How else could she be going in so fast? I wondered.

I knocked.

27

"Monsignor," Father Paul exclaimed warmly as soon as the door was open. He shook my hand. "I expected you last night."

Still grasping his hand, which was strong and calloused from what must have been hard work, "I was very tired when I arrived." By way of explanation, "Jet lag."

"Yes." He smiled forthrightly. "I wouldn't know, but I've read about it." He laughed, "In magazines."

"Soon you will know firsthand." The voice was German. She was sprawled out in a chair, her legs dangling over one arm. Sunlight from the window bounced off the metal-studded apparatus fastened around her thigh, creating a chorus line of mirrored light that obscenely danced up the wall and onto the ceiling in time with the agitated syncopation of her leg.

I released his hand.

"We'll have to see about that," Father Paul answered with what seemed mild embarrassment.

"You will." She leaned her head back, as if she were some kind of cheap rock-and-roll seer. "I see it very clearly."

"The question is, what does God see?" Odd, how time alters your perspective. I think at the time I found that reply glib. Perhaps even shallow. But now it seems to me that Father Paul was able to say things like that without... well, it's that things like that came to his lips quite naturally. Without being mere formulae. Many priests say things like that, but they have the ring of "Good morning," or "How are you?" With Father Paul that was not the case.

Perhaps the fact that she was there, sprawled across the chair as if she belonged there, altered my perception. I remember being struck by the contrast between his simple blue eyes, which seemed to reach out to touch everything around them, and hers, masked by those glowing, black aviators. There was no doubt in my mind that she had been sent directly from hell or was soon to be there. Was Father Paul completely blind? I wondered.

"Monsignor Babulieski, this is Dietra Christian." She nodded without rising from the blue brocade chair, whose angelic Victorian wings hovered behind her as if repelled by her mere touch. "She has come to help us from Europe. As you have, Monsignor." Self-consciously, he added, "I didn't realize what we are doing was so widely known."

"You can't hide in St. Pierre, Minnesota, forever," she offered reprovingly. The thick German "Minnesota" sounded like a province on Mars.

"Apparently not." Smiling, he turned to me. "Have you ever been to Minnesota?"

Absently, I replied, "No," while I tried to engineer some way to get her on her way so that Father Paul and I could talk privately. Surely it must have been obvious that I had just arrived. She lounged there behind her impenetrable aviators, dressed in that permanent half-smile inflicted by the safety pin.

"It gets quite cold there. And everyone knows it. It brings the best out in them." He looked directly at me.

"Oh." The look left me unsure how to proceed. "I guess it would. God's presence seems more apparent in times of adversity." I had been about to announce (in some obvious way, but I wasn't sure exactly how) that I had just arrived from the Vatican, but his "It brings out the best in them" seemed to be subtly aimed at me.

What kind of help could she be offering? She was the kind of theatrical, purposeless obscenity that seemed to thrive in the West. I vacillated between abhorrence and pity.

As if he were reading my mind, he explained, "Dietra has been with me almost from the beginning. From St. Pierre." In a way that suggested that he himself was still not sure why, "She appeared on our doorstep the week after the convoy incident."

Looking out the window, which seemed large enough to admit the entire city, "I knew you were the one."

After an awkward silence, "We'll leave that judgment to God."

Still staring out into the Manhattan sky, snarling (perhaps it was the safety pin in her cheek? That shiny, inch-long sliver of steel seemed to be the source of all expression in her face), "I did. I knew," she persisted, as if she had been the author of some profound insight.

Father Paul sat on the edge of the sofa and brushed his fingers through his hair. Suddenly he appeared completely exhausted. You could see white furrows left behind by his fingertips as he massaged his temples. Odd, only seconds before he had seemed full of energy. And much younger. Almost too young. Too innocent. But at that moment, crouched on the sofa with his head in his hands, he looked all of his thirty-one years and more.

"Did you not sleep? No." She rose. "Of course not. You never do

29

the night before." Her voice was very lush and German. "Well, there's no reason for you to arrive before two. Come."

"I'll be fine." Digging his fingers into his temples, "I will."

"Of course you will. But, you had better rest here." She gently pushed him back onto the sofa. "Just for a while."

"Yes." He closed his eyes.

"He must rest now," she said, to me. The leather strap tightly cinched around her thigh glistened in the sunlight for an instant as she stepped across the coffee table. Pulling the drapes to without resorting to the drawstring, she thought out loud, "If he doesn't he won't be worth a damn." When she recrossed the coffee table, I found myself backpedaling toward the foyer, facing her as we both moved across the thick carpet, until the doorknob knifed into my back.

With that same snarl, but without recrimination, as if she were simply reporting a fact, she said, "All that damned praying." She opened the door. "It's a wonder he has the strength for anything important."

As I was about to reply, she pushed the door shut. All along I had supposed she was going out with me, but she stopped at the door and just shut it, leaving me there alone in the hall facing the blank door.

What strange behavior, I thought. He certainly knew that I had been dispatched from the Vatican. He had seemed quite pleased to see me.

I actually raised my fist to rap on the door. To bring her out. Why, I hadn't even shown him the newspaper. I slipped it from under my arm and opened it. "NO," the headline proclaimed in bold type. Beneath it was a photograph of a large, grassy park: thousands of people camped out in Central Park last night in anticipation of today's Festival of Peace. The photograph showed scores of people sprawled out on the grass in sleeping bags, or just wrapped in blankets. A skinny, bald man of about forty was holding a sign with "NO" written on it. He was squinting. Perhaps the flash of the camera had produced the comical squint. He looked as if the bright light had suddenly awakened him. The O had that same diagonal slash through it.

I examined the photograph for another second or two before slipping the paper back under my arm. Perhaps I would get a firsthand look at all this, I decided.

By the time I arrived at Central Park there were thousands of people there. (I had stopped several times to sample more food from the street vendors that barraged passersby with temptation after temptation, and then I was punished for my gluttony by a nearly uncontrollable need for a toilet. Perhaps it was the hot dogs? There are no public toilets in New York City! I was forced to race back to my hotel. The sight of a hunchbacked priest racing down Fifth Avenue with his cassock hiked up to his knees seemed to rouse no interest. They chatted and looked in the packed, gaudy store windows, paying me no mind at all. I tried to pass through the lobby as calmly as circumstances would allow, but at the last minute I had to burst across the clickety-clack terrazzo to the bar, where the barman was kind enough to direct me to the toilet. After that experience I treated myself to a brandy and a taxi.)

As I entered the park, I cursed my way past the vendors that hawked their temptations from underneath striped, multicolored umbrellas, all the while vowing that I would not be victimized by them again. Fifty meters past the entrance I was greeted by a long, silent row of portable toilets that had evidently been placed there for the occasion. I was too angry to allow myself to curse.

Plastic disks zipped by like playful birds (Frisbees! Now I occasionally pick one up during recreation period).

Roller skaters rumbled down the old walkways, holding hands and laughing. Here and there someone was nestled in the grass with a book. All in all, near the entrance, it was not very different from a summer day in Poland. Except for the Frisbees. And the roller skaters. (They were not children but adults!) I can remember being nearly overwhelmed by nostalgia for an instant; and swept away, as I sometimes am, by the rush of feeling that flows from the simple truth that people everywhere are so much alike. As I worked my way to what seemed to be the center of the park, navigating more by the sound of music than the map of Central Park that was in Fodor's New York City, the crowd got more and more tightly packed, until, surrounded by a mass of humanity as tightly packed as stalks of wheat in a field, I could see nothing except torsos and blue sky.

Suddenly I was suffocating. The air was packed with sweat and suntan oil. And laughter. Everyone was overflowing with laughter. They were absurdly happy. You would think they had already achieved their objective.

The only visible escape was a small, grassy knoll overlooking the crowd. Shielding myself from the swarm of bare chests and backs with my extended hands, I fought my way to one of the cool granite boulders scattered across the green incline. The one I sat on was warm from the sun. After a second or two I was breathing fine again. The sky was crystal-clear. Isn't it amazing how those moments of panic which come upon one so suddenly and seem so claustrophobically intense (Is this going to last forever? Am I about to keel over in a stupid faint? Am I about to die?) can vanish without a trace?

From my vantage point I could see for half a kilometer. Everywhere there were people. As I soon discovered, even my little knoll was inhabited. A boy and girl were stretched out between two boulders embracing. I stepped to the left so that they would be hidden from my view. The girl giggled. Her bare calf waved at me from between the two boulders. I moved to a half-shaded spot a little farther away.

Small, swaying figures encircled the wooden platform that jutted from the opposing knoll like a Brobdingnagian banquet table. A tide of music rolled at me from the speakers attached to its legs. I tried to understand the lyrics, but my English failed me. Even then I was quite fluent, but songs like that were impossible to unscramble.

How different it was from those Solidarity days. Oh, there was song. And guitars. Many of them happy songs. But the singers were workers. And the songs, even if they were later in the night love songs, were blessed with an indisputable sincerity. And the singers were real people. This scene unfolding before me was more like a circus. Not an ordinary circus, where the performers and crowd are distinct, but some disturbing concoction of a circus in which everyone was simultaneously performer and audience.

Just two or three meters in front of me a muddy, unkempt young man jack-in-the-boxed from between two half-buried boulders. A hairy head was locked in the elbow of his arm. Evidently he, and the head, and what was attached to it, had spent the night in the embrace of the rocks. He screamed, in cadence with the music, "Three, two, one. Where is everyone?"

So those were the words.

A safety pin was tightly fastened in his cheek.

Yes, those were the words. It was easy once you heard it, so that your brain could remind your ears what to hear.

"Three, two, one. Where is everyone?" he mouthed, silently drowning in an electric-guitar wave.

With an abrupt jerk he yanked the head upward and kissed the open mouth a second after the words stopped spewing out. He pulled open his companion's shirt and thrust his hand inside. I wanted to look away, but I found my eyes locked to his muddy, groping hand. There were no breasts. The bare chest was breastless white.

Suddenly, he began to sing, "Three, two, one. Where is everyone?"

His companion picked up the chant, hips bouncing back and forth, the grass-stained, muddy hand now planted on his backside.

There was a bright red bruise on the small one's neck. I felt myself cringe as it struck me that the lurid red mark had been inflicted by teeth.

After lifting the hem of my cassock I stepped over to the next rock, where I perched while the legions of peace multiplied until the grassy knoll was asphalted with bodies.

Peace? The air was dense with racket. Screams. Chants. Laughter. Music. Or what passed for music in the West. All that talk of freedom. It always seemed to end in some kind of mindless waste.

Peace? Such a contemplative word. A circus. That's what it was. Or worse, the tremblings of hell waiting for Lucifer to scream out his defiance.

"Three, two, one." The explosion. "Where is everyone?"

The two creatures who had risen from between the muddy granite boulders faced each other and threw up their hands in silent-movie despair before repeating, "Where is everyone?" As if the convenient position of their hands made the idea irresistible, they began to dance, their palms caressing each other through half a meter of air.

Peace? The banners proclaimed peace; screamed yes to life. The rest, I decided, was too ugly to have anything to do with peace, too vulgar to have anything to do with what God had created and called life.

Father Paul's entourage arrived half an hour later, Dietra Christian clearing the way. Without actually touching anyone, with a wave of her hand through the air as if she were a medieval sorceress, she tore open a wound in the mass of flesh surrounding the platform, through which they passed like a shiny new knife. The wound instantly healed behind them. Flanking Father Paul were two mimes clothed in green, muddy wrappings. Disentombed mummies? Angels of

33

death? They wore gas masks and ridiculous flippers on their feet, like the ones skin divers wear. How silly, I remember thinking. But they did rouse an odd, prickling chill. Silly or not, they were death.

She sat behind him, cross-legged, a little to the left. The safety pin glistened in her cheek.

"Hello." He offered the salutation with a tinge of embarrassment. He shuffled his feet a few times.

"No," they replied almost in unison, the sound rolling across the densely packed field and up the hill toward me, so that the "o" was bizarrely long and quivering.

He raised his hand to restrain them.

"No to death. No to death."

The chant was voluminous, overwhelming.

"Yes to life. Yes to life."

A young girl, her bare breasts rumbling around her chest, climbed up on the platform and ran toward Father Paul. There was an instant of suspense. Even her breasts seemed poised silently for a second, frozen. "Yes," she screamed. "Yes." You could hear her very clearly. The crowd was transfixed.

Before she could utter another "Yes," Dietra Christian jumped to her feet and, with the girl in the crook of her bare, muscular arm, toted her off like a sack of potatoes. She unceremoniously dropped her off the far side of the platform. She might have been unloading a truck. Had anyone else taken his eyes off the center of the stage? Perhaps not.

The girl lay there for a second or two, her arm uncomfortably twisted behind her head, before staggering to her feet.

"Yes to life," Father Paul responded, as if they were celebrating some strange mass. Had he not seen the girl? (She was now clapping her hands over her head, dancing, her bare breasts jiggling above the still-tucked-in T-shirt that had been pushed down over her shoulders and left to hang meaninglessly around her waist.)

"Yes to life."

He looked directly at me (Did everyone there feel the same way?) for a second or two before offering, conversationally, "All it takes is a little ... courage. A small gamble." After half a measure of silence, "Or is it even a gamble?"

Like grim schoolchildren, they responded "No."

34

"Let God decide it. Put it in His hands. Let the loving hands of Jesus Christ, the hands that shed blood for us so that we might live forever, let those hands decide it. Is that really gambling?" Silence. "No. Because Jesus Christ is love. And our salvation."

Later, they chanted, "No to death; yes to life." This peculiar doxology was repeated over and over until the entire assemblage spoke in one voice.

"Say it to Washington. Say it to Moscow. Say it to the world."

"No to death; yes to life."

Now, even now, half a dozen years later, I can remember the confusion induced by that one afternoon in Central Park. It was hard to see the hand of God in what I had witnessed. There was something evil about it. But I wasn't sure of that then. No. Not then. That came later. It was more that it was comical. In the grand sense of comedy. Comedy that exposes human foible. The propensity for the silly. Still, there was something else to it. It was as if a long way away the earth were trembling and quaking so violently that even there, on that grassy knoll, the movement of the earth could be felt.

An hour later I was lost in the intoxicating complexity of New York City. The streets were crammed with people eating and buying and talking. Where were the police? I remember asking to myself. Why had there been none? Oh, there had been a few uniformed ones. They wore light blue short-sleeved shirts. I remembered that as I strolled along Fifth Avenue. But where were the secret police? The so-easy-to-identify, large-overcoated police that must have been there? It was something I was so used to, like an old friend's mustache or wire-rimmed glasses, that it was only later that I sensed its absence. There had been none. Of course, that night I was sure they had been there. In the crowd, disguised. I was sure that it was only my naiveté about things American that made their presence impossible to detect. In fact, I made up my mind, while I was peering into the window of Saks (I had never seen anything like that!), to pay special attention the next time. Then they would be as obvious as pictures in a mosque. I decided to make a little game of it. Like poor Glotkyn, I would see how many I could count. Of course, in Gdansk that was not much of a challenge. But that was Glotkyn. A shipbuilder in a city of shipbuilders, he was too straightforward for the times we live in. So he went in the initial crackdown. "There's one," he would laugh out loud. "And another."

35

While pointing, he would announce, "Ivan's on the phone. Do you want to take it here? You're right, better at home." He would hang up the phone with a tongue-created click. Those Solidarity men had guts.

The windows were full of things. Glittering. Shiny. New. It must have taken horrendous exploitation to create all of this, I marveled.

And the streets were full of vendors selling food. I tried to fight off the temptation, but in the end I succumbed. First a glass of orange juice. It was freshly squeezed. And marvelous. And then teriyaki. And then pizza. Just a slice.

As penance I walked another hour, but that led to more eating. That night, lying in bed, hiding under the sheet like an engorged tick, I resolved to control myself. I was scolding myself with "It's one thing to regain a healthy appetite, but another to . . ." when it came to me: I had never eaten like that until they had rammed that stick down my throat. Yes, it all stemmed from that, I concluded. Now, suddenly, I was reclaiming all the food they had robbed me of. I could feel the back of my neck sweating into the pillowcase.

When the sky began to lighten, I splashed water on my face and prayed. What was I to do about Father Paul? "Surely, God, You will guide me. Why else am I here?" I found myself repeating several times out loud.

But I felt no more reconciled. Or less confused. Perhaps it was just me. Prayer had been everything to me in the basement of the Gdansk police station. Afterward I felt completely renewed. Ready for the next challenge. Ready to give up my life. Ready even for the humiliation of the club.

Was it that my life was in jeopardy? That I was standing on the edge of the knife? Why in this case was prayer so much less efficacious? God was no less powerful, so it must be me. That itself seemed a subject for thoughtful prayer.

Jesus Christ would guide me. Of that I was certain.

Alex reread the last paragraph. Who was this Jesus Christ? Originally Alex had been sure he was a general. Why? He began to thumb back. Where had that been? An army? Yes, he remembered clearly: the army of Jesus Christ. So he must be a general. Or something like that. He thumbed around for a few seconds before deciding that the giant oaks had choked off too much light for him to find anything.

36

And New York City? It sounded like stories he had heard about Moscow, he concluded, while tightly wrapping the book in the plastic bag. Yes. It sounded a great deal like Moscow. But that didn't make sense, really. The man had said he was in America. And, as best he could tell, America before the Great Uprising.

Quite suddenly there was a noise. A quick sharp sound. It occurred just as he was crawling into a thick oleander cluster to bury The Book. Just as it became evident that the events in The Book were taking place long ago. Perhaps long before the Great Uprising. He lay very flat and still. Waiting. But all he could hear was the breeze. And far off the surf. But nothing else. Perhaps the wind had knocked down a branch. It blew harder late in the afternoon. He quietly rolled over on his side so that he could survey the rim of the dune. Nothing. He searched the other hemisphere. It must have been the wind. Or a bird.

He quietly scooped out a tomb for The Book and shoved it in before gently strangling the crinkly plastic with a handful of sand. When the hard-packed tomb was complete he slipped out from under the oleanders on all fours and crouched in the cavernous center of the dune. His heart sounded as if it were the boiler room of a ship: boom, boom; boom, boom.

Dodging the outstretched, immobile arms of the tireless old wrestlers, he burst up the side of the dune, its bone-dry walls sucking him in up to his ankles. Outside it was still shockingly bright. And desolate. There couldn't have been anyone there. The only footprints on the dune were his own.

He ran as fast as he could. It was the only way he could catch up with his heart.

He had run half a kilometer, splashing through the shallow, wormlike trough of water left behind by the receding tide, before he realized he was wearing his sneakers. They were as heavy as sunken boats. Only when he sat to remove them, panting, straining to pull them off without loosening the laces, did he look back at the dune, which, as always, seemed to be regarding him and the rest of its domain with a kind of detached superiority that proclaimed, "I'll be here long after you are gone."

Suddenly he was attacked by profound disappointment: The Book didn't make any sense at all. Not really. And it wasn't much of a

37

mystery. Why, it didn't hold a candle to *The Cleft Foot*. Even the simple-minded stories from *Tales of Vigilance*, which they used to read out loud at Young Pioneers meetings, were more like real mysteries.

He stared at the arrogant old dune for a moment or two, then pushed off with one hand and resumed running.

Well, even if it wasn't a real mystery, it was after all a book. In a way, just having it seemed to make up for any of its deficiencies. Yes, there was something hard to understand, but at the same time gratifying, about just having it, he decided, as his bare feet glided across the sand, occasionally hitting the water, as he straightened out the mindless undulations in the ocean's contour.

Perhaps, he speculated, after finding a piece of the sun stuck between a rooftop and a clump of oleanders, she would still be there. That would be perfect.

He pushed harder, his eyes locked far up the beach on the pink-orange, ice-cream-sundae surf.

Long before any features were discernible he could tell it was her. As always, alone, her hair glistening, she recklessly crashed against the breakers, throwing herself into them as if fifty kilos of flesh could demolish a ton of water.

By the time he reached her she was sloshing through the ankle-deep water, contemplatively, her face obscured by a sheet of wet, silver-streaked blond curls.

"Finished?" he struggled, out of breath, unabashedly showing his disappointment.

"Worn out." She wrapped her wet arm around his shoulder and aimed him toward the house. "Anyway, it's time for Nurov's dinner."

Attempting to turn her around by pivoting on his heel in the damp sand, "Corinne can take care of that."

"No."

"That's what she's for." Sensing her disapproval, "Well, it is." He pulled her back toward the ocean.

Matter of factly, "He likes it better when I do it."

"Just for a minute." There was no point in pleading. Besides, when she was detached like that, being with her was worse than being alone. Changing his tone, as if he were reporting the weather, "I'm drenched."

"I know." She playfully covered her nose with her thumb and fore-finger.

Sensing that she might come around, "Well, then it's your duty to wash me."

"My duty. We'll," she slipped her leg between his, "see about that."

Dodging her attempt to trip him, "No you don't. See? I know all your tricks."

"Do you now." She bumped him with her hip while pulling simultaneously with the arm that had been limply resting on his shoulder, spinning him half around before they tumbled into the sand, laughing. It always amazed him that she could be happy all over again that fast, in the snap of a finger.

Sitting upright, looking down at her muddy chest, "Now see what you've done." She jumped up and said slyly, "Looks like I'll have to rinse off," before bolting toward the water.

He raced after her, plowing through the breakers to where the ocean was still. He was the only one whom she ever let accompany her. Nurov was a creature of the land; and she was, in his mind, a moody half-mermaid. Her green bathing suit shimmered as she arched before vanishing into the water.

He scanned the water's surface, waiting impatiently for her to come back.

She could stay down so damned long.

Where was she? Why did she love to torture him like that? The surface of the water was impenetrable. He slid under the water. So close to the breakers you could see nothing, but you could feel the hint of undertow that constantly tugged you toward Fort Sumter once you got out past the sandbar. He came up for air and went back down. Nothing. When he resurfaced she was there, within arm's reach: effortlessly treading water while she examined him. He brushed the hair from his forehead.

"Don't you look Russian, though," she offered thoughtfully.

Not knowing how to react, he replied awkwardly, "Shouldn't I?"

Running her thumb across the birthmark on his forehead, "Oh, yes. Sonia Ouspenskaya would be very proud." When she said the name it was with a confusing mixture of awe and annoyance that left Alex slightly embarrassed. "But it's how you feel that counts," she persisted enigmatically, before swimming off into the breakers.

Alex could feel the birthmark heating up. A touch would do that. Sometimes just a glance was enough.

The sun was almost down.

She squeezed the water out of her hair as they clumped their way down the walkway to the house.

She slid her shoes under the step and, after pushing the door open, called out cheerfully, in Russian, "Nurov? We're back." Just inside the door there were towels on the line waiting for them. Without stopping, she wrapped a large lemon-colored one around her hair in a turban. Buffing his shoulders as he walked, he followed her into the kitchen, where Corinne was chopping vegetables. In English, "How wonderful, Corinne." She paused to examine the vegetables. "They're very nice. Asparagus, Alex."

Still chopping, "The bus broke down again."

"You're a gem, Corinne. We haven't had asparagus in an age." She continued on into the living room. "Nurov?" In Russian, "It's too late to be working. You know you get indigestion when you work right up to dinner. Corinne is preparing the most beautiful asparagus in the world."

Alex leaned against the kitchen doorframe.

"This dinner won't be long," Corinne offered, her virtuoso hands advancing across the cutting board as if it were a piano. For Corinne that was a day's talking.

On his way to take a shower he could hear muffled laughter from his father's study.

Dinner was torture. He tried to focus on the paper. If he had only started right after school. Then it would be finished. He had no trouble imagining just how wonderful that would feel. But he couldn't bring himself to think about the paper itself.

On the one hand, The Book kept creeping in. At that moment, with his father right across from him, just thinking about The Book gave him a chill. But every time he pushed it out of his mind it slithered back in.

And even though his mother was right there, almost within reach, she seemed so far away. At least from him.

Nurov, warmly flushed from several glasses of vodka—or was it from laughing with his mother?—twice inquired, "Daisy, our son looks as though he has just been sentenced to ten years at Suvatsky

Crater. Or has he fallen in love?" Each time he laughed. It was the kind of laugh that he reserved for their table or the study. He had heard his father laugh in public only a few times, and that was a very different laugh.

The second time he replied, "I have a paper to write."

Nurov excused him from the table with, "Oh? Well, you'd better get to it."

"I think I'll need to use the encyclopedia," he requested cautiously.

"The door is open."

"I'll just take the ones I need to my room."

"I'll have Corinne wrap that for you, Alex," his mother offered while he was crossing the dining room.

"Thank you, Mother," he found himself replying with stilted formality.

"I'm sure you'll be starving by the time you finish."

Before he could reach the study door they had begun laughing again.

The room was nearly square. The wall facing his father's desk contained half a dozen built-in shelves that were crammed with thick, official-looking books, the encyclopedia, several dictionaries, and an atlas.

A few other books were stacked on the desk. They had small scraps of paper jutting from them. It was not really clear to Alex what his father did with the books. They came and went in his father's briefcase. Nurov never mentioned what he did with the books; no one asked.

It wasn't that he hadn't seen tons of books. After all, there were his textbooks. And all the standard reference books. It was that the books his father brought home were so old. Much older even than his mysteries. Not necessarily as frayed. Or ragged. But clearly older. And clearly, although no one had ever said so, unauthorized.

Alex walked to the far side of the bookshelf. Just the encyclopedia would be enough. There was no point in going overboard. He scanned the CCCP/USSA Encyclopedia until he found "GO-GZ." What could start with GZ? he wondered. Nothing. Not in English.

He balanced the encyclopedia on the corner of the desk. Like some superpolite, alien dinner guests the computer terminal stared mutely across the smooth oak surface. It was the only one he had

41

ever seen. In fact, he wasn't even sure what it did. Occasionally computers were mentioned in school, but there were none there, or, for that matter, anywhere else he was aware of except for this room. He had heard there were many more in Moscow. But there was no way to know if that was really true.

Occasionally, when he was smaller, when he had entered to say good night to his father, the screen had been brightly lit, usually in half a dozen colors. Even then he knew that it wasn't just a television, but beyond that bit of negative information the silent, bodiless head was a complete mystery.

In order to make room for the encyclopedia he reached out to push the stack of books farther back. They were obviously very old. The top one was called *Treasure Island*. The cover was leather. He tilted his head to the side to read the other titles. The second was called *The Quest of the Historical Jesus*. Below that "Schweitzer" was printed. Without touching it, his head still turned to the side, he examined its back. "The Quest of the Historical Jesus?" he repeated to himself. At the bottom in white ink someone had written "BT303"; and below that "S42." A small slip of paper had been inserted about halfway through the book. Bright, birthday-blue, it looked a little silly jutting out from the antique binding. He almost reached out to push the top book aside so that he could get a better look. Instead he was content to examine the binding, to reread the title, and the author, and the hand-printed numerals below that.

After a moment's thought he went over to the *CCCP/USSA Encyclopedia* and extracted the volume including the J's. There was nothing under "Jesus." Or "Jesus Christ," for that matter. He tried the C's. Again there was nothing. Funny. There was nothing at all. It must have been a made-up name. An invention. Just before returning it to the shelf, in a burst of inspiration, he looked up Paul Creticos. Of course there would be nothing there. That must have been made up too.

CRETICOS, PAUL (40–81) Born: Pierre, Minnesota. A dedicated Marxist-Leninist, Paul Creticos was an early (but minor) participant in the Great Uprising. Posthumously awarded the Lenin Peace Prize (83).

He quickly shut the encyclopedia and slid it back into the shelf. At least he had been right about one thing. The Book took place before the Great Uprising. That was interesting. But how much of it was made up and how much of it was true? That was the kind of thing he was sure his father would know. But there was no way to ask him. At least not directly.

When Alex leaned over to pick up the encyclopedia he had left on the desk, *The Quest of the Historical Jesus* was staring right at him. He reached out to push aside the book on top of it.

"So, how's it going?"

Startled, "Fine, I guess." He stood, his hand pulled tightly back to his side.

"No, stay. I'll get those out of your way." Nurov deftly lifted the stack of books. "There. Now you have a little room to breathe." He inserted the books in a file drawer and locked it. "So," looking over Alex's shoulder, "what's your topic?"

Opening the encyclopedia, "The Great Uprising." Awkwardly, "Class oppression. Before then." He quickly added, "In America," realizing as he did so that it was unnecessary. He could feel his cheeks warming.

"Don't," placing his hand on Alex's shoulder, "your textbooks cover that?"

"Yes." Uncomfortably, "But I wanted to use the most authoritative sources I could find."

"Authoritative." He could feel Nurov's fingertip tapping lightly on his shoulder. It felt as if it, the fingertip, in its mindless, monotonous tapping, could suck the truth right out of him. Why should he feel as if he were lying when he wasn't? "So? You have a problem. And the solution is . . . at your fingertips." After a moment's thought, "Yes, why not? Why not now?"

Dragging his fingers across Alex until they dropped reluctantly off his shoulder, Nurov stretched to flick a red toggle switch under the screen. It immediately came to life.

MONDAY OCTOBER 25, 143
PLEASE ENTER YOUR AUTHORIZATION CODE: _ _ _ _ _

Nurov's forefinger methodically crisscrossed the keyboard, advancing a small white bar along the blank authorization code. Each key-

43

stroke evoked a soft musical chime that reminded him of his mother's music box. He could remember opening and closing it for hours at a time while he filled sheets of blank paper with crayon. The sound was just as soft and delicate, but each stroke produced a chime that was identical with its predecessor. It was certainly not music.

PLEASE ENTER YOUR AUTHORIZATION CODE: <u>m</u> <u>n</u> <u>O</u> <u>O</u> <u>1</u>

"This is something you will encounter next year." Proudly adding, "At Moscow University." He teetered for a second or two before anchoring himself to the desk with his left palm. "You might as well see it now. We don't want them thinking you are too provincial, do we?" He turned to face Alex, examining him carefully for a second or two, before adding, "This will have to be our little secret. Father and son."

He raised his fingers to his lips. "Father and son."

Alex nodded.

"No one else." Nurov's head bobbed back and forth a few times, as if he were agreeing with himself.

The small white bar had been silently resting at the end of the line. Nurov struck the keyboard one more time.

PASSWORD?

The white bar chimed its way across the screen, but nothing appeared above it.

GOOD EVENING, VICE-MINISTER NUROV.
WHAT CAN I DO FOR YOU?

"See, Alex? We're friends, me and this old fellow."

bibliographical search
SUBJECT/AUTHOR/TITLE?
subject
DO YOU WISH TO BE PROMPTED?
no
ENTER SUBJECT.
great uprising

After a moment:

```
THERE ARE 3470 TITLES ON THE SUBJECT GREAT UPRISING.
DO YOU WISH TO LIST THEM ALL?
```

"When is your essay due?" Nurov asked with a laugh.

Awestruck, "Tomorrow."

"Then I don't suppose you have time for all of these," he injected before adding, "No," as he typed it. "No," he repeated, more thoughtfully, before facing Alex. "This is not the kind of thing that should be approached," he searched for a moment, "casually. You do understand that, don't you?"

"Yes, sir."

After a moment, "Who assigned this?"

"Brownsky," he answered derisively.

"Do I know him?"

"No." Reflexively, "He's an American."

"Yes, apparently so." Turning back to the screen, "Brownsky? One of those, eh? Yes, one of those."

Nurov's "no" still glared at them. Why hadn't the computer responded? Before the thought died, almost as a reply to the unspoken question, Nurov completed the line.

```
no/trim by source? periodical
THERE ARE 2668 PERIODICAL TITLES ON THE SUBJECT
GREAT UPRISING.
DO YOU WISH TO LIST THEM ALL?
no/classify
LEVEL 1:
    ORIGINS
    GENERAL HISTORY
    CHRONOLOGY
    PERSONAL ACCOUNTS
    CONDITIONS PRECEDING
    CONSEQUENCES OF
```

Nurov moved the white bar to CONDITIONS PRECEDING and struck the keyboard.

```
THERE ARE 476 PERIODICAL TITLES ON THE SUBJECT GREAT
UPRISING/CONDITIONS PRECEDING.
DO YOU WISH TO LIST THEM ALL?
```

After entering "no/trim by date" he paused. "And we want the most authoritative sources." He enunciated the word "authoritative" in a teasing, overly careful way. "And what does that mean?" He turned his face, which was slightly flushed from leaning over the keyboard, and waited for Alex to reply. There were hundreds of pencil-thin lines racing from his nostrils to his cheeks. When he repeated the question it arrived on a warm vodka cloud.

"Just . . . authoritative." Collecting himself, "The Party's most current position."

Toying, "Current position?" He faced the screen. "That was 'the most current,' wasn't it?"

```
no/trim by date > 140
```

"Is that current enough?" he asked, still toying with him, but with unconcealed pride.

```
THERE ARE 7 PERIODICAL TITLES AFTER 140 ON THE
SUBJECT GREAT UPRISING/CONDITIONS PRECEDING.
DO YOU WISH TO LIST THEM ALL?
yes
```

Nurov pivoted on his heel and, as if Alex were audience to some great impresario about to introduce an elephant from Africa or a woman with three arms, he pressed a light blue key with his right forefinger. Had he pressed that key before? At the end of each line? Most of the time Alex had been hypnotized by the screen itself, so Nurov's hands, and certainly the particular destinations of his fingers, had operated in that opaque world just beyond attention.

"All of the most authoritative sources." After a moment he added, almost sarcastically, "At your fingertips."

Seven multicolored citations appeared on the screen.

Before he could respond, Nurov, supporting himself on the desktop with his right hand, inserted his face between the screen and Alex.

46

The electronic backdrop invested his ragged head with a frightening red-and-blue corona that splashed a light scar onto his cheek when he tilted his head. The illusory scar, which whimsically appeared and disappeared with each movement of his head, perfectly complemented the real but invisible crescent splash on Nurov's forehead. He found himself reaching to his own forehead. Touching it. Spontaneously. Confirming that his patrimony was indeed there. He traced out the narrow red flesh continent that hid beneath his hair in a sea of white.

"Be sure of one thing. There is one and only one Party position on anything. Anything." Harshly, "The Great Uprising. The price of pigs. Anything. And never," his face enlarged as it zoomed in on Alex, "never imply, never in fact think, that there is more than that one position. And never let anyone think," he pressed his fingertip against Alex's lips, "anyone, your father, your mother, your best friend, never let anyone think that a thought like that has ever crossed your mind." His finger still pressed to Alex's lips. "Do you understand that?"

Alex nodded.

"Good."

Nurov released his lips and turned toward the screen. "Let's see," he said convivially. "Something, yes, that should do." He typed a "k" in front of the second entry, and the fifth. And then the blue key. The screen flickered; the other entries vanished. Poof. Gone, as if they had never existed. This was a whole new way for things to be. Insubstantial. At your fingertips. And then gone! Like the palmetto log on the beach, but this was a beach where the tide came and went at the whim of the blue key.

"Which one do you want first?"

Flustered, "Either."

"There's nothing to it." Wrapping his left arm around Alex, he pulled him closer to the screen. "First," he raised his right forefinger, "first observe the arrow keys." He pressed the one pointing downward. "See? Nothing to it."

The screen looked the same.

"Now, you try it." He took Alex's right hand with his and steered it to the arrow keys. "Press. See?"

"Why doesn't anything happen?"

Laughing, "Watch the cursor."

The little white bar bounced back and forth between the two citations, occupying the blank preceding the title.

"The cursor?"

"Yes. And do you know why they call it that? No? Because," he laughed very loudly, "using it will make you curse."

Alex laughed too, but he wasn't really sure why.

"Yes, using it will make you curse." He squeezed Alex to him as if he were deflating a beach toy.

After a minute or two, his face still bright red, Nurov persisted, "Which one will it be first?"

Alex pointed to the top one.

"Just what I would have chosen." He laughed again. "Now, observe." Nurov typed a "d" in the blank space before depressing the blue key.

Accompanying a rap on the half-open study door, "Nurov?"

His father unhurriedly turned the swivel-necked screen away from the door before answering, "Yes."

The door seemed to open of its own volition. Her nightgown gathered in her fingertips so that its wisteria-blue hem skimmed effortlessly across the floor, "I think I'm going to rest." A large wooden comb held her hair tightly to her temples, narrowing her face, enlarging her eyes.

"Ah, Daisy, I won't be but a minute."

Gently, "No matter." Her head remained perfectly level as she approached. He had never seen anyone else who could walk without even the slightest up-and-down motion. Her face glided toward them as if they were in the lens of a zooming television camera.

Nurov met her a step or two away from the desk. She fluffed the hair above his ear as she glided by, playfully, but without much energy.

The silk was cool to the touch. She pressed her cheek to his for a moment before saying good night with her eyes, which her languid eyelids had converted into green half-moons. Only her pinpoint black pupils seemed alive. It was a look of total relaxation, indifference, disregard. Alex had seen it a thousand times.

"I won't be long," Nurov repeated, following her through the study door.

America Before the Great Uprising: Slavery, Serfdom, and Privilege, by M. N. Nurov, Vice-Minister of Information, Southeastern District. Proceedings of the 64th Convocation of the Young Socialist Pioneers of America.

[Vice Minister Nurov was introduced by S. A. Karpolovsky and was warmly greeted by his youthful comrades.]

America before the Great Uprising.

So, what was it like? you ask. What was it really like? Oh, not as terrible as you might think; not if you were in the driver's seat. [laughter] I will climb to the top. To the top. On the shoulders of my comrades. So I'm wearing boots. [laughter] Do you expect me to get blisters? [laughter] I won't be on your shoulders but a moment, comrade. You'll see. Why, in a moment I'll be way up there and you won't feel a thing. At least not much. [laughter]

That, young comrades, is the engine that drove America then. Greed. Exploitation. Disregard for fellow comrades. That was America before the Great Uprising! [applause]

"Finished with that page?"

Startled, "Yes."

Looming over him, leaning toward the screen, Nurov seemed larger than life. Even the question seemed to ring out as if it were intended to fill a vast hall full of cheering Young Pioneers.

"Just press the space bar to page. Like this."

Or at least that was half of it. There was also war. Yes, war. There was war. In Africa. In Asia. In South America. It was the dialectic of the time. War fed the capitalist regimes, bloating them, and at the same time, bleeding them until, inevitably, they collapsed.

Some of you looked puzzled. Yes, puzzled. That is because you have never seen war, comrades. I know it is hard for you to imagine war. Indeed, I myself have never seen war. And I never will. And you never will. The Party,

49

as the vehicle of history, will see to that. [applause] The Party, and the Russian Hegemony, has ensured that you and I will never see war. [applause]

Is war then only a historical curiosity to be mulled over with detachment by scholars? No. No. [No] No. [No] It is crucial that war be seen for the horror that it was. And that it be seen rightly. War was the glue that held together the old apparatus of oppression and privilege. War. And the threat of war. The fear of war. Your great-grandfathers, when they were youths like you, and younger, much younger, went to sleep at night greeted by nightmares of war. Of destruction. Of annihilation.

Yes. Annihilation. Because that was the age of the bomb. The age when children dreamed not of sugar plums but of annihilation.

The photographs were ugly, burned brown. Nothing was standing. Like the blown-off arms of separated lovers, twisted steel beams reached for one another across nonexistent buildings. It was so sad. "Nagasaki. Hiroshima," he responded, still able to conjure up the dead old photographs, as well as the answer to the classroom question.

"So?"

"It's," struggling, "impressive. Very impressive."

"Impressive?" Nurov depressed the space bar. "Just impressive?"

Genuinely, "I wish I'd been there."

"No," he laughed, "not the address." More to himself, "I've given that address a hundred times." His hand resting on the terminal as if it were an old friend's shoulder, "What do you think of this, the DAL system?" When he asked the question his eyes penetrated Alex in that automatic, thorough way that accompanied any question his father asked.

"It's," he searched, "it's amazing."

"Yes."

Nurov waited for him to say more.

"You just press a few buttons, and bam? What you want is there?"

With obvious self-satisfaction, "Yes, bam." He sat heavily on the edge of the desk. "Everything is right at your fingertips. Everything.

50

Right at your fingertips." He slowly danced his fingers across an imaginary keyboard.

In disbelief, "Everything?"

"Soon. Very soon." Standing, "But now is not the time for that. Perhaps later." Nurov glanced at the door. Not, apparently, because he heard something, or thought someone was there; it appeared to be only an indication that his mother was competing for Nurov's attention.

"And there will be no books at all then?"

Penetratingly, "Oh, there'll always be books." He continued, "How could we get by without books?" There was a long moment of silence while he crossed over to the terminal. Patting the plastic-topped screen, "They'll all be in here. Right in here." Nurov bent over the keyboard, his face six inches from the screen.

"So there'll be no need for real books?"

Emphatically, "These are real books. Everything in here is real."

Reflexively, "And what will happen to the," avoiding the phrase he had used previously, "the old ones?"

"There will be no need for them. There will be," he patted the top of the screen again, "millions of these. Millions. So there will really be more books than ever before. Many more. The Party will make sure of that." Confidentially, "In fact, your school will have one very soon. Perhaps before you finish the year." Proudly, "Perhaps before you leave for Moscow University."

Cautiously, but with an undisguised sense of discovery, "So that's what you do with the books. Put them in there."

"No." Probing Alex's eyes, "Someone else does that."

He resisted the urge to ask anything else. After a moment Nurov turned back to the screen. "The space bar pages. See?"

Nurov showed him how to retrieve the other citation, making him walk through the steps several times before standing upright. "I'll turn it off later. After you've finished." He paused at the door for a second, as if he wished to stay longer, to show him more, but after saying, "Don't be too late," he vanished into the hallway toward his wife's room.

Alex copied down most of his father's address, picked up the volume of the encyclopedia, and left the Martian-necked terminal to stare blindly into the empty room. Lying in bed with the encyclopedia propped in his lap he could still see the screen. "Good evening, Vice-Minister Nurov," he repeated ominously.

What an incredible idea! How could something that small hold so many books? He picked up the encyclopedia, gauging its weight as he lifted it. That seemed so farfetched. But he had seen it with his own eyes. And his father had showed it to him. Father and son, he reflected. Father and son. Everything had changed so much since the news about Moscow University. Everything. He could almost feel his father's fingers pressing against his lips. Everything was completely different.

Quite suddenly The Book popped up. Out of nowhere, unexpectedly, just as it had a dozen times in two days, it just appeared in his mind. It was amazingly insidious. Bam. It was just there.

The next time they went to Saluda he would just put it back where he had found it.

Without thinking any more about it he began the paper: America before the Great Uprising. So, what was it like? you ask. What was it really like?

As he was dozing off it crossed his mind: The Book might someday be the last real book. Years from now, when every other book was part of DAL's gigantic memory, The Book would be there, tucked away in its tiny rock niche, hidden in the clump of mountain laurel that had been a treehouse, a command post for Martian surveillance, and later just a place to reread decaying old mysteries.

How long had it been there?

Questions. Questions. That was what was wrong with the book. It led to questions. And more questions. And more. Until you were buried in an avalanche of questions. It was better not to think about it at all.

Still, when he went to sleep, it was there, right in the middle of his head tucked away in the kind of place a chipmunk or rabbit might live. Funny, he thought, in that stupid, sleepy way that overwhelms you late at night. How funny. The last real book tucked away in a rabbit's house. Or a chipmunk's.

Chapter
2

When he looked up, Martina Antipova was there, in the aisle, not more than two meters away. What was she doing on the bus? She always raced by them on the high bridge, looking very cool and relaxed, in a long, shiny chauffeur-driven Zlotny that zipped past the straining old school bus like an ice-cream-cool meteor.

With a blinding smile, "An assignment?" Her voice was deeper than he had expected; more round. And very Russian.

"Yes," he replied with undisguised surprise, before adding, with more composure, "For Brownsky."

"It must be important." Before he could reply, she turned back toward the front of the bus and blurted out, "Fede, I've saved a seat for you." With that she slid into the window seat across the aisle from him, all the while smiling that blinding, effortless smile down the aisle to the beige flesh avalanche rolling toward them.

After Fede had collapsed into the seat with a fierce grunt, "Well, what do you think?"

Fede adjusted her jumpsuit. Its zipper swerved down her stomach as if it were a dangerous mountain road.

"Well?"

Expelling a huge breath and rotating so that Martina Antipova was completely eclipsed, "Give me a minute."

After their heads moved together he could hear nothing else. But he still couldn't bring himself to finish copying the paper. The time evaporated while he guessed what they were saying.

He expected her, when she stepped out into the aisle, to speak, or nod, or offer some hint of recognition, for after all she had been the

53

one to speak to him earlier; but she glided after her monstrous friend as if he weren't there, the sleek muscles rippling musically up and down her back as she walked.

It was not until they reached the door, when she turned to toss her braid over her shoulder, that she looked at him. It was, he was sure, a look. Not an accident. Or reflex. But while he was still smiling acknowledgment she turned back to her friend to say something. As they vanished up the stairwell he could hear her sumptuous voice blending into all the others.

Before class began he finished copying the fourth page of his essay, sliding it into his notebook as he stood with the others to greet Kerelsky. Kerelsky was a true Russian. Not as impressive as you might expect, but, nevertheless, a true Russian.

"You may begin the recitation, Comrade Nurov," he requested. Even though he was no more than thirty, Kerelsky was as pale as a corpse. A red-orange cap of hair covered his head like moss.

"Yes, sir." He fumbled open his notes.

"When class begins, class begins," Kerelsky offered dryly, almost philosophically, and with a kind of boredom that only Kerelsky could exhibit. He must have been talking to Brownsky. That was the last thing he needed.

"Yes, sir." He stood at his desk. "'Revolutionary Zeal,' by S. T. Dramolov." He took a deep breath. He was the Russian man on the street. A Leningrad tram conductor. A student at Moscow University. The whole time his forehead was remarkably cool.

"What was the title of that," twisting his mouth, "poem, comrade?"

"'Revolutionary Zeal,'" he replied hesitantly, his forehead starting to warm.

"Yes, quite right." In that same bored way, "Why did you read it as if it were a Moscow grain report?"

Kerelsky was inclined to make remarks like that. Remarks that struck Alex as being vaguely unpatriotic. On the one hand, "Revolutionary Zeal," and on the other, innuendos about the grain harvest. Or at least it seemed so. Not a very good example for a true Russian to set, he decided. Still there was something about him. Something —well, a little impressive.

Alex sat, in response to a wave of Kerelsky's hand.

Marking in his notebook, "The phrasing was fine." From Kerelsky that was high praise.

The next two poems were read with a lot of revolutionary zeal, even though the second was entitled "Summer Solstice." None sounded, he was sure, more truly Russian than his. Of course, that wasn't really surprising. Most of them had spent no more than a month out of every two years in Russia. And some less than that. Oh, there were a few new ones. But most, like Gregorov, and Myslov, had spent no more than six or eight months in Russia altogether. And those as tourist. Or visiting relatives. Or, as in his case, as infants. Odd. They still thought of themselves as completely Russian. And they were.

While they read, Kerelsky occupied himself by twisting a tuft of hair over his ear, winding it tighter and tighter as if his head were a wind-up toy powered by a spring.

After the bell, while Alex remained at his desk to copy the last page of the essay, Kerelsky sat looking into the empty room, still, it appeared to Alex, in a state of shock from the recitation. But then, Kerelsky seemed to be perpetually disappointed. Or distracted. Or privately amused. As if he knew something that no one else did. Some secret that made everything and everyone a joke. Or fraud. He was, Alex was sure, a Russian who would rather be in Russia.

He waited for Alex to reach the door to speak: "I understand you will be at Moscow University next year." Alex pivoted. "Congratulations."

"Thank you."

Rolling the ball of hair between his forefinger and thumb, "Quite an honor."

Awkwardly, "Yes. Thank you."

Again stopping him after he had turned, "You will be the object of considerable . . . scrutiny." When Alex looked over his shoulder, Kerelsky was absently winding up his head in preparation for his next class.

Alex escaped into the hallway.

When he arrived at Brownsky's class, after repeating, in as many ways as he could in the five-minute span it took to get there, "America before the Great Uprising. So, what was it like? you ask. What was it really like?" Brownsky merely pointed an arched finger at his desktop, indicating where the paper was to be placed.

A cool breeze blew across his face as he walked back to his desk. He was sure Brownsky had said he would have to read it. Yes. Gregorov had that disappointed look on his face.

Before he reached his desk he was daydreaming about Martina Antipova's blood-red shorts. And the guitar-string tendon that stretched down the inside of her thigh.

Later, they were in the throes of the Great Uprising:

"History is propelled by scientifically identifiable forces, a dialectic discovered by Marx. Elaborated by Lenin, as well as the other great scientists of socialist thought. Note the word 'scientist.' These men were not philosophers engaged in speculation. Or mumbo-jumbo priests."

The hunchbacked priest popped into his mind. The phrase. Not the man. Or a picture of the man. Just the phrase: the hunchbacked priest. Mumbo-jumbo, hunchbacked priest. And then a picture. Of sorts. At least the hunchback. No man to go with it. Just a hunchback. Draped in black. Why black? he wondered.

"They were engaged in the tough business of science. Think of the revolutionary conclusion they reached: the destiny of man is scientifically determined; the instrument of history is the Party. We are all part of, in fact the culmination of, a great, unstoppable process."

He stopped to wipe his nose. The world of shrubs and trees and grass didn't seem to be the right place for him. "How does it feel to be part of something as momentous as that?" he asked through the large-as-a-sail white handkerchief that was always in his hand or waiting nearby in his pocket.

Myslov chirped, "Wonderful, sir."

Brownsky waited.

"To be part of history organizes each day."

"Quite right, Myslov. Quite right."

It was just like Myslov to respond with an elementary-school proverb.

"Now, let us focus on America. It may be hard for us to believe, but America, the city of Charleston, was a very different place before the Great Uprising."

Charleston was always the example. Was that just Brownsky? Or because that was where they were? No. There was more to it than that. It was the city itself. It was, after all, on the surface, a perfect

56

example, with its old, arrogant houses that stood overlooking Battery Park and the two rivers that joined there like unrepentant backsliders. Not that he regretted living in a place that so perfectly exemplified the errors of the past. That just made it easier to see the truth. But sometimes it did feel a little odd to be in a place that had been the focus of so much evil.

"Very different. But beneath the surface the forces of history were heating to the point of explosion. And nothing could stop it. Nothing. Marx and Lenin make it clear that only what happened could have happened.

"The question is, what were the ingredients that when brought together made this explosion a certainty? Just as a chemist might isolate the ingredients in gunpowder, scientific socialism asks: what were the forces that made the Great Uprising inevitable? Why the explosion?" Brownsky said "explosion" with such force that the room rumbled.

He enumerated with his fingers.

"First, slavery. Owned black labor that scrubbed floors, swept streets, harvested the crops.

"The working masses. Not much better off than slaves. White slaves, if you will.

"The unemployed masses. One of the many," he chuckled sarcastically, "contradictions of capitalism. Starving, their unwanted labor wasting away with their unfed flesh.

"The criminals. Yes, even they played a role in the history's march. Thieves, muggers, murderers, they covered the streets like sores on a syphilitic corpse. Pity them."

Brownsky looked up while he paged forward in his notes. His face was beaded with sweat, flushed, transported by conviction.

"They were also victims."

Alex looked around the room at his classmates as they impassively copied down Brownsky's words. They were not really bored, but in a state of functional awareness somewhere between boredom and interest, a state in which words are copied, questions are answered. It was as if Brownsky were trying to rouse them with the color blue. The sky was full of it every day, but it was too far away, or too obvious, to really matter at all.

"And lastly, the privileged: the property owners, the capitalists, the weapons manufacturers, the users of labor, and their paid vultures.

Lawyers. Politicians. Priests." Alex was sure he had seen a picture of a priest. In one of his textbooks. Yes. Perhaps it had been a photograph. Yes. And he was wearing a headdress. Or was that an Indian chief? Perhaps it was in the encyclopedia? Odd he hadn't thought of that when he was reading The Book. That hadn't been the picture that came to mind at all when he had been reading The Book.

With a smile, "They were sitting on a bomb ready to explode and," he paused dramatically, "they didn't know it. They didn't know it at all."

The bell rang.

"Oh," Brownsky exclaimed, before adding with a touch of embarrassment, "Enjoy your lunch, comrades."

Myslov paused at Brownsky's desk to say, "A stirring lecture, sir," before scurrying down the hall toward the cafeteria.

For the first time he felt a little sorry for Brownsky.

Skating along the icy hall floor, flanked by successive wall-sized photographs of the heroes of the revolution, he vowed to be more serious about history. Perhaps Gregorov had been, albeit accidentally, on the mark; perhaps history was indeed the queen of the sciences.

She was on the other side of a sea of grass. After drying her palm on the hem of her shorts she grasped the javelin firmly and began trotting toward him. Her perspiration-dampened face glistened in the sun as she accelerated. Snap. He loved the way her body snapped when she released. And she always smiled afterward. No matter whether the toss was long or short. Apparently the smile was a completely natural consequence of the act itself. As natural as the run. And the snap.

The javelin flew past the doorway he was occupying.

He could smell the fresh-cut grass as he kicked up small, damp clumps of it with his feet. It smelled faintly stale. Like it had been cooking in the sun.

"Nice toss," he offered as their paths crossed.

Without slowing down she slipped the headband from her hair with her thumb. "Thank you." She stopped, leaned forward, and vigorously shook her head, creating a showering sweat rainstorm that lit up in the sun like fireworks.

"You must be very serious about the," he paused for a second, "about sports."

58

With a puzzled smile, "Yes."

Her hair was thick and damp. He could almost smell it, mingling with the just-that-morning-cut grass.

"Throwing the javelin, I mean."

"Yes."

She smiled, mopping her neck with the terry-cloth headband, making no attempt to shade her eyes. The smile said nothing at all, beyond "Hello."

Awkwardly, "I've noticed you out here. While I'm eating lunch." He pointed up toward the cafeteria.

"Oh." She began trotting toward the javelin.

"You ought to be on the cover of *Soviet Sports*," he blurted out. He immediately regretted saying something that dumb. It was the kind of thing Myslov might say in one of his attacks of friendship.

She stopped for a moment, apparently in response to what he had said, before announcing, "I have two more tosses." She immediately trotted off toward the javelin.

He waited in the shade of the building. The second toss left her not far away, where she sat cross-legged to rub down the javelin with a small blue cloth that had been tucked in the back of her shorts.

Approaching, "That was quite a throw."

"No."

He stopped a foot or two away.

"No." With annoyance, "I've completely lost my concentration." She pumped up and down along the entire upper half of the shaft in long, vigorous strokes for half a minute before looking up. Apparently her attention had been caught by the sandwich which dangled helplessly at his side. She repeated, "Completely."

"Sorry." Realizing that the sandwich was dangling in her face, "My lunch. Would you care for some? I can cut it in half."

She looked as if she might get ill. "No. Five minutes ago I could feel it. It was there. I was a javelin thrower."

He wasn't sure what to say.

She stood without pushing off, her crossed legs raising her as effortlessly as a pneumatic service-station jack raises a Zlotny for an oil change.

"It'll come back," he offered consolingly, still not sure what if anything she had lost.

Unconvinced, "Hmmm."

The spear balanced on her shoulder, she walked dejectedly to the far side of the portico. Twice she stopped to kick ruefully at the grass, each time precipitating a small shower of freshly mowed stubble that evoked that same slightly cooked, decayed smell he had noticed crossing the field. She sat against the wall in the brick elbow created by the portico and unzipped a canvas bag that had been left resting against the wall. She pulled out a spoon and polished it with the tail of her T-shirt before extracting a cardboard cup of yogurt.

He carefully chewed several bites of his sandwich before venturing, "So, what do you think of it?" She looked a little puzzled. "Here. America."

With a shrug, "A little old." After a moment, "Run-down."

"Run-down?"

"Yes."

"Compared to Moscow?"

Smiling, "Yes. Or Leningrad. Or Grognesk."

"Grognesk?"

Matter-of-factly, "That's a fishing resort in the Urals."

Embarrassed, "Oh."

He sat there quietly while she ate the yogurt, watching her discreetly run her tongue through each cool spoonful after her mouth was closed. When the container was empty, she remarked, "You haven't told me your name."

"Actually we met this morning, or almost did."

"I know." She leaned her head against the brick wall and closed her eyes.

"Alex. Alexander Mikhailovich Nurov." He emphasized the "Mikhailovich Nurov," but she evidently had not been there long enough for that to mean anything to her.

"I am Martina Antipova."

He prevented himself from blurting out, "Yes, I know," contenting himself instead with merely smiling.

Her hands still closed, "So, you must be what they call an old hand?"

"Yes, I'm afraid so."

"You shouldn't be. Apologetic, I mean." Her broad cheekbones seemed to be melting into the wall. "We each have our duty."

Starting to rise, "Yes."

"I am visualizing," she said, in a clear effort to restrain him. "I always visualize afterward."

He slid back down the wall onto the grass.

"So, I suppose you know everything there is to know about Charleston?"

"Yes. I guess." Taking advantage of the fact that her eyes were still closed, "I could show you around the old part of town. If you haven't seen it."

Opening her eyes, "I haven't."

"It's interesting," he replied in a way that implied he knew more about the old part of town than he did.

Rising, the javelin firmly in hand, as if the key to success with it was to remain as close to it as possible, "Time for my shower." She bent at the waist to pick up the canvas bag.

"It only takes an hour or so."

She was already in the stairwell when he offered, "We could today. If you wanted to catch a later bus."

Bounding up the stairs two at a time, "If you like."

"Then, why don't we meet," looking up the stairwell, "here. After school?"

Her round voice, sounding immensely Russian, echoed down the staircase, "Yes. After school."

But by four o'clock, when she hadn't arrived, after he had checked around the front twice, he left.

She must have talked to someone. Like her hideous friend, Fede. So what? After all, he was an Ouspensky. As well as a Nurov. That more than made up for being Russamsky. If that's what she wanted to think he was.

Chapter

3

     The blonde walked with her head down, the atrophied purple arms of a sweatshirt dangling from around her neck onto her tiny breasts. Her hair was so short and greasy that it rested dead against her cheeks instead of bouncing with her head as it bobbed up and down. Her hands were jammed into the front pockets of her jumpsuit, giving the impression that it was midwinter.

He paused at the open doors of a fruit stand.

Behind her the narrow straight-as-a-rifle-shot street was chopped into irregular asphalt oases by the dozens of listless lines that sprang from the shop doors. Above the lines, smiling billboard clouds filled with lean tan faces rained down enthusiasm. Dedication. Hard work. But, as if they were protected by invisible umbrellas, face after face retained that same bored listlessness as the messages fell pointlessly onto the smooth black asphalt.

When she got closer he occupied himself with an empty basket. Above it a triangular sliver of masonry hung precariously, ready to guillotine an inquisitive hand. That was the kind of thing that ought to be reported, but for some reason was not. Instead, problems like that waited for the next man to report them. And the next. And next. Until a long, senseless chain of nonreports had been created. For this tear in the wall. And the next. And the next. Perhaps when the building collapsed someone would notice? He felt like walking up to the clerk and saying, "Why haven't you reported that, comrade? Don't you know that if you did it would be taken care of?" The clerk was sitting behind the counter half asleep. Why were they like that? Couldn't they see that if they were willing to work everything would go so much better? There wouldn't be all these damned lines. Not if everyone was willing to do his duty and work.

She pushed by, her hands still in her pockets, her head still down. From close up she wasn't very pretty. You could see the bones poking through her jumpsuit. At the hips. And even her shoulders, through the draped sweatshirt. But when she walked there was a lingering, almost imperceptible sway that, long before she was sharply visible, had arrested his imagination.

He let her get a few meters in front of him before following. The fascinating sway seemed even more pronounced. Perhaps she had realized he was there?

Alex slowed down.

She stopped at the window of a shoe outlet. The sign above the door merely said SHOES, or once had, before the "S" had peeled off. Now one had to stop and look into the window for the sign to make any sense. Or know beforehand that there were shoes inside.

Perhaps it was run-down. Odd that had never really occurred to him before. It had seemed perfectly natural. Now, just looking around him produced a mild embarrassment that arose not just because she was right, but because, for some reason, he had never noticed. No wonder Martina Antipova thought they were all such bumpkins.

She slid through a line as if it were a crack in the wall, but when he attempted to follow an old woman grimaced, mean-eyed, saying silently, "You can't have my spot. No. Go to the back. Or at least behind me." He looked her directly in the eye, until, sensing perhaps that he was Russian—and only passing through—she stepped back, her shopping bag tightly in her white-knuckled fist.

When he emerged she was sitting on the steps of a large, gray stucco building. It was one of those left over from before the Great Uprising. In itself that was not especially unusual. Nor were the four large, rather stately columns that looked down over the stairs as they flowed into the sidewalk. It was the tower that distinguished it. A flat-topped masonry tower which squatted in the dead center of the street side of the gently pitched roof. It was three, perhaps four, meters tall. Tucked away in that inconvenient place, it seemed to serve no useful purpose. No useful purpose at all.

63

She sat with her elbows on her knees, her chin cupped in her hands.

He measured the tower several times with his eyes before crossing the street. He looked up at it from the corner. The barren street corner offered him nothing else to pretend to do.

Just as he was about to pass by, "Nice day."

It wasn't clear whether what she had said was a question or just a remark. He wasn't even certain it was directed to him.

"Wouldn't you say?" She wiped her nose with the back of her hand.

"Yes." Feeling compelled to explain what he was doing, "I'm just walking, enjoying it."

As if it were quite an achievement, "I've been getting coffee."

She reached under her arm into the pocket of the purple sweatshirt to extract a small brown paper bag. Holding the bag between her forefinger and thumb, "Two hours."

"Oh. I guess that is sort of long."

With surprise, "No. It's coffee. Real coffee." Proudly, "One tenth of a kilo. And it's full weight." She bounced the paper bag in her open palm. "I can tell things like that. My hand is a scale."

What an odd remark, he thought.

"I'm serious." She must have seen the surprise. "It is."

"This is no place to loiter," a voice exploded from above them. Standing between the columns the policeman seemed especially large and official.

Alex replied, "We're just enjoying the sun."

"Enjoy it somewhere else."

"There's no . . ." he began before the young woman slid her arm through his while saying, "Come on, we can walk."

"He's American SP. He has . . ."

In a whisper, while tugging on his arm, "Are you crazy?" Looking over her shoulder, "Let's go sit by the river." He could feel the gentle sway as she led him down the sidewalk. "Do you want to land up in one of those places?" Pulling her head back so that she could look him squarely in the face, "You're not out on leave or something? No, you're not that much of a loon. Well, you'd better be a little more careful or you're going to land up in one of those places."

He kept expecting her to withdraw her arm, but she left it there, looped around his like a pasty, skin-covered rope, until they were on the boomerang-shaped concrete walkway that hugged the point where the river that had been on their left joined another broad, tidal river. The confluence of these rivers formed a lazy, smooth harbor that stretched four or five kilometers to Mt. Pleasant. Behind them was a line of ancient houses that presided over the harbor like self-satisfied old ladies.

Sliding under the metal railing so that her feet were just above the water, "I'm pooped. I haven't been feeling well." As if it were a prescription for feeling better, "Would you like a cup of coffee?"

"Yes." Awkwardly, "Sure."

"I might even have something sweet?" she added, her head tilted to the side playfully, as if the question were some kind of test. Not a serious one, but one that might arise in a game that children play, where failure to provide the right answer, or adhere to the right form or some silly rule, results in a penalty or punishment like stepping back three paces or shutting one's eyes while everyone hides.

Her apartment was one of those odd, flat-topped towers. It was at the top of three flights of clanking metal stairs that were clearly an afterthought concocted long after the building had been erected. The black exoskeleton enveloped two adjacent sides of the building, the three ascents connected by two slatted catwalks riveted to the bricks by huge, rust-sweating bolts.

"Well?" she inquired proudly.

If the door had opened inward there would have been nowhere to stand while you shut it.

"Very comfortable."

Along one wall there was a counter on which a hot plate, small refrigerator, and sink were crammed. A rolled narrow mattress secured by a rope had been pushed into the far corner under the counter. The only furniture was a small rocking chair.

Pointing to the chair, while water roared into an aluminum teapot, "You'll like that."

And he did. Odd she would know that. The chair was a scaled-down version of the chairs at the Saluda house: a half-dozen huge, straight-backed rockers lined up on the porch like soldiers. He would sit in one, and then another, until he had sat in them all, leaving the unoccupied ones emptily rocking back and forth.

Just as she leaned against the counter to wait for the coffee, "Oh, damn. I promised you something sweet."

To the pale yellow handprints that had been worn in the seat of her jumpsuit, "Don't go to any trouble."

"A promise is a promise." Gravely searching the countertop refrigerator, "You learn that swapping. You can ask anyone." She pulled out a palm-sized foil package, crumpled it open at the top, and rested it against the teapot so that it shared the eye. "If I promise something, it's there." With finality, "Full weight."

"Where do you work?" he inquired after searching a second for something to say.

Energetically, "I'm no parasite, if that's what you mean."

"I didn't mean that at all."

"I've been sick. That's why I wasn't at work today." Emphatically, "I have a doctor's excuse."

"I'm sure you do," he replied feebly.

"Well, I don't want anybody thinking I'm a parasite." Facing him, resting her butt against the counter, "I'm a clerk. A file clerk. But a," she paused, "a friend of mine has promised me a better job. A much better job." After a moment, clearly for effect, she added, "At the submarine base."

Agreeably, "I guess that would be better."

"He's very good at arranging things like that," she added, leaving no doubt that she considered that immensely important.

Coolly, "I'll bet."

She tucked her hands behind her back so that she rested against them instead of the counter. "He's a Russian," she announced. When he did not respond, she added, "They're not so bad. Not when you get to know them."

"No." Feeling a little strange, "I guess not."

"And they can, well," she turned her attention to the foil-wrapped package, tapping it away from the hot eye with her fingertip, "do things for you. Things that no one else can do." She snapped her fingers. "Just like that."

"I guess they can."

"You really are a loony out on leave if you don't know that."

She served the coffee with great attention to detail and ceremony, in mismatched cups, saving the one with the large chip for herself.

She spread a large pat of margarine on the sweet roll before breaking it in two. When she dipped hers in the hot coffee before biting into it he followed suit. It was warm and sugary.

Pinching off a crumb of mold, "Not bad, eh?"

"Delicious," he agreed.

When they had finished he stood to look through the window.

"No need to hurry off," she said quickly, leaving no doubt that for some reason she wanted company.

"I wasn't really thinking about that." Comfortably leaning against the high windowsill, "The view is great. You can see the river quite clearly. Through the branches."

In the form of an explanation, "I can't have sex." Matter-of-factly, "Not for another week."

He watched a boat skim between the branches of a monstrous oak.

"I had an abortion last week," she continued, as if she were delivering the evening news.

The bus broke down on the bridge. You could always tell when it was going to fail: the pitch of the electric motor rose from a shrill soprano until it just vanished into nothing. The driver radioed for a replacement and propped his feet on the dashboard.

After watching the bottom half of his pencil flutter, like a busted, out-of-control moon shuttle, into the sixty meters of blackness that separated them from the river, Alex occupied himself with the taste of melted sugar and the unfamiliar, lingering coffee buzz that zipped up and down his arms like an electric breeze.

It was not until he was boarding the replacement bus that it dawned on him that he didn't even know her name. Well, it probably didn't matter. He would never see her again. No. There was no reason to. She was so strange. All American girls couldn't be that strange, could they? No. There was more to it than that. Calling him a loon. Why, she didn't even realize he was Russian. She was the loon. Maybe she was the one out on leave. Just the thought made him shudder.

But then, until she had mentioned sex, he was feeling quite relaxed. In the rocking chair that reminded him of the big Saluda house. Even drinking coffee. And there was that hint of excitement.

Sprawling, concrete-coated Mt. Pleasant and the long asphalt arm that reached out to the island across the marsh slipped by disguised as sweet rolls and coffee. He barely opened his eyes at the gate, even though one of the guards boarded the bus and shined a light under each seat before letting them pass. What did he expect to find? In the thousand times Alex had seen that, not once had anyone been under one of the seats.

After loping to the door, he stopped and took a deep breath to prepare himself. It never paid to be late for dinner.

As soon as he opened the door he could hear them:

With firmness, "That would be unwise. Very unwise."

"Anything else, Nurov, would be to deny his destiny."

"Destiny? You sound like some old witch."

Dryly, "I wish I were."

"The period of planned technological development is ending," he offered, as if it were the beginning of a long lecture.

"Are we tiring of the traditional virtues?"

Ignoring her, "The point is, there will be many opportunities. In science and engineering. And," he spoke emphatically, "they are not political. At least not obviously. There is no point in having him take risks." Expelling a breath of air, "To land up stuck like me."

"I didn't have a son to have him stuck in a Zlotny factory."

"A lot worse things could happen. A lot worse." Affecting calmness, "I know this is a message. But only a message." He lowered his voice. "Perhaps they are recognizing what I have done. But don't make too much of it."

"This is an opportunity, not a message. And he will be the one who must be ready to seize it."

"He has already been accepted in the Polytechnic Division."

"But now—now that we know he will be accepted—why not apply to the Division of Government Studies and Marxist Analysis?" When he refused to reply, she continued, "I'm sure Sonia Ouspenskaya would approve."

With an agonized hiss, "Leave my grandmother out of this."

"She is in this." Whispering, "We both know that." Continuing to whisper, "She would approve."

Sarcastically, "Since when do seventeen years of silence evidence approval?"

His mother did not reply. She simply sat there. Looking very cool

68

and relaxed. Except that her finger was lightly tapping against the tablecloth.

With finality, "He will study engineering. I will not sacrifice him to satisfy some," Nurov searched for a moment, "religious whim."

Disgustedly, "Religious? Is that how my opinions are received?"

So that they would be certain to hear him, "Hello, Corinne."

She muttered something into a large pot without removing her head from it.

"Your dinner is getting cold," Nurov reprimanded, before Alex could get to his chair.

"Sorry, Father. The bus broke down."

Seizing the opportunity that Alex had presented, "Perhaps what we need in this country is a few engineers. Then perhaps," he gloated, "the damned buses would run on time."

"I missed our swim," his mother replied, as if Nurov had not spoken at all. She rose and, her gown in her fingertips, crossed over to Alex and kissed him on the cheek. "The clinic was a madhouse today. A swim would have been relaxing." Without turning, "Good night, Nurov."

Her pale gown was as thin and blue as ice on a windowpane. It caressed the floor behind her as she vanished down the hallway.

After an awkward minute or two, "So, how did your paper go? Now that you are able to use the most authoritative sources."

"Fine," he replied uncertainly.

Carving a slice of meat for Alex, "Just fine?"

"Well, I didn't actually have to present it."

"Oh." He dropped the wet meat on Alex's extended plate.

"Yes. It was kind of odd. That's not really like Brownsky."

Chewing, quietly, "Really. What is really like Brownsky?"

"Oh, I don't know. The usual." On the spur of the moment, "He gave a rousing lecture today. On conditions leading up to the Great Uprising."

"You were moved, then?"

Not knowing how to respond, "Well, it was more exciting than usual." Was the question merely sarcasm? "Sometimes history can be a little," he searched, "repetitious."

His father laughed very loudly.

"But, I'm finding it more to my liking. A lot more."

Grimly, "That's fine. But remember your talent lies in science and engineering." He smiled. "The Party will have need, great need, for engineers."

Alex nodded while cutting into his meat.

"When you have finished your dinner I'll show you more about the DAL system."

"DAL?" Alex repeated.

"Your friend from last night."

"The computer?"

"That interest you, then?" Nurov inquired in a way that actually seemed more like a statement than a question.

"Yes." He continued while his father rounded the table, "Very much."

"Good," Nurov remarked without a hint of sarcasm.

He hurried down the last few bites of his dinner before following after his father, who was already seated at the screen, his face coated with the unnatural patina the screen gave to everything nearby.

PLEASE ENTER YOUR AUTHORIZATION CODE: m n 0 0 1
PASSWORD?

While his fingers moved across the keyboard, "So, what would you like to see?"

GOOD EVENING, VICE-MINISTER NUROV.
WHAT CAN I DO FOR YOU?

"Ah," Alex stammered, having no idea what the choices were.

"There must be something you want to know." He always became tongue-tied when Nurov behaved that way. "Something that interests you?" Peering into the screen, "Nothing to rival an afternoon swim, I'm sure. Let's see." He spun around in the swivel chair so that his face was suddenly right in Alex's. "Physics? How does that sound?"

Stammering, "Okay."

"So?" After waiting, "What are you studying right now?"

Alex's mind went totally blank.

"Well? Don't tell me you've been doing calculus problems in that class too."

70

That explained why he hadn't had to read the paper.

"We're waiting."

"Most of the problems have been about," Alex searched, "mechanics. You know, things like inclined planes and screws."

"Well," turning back to the screen, "let's see what my old friend has to say about that."

"And pulleys," Alex added lamely.

"Well, of course. And pulleys. The most authoritative sources on pulleys." Nurov's fingers glided across the keyboard. "And screws. And et cetera. Let's hope we have clearance for something that," he hesitated, "exciting."

There were 12,850 citations on mechanics. Nurov selected four tutorials: the computer posed questions.

They took turns responding. Each time Alex missed a question Nurov would say, "Damned American schools," or "What do they do there all day, whittle?"

As always, Alex did not know whether to laugh, or be very quiet; but, in the end, the paralysis inflicted by remarks like that subsided enough for him to at least attempt an answer.

"Alexander," his father said when they were finished, leaning back in his swivel chair, "your mother is going to be talking to you." He probed Alex's eyes with his. "If she hasn't already." The eyes continued to interrogate him. "She can be very persuasive. Very. Don't let her confuse you with, well, her fantasies. Do you know what I'm driving at?"

"Yes, I think so," he replied, although he didn't. At least not completely. But he would have said yes no matter what. Talking about her, to his father, produced an odd, prickly feeling, akin to the one you get just before you're going to throw up. He would have said yes to anything to rid himself of that feeling.

"Good. You'll make a fine engineer. This here," he tapped the top of the terminal, "will help prepare you. Moscow will be very different."

"More competitive. I know."

"That and other things as well."

"I know."

"No." Quietly, "You don't know at all. It will be like being alive after being dead." Nurov rose. "I'll get you a password. So that you will have access to the DAL system on your own."

"Thank you," Alex replied, containing his amazement.

Philosophically, as if Alex were somehow missing something, "That way you should be more than ready by next fall."

"I will be," Alex assured him.

His hand extended to switch off the terminal, "Do you understand the enormity of this?" The "this" clearly referred to the machine he was touching. It was said with a kind of certainty. And gravity.

A crackle and the screen was empty.

"For the first time," Nurov walked toward the study door, "the Party will completely control history." Dimming the light, "And through it the future. The truth will no longer be hostage to lies and distortions." In the dark, "It will alter the world."

Suddenly sounding very tired, his back to Alex as he walked down the hall, "Good night, Alexander."

His voice had been riddled with disappointment. Perhaps he didn't realize that Alex understood. Or that he appreciated what was being offered to him. Or maybe it was that long-standing disappointment that seemed to chronically afflict him. He had given up so much. Alex wanted to say something. To let him know that he understood.

"Good night, Father."

That night Alex resolved to be truly Russian. To make it all worthwhile.

That meant he must think like a Russian. That he must think the right thoughts. That he must obey the dictates of the Party. After all, the Party's leadership knew. They had thought it all through.

It was hard to tell when the idea first hit. Maybe when he passed by the kitchen. No. It just seemed to be there, waiting for him, the moment he woke up.

Actually it was the kind of Saturday morning made for hiding out in the dune with a sandwich and one of his mysteries. But they had been read into the ground. And there was The Book. If it was there, in the dune, within reach, he wouldn't be able to stop himself from reading it.

And his father's study had been locked. "AN001," he tapped out on the shiny aluminum seat back of the bus. Just one character different from his father's, he thought proudly, struck as he did so by how much everything had changed. Just because he had been admitted to Moscow University. He tapped out the password.

And then he nervously patted the invisible lump in his breast pocket while the bus crept over the bridge.

Rather than wait for a transfer he went on foot from Gorky Street, shaking the excitement out of his hands with an occasional snap as he walked. At Battery Park he stopped for a second to listen to part of a carriage tour. Even the driver's abominable Russian offered only a second's diversion. Take a deep breath, he said to himself. That always works at the free-throw line. And it did. But only for a second or two.

The metal stairs hummed an embarrassing fanfare as he climbed. When it subsided, he knocked.

The horse-drawn carriage he had passed at Battery Park was in front of the Governor's residence. The driver, his period top hat pushed casually back, his foot resting on the seat, was continuing his sightseeing speech. Perhaps the young woman was still wondering what a mint julep was? No. Her hand was resting on the Russian officer's knee while she daydreamed.

He knocked again.

The carriage was advancing now. Very slowly. The driver still talking, uttering that same awful Russian Alex had heard as he passed by.

There was a sharp rap on the windowpane.

Her small, naked breasts were squashed against the glass.

"I can come back later," he forced out, returning his eyes to the Battery.

He could hear the door open.

"I didn't mean to wake you."

Melting into the door, "Oh? You?" A small tear jutted out from the hip of her underpants.

"I was just walking around."

Receding into the shadows, "I'd offer you some coffee, but," collapsing cross-legged onto the small mattress, which had been pulled from under the counter, "there's none. Not a damned drop."

With a sudden burst of confidence, "I brought some."

"And," curling up like a hairless kitten, "I'm worthless without my coffee."

73

Before he could extract the plastic bag from his breast pocket, she had shut her eyes.

"I'm sure it will wake you right up," he offered, his voice trailing off disappointedly when she began to snore.

He stood there for a moment, feeling superfluous, before stepping up to the counter and, mimicking what he had seen her do on the previous Tuesday, emptied the old grounds from the coffee maker, retrieving the soggy brown paper filter before pasting it back into place. After pouring in the coffee grounds and putting the water on, he retreated to the rocking chair to wait while she slept, a crumpled sheet pressed in a tight ball against her chest as if it were a life preserver in a crystal-clear, sleepy sea.

Odd. He had been terrified on the way over, but now, even though she was lying there wearing only underpants, he felt fine.

"Your morning coffee," he announced proudly while placing the cup on the floor by the mattress.

But she didn't budge. After a few sips from his cup he leaned forward and inched hers closer to her nose. "Your morning coffee," he repeated, more loudly.

Apparently she could sleep through anything.

Later, on his way to refill his cup, as he straddled her, she murmured, "Those grounds are dead."

He quickly stepped the rest of the way across her.

Rolling onto her back, the tightly balled sheet in the cusp of her elbow, "Completely dead."

"No." With satisfaction, "I made it just the way you did. At least I think I did."

"How long have I been out?" Without waiting for an answer, "You're really drinking that stuff? You must have plenty of imagination." She raised up on her elbow.

"It's fresh." He gestured toward her cup. "At least I think it is."

"Really?" she inquired suspiciously. "Fresh?" The crumpled sheet fell carelessly aside when she reached for the cup.

After convincing herself it was real, and fresh, she stretched out on her back and, using her belly as a table, sipped intermittently from the cup.

Twice he brought her refills.

All the while her nipples jutted up like pencil erasers.

74

"There's room here," she said on his way back from placing his cup in the sink. She slid over onto her elbow and extended her empty cup to him.

After stacking her cup on his he sat on the edge of the inch-thick mattress.

"So, you live at home," she remarked, as if that had been the topic of conversation for the last half hour. Proudly, "It's not easy to find a place of you own."

"I suppose."

"You have the oddest ideas." Wrinkling her nose, "Many brothers and sisters?"

He shook his head.

"Then that's not so bad."

After a moment she picked up his hand and placed it on her breast. Perhaps she had noticed him looking. It was as sticky as warm marshmallow.

"What does your mother do?"

Cautiously, "She's a doctor."

"Oh? Is that what you're going to be? A doctor?"

"No." He began to knead her breast. Tentatively.

"What then?"

"An engineer." He slid his hand down her side. "Perhaps an," stumbling, "an aeronautical engineer." He stopped the advance of his hand, as if his stumbling on the word would somehow make her conscious of its location.

"An engineer," she repeated, convincing herself that was a reasonable thing to be. He slid his thumb inside the elastic band of her underpants. "You must be one of those brains." His thumb grazed across her pubic hair. "Is that what you are?" she pressed, while extracting his hand.

Awkwardly, "No. I guess."

Matter-of-factly, as she put the hand back on her breast, "I can't do that. I won't get more pills until I go back to the clinic. And," she gently squeezed his hand into the shallow layer of flesh so that he could feel the nipple rising into his hand from her ribs, "one more abortion and it's a reeducation center for sure." Suddenly, as if it were necessary to append an afterthought, "Not that I wouldn't deserve it. But . . ." She ended the sentence with a shrug instead of words.

How could she be so unaffected? he wondered. After all, his hand was on her breast.

"Smile, and maybe," she tilted her head back, "I'll do something nice for you."

Caught off balance, he smiled without meaning to.

"If you knew what I had in mind, that smile would be bigger," she said with complete assurance. Before he could reply she reached over and unzipped his jumpsuit. "So, you're one of those school brains? I remember them." Inserting her hand into the meter-long incision in his jumpsuit, "Always sniffing up to the teacher." She slid her hand across his belly, grazing his erect penis before clamping her hand around his testicles. "I remember them."

She raised herself up onto her haunches, her spidery legs bent at the knees, and slipped her head into his jumpsuit. "Yes," she sighed, her voice muffled by the jumpsuit, "they were a pain." He felt the breath of the last word before she slid him into her mouth.

Just before he was about to ejaculate she shifted her hand from his testicles to the shaft of his penis, clamping him shut.

After abruptly removing her mouth, "So, is that what you are?" She squeezed tightly with her fist, while pumping up and down. "Is it?" she pouted, as she began to massage his testicles with her other hand.

When, on the way up, she snapped her thumb across him it sounded like a match striking.

Pumping, "Ready?" The question floated hypnotically toward him. "Ready?" she smiled, rolling his testicles from finger to finger. "Ready?"

When she let go of him, he came, his penis flopping around like a trout on the floor of a boat, gagging on a hook.

She leaned back so that her butt rested on her heels. "Look at all that wasted love. But I don't think you're going to miss it at all." As if she were a child fingerpainting, her lips in a rapt pout, she smeared the ejaculate into his belly until it formed a slick, dry veneer.

He was lying there, still enjoying being totally mystified, when, after craning to look at the clock, she announced, "Time for you to go. My friend will be here soon."

The pain must have registered on his face.

She bent back down and drew him into her mouth for a second

76

before releasing him with a loud smack. "Hmmm," she said, evidently pleased with herself for making him hard again. "Now up." She raced the cool zipper up to his throat and gave his crotch a gentle pat before standing and opening the door.

"Bye."

"Bye," he echoed lamely, while taking the two steps to the open air.

How could he feel so good one minute and so lost the next? he mused, while descending, his hand on the rusty railing, his eyes sifting the carriage and tourists through the gaps in the water oaks.

Suddenly the landing overhead exploded into a metal thunder storm. And there she was, her half-zipped jumpsuit snapping open and shut like a yellow kite on a March day. In a loud whisper, "I don't know your name."

"Oh." Confused, "Alex. Or Alexander."

"Well, Alex, come back soon and we'll finish the rest of the coffee." Retreating, "I'm Celeste."

She must have found the plastic bag, he concluded as the door shut. He had left it tightly sealed, resting against the wall behind the coffee maker. Odd she had found it so fast. A picture of her discovering it flashed through his mind; and of her racing to slip on her clothes. For some reason, just that picture of her racing around served to make her more real. And understandable. Which made him feel better. Much better.

Still, he decided, while staring up into the empty landing, I should have told her I was Russian. After all, I am.

Chapter 4

It was November 7. A very big day. In honor of the 143rd anniversary of the Bolshevik Revolution, the Governor was hosting a garden party. And, for the first time, Alex was invited. He had spent most of the week trying to imagine what it would be like.

Wryly, "Well, Alex, are you ready for your first grown-up social event?"

That was the first mention of the reception made since his father had read the invitation at dinner the preceding week. It was something that happened each year. For reasons she never revealed, or even commented on, his mother hated occasions like the Governor's reception. So, until the last minute, nothing was said.

Rising, before Alex could answer, "Perhaps I'll call the clinic."

"Let them call you." More gently, "If there's an emergency they will reach you."

"Not if . . ."

With a laugh, "Your penance can wait one day."

His father was fond of saying things like that. Things that seemed to make no sense at all.

"So, Daisy, what are you planning to wear?" Nurov was unshaved. Greasy black flames of hair curled around and into his ears. The hair was pushed back off his forehead, exposing the bright crescent birthmark that usually lurked invisibly behind a fold of black hair.

Pushing aside her plate of untouched breakfast fruit, "Perhaps I'll go naked this year." With her gown characteristically raised in her fingertips she glided down the hallway. For the first time Alex realized how truly thin and transparent the gown was.

78

From halfway down the hall, nearly imperceptibly, her back to them, "I'll go as the naked American whore revealed."

"And what are you going to wear, Alex?"

Embarrassed, "Ah, I don't know."

Nurov stared at him for a moment. He looked as if he had been awake for days.

"Something new, I guess."

Pushing up from the table with his palm, "Something new. Why not?"

There was really no answer to that.

After his father disappeared down the hallway, Alex drifted into the viewing room. Reruns of the parade were on. In close-up the figures were nearly life-size. Alex stretched out on the carpet a few feet from the screen so that the towering Young Pioneers who silently marched past the Kremlin wall almost stepped on his toes.

He raised his foot to trip one. The electronic image tromped adroitly by, followed by his successor. And then his successor. Each obliviously stepping over Alex's raised foot. . . .

When his father had entered the room, Alex had been half asleep, wondering in that drugged, slow way what the Governor's reception would be like, who would be there, who would not.

Just the day before on the bus he had overheard Martina Antipova say to her fat friend Fede, in her confident, fresh-from-Moscow way, "It will probably be a big bore." Did that mean she would be there? Or that it wasn't really worth the trouble? Or that the daughter of the naval attaché was not invited?

Alex could smell him, no, not that, somehow sense that he was there before he opened his eyes. For an instant he lay there very still, as he had every year until seven or eight years ago, waiting for his father to lift him up bedclothes and all and carry him into the viewing room to watch the huge parade live from Moscow. Then the event had been awe-inspiring: soldiers and Young Pioneers and workers of every sort marching past the Kremlin wall to be reviewed by the Party leadership.

"Alex." A moment of silence. "The parade has begun." Rather loudly, "Live from Moscow." Laughing, "Your last chance to see it live without being there." He sat up. Until then he had been lying there, rigidly waiting to be scooped up and carried into the viewing room. His father laughed again, more loudly. In his sleepiness Alex had thought for an instant that he was laughing at him for lying there like a little boy. For mistaking the time. But he had only been laughing at his joke.

They watched it together. The commentator turned off.

Only once did his father say anything at all, and that was "Perhaps you should toast the General Secretary." He got a glass for Alex and poured it half full of vodka. "To the health of the General Secretary." Lifting his glass. "Good health, Fyodor Alexandrovich Ouspensky." His father emptied the glass before looking over at him. He nodded.

It was ice-cold. And then so hot the fumes burned the inside of his nose.

"Didn't my great-uncle wave to us, Alexander? I'm certain he did. Isn't television a marvelous device? The way it brings families together." He nodded again, encouraging Alex to empty his glass.

His father's glass exploded against the base of the wall a meter away from the television.

"Go ahead. The General Secretary is waiting."

Alex threw his glass against the wall.

"To the General Secretary."

He had almost thrown up. Right on the spot. From the vodka. And the anxiety. And the odd, prickly excitement that accompanied shattering the glass. But he had held it back, half swallowing the sweet acid backwash as it rose in his throat.

The glass was still there, from the night before, where it had showered back onto the carpet. The shiny, dangerous-looking shards were patienty waiting for Corinne to vacuum them up.

He massaged his temples. His brain felt swollen and fat as if it had sponged up the vodka. That same uneasy sense of nausea that had struck just as his glass hit the wall returned. He shut his eyes, letting the marchers silently tromp by on the other side of his eyelids until he was asleep.

"Alexander, I thought you were dressing."

He turned his head so that she was perpendicular to his line of sight. Her hair was pulled back tightly, held in place by a brightly painted wooden comb; it was very blond, almost radiant.

He rubbed his eyes.

Musically, "You'd better wash up before Nurov sees you."

He sat up.

She was clasping a thin diamond choke around her neck. It rested securely against the red velour strip that encircled her neck in honor of the occasion.

"Hurry." Again what she said didn't really match the way she said it. She said, "Hurry," but in a way that meant "Hurry slowly. Or not at all." She was smiling, serenely, her eyes half hidden behind her eyelids, as if she were a very beautiful, wise fairy queen and he were a woodsman's son or a princely frog.

"What time is it?"

From the doorway, "Very late."

He stared up at a phalanx of agricultural workers from the Ukraine. The banner proclaiming their origin stretched across twenty of them. The last two rows supported a huge color portrait with the caption "Long Live General Secretary Ouspensky."

The General Secretary reciprocated by raising his hand to his shoulder.

Alex examined the face very carefully. Apart from the characteristic birthmark, it didn't really resemble his father's at all. Or his. No, not at all. Except for the eyes, perhaps. And then only in the way they seemed to say nothing. The General Secretary's eyes, like his father's, seemed to drink in everything around them, to inquire, to evaluate; but they said nothing themselves.

On the way to the Governor's reception he sat facing them so that his back rested against the driver's. He found himself studying his father, searching for some hint of resemblance. Only the eyes. When the Zlotny slowed down at the checkpoint guarding the inland-waterway bridge, Nurov tilted his head so that the guard could see his face.

The guard waved them on.

The eyes had said, "Can't you see this is Vice-Minister Nurov? There's no reason to delay us." But they said nothing else. Not "Hello." Or "Goodbye." Or anything like that.

"What a marvelous day for the reception," Nurov said as the Zlotny accelerated. "Don't you think, Daisy?"

And it was. Not a trace of summer haze lingered in the sky. It was a perfect blue.

"Yes." She patted his thigh with her fingertips. The diamond choke sparkled. In each earlobe a tiny sparkle answered, as if each was a distant star-based transmitter responding to the hundreds of tiny transmitters clustered around her neck.

While they chatted, Alex watched the guard post vanish into the blue sky. And then the high bridge. From the apex of the second span he looked down at the bus which was parked on the little ledge set aside for emergencies. Through the opaque white roof, he could see the driver with his feet propped up on the dashboard sleepily waiting for another bus to rescue his passengers.

Playfully, "Now, Nurov, I want you to promise that you won't gorge on oysters."

"Why should I promise any such thing?"

"Because," tapping his thigh, "they don't agree with you. And I'll be too exhausted to doctor you all night."

"And why not?" With an edge, "You seem to have plenty of time to doctor the locals." The designation "local" was one often chosen by his father as some sort of inoffensive substitute for "American." Or was that really it? When he used it the word sounded like the name of some ancient, distant Indian tribe with strange unfathomable customs which by its sheer distance could not include Alexander or his mother. After a moment, as if he did not wish to let the conversation take a bad turn, he added, "Besides, you know that's not the effect they have at all."

"Is that so?" With a smile, "We'll have to see about that, won't we?"

Suddenly feeling a tinge of embarrassment, Alex removed his eyes to the window: the second veranda was already filled with milling guests.

"Yes." The Zlotny bumped as it entered the driveway. With a laugh, "I'll remember your offer." He looked through the air-conditioning-fogged glass at the security policeman who controlled the gate. "Or was that a challenge?"

Without a word the security policeman motioned for the gate to be opened.

"The oysters will be the challenge, Nurov." As the driver zipped the last twenty meters to the roof-covered side entrance, "I never am."

• • •

82

They were greeted by the Governor and his wife under the watchful eye of the General Secretary—whose gigantic portrait sternly looked down on life-size swatches of blue and yellow as they floated across the foyer like bright summer clouds. Only the small strips of red that adorned the women—on their throats or chests—seemed consistent with the General Secretary's sober countenance.

As soon as the Governor's wife withdrew her cold, wisteria hand, Alex escaped to the balcony by means of the lazy stairway that flanked the lower porch. He looked across Battery Park for a second. Across yet another somber likeness of the General Secretary. The park contained several dozen plainclothes security police. Yet another dozen in uniform were arranged around the gate. What did they expect to see? Oh, there were loonies who sometimes attempted some kind of disruption. He had heard of them. But he had never actually witnessed any kind of disturbance. And certainly no act of violence. It was hard to undersand why the authorities overreacted like that. Of course, they knew more about things like that than he did. They had the facts. But deep down inside he was sure that all these precautions were, well, the kinds of things old people did—like checking the faucet twice at night to make sure it wasn't dripping.

He circled around to the back. The party spread across the entire lawn. The guests accumulated in small eddies around oyster-stacked charcoal roasters and long food-cluttered tables.

His mother stood a meter or two from his father while he devoured oysters. A small, blunt knife in one hand, a muddy glove in the other, he resembled an aging, crafty gladiator waiting for his opponent to blunder, as he slid the blade into a succession of immobilized oysters.

His mother stood there, just far enough away so that no debris would splash on her immaculate blue jumpsuit. It was impossible for Alex to understand why she didn't want to be there. She was by far the most beautiful woman there. And the most composed. Yes, that was it: a kind of cool, relaxed composure that by its very nature became the focus of everything around it, so that the people and lawn furniture, even the smooth, grassy lawn, seemed to fold around her like objects in a picture.

The guests divided neatly into three distinct groups: the "old hands," the Russians, like his family, who had been in the States forever, or what might as well have been forever; the newly arrived Russians, along with those who were there temporarily to conduct Party or State business; and the Americans.

The balcony he was on seemed to be reserved for the newly arrived, who split their time between rather surreptitiously chatting with one another and gawking at the guests below. Most of them adopted that bored mask that announced, "I've been to much bigger and better affairs in Moscow or Leningrad or Gorky."

The old hands for the most part congregated around the long corrugated-metal sheet that had been laid out to serve the oysters. Completely at home, they ate and drank and talked. A few wandered about, spending a few minutes with a local official or some acquaintance; or they climbed the stairs to the high veranda to mingle with their more distinctly Russian comrades, so that they could hear the latest gossip or inside tip from the capital.

The locals, American Party members, members of the State government, were huddled over in the far corner of the lawn near the wall. Occasionally one would venture over to the oysters or the bar. He caught several of the women stealing glances at the guests on the veranda. Perhaps they were studying the latest fashions from Moscow; perhaps they were just curious in general.

On the blurry edge separating the Americans from the old hands, one foot characteristically on each side of the imaginary line dividing the two, he spotted Myslov. He was standing there, looking thin and pasty, peering up at the veranda through his thick-as-bottle-bottom glasses. Alexander slid behind the column. He was in no mood to baby-sit. He crept toward the wall so that three or four bodies separated him from the railing and made his way back to far edge of the veranda near the stairwell.

It dawned on him, just as he reached the stairwell, that Celeste's apartment was visible. The flat-topped, square little room was nestled in the crotch of a huge oak as if it were a birdhouse. He stared at it for a moment, convincing himself that it really was her apartment, wondering, while he looked, if she was even aware that there was a grand event like this taking place right under her nose. No. Suddenly he felt a little funny just thinking about her. Not for any reason he could figure out, and, certainly, there was no reason to, he decided, before returning his attention to the party.

An older woman, very crusty and Russian, was at Alex's elbow. From time to time she leaned over to make an observation to her companion.

"They seem quite contained," her companion remarked, with what could have passed for disappointment.

"Oh, yes. While we're here. But later don't be so sure. I've heard about what goes on here."

He found himself touching the woman's dried-out elbow so that he could hear.

"Why, in this district alone there are a million abortions a year. And," she took a deep breath, "even then most of the babies are illegitimate."

Grimly, "I've heard that."

"And still, they marry them."

"Well," with a laugh, "you know what fools men can be. Sometimes I think their brains are between their legs."

In a nearly inaudible whisper, "There's one there. My sister knows his family well. Connected to the Shrevovskys, I believe. They are destroyed. Simply destroyed." He looked down at Myslov's father. His hands in his pockets, the same apparently hereditary glasses snugly against his nose, he seemed clearly detached from the tragedy that had descended upon him.

"It's not as if he were an army sergeant or something. He had a very promising career." With finality, "They are destroyed. Just destroyed. My sister tells me they are the saddest family she has ever known."

"How awful. And she's known them all along?"

"Well, no. Only recently, I think."

When the woman turned from the railing and headed for the punch bowl, he pivoted to follow her and instantly collided with a solid female body, chest to chest. Their foreheads clicked together.

"Excuse me."

A small red bump immediately began to form on Martina Antipova's forehead.

"Are you all right?"

"Yes." She smiled. "I'm fine."

"We'd better see to that."

A little dazed, "See to what?"

"There's a bump." Reaching toward her forehead, but stopping short of touching it, "Right there."

"Yes. I can feel it. Does it look awful?"

Slightly embarrassed, "No. Not at all."

She smiled again.

"But why don't you sit here for a moment. Against the railing. There. I'll be right back."

He picked a small piece of ice from the punchbowl and applied it to her forehead.

After a moment, "That's cold."

"But it'll stop the swelling." Stiffly, "I've used it on sprained ankles before. It helps."

"Yes. I'm sure it does." Conversationally, her head tilted back so that the melting ice ran down her temple instead of in her eye, "So how did you sprain your ankle."

"Basketball."

"Basketball?" she echoed with mild disbelief.

Defensively, "Yes. I play on the team."

"Oh." As if she were now talking to someone in the same club, "You're an athlete."

"Well," unsure how to respond, "yes. I guess I am."

With what he decided was a kind of tactlessness that suited her perfectly, "Guard?"

"Yes."

She nodded her head as if she had just figured out something difficult.

While Alex was holding Lieutenant Commander Antipov's punch cup under a ladle, he heard Myslov's voice. "Quite a gathering, isn't it?" He was directly below, blindly staring up at him.

After glancing back toward Martina Antipova and her father, "Yes."

"Perhaps I'll join you up there."

"No." In a hoarse whisper, "There's really nothing exciting going on up here. I'll be down there in a minute."

"Shall I wait here then?"

"Yes."

After holding Martina's cup under the mechanical black hand, which neatly filled it to the top before moving on to another jiggling, impatient cup, he hurried back to them, the whole time taken by the silly feeling that they might at any moment vanish before his eyes.

She nearly emptied the cup in a single swallow.

"So, you are a basketball player," Lieutenant Commander Antipov remarked. His uniform was blindingly white. On it there was only one medal: the Order of Lenin. "A very good sport. An Olympic sport."

Alex nodded.

"The Soviet team has won the last three times, I believe."

"Yes," he replied, although he wasn't sure of that at all.

"The Cuban team is also good."

He took a swallow of punch.

"But of course the Soviet team usually prevails."

"That's true," Alex agreed.

Martina Antipova absently pivoted back and forth at the waist. Was she bored? he wondered. Or just warming up for some imaginary athletic competition? Her brocade-encased ribs rose like a staircase, slowly, inevitably transforming into breasts. In spite of their circumference her breasts did not jut out at all. Instead they clung tightly to her muscular chest. Still, in the small vee in the neck of her jumpsuit a distinct cleavage was visible.

"Ah, there you are, Alexander." Like some creature from a science fiction film, Myslov's huge glasses ascended the stairwell accompanied by his reedy, thin voice, which seemed to be coming not so much from Myslov as from the slatted wooden walls of the stairwell. "I should have guessed you'd been detained." Breathlessly, "I was afraid you'd gone around the other way. And I'd missed you."

He introduced them to Myslov.

Shaking Lieutenant Commander Antipov's hand, "So you are the naval attaché to the Soviet embassy." Sounding absurdly worldly, "Nothing escapes notice here. We're all constantly starved for news."

"I suppose so," Lieutenant Commander Antipov replied noncommittally.

"I'm still dreadfully thirsty," Martina Antipova announced. "How about you, Alex?" She looked him squarely in the eye. It was that same look he recalled from the bus. Very grown-up. And clearly a look.

Before Myslov could get out that there was a bar on the balcony she had descended halfway to the lower porch.

"Can we bring you anything, sir?" Alex inquired of her father.

She frowned.

"Yes." Oblivious to his daughter's frown, "Another punch."

Alex nodded compliantly and then descended the stairs.

"Who is that little worm?" Martina Antipova demanded before they had turned the corner.

"Myslov?"

"Myslov." She shuddered. "If I ever have to hear that name again I think I'll be ill."

"He's not as," he began before interrupting himself to continue, "yes, he's as bad as you might think. Worse." Searching for some way to explain him, "He's like a stray dog." He realized as he was speaking that she was not the type to pick up stray animals. "He's not really someone that I spend a lot of time with." Guiltily, "But he's harmless."

As if she had never heard of Myslov, "Look at that bird." She carved off the duck's leg with one stroke of a long knife and sank her teeth into the juicy brown meat. "Ah," she exclaimed, from deep down in her throat. "Poison." Just before biting into the drumstick one more time, "Absolute poison." She tossed the mangled leg onto the linen tablecloth. "If my coach saw that he would kill me." By way of explanation, "You can't run a Zlotny on horse piss."

He couldn't decide whether to laugh or what.

"This will have to be our little secret." She smiled, her lips glistening from the meat.

"Sure," Alex promised soberly, happy to be included in her private thoughts.

As if she were inspecting tires on an assembly line, "Too rich." Curling her nose, "The glaze on that ham looks too rich."

"Yes, it's too thick." Conversationally, "I don't really care for extra-rich foods."

"Poison."

The left half of the ham had been scavenged to the bone by the less health-conscious guests; the right sported six or seven fresh wounds. She tore off a piece of glazed flesh.

"Too rich." As she inserted the entire piece, which was the length of her index finger, into her mouth, she repeated, "Too rich."

Instead of washing away the shiny fat residue, the punch left a liquid film on her lips which exploded in the sunlight as they strolled along the balcony past the stairwell. He did not look up to see if Myslov and her father were still there at the crest of the stairs waiting. He merely followed her along the lower veranda as it melted into the shady windward side of the house, where they sat on the railing and talked for half an hour. She explained the mechanics of javelin throwing thoroughly, emphasizing the importance of mental preparation and concentration. She was certain they were the key to success, and Alex couldn't help but agree, since she was from head to toe the prototype of athletic perfection.

"The crucial part is to be able to see yourself doing it perfectly." She licked her lips. "In the morning, in the shower, with my eyes closed and the water splashing into my face. That's the best time. First I pick it up, letting the grip slide comfortably into my hand. I close my hand, slowly, but not too tightly, so that my fingers slip around it naturally. I want it to feel completely at home in my hand. Then I lift it up to my shoulder, sensing its weight, locating the balance point. And I begin to trot. Slowly. I can feel it bouncing up and down gently in my hand. Up and down. Up and down. Until I'm nearly running. Finally, when it explodes from my hand I can feel every muscle in my body pushing, cooperating. And if it's a perfect throw I can feel it tingle up and down my body. And suddenly I'm covered with goose bumps. Goose bumps. Isn't that odd?"

Hoarsely, "I guess."

"And then," with a laugh, "it's 'Martina, your breakfast won't wait all day.'" Matter-of-factly, "And I haven't washed my hair yet."

"Alexander. So here you are." His mother was a few meters away making her way toward them across the grassy lawn. "Nurov doesn't think we should linger past three o'clock."

With a noticeable tinge of disappointment, "Mother." He slid off the railing. Stiffly, "Mother. Martina Antipova. Martina, my—"

Interrupting, "Daisy Simpson Nurova." He had never heard her formally introduce herself. Did she always use her father's name when she introduced herself? he wondered. In any case it seemed to make no impression on Martina Antipova.

Extending her hand, "Madam Nurova."

They shook hands over the railing.

"The car is being brought around," she offered. The midday's playful freshness had vanished. After releasing Martina Antipova's hand she turned to recross the lawn.

He was about to speak when she turned and said offhandedly, "You might like to invite your friend to late lunch. And a swim. I'm sure Corinne would love to have something to do." Her hand had been casually tucked in her pocket while she spoke; she removed it and, cocking it to the side in a gesture that said, "You may want to; you may not," she added, "We'll be having late lunch at the ambassador's."

She crossed the lawn, weaving her way through the expanding mass of "locals," who he realized were no longer huddled in the far corner near the fence. Many of the adventurous ones had drifted over to encircle the metal table used to serve the oysters. Others had staked out claims in the smooth green side yard only a dozen or so meters from the veranda. He could hear them laughing and talking. Perhaps the alcohol had made them braver, he surmised.

On the way back his mother rested her head against the seat, grimacing each time the driver hit one of the thousands of potholes that scarred the road like ancient, picked-over zits. After a particularly nasty bump, just as they were descending from the last hump of the big bridge, she remarked, "I take it the amazon belongs to the new naval attaché?"

Before her interjection his father had been offering imaginary responses to the Governor's tedious recapitulation of the next five-year plan. "Perhaps you should start with the next five-year plan; we can start right after you finish talking about it. That might leave us just enough time. Why does the Vice-Minister of Information have to be on the editorial board of USSA *Today*? It's worse than being a pimp!"

When she spoke, Alex assumed it was going to be a reprimand for using the word "pimp."

His father immediately echoed, "Amazon?" He repeated the word as if it were brand-new to him. "Amazon?"

"Actually," she lowered her eyes, "a glorious example of socialist, or should I say Soviet, womanhood." Apparently sensing without opening her eyes that Nurov was lost, "Our son's luncheon guest. She is coming over?"

"Yes," he responded. "It's," he looked out the window, "no big deal."

90

With interest, "The new naval attaché's daughter." He was tapping his finger on his knee when Alex returned his eyes to the car.

From what could have been construed to be a deep sleep, "Oh, I doubt if she's KGB too. Although," she paused, eyes in focus, "one never knows."

Why had she made it so easy to invite her, in fact created the opportunity, and then tried to ruin it?

Nothing else was said the rest of the way back.

"Just tell Corinne what you would like her to fix," his mother suggested mechanically as she disappeared down the hall.

"We've been eating all day." Just as the bedroom door shut, "I think we'll just walk on the beach."

"So. A rendezvous?" his father inquired, making the whole thing sound as evil as possible.

Alex stormed off to his room and slammed the door. Damn! Why did they have to make such a big deal out of it?

At that moment it occurred to him that she might not show up. Until then it had not crossed his mind. Even though the other time she had left him there waiting at the back stairs to the cafeteria. He tried to reconstruct the expression on her face. She would be there. But then the last time there had been no reason to believe she wouldn't be.

Odd, he had been very angry about that. He hadn't spoken to her again since. Not that there had been any real opportunities. But he could have: on the bus, or on the playing field. He had watched her throw only once since then. After that he had decided that she wasn't worth watching. But when he ran into her at the reception he never even thought about it. Maybe it was the collision. He laughed. Amnesia?

He changed into shorts and after a moment's reflection got a heavy cotton sweater, which he tossed over his shoulder.

Had they left already for the ambassador's? He hoped so. There was no sign of them. Perhaps they had left. There was no point in their being there if she didn't show up. If she didn't he'd just act as if she had.

"So," raising his busy eyebrow, "how was your rendezvous, Alexander?"

"Marvelous. She gave me a blow job out on the beach. Block Commander Gregorov was most impressed. Perhaps he can show the video at the next meeting of the Young Pioneers."

Wearing that serene, careless smile that she put on as easily as lipstick, "A true amazon."

"Yes," he answered out loud as he lowered himself onto a large cushion in front of the television.

He was hard. He could see the ridge of flesh pushing up against his zipper. He ran the palm of his hand across himself, disguising it as part of a long, bone-cracking stretch.

They must have gone.

He could feel himself pressing against the zipper.

"Your mama says you want lunch."

He quickly rolled over onto his stomach.

Persisting, "Is that so?"

Corinne was standing at the door, her hands on her hips. "Do you want me to fix you something or not?" Her finger tapped restlessly against her hip.

"No."

When she frowned, the creases around her eyes resembled chocolate pudding when you press down on the skin with your spoon.

"No lunch at all?"

"I've been eating all day."

"I hate to ask what."

"Maybe after I get back from the beach," he offered.

"The beach. The wind's blowing out there." On her way to the kitchen, "You'd better find something to hold on to."

"I'm not that skinny," he hollered, still lying uncomfortably on his stomach.

He let the doorbell ring twice before rising. After a few steps he stopped. "Corinne, there's someone at the door." He flicked on the television and sat in one of the huge Afghan chairs that were casually arranged around the wall-size screen.

A young woman with gray-streaked, cropped hair: "What light can you shed on the motivational problem of the American worker?"

A bald man: "Fortunately, we have the science of socialist psychology to aid us in understanding the afflicted worker. We needn't be too judgmental, mind . . ."

Pretentiously, "Someone to see you, Mr. Nurov."

He flicked the channel.

92

"I'll be in the kitchen."

Affecting casualness, "Oh, hi. Thank you, Corinne."

"The Uzbek Trials. Great."

"Yes. They've been pretty exciting."

She seated herself on one of the Afghan chairs.

"So, what's been happening?"

Improvising, while looking up at the screen, "Running. Mostly running."

Spontaneously, "Running can be a little dull. At least on the screen." After a moment, "Have the field events already taken place?"

Thoughtfully, "I think so."

"It took Father forever to escape from the reception." Leaning back in the large chair, "But I guess things like that are part of his job. Wouldn't you hate spending all your time socializing with people like that?"

Was that what the KGB did? Socialize? Of course, there was no certainty that he was KGB. That was just a supposition. Cautiously, "Everyone has his role."

"I suppose."

On their way through the kitchen, Corinne handed him a tightly wrapped plastic bag.

"This'll give you something to do out there."

He indicated his displeasure by frowning.

In a whisper, "Make sure you," she glanced at Martina Antipova, "get some of this."

Philosophically, "Thank you, Corinne."

Right away he knew he would take her to the old dune. At the end of the walkway there it was, looming like a miles-distant white volcano, spewing green lava and smoke that remained photographically in place until the seasons changed the spew to ugly brown.

As soon as they reached the water she began to trot, reaching down on the move to roll up her trouser legs.

"It seems like I've been sitting and standing for eternity," she screamed out before plunging into the ankle-deep surf. "What we need is a swim."

Running along on the sand, "In that water? You must be loony."

Insulted, "What?"

He smiled, "It's too cold."

"Oh." She threw her head back and began galloping through the water, her hair bouncing against her back like a show horse's braided mane. He could see her legs flexing against the wet thighs of her jumpsuit.

Effortlessly, just as they were about to reach the old dune, "I never get up this far. After video sessions and the weights it's almost dark."

"You do that every day?"

He glanced to his left as they passed by the old dune.

"Yes. I have to study the videotapes to perfect my form. Every day at three. That's part of the discipline."

Every day? I wonder if that's where she was that day, he puzzled, while picking up a broken shell and skipping it across the water until it was gobbled up by a small wave. He had been so dumb about it. He should have asked. Or figured out that it was something like that. Still, you would think she would have brought it up. Of course, there really hadn't been much of an opportunity. No. Today had been the first real opportunity. And it would be foolish to ruin things by bringing that up, just when they were going so well.

When they rounded the bend the beach very soon gave way to marsh weeds and silt. She stopped.

"No more?"

"The inland waterway," he said, pointing across the inlet to the narrow river that cropped up between two long rows of marsh weeds and oyster banks.

She shrugged and waded to shore. The water had splashed up over her thighs as high up as the vee of her crotch. It was running down through the fabric so that it collected in the big cuffs she had made. Water sloshed out of them when she walked.

"Time for lunch."

Making a face, "I'm not hungry."

"Well, come on anyway. I'll show you something."

He led her the back way so that they scaled the old dune from the dark side, following a rising elliptical path to the bushy rim.

She peered suspiciously into the bowels of the old dune.

"Come on, but look out for stickers."

He half climbed and half slid down the interior wall, which gradually flattened out into a circular space shaded by a large water oak umbrella.

94

She was still standing on the rim.

"Come on."

"Are you sure there aren't snakes in there?"

Stretching out on his back in the sand, "If there are they'll get me."

She cautiously descended, sinking into the soft interior wall up to her cuffs, which were spilling sand instead of water when she reached the bottom. She sat facing him, her thighs drawn up against her chest, her chin resting on her kneecaps.

Alex opened the crinkly green lunch bag. "Well, what's this?"

She dropped the sandwich he offered her into her lap.

Without lifting her chin she surveyed the interior of the old dune. "So this is your hideout?"

Carefully, "No. I used to come here some when I was a kid."

Matter-of-factly, "Yes, I guess it would be antisocial to come here too often."

"Damn. We didn't bring anything to drink."

After watching him eat for a while, "If you lick your lips it's easier." Lowering her head so that she was looking into her lap, "It's easier to chew."

He licked his lips. "Yes, that does help."

"There's an apple," he added after swallowing.

Still looking down, "No, I'm not hungry."

He took one bite from the apple and tossed it back into the bag. "If you're cold we can go."

"No."

"I mean, you're wet."

"No, we can stay."

He hesitantly slid his hands onto her shins, wrapping his fingers around so that they loosely encircled her calves. After a moment he began to massage the length of her calf and then upward past the wet cuffs until his fingertips touched the back of her knees.

Thrusting her legs forward so that they were on either side of him, "That tickles."

"Oh." He withdrew his hands.

Her head still down, her hands at her sides palm down in the sand, "But you don't have to stop." Inclining her head slightly, "It was making me warmer."

He slid his hands back onto her calves.

When he kissed her she kept her lips tightly together, but followed his lips for a few centimeters as he withdrew.

Forthrightly, "Was that good?"

"Yes."

"It was?"

"Very."

Leaning toward him with her eyes half closed, "Again?"

She slid her tongue across the edge of his lip.

"I've kissed boys before." Looking directly at him, "I thought you should know."

He tugged her toward him by the lapels.

In a sober, forthright fashion that suggested she was repeating something from a Young Pioneers meeting, "It's important to discuss things like that."

She opened her mouth on the next kiss. He could feel her suck in a mouthful of air as he slid his hands from the lapels onto her breasts. He kept his mouth on hers while he caressed her. After a moment she pushed his hands down, and, while holding them firmly so that his palms rested in the sand, announced, "I'm wearing an athletic brassiere."

He stopped trying to raise his hands from the sand.

"It's . . ." She paused. "Would you like to see my breasts?"

Containing himself, "Yes."

She unzipped the jumpsuit to her navel and extracted each arm from the sleeve, leaving the bodice in place on her shoulders, her arms crossed inside. "Look away."

He turned his head to the side.

"Are your eyes shut?"

"Yes, but this . . ." He could hear the snap of her hair as the elastic bra slipped over her head.

"It looks, well, it smashes me down." After what seemed forever, "You can turn back now."

Her breasts were right there, returning his stare like myopic, rusty eyes.

She sat there silently, her hands buried in the sand at her sides, the jumpsuit crumpled around her waist like leaves around a flower stem.

He lifted his hand, realized that it was covered with sand, and began wiping it on his hip.

As if she were conducting a tour of Grand Canyon, "What do you think?"

"They're beautiful."

Looking down, "Yes, I suppose they are." She picked up the bra from the sand and shook it. It was heavy elastic, with wide straps the texture of thick gauze. The whole apparatus looked more like some kind of orthopedic device than a garment. "I have to wear this to throw, so I wear it all the time. So it will feel completely natural. That's very important. For everything that is part of the throw to be natural. To be second nature. Sometimes I even sleep in it."

He smiled.

"You think that's silly?"

"No," he paused, "I was thinking that it might lead to an explosion."

She didn't laugh.

"I mean, they're . . ." he wavered.

Seriously, "Too large?"

"No."

Haughtily, "My boyfriend in Moscow likes to look at them for hours. He does. And," she paused, "he puts them in his mouth. He loves to do that."

Angrily pulling his knees up against his chest, "Who gives a damn about your boyfriend. And what he did to your tits."

She shook the bra again before lifting it up over her head. "There's no reason to be nasty." After slowly inserting one arm in the apparatus, "You can if you want. You can put them in your mouth if you want."

She reclined in the sand, her head resting in her open hand while he devoured her right breast, both hands wrapped around it like the base of a warm, nipple-topped sundae. When he tried to slide one hand down across her belly into the crotch of her jumpsuit she retrieved his hand. The nipple became long and hard, and after a while she moaned just for an instant, very deeply. It sounded like Russian, as if you could moan in one language rather than another.

He could feel small goose bumps begin to rise on her belly. He slid his hand down across them into the tight vee where the zipper pressed against her flesh. He could feel it dig into the back of his hand as his fingers flowed across her pubic hair. Her crotch was wet.

Immediately, she clamped her hand around his wrist and pulled him away. The upward pull dragged his fingers across her lips.

And she screamed. Or almost did. It was one deep, short gasp. Again distinctly Russian. Perhaps she had uttered a word. A Russian word.

He lifted his head. Her chest and belly were covered with goose bumps.

She wrapped her hand around his neck and drew him to her, pressing him hard against her chest.

"What a throw. Ahhh, what a throw."

He attempted to pull free so that he could look at her, but she held him tightly against her. When she finally released him, she repeated, "What a throw." Her lips trembled slightly when she said it, as if she were about to explode.

He slid his thumbs into the sides of her jumpsuit in an attempt to push it over her hips. She pressed her butt down into the sand.

Sounding lightly drugged, "No."

He pushed down with his thumbs.

"Alexander." She sat up, trapping his thumbs between her jumpsuit and her hips. "That's . . ." She paused for a moment before pulling up on his hands. "You know you can't do that." Holding him by the wrists, "I'm not some American whore, you know."

Yanking his hands away, "No, you're just a Russian whore for your Russian boyfriend."

He could feel his fist tighten into a ball.

Firmly, her shoulders erect, "I'm not going to end up in a reeducation center for. . ." She stopped. A moment later she picked up the brassiere, shook out the sand, and slipped it over her head. "You seem to have lost sight of what the Party expects of its youth, Alexander," she pronounced soberly. "Is that what happens here?" Snapping the elastic side panels in place, "Well, that will not happen to me. Never. As an athlete my first responsibility is to the Party. I will never forget that."

"Unless your Russian boyfriend is around, so you can be a fat Russian whore for him."

She climbed halfway up the sand embankment before facing him. "I don't have a boyfriend in Moscow," she confessed earnestly. "Or anywhere." She vanished over the rim of the dune.

Alex crumpled onto the sandy floor of the old dune. In a long, sarcastic scream, "Liar!" He stretched out facedown in the cool sand, repeating several times, "Liar! Liar!"

He lay there very still for a while, repeating the word, his arms stretched out against the belly of the old dune as if it were a live, comforting thing.

Her still-wrapped, smashed sandwich was just out of reach. It must have fallen, disregarded, when she stood. He rose, picked it up, and stuffed it into the green lunch bag, pressing it downward until he could hear the plastic bottom stretching.

American whore. Maybe she hadn't meant anything by that. Probably to her it was just an expression. It didn't even make any sense for that to make him so angry. No sense at all.

With the bag in his lap he leaned against the base of the gnarled oak tree. Perhaps it was the plastic bag that reminded him. Or just the fact that it was buried a meter away. He was sure that if he had had one of his old mysteries there he would have settled for that. After putting aside the lunch bag he crawled around to the other side of the tree and exhumed The Book. The tightly wrapped plastic had kept it very dry.

"The Plot to Kill Paul Creticos," he repeated to himself. What did that mean? It wasn't a mystery. And it wasn't history. No. Too many things were made up. And the method was completely wrong. It wasn't scientific at all. What would Brownsky say? Or Gregorov? He shuddered. The little policeman would love to know that he had it sitting there right in his lap.

Yes, that would make Gregorov's day. He would have something to brag about at the next meeting of the Young Pioneers. He could brag how he had saved the Party from corruption. Or destruction. The more so, since The Book was about America. More than that, it was about America before the Great Uprising. And there was something strange about it. Something slightly off. That was just the kind of thing that would drive the orderly little policeman up the wall. Not that he would actually read it. No. He would just dutifully turn it over like a good little policeman, so that it could be destroyed. Yes. That's what would happen to it, he decided. Or would it be put into the DAL system first? Yes. That made sense. That's where it would land up.

He could hear Gregorov gloating over it at lunch with them hanging on his every word. Repeating it, in his offhand, subtle way: never mentioning, or having to mention, that Alex was a Russamsky. No. that would be left completely to innuendo.

Alex bounced The Book in his lap, balancing it in his hand. So that was what it was all about? Maybe.

Suddenly he had the urge to tell his mother about it. But that would be too dangerous. Not to him. She would just insist that he . . . What? It wasn't clear what she would say, apart from "I'm a doctor. What do I know about history?"

But she would insist that he do something with it. He could almost hear her say, "Ask Nurov. That is his specialty." No. She wouldn't risk that. But she would insist that he get rid of it.

And he would never really know what she thought of it. No. She had a knack for not revealing things like that. Nevertheless, it would be hard for her not to be curious. She never seemed really curious about anything, but, being an American, or least having been born one, would have to make her a little curious about what it was like then. How could she not be?

He carefully zipped up his jacket around The Book and walked home.

Chapter 5

They had not returned from the ambassador's yet.

He disguised the bed with several notebooks and, along with the *CCCP Dictionary*, slid under the spread, draping it over his shoulder so that it created a small plaid cavern. He rested The Book on its side against his knees in the directed gaze of the bedpost lamp.

He reread "The Beginning." He looked up Paul Creticos in the biographical section of the *CCCP Dictionary*. Two lines. There was no entry for Piotr Babulieski. Or Gustavus Roman. Or Cardinal Rudolfo. Or Dietra Christian. Or Jesus Christ. There was an entry for New York. But he had already heard of New York. Every schoolboy knew it was a state. But there was no New York City. Either under geographical names or on the map.

> **priest** (prēst) *n*: a person whose function was to make sacrificial offerings. See SHAMAN, WITCH DOCTOR.

So far there had been no mention of sacrificial offerings, whatever they were.

FATHER PAUL'S CONFESSOR

On my second day in New York City I discovered the computer store. It was really quite by accident. I was roaming about, considering exactly how to approach Father Paul, and there it was: Computer Village.

101

There were thatched huts and vines. And a large cardboard cutout of a man wearing a pith helmet.

I had been staring through the window at the fake thatch-covered display stands for several minutes when the clerk unlocked the door. Why was it locked? I wondered.

"Good morning, Father. Is there anything in particular you would like to see?" the young man asked, smiling from under a large tan pith helmet. The offer seemed quite genuine.

"No," I replied, attempting a step down the sidewalk.

"Well, perhaps you'd just like to browse." His eyes were soft, friendly blue. Without being sure quite why, I was inside. "Holler if there's anything I can show you."

"Yes, I will," I assured him, certain that I would not. "I won't be but a minute anyway."

Displaying his raised palms, the young man offered, "Just make yourself at home." He vanished behind a row of shelves. They were decorated with pieces of vine and other tropical debris. A large banner offered: "Let us lead you through the hardware jungle!"

The hardware jungle? I mused.

In black, on a sky-blue screen: HELLO. I'M YOUR IBM PC. DEPRESS THE SPACE BAR AND I'LL SHOW YOU WHAT I CAN DO.

I looked down at the keyboard. It was not very different from the old Smith-Corona I'm using right now. More sculptured. More space-age. But basically the same.

"The nuns at St. Agnes's just got three of those," remarked a disembodied voice. With enough gravity to let me know it was important, the voice added, "They're networking."

"Oh," I replied noncommittally.

I circled around the row of shelves to ask the bodiless voice to unlock the door. There was no one there. At least not in that aisle.

In bright, jagged letters: "Buck Rogers and the Planet of Zoom." A blue spaceship fluttered back and forth across the screen, dodging streams of alien lasers.

"That's a great game."

"Game?"

"It's arcade-quality."

"Arcade-quality?" I repeated, having no idea what that meant. Where the hell are you? I nearly blurted out.

102

"Absolutely. Pick up the joystick."

I had no idea what a joystick was, and I had no plans to find out.

"Try level two. That is, unless you play a lot." In that slightly moralizing tone that the laity reserve for the clergy, he questioned, "You don't play a lot, do you?"

"No," I mumbled. "I'm afraid I have to go, anyway." I made a point of sounding decisive. "I have an appointment. Or I'd stay."

"Only takes a minute." And there he was. "Especially if you haven't played much."

Perhaps he mistook my confusion for wavering.

"The control pad is super." He slapped the joystick in my hand. "The sides are speed. The stick is direction." More to himself, "Level one. Two players. Planet of Zoom, here we come." He smiled. "Ready?"

The screen flashed, and suddenly I was flying.

"Try the joystick," he prompted gently.

"Ah, the joystick. Yes."

He reached over and twisted the golf-tee-shaped knob.

Before I knew it, it was lunchtime and I had written my name and score in the hall of fame.

"Have a nice day, Father," the young man chimed while unlocking the door.

"Yes. And you do the same."

He pressed a card into my hand and locked the door.

I almost rapped on the glass to ask: "Why do you lock up in the middle of the day?"

(Later I found out that they were screening everyone who entered. So that robbers—or street people—could be kept out. Provided the robber wasn't wearing a three-piece suit. Or clerical collar. I am glad I didn't ask then. As it was, my preconceptions about America were melting.)

I glanced through the window on my way by. The clerk had already climbed up a ladder to retrieve more boxes. More, I thought. There must have been fifty smiling, blank terminals on display already.

What in the world were the nuns at St. Agnes's doing with three of them? I puzzled. That didn't make any sense at all. A convent is a serene, contemplative place. Smiling nuns battling their way across

103

the Planet of Zoom with joysticks in their hands seemed, well, if not wrong, a little too unconventional.

My gluttony persisted unabated: I ate two hot dogs and a slice of pizza, and then a teriyaki on a wooden stick.

Perhaps, I decided while sliding the last of the teriyaki up the stick, I would visit St. Agnes's. After all, there was probably a quite logical explanation. And I needed time to think of the best way to deal with Father Paul. Before I spoke with him again I wanted to have it all clearly worked out. So that there would be no misunderstanding. His heart was clearly in the right place. He had the vocation. But his methods were, well, inappropriate. Another little side trip would give me more time to work it all out. I would just let the problem percolate in the back of my mind. On simmer, if you will.

Of course, I had been quite wrong about St. Agnes's. At least my mental picture was overly imaginative. They didn't play Planet of Zoom at all. In fact, just asking that question produced an odd sort of nonreply. But, as is usually the case when a priest pays a visit to cloistered nuns, they were quite pleased to see me, although uncertain as to why I was there. And quite accommodating: they served me cookies and tea.

Sister Alice was in charge of the computers. With great relish she showed me how they were used to print letters from their mailing list.

"Each one is an original."

"An original?"

"Oh, yes. With the person's name. Dear Joseph. Or Matthew."

"Oh."

Making sure to impress me, she persisted, "Some even include a personal message."

"A personal message?"

"From the data base."

While Sister Alice demonstrated the device I wondered if all this wasn't some kind of deception.

"See. This one says, 'I'm sure since the passing of your beloved husband Charlie you feel closer to God. Here is a chance for you to help God in His work.' Isn't that nice?" She rubbed her finger under her nose as if it itched. "I'm sure it must be comforting."

I let her describe it to me without interruption. Preventing myself from commenting or moralizing.

104

It was a thorough tour. She even showed me how they kept their accounts. Evidently Sister Alice was very happy in her work.

"Why three?" I remember asking, having no real idea what the difference was between having one or two or three.

"We send out over eighty thousand prayer letters a month. By networking we can operate all three terminals at once, accessing the same data base. One of the sisters can be adding names to the mailing list. Another updating the files with new addresses or phone numbers. Another recording donations. And it's actually cheaper, about three thousand dollars cheaper." She stopped to scratch her nose. "Than three stand-alone systems."

"Three thousand dollars."

"Yes. And donations for our African mission have increased by forty-three percent in the last year." Beaming, "You can thank networking for that."

"I prefer to thank God," I replied as gently as I could.

"Of course, we all do," she agreed, but without the slightest hint of apology.

"Were Christ and the disciples to return today I'm sure they would be networking," I nearly remarked. Networking. I'm sure Sister Alice was wondering what I found so amusing. And the martyrs. And the saints. Networking. Perhaps in America. But certainly nowhere else, I concluded.

On my way back to the hotel, on the Lexington Avenue subway, which gorged on and then vomited a soup of black, dangerous bodies seasoned with an occasional three-piece suit, I rehearsed my conversation with Father Paul. I would be sympathetic: the Church has always been an instrument of peace. But I would be firm: the dignity of the Church and its representatives was something we must all cherish. It could not be squandered to satisfy some transient end.

When the door opened, I was greeted with "Nuclear-free toothpaste! That is the last thing the world needs. More toothpaste!"

Was there no way we could rid ourselves of her? I complained to myself, as I looked into the three faces crammed into the foyer.

"Monsignor, what a perfect time for you to arrive," Father Paul exclaimed, firmly shaking my hand. "This is Jack Hawkins. And this is Monsignor Babulieski."

"Hi. Nice to meet you," Jack Hawkins radiated, taking my hand as soon as Father Paul released it. Still holding on to my hand, but after a polite pause, he said, "Then we'll begin taping Tuesday."

"I'll be there," Father Paul replied.

"Nice to meet you," he repeated to me before stepping into the hall.

"Yes," I stammered.

"If the stars use it, the masses need it," Dietra Christian announced without a hint of sympathy for the masses or anyone else.

While Father Paul tried to explain, she hissed, after sprawling into her favorite chair, "Madison Avenue is now packaging a nuclear-free world." She had stopped to gag on the word. "The truth does not need to be packaged and sold." As if it were the last act of a never-ending Wagnerian opera, she railed, "I hope you are pleased. You have destroyed the last of my illusions."

"I'm hoping that nothing will really change," Father Paul soothed. "Except the numbers."

"Hopeful? With that adman turning you into something fresh and antiseptic that will slide down a hundred million suburban throats."

"Suburban throats have voices. And." He wavered briefly. "Fears. And votes."

She sneered, "Votes. Nothing of importance has ever been decided by a vote."

"And souls," he whispered. "They have souls."

As if she had been alerted by something in his voice, "Are you all right?"

"Yes. I'm fine," he replied with a drawn smile.

She stood. "Shall I massage your temples?"

"No."

Somewhat taken back by his refusal, she persisted, "Are you sure?"

"Yes." He pushed his hair back over his ear. "Monsignor Babulieski and I need a few minutes." As if he were dismissing a spoiled child, he appended, "Alone."

She stepped across the coffee table and without turning back disappeared into the foyer. A long moment later (perhaps she had paused to reconsider. I remember dreading she might just bound back into the room) the door slammed shut. Coincident with its crashing shut, as if precipitated by the tremor, the foyer light dimmed. It didn't actually go out, it only became weak and fluttery for a second, before returning to full strength.

At last we were alone.

He sat down, sinking comfortably into the sofa, and looking directly at me, smiled. It was a relaxed, oblivious smile without memory, without recollection.

I would not be put off by a smile, I decided. I looked him straight in the eye.

The smile sailed at me for a moment like a sturdy little boat anticipating a storm, but behind it, perhaps in the corners of his eyes, I could see fatigue. Perhaps concern.

I would never get a better opportunity.

"Would you mind taking my confession, Monsignor?" This surprising request was made in a matter-of-fact way. He might as well have been asking for a glass of water. Or the time of day.

Of course, there was no way I could say no. Had I wanted to.

"No, not at all," I struggled out, wondering why he had chosen that moment to make his request. But any uncertainty I had vanished as soon as I agreed. Suddenly I felt very pleased with myself. It was, in fact, the first time that I felt completely at ease around him. Up until then I had always felt slightly awkward in his presence. As if I were about to break an antique crystal glass. Or stumble on a crease in the rug. Perhaps it was because he was so perfect. Oh, not that he was a saint. I was sure he wasn't. At least not in the sense of popular hagiography. It was more than anything else because he was so physically perfect. So beautiful. In the beginning that made me feel like a huge wart.

"Do you miss your pastoral duties?" he inquired, almost as an afterthought.

"Yes," I replied candidly. "Often."

"I don't." He slid forward to the edge of the sofa so that our faces were quite near. "That is what I have to confess."

When we had finished, he walked me to the door.

"Candidly, Monsignor, what do you think of the idea of television spots?" he asked, just as he was opening the door for me.

At that time I had no real idea what a television spot was, but before I could respond the foyer light flickered and died.

"It seems that God has chosen to interrupt you." He laughed. "What do you suppose He is saying?" He laughed again. The laugh was very round and full. It didn't seem to fit him at all the way it filled the semidark void of the foyer with no clearly visible person to

attach it to. "Is that yea or nay?" He laughed again.

The light struggled back on.

"What do you think, Monsignor?"

Awkwardly, trying to laugh myself, I replied, "There must be a short in the fixture."

"Yes, I suppose so," he agreed, before adding forthrightly, "Too bad it's not God Himself signaling us with Morse code."

I stood uncomfortably at the door. We hadn't discussed the business about the T-shirts. Or Dietra Christian. Or any of the things that I found disturbing. That was my fault, of course. Prior to taking his confession I had them all arranged in a one-two-three list, ready to be ticked off. But the right moment never presented itself. I just couldn't find a way to get over that awkward transition to say, "You know, of course, that the Church is most concerned about the behavior, the decorum, if you will, of young priests." How unusual for me to be so passive, I thought. If anything I am usually too quick to speak out. But with Father Paul I was finding it quite difficult to be forceful.

He mollified me with, "Perhaps we can have supper together?"

"Yes," I blurted out almost too quickly. "That would," I could feel the sense of relief spreading slowly through my body, "give us an opportunity to discuss several matters that need," I floundered for an instant, "attention."

At least that was settled. I found myself humming contentedly as I sauntered in my herky-jerky, left-to-right way toward the elevator. Yes, things were going quite well. After all, the problems were, well, problems of style, not of substance. A long dinnertime discussion could resolve everything.

When I reached the elevator I was surprised to find her sitting there, cross-legged, beneath the large mirror that faced the elevator doors.

"So, his soul has been cleansed."

Refusing to be intimidated by her sarcasm, "Yes." I pushed the button to summon the elevator. Had she been listening?

Rising to her feet, "Do you really believe that?"

"Yes." How could she know I had taken his confession?

"You are a fool then."

Thinking, We will let God decide who the fool is, I waited with my back to her. When the elevator arrived she stepped on after me. Standing beside me in that shiny stainless-steel box she seemed enormously tall and powerful. As I reached around her to push the button

108

she snarled down at me. The skin around the safety pin was especially red and festering.

"If God is so wonderful, why did he give you that fucking hunchback?" A light spray rained down on me as she spoke.

Before I could answer, the lights went out. A second later the elevator droned to a halt.

"Was gibt?" she exclaimed in the blackness. When I remarked that the power had gone off, she hissed, "Brilliant. You must be a Jesuit."

We stood there for a minute or two. Then she demanded to know where the emergency light was.

It seemed that there should be one. But where?

And then she began screaming out that there ought to be a phone. I could hear her hands sliding along the wall, searching. After searching a moment alone she inquired sarcastically, "Are you going to help, or are you going to stand there like a fool waiting for God to rescue us?"

"Don't think you are mocking God," I responded confidently. "It can't be done."

While her hands feverishly explored the elevator's walls, I explained that I had called upon God. When I needed His help.

She replied jeeringly, "And I suppose he answered like that." Her fingers snapped in the dark.

"Yes," I replied simply.

When it was evident she expected me to say more I added, "I am alive. Therein lies the proof."

Contemptuously, "I didn't realize being a priest was so dangerous."

"That depends upon where you are a priest."

"You mean the East?" She resumed her search of the walls with her hands. "At least they see you for the fools you are. Besides, all that trumped-up persecution gives you something to whine about. It's better than just being ignored. You will soon discover that truth now that you are in the land of the golden arches."

Before I could protest she slammed her fist against the wall, or kicked it. "Where is that goddam phone?" As if she were a disappointed child, "There is always a phone. There's some kind of law. Isn't there some kind of law?"

I chose not to reply.

She continued to search for a few minutes. I could smell her sweating. Breathing.

"Do you have any fucking ideas, Jesuit?" she panted.

109

I decided to let her stew.

More evenly, "How long do you think it will take them to realize we are in here?"

I breathed as quietly as I could.

"Have you passed out from fear, Jesuit?" The ensuing laughter rattled against the stainless-steel walls. "Afraid of the dark," she taunted. I could still hear her hands sliding along the walls.

"Ah, here it is. Yes." I could feel the change in her voice. "Now we can inform someone. Hello. Hello. Where the fuck are they? Do you suppose this thing is broken?"

I mopped my brow with a handkerchief. It was getting quite close. I tried to imagine that (since they were invisible) the walls were far away. I was used to playing games in cells. The little games that keep you sane. In fact, that is the formula. Little games. And prayer. That's what keeps you going.

"Do you suppose air comes in here? Fresh air?" she wondered out loud, before threateningly demanding I reply—and then grabbing my arm. "Just as I suspected." She slid her fingers down my sleeve toward my hand. "Wasting your time with a rosary!" she taunted as if she had just made a damning discovery.

She seized my empty hand, then grabbed at the other.

"Have you lost your mind?" I exclaimed.

Without saying anything she withdrew her hand. I could hear her step back into the wall before sliding downward onto the floor.

She must have been sitting there on the floor, for three or four minutes, when she whined, "Do you know what it means to be a Green?"

I had heard of them.

She began to talk of the sky and air. And of the green, full earth. The image was so gutturally verdant I could see her freshly scrubbed, hiking through the Black Forest in lederhosen. "Beautifully green. The way it was before they corrupted it."

"They" was one of her favorite epithets.

She took a deep breath. "I hate them for it. God, I hate them for it." And "them."

She began to weep.

The last thing we needed was for her to become hysterical. To calm her I suggested she imagine she was in front of that monstrous window, looking out into the sky.

110

The weeping stopped. Perhaps because of the mind game. Perhaps it was the sound of a voice.

I sat down on the floor.

"Do you think it will take them long to figure out we're here?" she puzzled out loud.

"No," I consoled before assuring her that the power would pop back on any second. The darkness made it much easier to talk: her violent, ugly garb and that festering pin were not staring you in the face. "In a city full of elevators they must deal with problems like this every day," I explained soothingly.

"Yes," she replied, in a slightly different tone. As if something had just occurred to her, she demanded, "Have they sent you here to stop him?"

It took me a second to figure out what she was talking about.

"If I thought that, I'd kill you. Right now."

I stumbled for a second (not out of fear, mind you. No. It was just that I was having difficulty finding the right words. Or perhaps I was no longer sure myself?) before pointing out that I was not there to explain myself to her.

I could hear her boots grinding against the floor as she stood. "I'll know soon enough," she summed up mystically. "Soon enough."

I stood.

"No matter which side has sent you."

Which side? How could I let that pass? "I have come to protect the interest of the Church."

"The Pope is just another capitalist. The same!" She snapped her fingers disdainfully. "They are both trying to strangle us to death. The East. The West. Different slogans, but there is not an ounce of difference between them. Their agenda is the same: strangle us with technology, until we are living like pet orchids in a hothouse. Pet orchids waiting to be slowly poisoned by radiation. Or incinerated. Poof!"

I had heard it all before.

"East and West. Capitalist. Communist. Just a schizophrenic staring at himself in a cracked mirror," she spit out.

Political ranting like that always put me to sleep. It was so tedious. And pointless.

"Have I offended you? Yes. No doubt." As if she were prying open an old can of sardines, she asked, "Your sympathies lie with the East, then? You are of the East. That would make sense. Or with the capitalist Church?"

"My sympathies lie with Jesus Christ," I announced.

"So you refuse to be hounded into a phony choice too. I commend you. Too many people seem to think that those are the choices. Not so."

How was one to choose between a system based on greed and another based on betrayal? Not a point to ponder, I had long ago decided. There was no doubt that socialism was right. It was a natural consequence of Christian charity. It came from the heart. But to reform it? To bring Christ back into the center of it? That was the challenge I had dedicated my life to.

"The only choice is the preservation of the earth. Why can't they see what they are doing? Can they be blind?" She began to shuffle about. "How can they not see? Do you know that in ten years the rain forest will be gone? Destroyed. The Black Forest is half dead. Don't they know they are raping the earth?"

When she paused, I asked why—if she had so much respect for life—had she inserted that pin in her cheek. The question just popped out. Unexpectedly. Perhaps it was prompted by her use of the word "rape."

"It is my penance."

I didn't understand.

"I was for a long time one of them. I ate at their table," she explained.

I asked her if she had undergone some sort of conversion.

"Yes," she laughed lightly, I think at herself, before recollecting how devout she had been as a child. And that she had even considered becoming a nun.

You can't imagine how commonplace that revelation is. Or its brother, "I thought about the priesthood when I was young." It seems to come up most often after a few glasses of vodka. "Yes. I sometimes wish I had. Except for the vow," a raised eyebrow, a downward tilt of the head, "I think I would have. Yes. If it weren't for that I would have." Which, I often wanted to reply, was like saying I'd like to be a pilot, if you can assure me we will never leave the ground.

"But I decided to become a whore instead," she announced matter-of-factly. "I must have fucked a thousand men. With my
112

mouth. With my ass. Anything they wanted. Any place they wanted. I would have let them drive their dick into my heart like a stake if they were willing to pay."

Refusing to be shocked, I observed that poverty drives people to all sorts of things.

"I was rich." She began, in the form of a revelation, "Very rich. My father is in the Bundestag."

I waited.

"I decided that if he could be a whore for the capitalists, I could be a whore too." She laughed. "And a capitalist."

I began to feel very uneasy.

"Of sorts. For the Bavarian side election I raised sixty thousand marks. In a month. I must have gone down on, let's see, six hundred men." There was unmistakable pride in her voice. "And not a one of them would have given a pfennig on their own.

"Fucking elections," she spit out angrily. "What a sham. What have elections ever achieved?" When I did not reply, she persisted, "Has an election ever achieved anything?"

I refused to be drawn into a discussion of popular democracy, but I had my doubts that the truth should be held hostage to popular whim.

"Not one goddam tree has ever been saved by an election," she whined. "Not one." She slammed her fist against the wall, sending a shock wave through our little cell. "I'll wager you agree. After all, the Church is not exactly the home of democracy, is it?"

I could hear her pick up the phone again. "They are satisfied with just one election. If you can call that an election."

Refusing to engage in debate, I asked if the phone was still dead.

"Yes," she replied weakly.

After we had been sitting quietly for half an hour, she asked if I could smell anything?

"No," I replied, although I could smell sweat and stale, rebreathed air.

She repeated the question, and when I reassured her that the air was only stale she inquired, "Are you always so calm?"

There were times when I certainly had not been, I admitted.

"I don't like small places like this," she complained agitatedly. "They upset me."

When I again suggested she look out the window, she speculated

113

gravely, "I must have been locked up. When I was young. By a maid. Or cook. Do you think that's possible?"

Another false idol.

"So, which side is the window on?" she asked rather deliberately.

"It's in front of you."

"Of course." Cautiously, "Are you sure you don't smell anything?" She stood. "I smell fire."

"No. I would smell that too. Besides, our eyes would burn. From the smoke."

"Mine are burning." By way of explanation, she added, "I am very sensitive to things like that."

"The air is somewhat stale in here. That's all."

"Goddammit, would you answer the phone! There's a fire here." Spent, she remarked thoughtfully, "If there were a fire there would be no one here to answer the phone. That would explain why there is no one there to answer."

"I don't know where the phone goes," I deflected her before returning to the pin in her cheek. "Penance. I understand that. For selling yourself to men?"

"No. No. No."

At least she had been distracted from the imaginary fire.

"No. It is atonement for eating at their table for sixteen years."

"Their table?"

"The pigs who are raping the world."

"Certainly that is no crime. You were a child."

"Rape is rape. Collaborating with rapists is rape. Eating at the table of rapists is rape."

"Penance for merely being a child seems a little harsh," I observed.

"Call it original sin, if you wish." She reasoned out loud, as if she had discovered something, "That's what it is, isn't it: a kind of original sin."

I was beginning to wonder if I could smell something myself.

"Also, it reminds me." I imagined that she was pausing to reach up and touch the pin. "That I should be willing to accept pain until we have succeeded in stopping them. This prevents me from forgetting."

Yes. That seemed certain.

"Actually, I have taken a vow. A blood vow," she continued soberly.

She was misplaced in time: she should have been the witch for

114

some Viking raider; she would have stood at the bow, astride some hideous Norse god, spitting into the wind.

"I will never feel real pleasure again until we have succeeded. Never."

I put my hand on the aluminum wall. No. It was not especially warm. Not really.

"Never."

But the air was a little acrid.

"Do you believe sacrifice—renunciation—can alter the world?" she philosophized. Before I could reply she answered for me, "You must. Of course. A priest would have to agree. Perhaps we are not as different as we think."

That was not a comparison I enjoyed.

"Yes. Perhaps that is the case." She drummed her fingers on the wall. "Yes."

As calmly as possible I asked if she thought there might be a hatch in the ceiling.

"Perhaps," she offered distractedly, apparently still caught up in her own ruminations about the pin in her cheek, before objecting, "But what good would that do?"

Firmly, calmly, as a captain might speak to his lieutenants I warned, "I am beginning to think that I can smell smoke."

"Scheisse!" She collapsed onto the floor. "Do you believe he is safe?" she moaned.

"Who?" I asked before realizing she meant Father Paul.

"There was no alarm," she reasoned out loud.

Cautiously, "I am not even sure I smell smoke. It could just be my imagination."

"No. It is here. Hiding in the darkness. Slowly poisoning us. I can sense it."

I peered into the blackness at the ceiling. Perhaps there was a hatch? I tried to picture all the elevators I had ridden in. Hadn't there always been something like that in the ceiling?

"I think we should try to open the hatch," I announced.

"What floor do you think we are on?"

"What difference does that make?" I replied, annoyed that she would ask such a nonsensical question.

"Try to remember. Did we descend at all?"

"I don't know," I replied with irritation.

"Perhaps we can warn him."

With consternation, "This hotel is full of people who can warn him." I was about to add, "We had better worry about ourselves," when I realized that disguising our efforts as an attempt to rescue Father Paul might be just the tonic we needed to prevent her from panicking. "But it does seem we would have heard something in here. An alarm. Something."

"He sometimes sleeps quite heavily. Like the dead."

"I will have to lift you on my shoulders. And you can search for the opening with your hands." Before she could protest I added, "I am much stronger than you suspect. My legs are quite powerful."

Her thighs clamped around my neck, she rested on my broad, hunched back as if it were a saddle, while I systematically traversed the elevator in small, cautious steps.

I could smell her pungent femininity through her jeans: sweet, slightly decayed. I tried to hold my breath, but that was impossible. It overwhelmed the smoke, or what I imagined was smoke. My stomach inched up toward my mouth. Several times we began to teeter, to which she responded, "Hold still, hold still," while she clamped her legs even more tightly around my neck, digging the metal studs that usually glistened from around her left thigh into my neck. I let the smell vanish into the pain. I concentrated on it; finally that's all there was. Gnawing, hot pain. That was something I could deal with. I had had experience.

The sound of the aluminum hatch striking the top of the elevator, followed by a curse, brought me back to the here and now.

There was no light.

Still astride me, lifting herself up into the opening, she began calling out for Father Paul. The words exploded like thunderclaps. "Hello! Hello!"

She waited.

"Hello! Paul! Hello!"

She struck the top of the elevator with her fist. Or forearm.

I slowly descended to my knees.

"Goddam!" she wailed, collapsing across me onto the floor, continuing to strike the elevator.

We sat there for what must have been five minutes. It's always hard

116

to tell time in the dark. The distinct smell of smoke drifted down onto us through the invisible opening in the roof of the elevator.

I could hear her weeping.

"They'll soon be here to get us." My voice seemed to explode into space. Straining to speak more softly, I offered, "Just look out that window."

"Would you grant me absolution, Father?"

I sat upright against the wall. "Are you ready to confess your sins?"

"Yes," she began.

"What is it," I stumbled for a second, still adjusting to the idea, "you want to—"

Abruptly, the lights came back on. A second later, while we were still squinting into the bright fluorescent ceiling, the elevator resumed its descent.

"I only offered it for him," she hissed, when we reached the lobby. She strutted across the terrazzo floor, the metal studs around her waist and thigh sparkling in the sunlight like fresh-cut diamonds.

There had been a power failure. All of Manhattan had been plunged into darkness for one hour and twelve minutes. Next day's New York Daily News: "City in Shroud of Night 72 Minutes."

From that day on, Dietra Christian hated me.

Nine months later there were an inordinate number of births in New York City.

MOTHER POLAND

During my second summer with Father Paul we went to Poland. That I was going home filled me with joy and satisfaction. And even fear. Not fear for my safety. No. There was no real danger for me there any longer. It was only the gnawing fear that the joy of being there would be overshadowed by old memories.

That we were permitted to deliver our message in the East was a tribute to our success. Notice that I now say "we." Clearly I had become one of them. What the press, to my annoyance, called the Children's Crusade. Certainly we were not all children. And the Children's Crusade had ended (although I wonder if they even knew that there had been a Children's Crusade!) rather unhappily.

117

When we arrived at the Warsaw airport we were desposited in a huge waiting room. Poland is full of huge waiting rooms. The officials there always feel more important when they can look out into a sea of waiting faces. That lets them know they are indispensable.

Since it was a warm June afternoon, they felt even more indispensable. And showed it by taking their time.

While immigration led members of our party out one by one, I wondered if I would be treated like all the rest. Or, as I was inclined to suspect, in some special way. By the time I was ushered through the door and down a maze of corridors to a small room I was drenched with sweat. Colonel Janovich was there. Along with an immigration official. Janovich had certainly not been there to greet the others.

"Ah, Monsignor Babulieski. Welcome home." He extended his right hand; a countervailing cigarette occupied his left.

Choosing not to reciprocate, I merely said, "Good morning."

He inserted his hand into his pocket. "I'm sure your old friends will be happy to see you."

I can remember being angry that it was hot enough for me to be wet with perspiration. I didn't want him to think that he was the cause of it.

Sitting behind a desk that nearly filled the room, he said, "Especially your old friend Ivan."

They had begun by forcing it down my throat. Usually a few minutes after I had eaten. When I discovered what they were doing I put off eating as long as I could. Sometimes for half the night. But after a while I would tear off a piece of bread. Or a small piece of sausage. As soon as I finished they would start walking down the hall to fetch me. I could hear their boots crisply marching. They draped me across a rough-cut table, one guard holding each arm, and inched the wooden club down my throat, agitating it like a plunger until the little bit of food I had eaten rose like debris from a clogged-up drain.

"Yes. You and Ivan were dear friends, weren't you?" Always Janovich's voice has that teasing, sensual ring to it. My stomach spontaneously turned over.

They had been doing that for several weeks when, out of boredom or design (maybe that's just the way things went, step by step), they (I can remember waiting, stretched out across the table, my mouth clamped shut in numb determination) shoved it up into my rectum.

118

I could feel the hard wood tearing away at my insides. Just as I was about to faint it was yanked out. And then reinserted.

"Look," a faceless boot laughed.

I could feel them all staring at my erect penis.

A voice scolded, "My, my."

The wooden stick was rammed in again.

"My, my."

Another, gleefully announced, "Look at that on the floor. What would the Holy Father say?"

My face was on fire from humiliation.

"So, not just a traitor to his country, but his sex."

They laughed hard; I could feel the laughing hand twisting the stick.

Back in my cell I wept. And prayed. Surely God could forgive me that.

Couldn't He?

The next time: "Well, your friend Ivan is here to see you." I could see the glee in their eyes. "He's missed you so much. You're his favorite."

I tried not to flush.

"Oh, don't be jealous. No, no. The others are, well, just business. But you, Father Babulieski, you are Ivan's favorite. His true love."

Another voice from the other side of the lights responded, "And he's so happy it's reciprocal."

Before that, after each interrogation (I call them that although there seemed nothing that they wanted to know) I had returned to my cell and prayed. Contemplated the martyrs. Reminded myself that they too had been scourged. Now each hour was spent in anticipation. Waiting. Counting the minutes until my next humiliation.

I considered suicide. I concocted several ways. In fact, I spent hours planning my suicide. Going over each detail. Just ramming my head into the wall would work, I decided. I pictured my head shattering like a ripe pumpkin. I watched each piece of orange debris fly across the room in slow motion. I felt myself vanish.

But in the end I was always there when they came to get me. And I submitted. Oh, my body resisted; it struggled. But my mind submitted. While they were doing it I found my mind slowing drifting (even while they jeered; even while they pounded on my exposed, de-

formed back with rubber sticks as if it were an ancient drum) into a kind of distant, euphoric place. And I always came.

And later, I always hated myself. And felt filthy.

"So what is your business?" he requested.

Well, things were quite different now, I said to myself. Quite different.

"Since when is the Polish KGB sent to meet official visitors?"

"When they are old traitors returning to stir up trouble."

"Well, I'm sure a Soviet marionette would be an expert on treason."

He held the cigarette to his mouth, allowing himself to be engulfed in its acrid blue smoke, before continuing, "I suggest you stay clear of your old friends. Although most of them are away at the moment. Except for your dear friend Ivan."

"Are you finished?" I responded coolly. At the time I remember thinking, with a sense of relief, How childish of him to taunt me about that. It is over. It is nothing but a dimly recollected nightmare.

Now I know that was not completely true. Things like that don't just go away.

A week later, six hundred and fifty thousand souls (and several hundred KGB) came to hear Father Paul in Gdansk. A million had seen him two days before in Warsaw.

It was like the high-flying days of Solidarity all over again. No. It was even more intense. More intoxicating.

And the authorities did nothing. They were, in fact, quite helpful. But what could they do with the whole world watching? This was not something that, like Solidarity, could be stamped out in the middle of the night.

I was not permitted to join them in Leningrad. Or Moscow. The Soviet authorities refused my application for a visa.

I took that opportunity to visit my old church. And some friends. Those that were not, as Colonel Janovich put it, "away." I was pleased to discover that Solidarity was not really dead. It lurked beneath Poland's skin like a rash ready to break out after a scratch or two. That discovery pleased me a great deal, but I offered them no real counsel. I had, I suppose, found bigger fish to fry. Reforming socialism could wait.

The only unsettling event of those five days occurred while I was celebrating mass at my old church in Gdansk.

120

"The German bitch is a Soviet agent."

Those words were uttered by a communicant. A man of about fifty. Placid. Not wild-eyed. His calloused hand brushed against mine with a sandpaper shock as he took the chalice, and, looking me directly in the eye, he said, "The German bitch is a Soviet agent."

I advanced the cup to the next communicant, and the man was gone. Vanished into a sea of capless heads.

But the thought stayed with me. Oh, I didn't believe it. Not really. But when you have experienced living in a society in which moles spend an entire lifetime burrowing, rooting around for the smallest morsel that can advance them, you learn to be careful.

When I met them in Prague I began to look at her in a brand-new light. Things that may have gone unnoticed before took on altogether new meanings. What an idea, I marveled. Could she be an agent? She was, on the surface, a most obvious example of Western decadence. What irony. Or was it too much to be believed? And to what purpose?

After a few days I began to discount it. No. She was just what she seemed: a decadent, foul-mouthed whore. An embarrassment, certainly. But no more.

And she did appear dedicated to Father Paul. Only she, it seemed, could rid him of those paralyzing headaches that sprang up from nowhere, leaving him immobilized until she arrived.

Within a week I was too busy with our crusade to give it any more thought. But the shipbuilder's words simmered beneath the surface, waiting for someone to turn up the flame.

In all, twenty-five million East Europeans saw Father Paul face to face. Ten times that many saw him on television. There. And in the rest of the world—only God knew. It was clear that Father Paul was achieving something incredible.

Some suggested that he was paving the way for the imminent return of Christ; others, that ignoring him would lead to the destruction preceding His return.

We were all giddy with success on the return flight to New York. The lobby of the Hilton was jammed with T-shirts, and foreheads, waiting to be autographed. Those who couldn't clutter around Father Paul whetted their insatiable curiosity (so insatiable that Jack Hawkins was already confidently predicting that Father Paul would be

121

Time *magazine's Man of the Year)* on me *(even the hunchbacked priest was becoming something of a celebrity—two paragraphs in Newsweek). I politely squeezed my way through to the elevator.*

"Good afternoon, Monsignor."

I nodded without really even looking up. This was the kind of evening I wanted to spend alone. Thanking God for the great success we had just experienced.

"Quite a circus, isn't it?"

The man who spoke was young. No more than twenty-five. And smoked a cigarette through a long, shiny holder that jutted out of the center of his mouth like a piece of modern sculpture.

"Perhaps I should introduce myself," he enunciated through closed teeth, before extending a card.

Fiorelli. Interview.

That was all it said. "Interview" was printed in hurried, exaggerated script.

"I can see no purpose in that," I replied firmly, wondering why he handed people that silly card instead of simply asking.

"Purpose?" He unbuttoned his coat, still leaving the collar turned up as if he were some old movie sleuth. "My readers are insatiably curious. About all sorts of things."

"No, my deformity was not caused by a beating inflicted by the KGB."

"Good." More to himself, he winced. "What a gruesome thought."

"Yes, I was raised in a Catholic orphanage," I continued drearily, stepping through the elevator doors as I spoke.

"Oh," he replied in a way that let me know that that was of no importance to him.

Perhaps he was interested in hearing something of substance. On the few occasions that had presented themselves I had tried to inform the world of the Church's views with regard to Father Paul's crusade. Usually with little effect.

"What were the hotels like?" I realized he was following me. "Was the service first-rate?" What a question, I reacted. Next he will be asking what the privies were like: were they well lighted? clean?

The mixture of confusion and displeasure I was feeling must have showed.

Trying a new tack, he inquired, "Did you see any films while you

122

were in Poland? The new Polish cinema is very exciting." Approaching earnestness, he continued, "You do find film exciting, don't you?"

I was about the push the door to in his face when I heard Dietra Christian's voice: "Monsignor Babulieski. Wait a moment." A second or two later she dropped a huge box at my feet. "From Father Paul."

Mystified, I gingerly tilted the box up on end.

"Perhaps you should call room service," he offered with his nose up against the box.

After informing him that a little work never hurt anyone I hoisted the box onto my back and carried it into the room.

"What do you suppose it is?" he inquired as if he belonged there.

I gave him a look indicating he should leave and bent over the box, looking for some obvious way to open it. I had not received many gifts. In fact, none that I could recall, apart from a few meager hand-me-downs near what was decided was my birthday. I carefully peeled off the tape securing the box and slipped off the lid, revealing a marblelike expanse of smooth Styrofoam that as much as anything resembled a pearl-white sarcophagus.

"My God, it's a computer," I roared, as soon as I had pried it open. "A computer," I repeated in disbelief. As if the little man and I were now old friends I exclaimed, "Can you believe that? A computer. Father Paul must have gotten tired of hearing about my excursions to Computer Village."

After excavating the Styrofoam box as carefully as one might an Egyptian pharaoh's tomb, I spread the directions on the floor, and while the little man, his collar still turned up, a scarf tightly wrapped around his throat, perched on the edge of the coffee table I assembled the computer. It took no more than ten minutes.

I inventoried out loud, "Frogger, Dungeons and Dragons, Word-Perfect, Spelling Bee, Superbasic, Maxisheet."

"So," he probed, "you are something of a hacker?"

"A what?" I asked back shortly. Surely it must be here. After all, he knew it was my favorite. "Dammit. It must be here somewhere."

"What is that?"

"Buck Rogers."

"Buck Rogers?"

"Yes. He knows it's my favorite."

"Oh."

And there it was, in an envelope along with a card. It had been taped to the side of the box like an inscription on a pharaoh's tomb. I read the card several times: "After nine hours in the air I am sure you are too tired to go on safari." It was signed "Paul."

"Aren't video games out now?" He wrinkled his nose in the way he had when I mentioned work.

I played half the night, beating him unmercifully, until, at two or three, he fell asleep propped up against the coffee table with his small round head pillowed by his coat collar.

After that I lay in bed for an hour or two feeling very good. It was only when I was about to fall asleep that I began to wonder: apart from a few books and my clothing (nothing extravagant, excepting perhaps my heavy coat), I had never owned anything at all. Certainly nothing like a computer. And the games (Dungeons and Dragons was almost as good as Buck Rogers) were, well, frivolous. There was no other way to characterize them. Harmless, perhaps. But frivolous.

I spent the remainder of the night on my knees in the cool, black wind, staring out through the opened glass sliding doors, praying. How could I part with it? After all, it had been a gift from Father Paul. Oh, he would understand if I had to give it up. Yes. He would. Yes. Unless he found giving it up too vain. Yes. Was the whole idea merely a conceit? Spiritual vanity?

By dawn I had decided to give it to an orphanage. Yes. They could put it to good use. I imagined what it would have been like to have something like that when I was a boy. How different from wandering down a country stream searching for God. Avoiding your reflection.

Odd, that was the first sacrifice I had ever made that hurt. In comparison all the rest were nothing.

When I stood, the little man was there, looking somewhat frumpy and disheveled. "Coffee," he exhaled weakly, as if it were his dying breath.

I offered generously, "Then we can have our interview."

"No. No." He opened his greatcoat. "It is done. Finis." Dangling against each hip was a large black cassette recorder. "It's all here. Naturally."

A CONSPIRACY TO KILL US ALL

The two weeks from August 9 to August 23 were the happiest period of my life. I mean that sincerely. We had just completed our tour of Poland and Eastern Europe. Which had been a smashing success.

And now we were immersed in planning a tour of the United States that was to commence with a gigantic rally in Central Park on September 9. I found that especially exciting and rewarding, since it served to commemorate my joining Father Paul's crusade two years previous. And in Central Park again! The irony of it all was not lost on me later. Or for that matter then. I found it hard to reconstruct in my mind those initial feelings of abhorrence, shock, and distrust. Oh, I could remember; I knew what I had felt. But two years later the words were lifeless tags. As distant as old relations you haven't seen since childhood. (On our tour of Poland, several cousins and uncles "appeared." Where had they been when I needed them? I had wanted to ask. Were they even real? I had wondered. I suppose it is easier to love the right hand of the Savior of the world than a hunch-backed infant. Odd, how God has a way of turning the world on its head.) You know you are supposed to know them. You even remember their names. But the recollection is only a trick. The shock? The abhorrence? Mere words, like the names of those long-lost cousins and uncles.

But God had decided that the smooth sailing was to end. He had plans for me.

The day it all began was August 23. Unless it was that Sunday in Gdansk? I guess I will never know for sure. It was morning. The man was wearing a hat. Rather large and slouchy. He said, "It is important that I have a few words with you."

"You will have to speak to Jack Hawkins. He handles public relations." Walking briskly, I informed him, "He schedules interviews."

"It is you I must see."

"I have nothing to say."

"I need your help," the man in the hat replied firmly.

The request did not sound desperate. No. It sounded much more like an order.

"Jack Hawkins."

"We need you," he insisted. "The survival of the world depends upon you."

What a grandiose claim, I remember thinking. The world? How absurd. But I stopped.

Half an hour later I was in a room on the fifty-third floor of a glass skyscraper, at a longish rectangular table, seated, with three men, including the man with the hat.

"That German woman, the one who calls herself Dietra Christian." The man with the hat paused. "She is KGB."

They all seemed to be gauging my reaction. Waiting.

"You don't seem surprised by that," he fished.

"Who are you?" I demanded.

"Friends." Smiling, he temporized with, "Beyond that it doesn't really matter." He slid one hand across the other as if he were washing them with air. Why did they feel dirty? I wondered to myself.

"I am sure of that. But whose?"

"Why, yours, of course. At least we are sympathetic to your views."

The two other men conferred, mouth to ear; then the three heads joined at the corner of the table.

The man with the hat: "We are taking a chance. Just talking to you. You do understand that?"

"A chance? No."

"We have no way of knowing for sure that you aren't one of them."

"One of who?" I offered obliquely.

"We have no way of knowing that you aren't KGB too. Or something like it."

I am sure I hissed. "I say damn you. You're the ones who look like policemen. The stench is international."

"Then it is of no importance to you that the woman is KGB?" He wiped the corner of his mouth with his fingertip. "Or that he might be too?"

"Paul Creticos?" Silence. "What a disgusting accusation."

Calmly, he informed me: "About her there is no doubt. We know exactly where she was trained. We know everything about her. Everything."

"Why are you telling me this?" I replied. I had learned long ago that with the police—and these certainly were the police—you volunteer nothing. Half the time they are just fishing. Waiting for some tiny morsel of truth to slash their teeth into.

126

"Because you can help us discover if he is KGB." Another man, rather old, perhaps sixty, had responded.

"I notice that you cannot even say his name. Only 'he.' "

The third man: "There is no point in all this pussyfooting around." He spoke to me. "He is KGB." His voice was seductively smooth. "You don't really think her being there is a coincidence? Why else would he have her there?" He wrapped his index finger around its neighbor. "They're like this."

The man with the hat leaned across the table toward me. "We don't really know for sure."

"What would your superiors think if they knew you were covering up something like this?" the man continued, his voice nauseatingly sweet. "This is not the same as editing a few indiscretions from your reports, Father." He leaned toward me while he spoke, as if we were suddenly very close.

What had he meant by that? Indiscretions? I had tried to give as faithful a picture of what was happening as I could. There was no point in dwelling on Father Paul's unorthodox methods. After all, the men in the curia were a long way away. It was not really practical to include facts that would require lengthy explanations. And distract them from the important work that was being achieved.

And how the hell did they know that I was reporting to the curia?

"This is not something that can be erased with a few Hail Marys, Father," he reiterated, his face still looming toward me.

Silencing his companion with a raised palm, the man with the hat whispered, "We just don't know for sure."

I made no attempt to hide my disgust. "You are attempting to recruit me to be a spy."

"Not exactly. No. We merely want you to keep your eyes open."

"You can be sure that Father Paul will," I began before stopping. There was something in the older one's eyes, a cold interest in what I was about to blurt out, that convinced me to stop.

Playing the role of the congenial host about to bid adieu to his guest, the man with the hat rose, and with my hand clasped into his, he walked me to the door and to the elevator, leaving his companions behind. "Just think about it a few days," he requested pleasantly. "If we're wrong, then what's the harm? We'll be the first to admit it if there's been some mistake. The first." Confidentially, through the cracked door of my cab, he sympathized, "I don't want to believe this any more than you do." He earnestly continued, his watery blue eyes riveted to mine, "You could do us a great favor just by proving that we're misinformed."

As the taxi lurched across town I vacillated between anger and weakness, a kind of sick, physical weakness that arises from dread. I kept trying to picture the face of the man in Gdansk. He had said exactly the same thing! Even the words, after you translated them, were the same. Or almost the same. "The German bitch is KGB."

Was that really possible?

Father Paul would have to be told. Immediately. It was time for him to see her for what she was anyway. Something should have been done about her in the beginning.

And certainly I should have said something in Eastern Europe. Of course, things had been going so smoothly. More than that. We were, at least in our unity of purpose, a family. All of us. Even she had her place. As the corrupt child; or androgynous prodigal son.

After this, nothing could be the same.

What reason did the man have to lie, though? If he were telling the truth, wouldn't he have remained to explain? No. Perhaps not. Perhaps that would have been too dangerous there.

Or perhaps he was just poisoning the well we drank from. After all, we had enemies.

When I entered Father Paul's rooms, there she was, as usual, sprawled out across the wing chair, vulgarly swinging her leg to and fro. Just the sight of her produced a chill.

"Hello, Monsignor. Help yourself." In a gesture befitting an androgynous, foul-smelling Satan she waved her hand in the direction of the coffee table at the foot of her chair. It was covered with fruit and bread and yogurt cups with spoons jutting from them. "I'm sorry that we don't have something from the golden arches for you," she sneered. "Can you still digest unadulterated food?"

That was as close as Dietra Christian could come to approximating cheerfulness.

"Is Paul here?"

She pointed over her shoulder.

"We've been feasting." She inserted a plastic spoon in her mouth and sucked the yogurt from it, causing the shiny safety pin to vanish into a crease in her cheek.

128

"I can see you have," I replied in as conversational a tone as I could manage. There was no point in revealing anything to her. Not then.

"Actually he is taking a nap."

"Really." I sat on the sofa. "Is it Stuttgart you're from?"

Raising one eyebrow, "Yes."

"I was just curious." I ran my fingers through my hair. "Odd you didn't visit there. While we were so near."

"Stuttgart? It's a fucking sewer." Continuing to eat yogurt, "Have you ever been to Stuttgart?"

"No."

What did I hope to find out? Certainly I was no detective. Funny, they (at least the ones on television) always know what to ask. Perhaps I was too used to people volunteering the truth to me. This business of trying to unearth secrets was a very new and uncomfortable idea.

"Well, Piotr." Father Paul stood at the door for a moment to stretch. "We've been waiting for you half the afternoon." His thick, blond hair looked as if it had been sculptured with hedge shears. Smiling like a little boy, he teased, "So where have you been?"

I almost blushed. "Just puttering about."

"On the Planet of Zoom?" he accused, still smiling. "You should have kept your computer, then you wouldn't have to skulk about like a kid playing hooky."

Smiling the lie, I agreed, "Yes, I suppose you're right."

We spent the afternoon marking a large map with Magic Marker circles. Above each circle Father Paul penciled in a date. When we had finished, humming like a car engine or buzzing like a jet plane, he connected the cities with a dashed green line.

As soon as he finished he leaned his back against the sofa and exclaimed, "Thank God that's over. Now we can rest."

The afternoon had been torture. Sessions like that were usually fun. In an odd sort of way. Father Paul was so light and gay. Sometimes he would compose limericks using the names of towns. Some more than a little risqué—which didn't offend me. After all, I had spent half my life with the shipworkers of Gdansk. Sometimes I used to wonder: was Christ so lighthearted with His disciples? Perhaps He was. I still like to think so.

But that afternoon I couldn't bring myself to laugh at all. Not genuinely. And Father Paul chided me for being such a stick-in-the-mud, even though I tried to pretend the right sort of lightness.

I decided that as soon as she left I would tell him. There was no other way.

But I didn't. The closest I could come was to ask him, in the most casual, conversational way I could, what he really knew about her. I tried to mask it as curiosity.

Putting his hand on my back, he replied, "I know there's been friction. After all, the two of you are so different. I'm happy that's behind us." He sat down on the edge of the sofa and pressed his fingertips on his temples.

"A headache?" I inquired.

"No. Just a little tired. Perhaps you could bring me a glass of water."

I carefully filled a glass with ice and water before wrapping the base with a paper napkin so that it wouldn't drip. "Maybe this will help."

"Oh, yes. That will do the trick."

He drank the entire glass of water in one long swallow, leaned his head back, and fell asleep. I covered him with the bedspread and let myself out.

Actually it was a good thing I hadn't told him, I decided. He wouldn't have believed it anyway. No. And he might have just mistaken an accusation like that for jealousy.

As far as Dietra Christian went, I decided to watch her very carefully.

That night the dreams began:

The table is not cold. The way wood is not cold. But a little rough, because it is a simple table.

At first there are only boots. No faces. I can feel the hands. There is something about them.

"Your friend Ivan has missed you, Father." The voice is succulently hypnotic.

"No," I reply. Or do I? Do I say that or just think it very loudly?

The hands pull me down against the table, and Ivan enters me from the rear.

"No."

"But Ivan loves you so much."

"No," I moan.

130

The hands pull more tightly. There is something about them. Something familiar.

I can see Janovich's face in the shadows. Always he is in the shadows. Smiling.

"No." I must be saying it.

The ring. Yes. The ring. It is her ring. I have seen it a thousand times. But how can that be? How can she be here?

"Was ist los, Father?"

I strain to raise my head and look to the right. Yes. It is her. The safety pin is blindingly bright. But I can tell it is her.

"No."

"But Ivan needs you. See? A little more? See how much Ivan loves you?"

"No."

The hand on the left also wears the ring. The same shining safety pin blinds me, its white light shattering into two perpendicular rainbows of transcendent color.

I ejaculate.

Laughter. One voice is familiar. Whose laughter is it? Janovich's? Yes. It must be. I try to concentrate, but I am too sleepy. When I force myself to look up, my chin chafing against the rough tabletop, the face in the shadows is not Janovich's but Father Paul's.

"Is that you?" I start to ask. But before I can the club is shoved down my throat. At first I am about to strangle. I can feel myself starting to black out, but before I can the stick is withdrawn slightly. Air. Air. And then back down.

Laughter. Gales of sick, devilish laughter.

"Come, Father. Isn't there something in there for us? Isn't there?"

Finally I vomit around the agitating club. Or do I wake up first?

It was always the same.

After the dreams began I never slept. Not really. At first I supposed that by taking a nap here and a nap there I could hide from them; but I couldn't. They were always there waiting for me, like thieves in some dark alley.

Odd, the dreams were much more frightening than the Gdansk police station ever was. There there was a kind of comforting inevitability, but the dreams always teased me with the false idea that they could be eluded.

They seem very happy about the dreams here. The way a surgeon is happy that everyone has a heart. Even my doctor says they hold the key to my recovery.

At any rate, I had to give up sleeping, which cast a strange shadow over everything. That strangeness was exacerbated by the sense of separation I felt. I was no longer one of them. Oh, I wasn't actually spying. But there were now two of me. The one who helped draw circles on maps and brought everyone tea; and the one who watched. Waiting for some slip.

Still I did not believe it. Oh, she might have been lying. She was capable of anything. But not Father Paul.

On September 2 they called. When I picked up the phone I had been lying in bed for a hour trying to sleep and then fighting it off. Yes. No. Yes. No.

"We must see you," the voice demanded politely.

The three of them were there. At the same table. Two on my right. One on my left. A television stared at us from across the table. This time I made a point of examining each one very carefully.

"Just tell us if you have seen this man." The lights dimmed. The man with the hat turned on the television with a remote-control device.

The picture was black-and-white. The pond at Central Park. Dietra Christian was standing near the water's edge watching the sail-boats. A man approached from her right and stood beside her.

"That man."

The picture froze.

He didn't look familiar at all.

"Have you seen him?"

"No," I offered reluctantly. Certainly there was no harm in that.

The man with the hat started the action again with his forefinger.

The man stood there for a while. Said a word or two. Since her back was to us, I couldn't even tell if she was responding.

He could have been saying, "Lovely day, isn't it?" There was no way to tell.

He froze the action several more times, but the man was as unfamiliar to me as ever.

"Try another," the older man with the nauseatingly sweet voice suggested.

132

This took place somewhere unfamiliar. There were several men. And Dietra Christian. They were all strangers. Eastern Europeans. Perhaps Poles, I surmised from their dress.

"Was this taken while we were in Poland?" I asked.

"Do you recognize this man?" was the reply I got.

The next sequence took place in the lobby of our hotel. That made me feel strangely uneasy. Could they do that? I wondered.

I recognized no one.

They withdrew, leaving me with the staring, blank television. After a moment, out of curiosity, I looked down at the remote-control unit. Very space-age, I remember remarking to myself as I reached over and touched one of the buttons. Nothing happened. I pressed another. It flickered on. I pressed another.

Father Paul was reclining on the sofa in his rooms. He was pressing his temples with his fingertips. Slowly rotating his hands, his eyes shut.

"Damn them. God damn them!" I hissed.

Dietra Christian entered the room from the bedroom. She spoke, but there was no sound. Father Paul continued to massage his temples. She stepped across the coffee table and sat on the floor beside the sofa.

I picked up the remote control.

She rested her hand on him. Gently. Her fingers not moving, just resting there, as if they were draped across a pillow. The hand rested there for what must have been a minute or two before she unzipped his pants and extracted his member. Again she paused, her hand wrapped firmly around him. Perhaps she was speaking. Perhaps not.

She leaned over him, so that he vanished behind her head. I looked away for a moment but returned to the screen, unable to prevent myself from watching.

His eyes were closed. His fingers still motionlessly touching the sides of his head. You could see the pain vanishing from his face. His mouth relaxed into a faint smile as she drew the pain from him.

"Are you certain that you have never seen any of those men?" the man with the hat inquired.

Startled by their sudden reappearance, I yanked my eyes from the television screen.

"I don't think he's playing straight with us," the one with the sweet voice replied.

133

"I have never seen them," I replied tiredly.

In a concerned way he inquired, "Are you sure you're well, Father?"

"I haven't been sleeping well," I replied as my eyes strayed back to the screen.

"Oh." He made a small noise with his tongue against the roof of his mouth. "Sorry to hear that."

Father Paul tensed for a moment and then broke into a large, exuberant smile that seemed to engulf his entire face.

"Those men are all Eastern Bloc agents. All of them."

After that I believed everything they said.

DIETRA CHRISTIAN'S CONFESSOR

"God forgive me," I repeated several times before sliding the pistol into my cassock. The cold steel stabbed into my side as sharply as a spear, eliciting a gasp.

How had this moment arrived?

Even now I wonder. I was so sure then. So sure.

Father Paul had been in his usual state: a raging headache (were they authentic? or merely inventions to have her mouth upon his cock?) that only she could cure.

"I'll have the car brought around," I offered. "And wait there."

What an odd look Dietra Christian gave me. As if to say, "Finally, you admit he is mine." Perhaps she had always thought that my motives were purely jealous. Perhaps.

In twenty minutes they were downstairs, laughing, the tension vanished. Father Paul's eyes gazed out onto the city, serenely blue. Antichrist! I remember thinking. How the serpent adorns himself with fine colors and beauty. Antichrist. Antichrist. I repeated that one-word litany while our limousine crawled up the west side of the park.

"My, Father, you are in a dark mood," Dietra Christian commented. "Today is the day of triumph. The beginning of the new day. Can't you feel it in your bones?"

"Yes," I replied succinctly to the last thing she said to me.

The black stretch limousine glided across the grass along a winding path carved out of reaching arms and ecstatic faces. They wanted to see, to touch, the man who was delivering peace to the world. They

134

settled for brushing their fingers across the glistening black car; a glance into the window; a smile.

Huge slashed NØs emblazoned thousands of T-shirts like crusaders' crosses.

From the platform, banner after banner proclaimed NØ.

The faces and arms receded into the horizon; they might have extended to the edge of the world for all you could see.

"No." The chorus was as loud as the heavenly host.

Antichrist, I repeated to myself.

"No."

He approached the microphone at the center of the stage with the same mild embarrassment he always exhibited. How beautiful it was. How beautiful he was.

Antichrist.

"Effortless, isn't it? So short. So easy. What do you say?"

"No."

He was phalanxed by two short rows of seats. I was on his right at the far end no more than ten feet away. Next to smiling, mindless Jack Hawkins. Was he one of them? Or just in it for the money? The joy of selling was smeared across his face like a whore's lipstick.

Dietra Christian, as always, sat cross-legged on the wooden platform guarding the stairs.

There were armed policemen sprinkled about like blue flowers. There had been threats.

I leaned forward and slipped my hand into the fold in my cassock. The pistol, which had been warmed by my flesh, was as damp as a bar of soap left overnight in the tub. I closed my fingers around it.

"No," they roared.

When I stood, Dietra Christian appeared puzzled for a second. She posed a question with her hand.

"Die, Antichrist!"

I waited until he turned to fire. The shot pierced his chest. His face showed not the slightest surprise. None. It was as if he had expected it. How could that be? Could he have known? No. That was absurd, I told myself. Why wasn't he terrified? I had pictured terror on his face. I had expected that beautiful, tan face to be distorted with ugly terror. To reveal itself! For an instant I was seized by doubt.

The second shot hit Dietra Christian directly in the face. She had interposed herself.

Her face exploded like a ripe tomato.

Prone, beneath the weight of half a dozen bodies, I could hear him: "If life is in you, I absolve—" he was giving her extreme unction. How could that be? I had seen the bullet strike him. "Antichrist! Blasphemer!" I tried to scream in a final fit of rage, but the weight of the bodies was too great. Or I was suddenly too weak to force the words out of my mouth.

And through it all I could hear him say: "The Lord has freed you from sin. May He bring you freely to His kingdom in Heaven. Glory to Him forever." Even though the commotion was deafening, and I was buried under half a dozen bodies.

I even supposed, right then, as I tried to block it out, that I was imagining it all. That I hadn't really seen him at all. That I couldn't really hear him at all.

But of course it was him.

THE INTERVIEW

The day before the trial, my interview appeared. Unchanged by events:

> Monsignor Piotr Babulieski was raised in Poland. One of the leading lights of the Polish Church during the rise and fall of Solidarity, he is now the strong right hand of Father Paul Creticos.
>
> Monsignor Babulieski's rooms in the New York Hilton are simply appointed. A long white brocade sofa faces the bed, over which a pale blue comforter is draped. A Bible is on the bedside table beneath a Tiffany lamp.
>
> The drapes are pulled back, displaying a breathtaking view of midtown Manhattan.
>
> FIORELLI: It must be great to be back stateside, Monsignor Babulieski.
>
> MONSIGNOR BABULIESKI: A little rest will certainly be nice.
>
> F: I'll bet. There's no place like home. Unless you like to travel. Of course, for you this last tour was a trip home, wasn't it?

136

MB: Yes. (MB is assembling an IBM home computer—a gift from Father Paul that has just been delivered.) That was quite pleasant.

F: Visiting home always is. I guess this is quite a surprise?

MB: (Excitedly) Yes. (MB seems a little embarrassed.) Video games are a passion of mine.

F: Oh, they've been the rage for some time now. Ryan (Ryan O'Neal) has a loft space downtown with an entire floor devoted to them. It's not far from here. You should drop by sometime.

MB: Yes, I suppose they have. That was one of my first great surprises here. (Laughing) You don't see home computers in Poland. And certainly not video games.

F: I've never thought about that. I notice you are wearing a traditional cassock. Do all priests in Poland still dress that way?

MB: No. (MB turns on the monitor.) Most are quite modern. Like Father Paul.

F: Yes. He wears only a collar.

MB: Yes. And usually jeans. In Poland a priest wouldn't wear jeans. They're too hard to find.

F: Yes, I've heard that you can sell Levi's there for fifty dollars a pair. No telling what you could get for Calvin Klein's.

MB: No. (MB slides a diskette into the slot; Buck Rogers and the Planet of Zoom lights up the screen.) This was the first game I ever played.

F: Really. It looks like a good one.

We play Buck Rogers until three A.M. Along with Frogger and Zip/Zap. We have Brazilian coffee sent up to the room. (It's delicious.) When I leave, MB is kneeling in front of the long, sliding glass doors praying. The sunrise is gorgeous.

FATHER PIOTR'S CONFESSOR

At first I was disturbed that they had assigned me to a woman. Not that I don't have complete confidence in the capabilities of women.

It was just that I wasn't sure a woman could understand me. After all, my vocation is a man's vocation. And there would be certain things that it would be awkward to communicate to a woman.

Actually I have become very fond of her. Oh, our relationship is no more than professional. Not really. How could it be otherwise? But within that context there is an obvious warmth.

The sessions began in her office. A small, cramped room with books stacked in piles here and there. And coffee cups. But soon we began to walk through the countryside.

It was the fall. The trees were bright red and yellow. The leaves crushed noisily under your feet when you walked, so we had to speak loudly and clearly. But that didn't matter. There was no one to hear.

She was very different from my court-appointed psychiatrist. He would just stare at me, asking questions, while he held a pencil up to his temple, twisting it like a drill. He had been hired to say I was insane. And he did. To him there was nothing else to concern himself with.

Dr. ———— was different. I don't think she really cared whether I was crazy or not. She, in fact, seemed quite at home with crazy people.

DR. ————: So, you have always felt, from the time you were a small child, that you were an instrument of God.

FATHER PIOTR: Aren't we all instruments of God?

DR.: Perhaps. But you felt that, well, something special was in store for you?

FP: Yes. (FP laughs) And there was, wasn't there?

DR.: Yes, I suppose there was. But. . .

FP: Why was I filled with that perpetual sense of anticipation? Why else would God have made me the way I am?

DR.: I don't think I understand.

FP: Even as a child I knew that I must have been made so ugly with a purpose.

DR: Interesting. And how old were you when this occurred to you?

FP: From the beginning. I have always felt that.

DR.: And now?

FP: Should I feel that God has abandoned me?

DR.: Do you?

138

FP: No.

DR.: Not at all?

FP: What good would faith be if it were so easily disposed of?

DR.: Who could argue with that? But your confidence has not been shaken at all?

FP: In what? Certainly my confidence in God is stronger than ever. In myself? It is true that I have been deceived. But man is weak. I more than most. But what has that to do with God?

DR.: (Warmly) Little, I confess.

(But on another day I broke down completely, ready to renounce God; accusing Him of participating in the deception that destroyed me; damning Him for making a fool of me.)

DR.: Why would God want you to commit murder?

FP: God would never want that.

DR.: Then you are convinced that murder is a sin? (I nod) Regardless of the circumstances?

FP: Absolutely.

DR.: Then why?

FP: Arrogance.

DR.: Arrogance?

FP: Yes. The most seductive sin. I was willing to go to hell—

DR.: Forgive me for interrupting, Father. I want to be sure I understand you. Then what you were doing was wrong?

FP: Completely.

DR.: And you knew that at the time?

FP: Yes.

DR.: And you still went ahead with it?

FP: Oh, yes. Someone had to. I was sure of that. At the time it was quite clear to me what they had in mind.

DR.: They?

FP: Does that sound too paranoid?

DR.: No. Not at all. I just wondered who they were.

FP: Father Paul. Dietra Christian. I was not sure who else. I was sure they had to be stopped.

DR.: For what reason? Did God tell you they had to be stopped?

FP: No. God has never bothered to speak to me directly.

DR.: Oh.

FP: It was just clear to me that I must stop them.

DR.: From what?

FP: They were, at least I was convinced they were, Soviet agents.

DR.: And?

FP: I know the Soviets. I got to know them very well in Poland. They are evil incarnate.

DR.: You really believe that?

FP: Yes.

DR.: And now?

FP: They are as changeless as Lucifer himself.

DR.: So that justified murder?

FP: No. God abhors murder.

DR.: I'm confused, Father.

FP: I took it upon myself. It was a mortal sin. I knew that at the time. But what was one man's soul when so much was at stake?

DR.: Interesting. And now?

FP: That it has been proved that I was a fool?

DR.: Perhaps that is a little strong.

FP: No. I was exactly that. The whole world knows it. I am only pleased that I failed.

(In the spring, tramping through damp leaves left over from the winter.)

FP: She once asked me if I believed sacrifice could change the world. We were stuck in an elevator.

DR.: An elevator?

FP: Yes. At the time I did not believe she was capable of anything bordering on sacrifice.

DR.: And now?

FP: She died for him. In a split second. Without hesitation.

DR.: Perhaps that explains it.

FP: No. She was completely devoted to him.

DR.: That impresses you?

FP: Of course. She was the most disgusting thing I have ever known. If she was capable of that, just think what that means for the rest of us.

140

(We walked for ten minutes without speaking.)

DR.: *What did you think they were going to do?*
FP: *Disarm the world.*
DR.: *And?*
FP: *It was a trick.*
DR.: *Oh.*
FP: *To destroy us.*
DR.: *They...*
FP: *To enslave us. It was a godless conspiracy to enslave us.*
DR.: *Oh. And only you could stop it.*
FP: *Yes.*
DR.: *And now?*
FP: *I thank God for making me such a poor shot.*

JUDAS RECONSIDERED

It is another beautiful day. I look out my window across the old Smith-Corona that Dr. ———— has lent me. The mountains are bright red again. Showered with sanguine God's beauty.

After spending the morning in front of the television, I am in a peculiar frame of mind. I have been following it from the beginning. We all do. The way fans follow soccer: ecstatic when their team is ahead, or on the attack—but susceptible to waves of paralyzing doubt; despondent when circumstances are reversed—but always full of hope.

Today they broadcast the ceremony. The dayroom was jammed. I wondered, actually for the first time, if any of them knew what role I had played in it all. Some might, I decided. After all, they weren't as crazy as you might think.

It was aboard ship. An aircraft carrier. You could see the wind tousling the General Secretary's hair as he stood there, somberly, next to the President, as they shoved the missiles overboard. One of each. Wrapped in flags as if they were men being buried at sea. It was so powerfully symbolic I nearly wept.

Now, as I have so many times over the last three years, I find myself asking which disciple's sacrifice was greatest. Was it not

141

Judas's? He gave up his soul. Was vilified. All for the eternal triumph of our Lord Jesus Christ.

Has not Father Paul's crusade been provided with a similar scapegoat? To its eternal glory!

My attempt at assassination has been perceived as Satan's last gasping attempt (through the CIA; where else could the man in the hat have come from?) to thwart the forces of peace. My, how it all falls into place!

Who could have believed it could happen? The timetable for dismantling the missiles is in today's paper. By Christmas we shall be free. You can feel it. Like the gasp of air as the seal on a coffin is broken.

Too bad I can't be standing beside him. But the hunchbacked priest has played his ugly part. A different one, but does the hammer question the hand that drives it?

Now I content myself with reading Moby-Dick *and long walks through the countryside.*

Peace.

> *Piotr Babulieski, S.J.*
> *Sacred Heart Sanitarium*
> *Saluda, N.C.*

Alex lay there for a moment, resting on his elbow, which was now painfully asleep. Sacred Heart Sanitarium. Just what kind of place was that?

> **sanitarium** (san-a-teŕ-ē-am) *n*: an institution for the care of invalids or convalescents, esp. psychiatric patients

A loony. Yes. Just the thought sent a shiver through him. Why would anyone write a story about a loony? That wasn't the kind of thing that was done.

He then paged through The Book. Slowly. One page at a time. Not reading. Just turning the pages.

The print style for what Piotr Babulieski called "The Interview" was completely different from the rest. Smaller. And printed in narrow columns. He reread it. What was Buck Rogers and the Planet of Zoom? he wondered. Something to do with computers. That was odd in itself. Had there been computers back then? Before the Great Uprising? He thought not, but there they were. At least in The Book. At Computer Village. What an odd place that was. And at St. Agnes's. Whatever that was. They played games on them. He tried to imagine just what that meant, but got nowhere.

Why was the paper different? he puzzled while rubbing his arm. Those faint thin lines that made it look as if The Book was printed on washed-out notebook paper were missing too. It almost looked as if it had been cut out of a magazine and pasted on the page. But there were no ridges. And the entire page had that same slippery surface that every other page in The Book had. But other than that it looked just like something from a magazine.

He realized he was thirsty.

After sliding The Book under his pillow, he left for the kitchen. They were back. His father was stretched out in the viewing room. Asleep. He quietly extracted a glass of water from the tap and drank it.

Instead of returning to his room he walked directly to hers. Past the study. Slowly. He wasn't even sure why.

The door, which must have been slightly ajar, pushed open like a veil when he reached out to knock.

There she was. Not in front of him but in the mirror that adorned her bathroom door. She was naked from the waist up, the white silk jumpsuit pushed down around her like wilted flower petals. The sink was in front of her. She was tapping the crease separating her forearm and biceps with her fingertips. Energetically. Her eyes fixed on that fine crease and the perpendicular roadway of veins that intersected it.

He reached for the door handle, but missed.

She stopped. Had she heard the sound of the door scraping across the rug? She leaned forward, disappearing from the mirror. And then, after reappearing, stood there for a second or two, looking straight ahead. It was a look of disgust. Still looking straight ahead at herself in the invisible medicine-cabinet mirror, she squeezed the syringe in her hand, sending a tiny jet from its tip. Pure disgust, which vanished into mild surprise, a kind of shock, and then a smile. A faint, quivering smile.

Her nipples got hard.

He could hear her gasp. And then slowly expel a mouthful of air as she extracted the syringe. The transparent chamber was tinged with blood.

She let her eyelids droop; she smiled. A second or two later her knees began to buckle—as if she were about to fall.

He gripped the door handle tightly, not sure what to do. Should he run over to try to catch her before she struck the floor? She righted herself by grasping the sink and turned toward him so that the face in the mirrored door stared directly at him, paralyzing him as a flashlight paralyzes a creek frog.

Her lip quivered above her incisor as she peered. "Is that you, Nurov? I told you I needed to be alone."

Alex receded into the darkness, pulling the door behind him.

Muffled by the door, in a girl's voice, "But if you insist, come in."

When he reached the kitchen, his father was there, standing at the tap. He turned to Alex. "You would think I'd be used to this damned water by now, wouldn't you?" Alex could hear him spit the water back into the sink.

Chapter 6

Corinne interrupted his last fitful moments of dream-infested sleep with, "You get in here, now, Alexander. Before your breakfast gets frostbite."

He pressed his face down into the pillow one last time, his eyes squashed against the inside of his lids, in an attempt to erase the dreams from them: he could still see her quivering lip; her goose-bump-encircled nipples staring at him from the mirror. He could feel his cheeks heat up. They must have been Martina Antipova's. No. Later, cold water on his face reminded him. They were not. Or even a dream. Although they were in the dream. But the dream was later. Which is where Martina Antipova came in. And the colonel. What was his name? He shuddered. No wonder Piotr Babulieski couldn't sleep. He buried his face in the towel for a second, trying to make the face reappear, but it wouldn't. Still, there was something about the face. Something familiar.

His father was at the table examining *The Spark*. Half an orange, a tumbler of water, and a slice of dry toast waited for his mother. The tumbler looked absurdly large next to the juicy, smiling orange.

"Alexander," he acknowledged.

"Good morning, Father."

Perhaps she wouldn't come. Sometimes she preferred to sleep in.

"Actually it's not. But one of the joys of youth is not knowing that."

Alex stabbed a potato and slowly rotated it on the tip of his fork, wondering if he could actually eat it.

"You're a little old to be playing with your food, aren't you?" his father offered from the other side of "Politburo Members Tour Volga."

Weakly, "I suppose."

"There's a very good article on proposed curriculum changes at Moscow University." He folded the tabloid in half with a deft, single-handed snap. "You should read it. It points out that there will be an expected shortfall of, let's see," he flipped open the paper, "yes, one hundred and twenty thousand engineers. Unless something is done now. Of course, the Party expects everyone to do his part."

"And everyone will," his mother responded, strolling across the room like a sleepy cat. "Nurov," she nodded. "Alex." She dragged her fingertips across his back on the way past, causing him to withdraw. "That potato," she paused, perhaps wondering why he had pulled back from her touch, "doesn't seem very afraid of you."

"Oh," he replied. It took him a second or two to figure out what she was driving at.

"An ice cube, please, Corinne," she requested. Stopping her at the door, "Just carry it in in your hand."

"You should be . . ." Nurov began, before changing (perhaps he was about to launch into a discussion of the Party's need for engineers?) course, "You look like you slept well, Daisy."

"I did. Spectacularly."

"Good," he replied genuinely. Whenever she was in a good mood Nurov seemed unable not to respond.

"I always sleep well on the week before we're going to the mountains. Just the thought relaxes me."

Alex nearly gagged on the potato.

Feigning not recollecting, "That is this weekend?"

Tartly, "You know it is."

"I thought perhaps it . . ."

"You can tease me all you want this morning, Nurov. It won't faze me a bit."

Sourly, "Then I won't."

"Suit yourself." Turning to Alex, "Is that cold?" Her green, half-open eyes were fixed on the remnant of fried potato on his fork.

Forcing himself to swallow, "No." The potato bounced against the rubbery inside of his stomach. "I guess not."

In the form of a reprimand, "Either it is, or it isn't."

146

Just as he inserted the other half of the potato into his mouth Corinne arrived with the ice cube. It glistened in her pink, chocolate-rimmed palm like a gemstone.

His mother nodded appreciatively. Was that in response to Corinne's dumping an ice cube in her glass? Or to him for eating the potato?

"Well, I think," she almost purred, "we should leave early Friday." When Nurov started to reply she hushed him with, "Don't say anything now. Just wait. And see how it goes." She squeezed the orange between her forefinger and thumb before sinking her teeth into the pulp. "Mmmm. Delicious."

"I'll see what I can—"

"Hush. Let's let that wait." Turning to Alex, "Have you thought about inviting someone to join us?"

"No."

"There's always Myslov. He could collect a few more specimens." She opened her eyes very wide and tilted her head back. "Of local flora," she continued, clearly trying to entice him into laughing.

"No," he replied coolly. She must have been able to tell he didn't want to be near her. Why wouldn't she just leave him alone?

In kind, "Suit yourself. But what will you do when Nurov and I wish to be alone?"

He felt his cheeks and throat flush with embarrassment. "All right. I'll ask someone," he blurted out angrily. "In fact, I have already mentioned it to Martina Antipova." To his surprise the name had just appeared out of nowhere. "She only needs," he continued more circumspectly, "to get her father's permission."

Ambiguously, "Perhaps I should call him."

"No. At least not yet. I think she would prefer to ask him herself."

"In her own way," Nurov interjected, before continuing philosophically, "As we all know, women have their own methods."

His mother responded with a peculiar look that signified neither approval nor disagreement and then rose. "I'll be late for clinic if I don't fly," she explained on her way to kiss Nurov's temple. Her voice skipped across the words but the lightness was gone.

"Musn't be late for penance," his father remarked dryly, her lips still touching him.

Alex was seized with the picture of Dietra Christian, her cheek

147

emblazoned with that bright, pus-surrounded safety pin. Penance. Is that what that meant?

She ran her hand across his head as she passed by.

He shook his head. Spontaneously. As if he were ridding himself of any remnant of her touch.

"You're not hungry this morning?" his father inquired. He was looking at Alex. Thoughtfully. His large, dark eyes probing. That shake of the head had gotten his attention.

Conversationally, "Not very."

"It's not right for a young man your age to be less than ravenous in the morning." Digging into a piece of ham, "Or any man for that matter."

Alex ate another potato.

"Have you and your mother been talking about," he paused, "your education?"

"No."

"I thought perhaps you had. She can be quite insistent, you know." Emphatically, "No."

"Really." Nurov had clearly taken note of the strength of his denial. "Well, don't let her upset you with her," he searched for a moment, "flights of imagination."

Alex had no idea what that meant.

"I know that you and she are very close. And there's nothing wrong with that." He leaned forward before continuing in a very confidential way, "A boy should be close to his mother. There is nothing wrong with their sharing," he paused again, "dreams. Mothers always dream for their sons."

Alex was finding it impossible to swallow the dry, chewed-up potato, which seemed to grow and grow as he chewed.

"They should. But the dreams should be rooted in reality."

Sweat began to form on his upper lip.

"You do understand what I mean?"

Alex wavered for a moment, stood, covered his mouth and ran to the bathroom. There was virtually nothing to throw up. Just the two potatoes. And warm spit.

They fussed over him to the point of distraction. First Corinne. Then his mother. Dressed in ready-for-clinic white, she examined his throat, the glands under his jaw. Took his temperature. Probed his underarms with her fingertips.

148

"No swelling," she puzzled. "And," she took a long, thoughtful breath, "no tickle response."

He refused to laugh, though he always had before—long after he was young enough to be fooled.

She stood. "Perhaps you should stay here for the day."

"No." Looking away. "I'm fine. There's no need for getting behind in school."

Smiling, "Promise you will call me at the clinic if you start feeling bad again."

"Yes."

She leaned down and kissed his cheek. Her lips were wet. He could feel the lipstick imprint they left behind.

"Promise?"

"Yes." He lifted his hand but fought off the urge to wipe the kiss off. "But there'll be no need to."

A little sadly, "Probably not."

"Well, I think you ought to just stay home in bed," Corinne offered authoritatively.

"I don't know if we should be taking advice from the woman who poisoned him."

"Poisoned him?" To herself, "What a thing to say."

Winking at Alex as she exited, "That's the only explanation, Corinne."

It was funny. The minute you stood back and looked. Without being affected. You could see the things she did. The tricks that made everybody love her. But if you were standing back, as he was at that moment, they didn't work at all. Not at all.

By the time he reached the bus stop he was feeling fine. Almost hungry.

Martina Antipova got on without the behemoth. She smiled before turning her head to the side as she strolled by. Her hair was still wet from the shower. Would his mother really call her parents? he wondered. Why had he said that? It was stupid. Plain stupid!

He surreptitiously glanced over his shoulder: she was looking straight ahead, dreamily, her eyes in that relaxed state the gentle motion of the electric bus seemed to induce. Just looking nearly made him gasp. She was so fit. And fresh. She really did belong on the cover of *Soviet Sports*.

149

His eyes straight ahead, aimed at the driver's back, he could nevertheless see her breasts. Gaping at him like nippled cantaloupes.

Alex positioned himself so that he could burst into the aisle right behind her.

"Good morning, Martina," he said as she passed.

"Good morning, Alexander."

He followed her out of the bus and into the building.

"Have a nice day, Alexander," she said before gliding up the stairs.

He stammered, "You too." Damn. He should have said something. Odd. It was as if she had completely forgotten Sunday afternoon. Or maybe she hadn't. After all, she had let him play with her breasts.

When he walked into Kerelsky's class there were three poems on the board. How strange, he thought. They had been assigned several things to read in the text. In fact, their assignments always came from the text.

Kerelsky himself was quite peculiar. First he read (actually recited, he never looked at the board) the poems himself, introducing the last with, "Here is something by a little-known Lithuanian poet who shall remain anonymous—permanently."

Later he sat there with a puzzled kind of smirk on his face while they recited. Limiting his sarcasm to a phrase or two, he just sat there, sidesaddle in his chair, his legs crossed. Right before the bell rang, he said, "Goodbye," instead of his usual sighing "Until tomorrow, comrades." He said it with such a strange finality that the entire class was affected. They sat there for a second. As if they were waiting for him to say something else. But he didn't. He simply sat there twisting his favorite strand of hair until it was as small as a piece of thread. When the bell rang they quickly exited, each looking at the other, with that "What is going on?" look on their faces.

Hoping to run into Martina Antipova, Alex took the far stairwell. But without luck. By the time he had circled back around through the maze of one-way stairs he was late.

"My, my. Comrade Nurov has decided to join us." Why did that damn Brownsky take such delight in humiliating him?

"Sorry, sir I—"

"No need to explain now. After class will be fine."

Damn. Lunch was his last chance to see her for the day.

150

"Yes, sir."

Gregorov raised a brow as if to say, "I've taken note of that."

As soon as Brownsky looked down at his notes, Alex responded with a silent "So what, Gregorov." But it was wasted. Gregorov was, with his usual single-minded efficiency, preparing to copy down every word Brownsky uttered.

"You ask," Brownsky looked up, "what were economic conditions in the United States prior to the Great Uprising? The answer is simple: there were the rich and the rest.

"You must remember—and I know this is difficult when you haven't experienced it—that then the United States was a class society. There were the oppressed and the oppressor; the many and the few; the starving and the overfed."

Piotr Babulieski popped to mind. The very comical picture of him racing down the street looking for a bathroom zoomed around in Alex's head. He almost laughed out loud. Odd, he considered. In The Book, Babulieski was constantly eating. There was food everywhere. Of course, that was in New York City. Alex guessed that fictitious places could have as much food as they wished. Yes. Even that idea suddenly seemed humorous. Perhaps that was the solution to the grain problem.

Brownsky stopped. The words had been zipping right by like anonymous Zlotnys past a dozing sentry, but the instant they stopped, Alex realized it.

"Would you care to share the source of your amusement, Alexander Mikhailovich?"

Why did Brownsky use that designation only when he was reprimanding him? Bravely, "I am not amused, sir."

"Oh? Then why did you laugh?"

"I didn't." Apologetically, "That was a sneeze, sir." He rubbed his nose convincingly.

Brownsky pulled down his glasses so that he could look over them.

"It won't happen again, sir."

He carefully listened to the remainder of the lecture, writing down the main points in his notebook. Actually, it was rather interesting. Funny, how he vacillated about history: one day it seemed so to the point, the next day not.

"The irony is that the great depression of the year twelve—just

151

twelve years after the Central Committee of the Communist Party set the Soviet Union on an irreversible course toward economic growth and prosperity—that great depression lasted until the Great Uprising. Sixty-five years. But such is the nature of capitalism."

Myslov raised his hand.

"Yes."

"The thing I don't understand, Mr. Brownsky, is, with the shining example of the Soviet Union to guide them, why they went on," he wavered for a second, "as they did. For so long."

Leave it to Myslov.

"A good question. There are a number of reasons. One is that the capitalist press consistently misrepresented what went on in Soviet Russia. As well as what went on in the United States. The press was much different from what it is today. Today the press serves the people. It enlightens them. Then it served the people's oppressors.

"Another . . ." Brownsky paused. "But we had better stop. Unless you'd like to skip lunch."

They chuckled politely.

"Enjoy your lunch, comrades."

The bell rang.

Alex waited at Brownsky's desk while he pressed flat a crumpled page of his notes. "Ah, yes. Comrade Nurov. Why were you late?"

"I had to stop in the bathroom on the way. I haven't been well."

"Perhaps you should have sneezed a few times while you were there, comrade."

Alex didn't know whether to laugh or not. He compromised by smiling.

"Enjoy your lunch, comrade."

Alex stood there a second or two longer before asking, "Did they have computers before the Great Uprising?"

Brownsky raised his eyes.

"I mean, had they been invented?"

"What makes you ask that?"

"I don't know. It just occurred to me. I was sure you would know."

"Oh, I do." He closed the folder with his notes inside. "The first computer was developed by a group headed by Sergei Malenkov in Soviet Estonia in the year sixty. Seventeen years prior to the Great Uprising."

152

"Thank you," he replied, before escaping into the hall. Why did you ask that? he repeated to himself as he descended the stairs. Are you out of your mind? Completely?

Still, for the entire afternoon he found himself musing about The Book. Every time he turned around it was there. Staring him right in the face.

What a strange story. Clearly there was something about the picture it painted of America that was off base. Nothing you could put your finger on. But it seemed exaggerated in some bizarre way. And that made it seem, well, not nearly so bad a place as he had imagined.

Just that thought—that perhaps it was not as bad a place as he had always supposed—made it seem all right to think about it. Nonsensical as it seemed, he usually felt faintly embarrassed by the fact that it had been such a terrible place. Not that he could do anything about what had happened sixty-some years ago.

But of course the whole thing might just be made up.

That was the thing about The Book. It seemed on the one hand to cause him to jump to all kinds of conclusions. And on the other, it stimulated a strange—and not especially welcome—curiosity. He couldn't remember being especially curious before. Oh, he was fond of mysteries. But this was a different kind of curiosity. Certainly he had never been especially curious about Americans. But now he found himself wondering about them.

On the spur of the moment he decided to catch a later bus. So that he could stroll around the old part of town. But instead of strolling he found himself going directly to her apartment. Even though he knew it was really something he shouldn't be doing.

Too bad he hadn't thought to bring something sweet, he said to himself as he clanged up the metal stairway. But then, that morning he had had no idea he would be going to see her. And there was the coffee. Surely some of that would be left. After all, it had only been since Saturday.

He rapped on the glass.

A second later the curtain was pushed aside. And there she was, an inch or two from the glass, looking at first a little puzzled, and then surprised.

She shook her head; pressed her finger to her lips.

153

That took him completely by surprise. He stood there for a second, trying not to look dumbfounded, while she moved her lips, soundlessly. "Come back later." Yes. She mouthed the words again. Then she smiled and let the curtain fall back over the window.

It was only as he was crossing the gravel that poked out from under the aged, but shiny, Zlotny nosed up against the stairs that he realized she had been wearing a Soviet navy blouse. Yes. That was precisely what it was. A nasty picture of her "friend," the submariner, invaded his mind. He was probably sitting there. Drinking the coffee Alex had brought.

He kicked at the gravel and then winced when one of the rough pebbles pinged off the Zlotny's bumper. After a few quick steps he thought, Serves him right. Around here that will rust in a week.

Without looking back he zipped down the block to the Battery and began crossing the small, square park that marked the confluence of the two rivers that formed the Charleston peninsula. A dozen life-size metal figures posed in a circle around the heroic figure of the General Secretary.

The plaque commemorating the Great Uprising said: Freedom. Justice. Socialism. He always felt quite good when he walked past it. It was so simple. And beautiful. And of course, the fact that his father's great-uncle stood, majestically, at the center of it all made up for a lot of the petty innuendos he had had to tolerate. Someday that would all change. Already he had been accepted to Moscow University. Which was no small step.

"Ready for a carriage tour, my man?"

"No," Alex stammered, feeling for an instant as if someone had been listening in on his most private thoughts.

The young man who had startled him was sitting on the steps leading up to the General Secretary's statue. Pushing back his black top hat with an extended forefinger, "My special price. Two rubles." The young man smiled, crooked-toothed, but convincingly. "My special, introductory, I'm-not-doing-anything-anyway price," he hesitated, "of one and a half rubles?"

Alex found himself staring curiously.

"Can you beat that?"

Alex stopped.

"Of course, the price is subject to negotiation."

154

Firmly establishing that the price was not really an issue, "One and one half rubles is fine."

"This way, comrade." He jumped up and adroitly descended the three or four marble steps that encircled the General Secretary. "Your carriage to the past awaits you." As if he were talking to himself but clearly for Alex's consumption, "If the beast will move without a carrot."

For reasons he wasn't sure of, Alex found that very funny.

The carriage was on the far side of the park, overlooking the river. With what Alex supposed was just the correct touch of period pomp, the young man bowed as he held the door to the low-slung open carriage. Without slowing down, Alex walked off the high curb onto a small wooden step, climbed into the carriage, and, stretching his arm out across the back of the seat, reclined in what he was sure was the appropriate Pre–Great Uprising fashion.

"You can call me Sasha, comrade," the young man announced, standing with one knee slightly elevated, the reins comfortably in his hand.

"Certainly, Sasha."

"My mother wanted me to be a Russian," he explained with a smile.

Coldly, "Oh."

"Actually," shaking the reins, "until you spoke, comrade, I supposed you were Russian."

"Really."

"Yes. A carrot later, my dear. First a little work." Slyly, "Horses don't seem to understand socialism very well, comrade."

Without meaning to, Alex started to laugh, but swallowed it. It wasn't really right to condone remarks like that with laughter.

Clearly playing to an audience, "They keep wanting a carrot before the five-year plan is completed. Daisy, as soon as we get home we will go over it again. I'm sure, given time, the correctness of it all will become clear to you." Looking over his shoulder while the carriage creaked along, "Me, I'm a dedicated socialist. I work." Proudly, or at least what seemed proudly, "I stamp out generator caps for Zlotnys. Thousands. Why, I was double my quota last week. And that was with a sore shoulder."

Sasha waited for a moment.

155

"Perhaps we'd better go this way first. Just to pick up a carrot for my stubborn, backsliding animal." Confidently, "If she doesn't shape up soon I shall be forced to turn her in."

Alex made it a point not to laugh.

"A few weeks in a reeducation center is what you need, my dear."

The horse began to trot. Was that possible? He watched Sasha carefully. Certainly that was some kind of trick.

"See? She's not utterly hopeless. She might learn to be a good socialist yet."

Still standing, the reins confidently looped across his palm, Sasha guided them down East Bay Street five or six blocks before slowly navigating the carriage onto a narrow side street.

"I'm afraid, comrade, before we can continue your tour, I'll require a small advance." His pale gray eyes were trapped in smile lines, but beneath the outward warmth they were as dead as a burned-out star. "My animal requires a carrot." Charmingly, "She is not the good socialist horse she ought to be."

With calculated coldness, "There are people who might wonder about that kind of joking around."

"Joking? I beg your pardon, comrade. I was only trying," he jumped down onto the sidewalk, "to explain the peculiar behavior of my horse. I," he was clearly waiting for money, "myself, am a dedicated, and patient, Marxist-Leninist worker."

Alex extracted a one-ruble coin and handed it down to him.

Turning, after tilting his hat to the side, "Comrade."

He flipped the coin in the air, very high, so that it dropped right over his shoulder and into his open hand as he walked. A second later he had disappeared down a shoulder-wide brick alleyway. What a strange bird he was, Alex decided. Insolent. And clearly antisocial. It was odd that someone hadn't reported him.

The building they had parked in front of was not a food distribution center. No. They were all farther up. In fact, the idea of searching for carrots down that little alley was ludicrous. He leaned back as far as he could in an attempt to look down the alley. The tidy, rectangular opening soon gave way to mixed brown-and-green overgrowth. Well, the carrots were his problem, Alex decided. If he didn't find any, and the horse wouldn't move, he would just demand back his ruble.

156

From the comfort of his carriage seat he surveyed the rest of the street. The four squat stucco buildings across from him had been chopped up into apartments. You could tell from the scale of the doors. Odd, everything he looked at today seemed to have two aspects: what you saw and what was. Why, today, was he so aware of that? he wondered.

From the narrow plaster-walled opening, "Well, my dear." Sasha held three wilted, green-tipped carrots over his head while he danced over to the horse. "Your petrol."

After the horse had consumed the carrots (she munched the carrots with such unhurried, almost bored, forbearance it was hard to believe the horse was hungry at all. Of course, she did eat all three carrots, limp green stalks and all), Sasha swung up into the driver's seat as effortlessly as a circus aerialist.

After they were under way, "I hadn't realized there was a food distribution center there."

"As a good socialist worker I knew it was my duty not to waste your entire morning, comrade, while I waited in line," he shook the reins meaningfully, "at one of our highly efficient state food distribution centers."

Alex replied with a stern stare that left no doubt that he did not approve of that kind of flip, antisocial behavior.

At each point of interest Sasha delivered a short spiel that was clearly not his, or even delivered in his true voice, but rather a quick, effortless drone that reminded Alex of the way schoolboys read poems in class. Occasionally Sasha would emphasize this word or that, perhaps "slave-holding capitalist" or "ruthless oppressor" or "dedicated servant of the working class, the Governor," in a way that led you to believe, at least for an instant, that he was not sincere. But at no time did he say anything that could be clearly construed to be antisocialist. Or anti-Soviet.

In the course of the tour Alex counted six of those strange flat-topped towers. Several, like Celeste's had been divided into small apartments that now resembled neatly stacked alphabet blocks. Others appeared to be used for storage. Or nothing at all. The buildings from which they sprang were each rather large, rectangular structures with big doors and columns. Several had marble stairs leading up to the doors.

"What are those?" he finally asked.

"That is the Board of Architectural Review, comrade," Sasha replied authoritatively.

Impatiently, "Yes, I can see that."

"They are responsible for preserving our heritage."

"I know. You just said that."

"Did I? Yes." Without the slightest hint of embarrassment, "I must have."

"Do you know what that was? This is an old building, isn't it?"

"Oh, yes, comrade."

Pointing, "That thing that juts out of the roof in such a funny way."

"Let's see." Sasha extracted a small, worn paperback book from his breast pocket. He thumbed through the little book for a minute or two. "Here we are: the Board of Architectural Review. Established by the people and the Party to manage the preservation of historical landmarks in the city of Charleston. The—"

Interrupting, "Doesn't that book say anything about what anything was?"

"Of course, comrade. It—"

"Never mind." Slumping back into the seat, "It doesn't matter." He glanced at his watch. "You can let me out here." He fished a half-ruble coin from his pocket and extended it. "I have to be somewhere."

Sasha replied, "Have a good day, comrade," but was already eyeing an approaching couple the way a cat eyes a lizard on a window screen.

"What a . . ." he began to himself, before he realized that he wasn't sure how to finish the thought. No wonder everything was such a mess. If that was the kind of workers the country had to depend on.

Before he had gone a block he made up his mind that if the Zlotny was still there, he would just catch the next bus. He was half tempted to do that anyway. Just to get it over with. Even if she had asked him to come back later. It would serve her right.

And there it was. Glistening in the late-afternoon sun. Well, at least there was one little ping in it. Thanks to him.

On the long, hypnotic ride over the bridge he made up his mind that that would be his last visit to see her. This sudden interest in Americans didn't make any sense anyway. And where would it get him? Certainly they were, well, anything but a good influence. Think of that ridiculous carriage driver, he reminded himself. It's a wonder he's not in a reeducation program now. And her? She certainly should have been at work instead of lounging around in that seaman's blouse. Which means she's some kind of parasite. And where would it get him to be found associating with people like that? That would certainly be a terrible embarrassment to his family. Especially considering he had just been accepted to Moscow University.

Yes.

Besides, the next day at lunch he would just ask Martina Antipova to join them for the weekend. He should have done that today. After all, she had been quite friendly on the bus that morning.

The lunch line was almost empty. He pointed, took what resulted, and strode toward the window, hoping that she would be out on the field.

Gregorov's group was huddled toward the center of their table, their shoulders out over their trays, making his passage by effortless. He was nearly past when Gregorov looked up. Confidentially, perhaps even with concern, "I suppose you have heard about Kerelsky?"

"No," Alex replied impatiently.

He smacked his lips lightly. "They took him off. Right in the middle of last period."

Impassively, "Oh. Was he ill?"

"You can ask that after yesterday," Gregorov paused, "and today."

He shrugged noncommittally while inching his way toward the window.

"I didn't turn him in, mind you. Apparently someone else did that. But surely, comrade, you must have noticed. This morning? He was loony as a bedbug."

Without responding, Alex took the last several steps to the window seat and deposited his tray.

"Of course, he always seemed a little strange to me," Gregorov persisted.

With finality, "Well, he was no favorite of mine either, comrade."

Gregorov raised his brow in that all-knowing way he was fond of and returned to his lunch. Evidently he had achieved what he had set out to.

After verifying that she was out throwing, he gulped down four or

159

five quick mouthfuls of his lunch, scooped up the tray, and zipped right past Myslov's "Hello, Alexander."

He didn't slow down until he was at the bottom of the back stairs, where he slipped through the door and waited under the portico for her to throw in his direction.

"Excellent throw," he offered.

"Not really." Shading her eyes, "That is you, Alexander Nurov, isn't it?"

"Yes."

"Too little elevation."

"If you say so."

Seriously, "One must be willing to be critical, self-critical, if one is going to improve."

"I suppose that is necessary."

Bending at the waist to extract the javelin from the ground, "It is." She stood there for a moment, her legs straight, her feet planted directly under her broad shoulders, the javelin rising at an angle from her left foot to her right hand, giving her the appearance of a determined ancient sentry.

"Have you had lunch?"

Not to be sidetracked, "It is a key part of being a dedicated athlete."

"Yes."

She brushed her hair back from her temple and smiled. "Would you like to keep me company while I eat?"

"Sure."

"I have two more throws."

"No problem. I like to watch," he blurted.

Puzzled, "Really? Watching sports never really affects me. It is not the same as participating."

Both throws were monumental. When Alex said so, she found something wrong with each of them. It was certainly her day to find ways to improve, he remarked to himself.

When he mentioned that they were going to the mountains for the weekend, she replied, "I guess it is much cooler there."

"Oh, yes," he agreed energetically.

"This heat is relentless."

"I'm afraid so."

Nostalgically, "In Russia now it is already snowing."

160

"That would be great, wouldn't it?"

"Yes, but I would have to train indoors. That is less effective."

"Is it?"

When he asked her if she would care to join them, she tilted her head to the side and then answered that she would have to talk to her father about it.

"Of course," he replied soberly.

"But," flashing a mouthful of glistening teeth, "he will say yes. He always does."

The afternoon flew by while he thought of all the places he would show her: old childhood streams that you crossed with your pants rolled up; big flat hunks of granite for sunbathing, where you could hear the water rush by a foot from your ears.

His mother was irritable and drawn during dinner.

He excused himself, saying he wanted to get started on the DAL system's physics and mathematics tutorials. "I'm going to work on them an hour a day. Without exception. By next fall that should be quite a lot."

"Remember we're going to Saluda this weekend."

"Yes. I will have to make the time up. In advance. It is time I displayed more dedication."

"Excellent," his father commented while carving a piece of roast.

From the door, "By the way, it seems very likely that Martina Antipova will be joining us this weekend."

His father nodded, his attention fixed on the recalcitrant piece of meat on his plate.

"I should know for sure in a day or two."

"Well, I'm sure we'll all have a marvelous time," his mother commented.

Soon after he got started, Nurov came to the study. On his way past the desk he raised his hand as if to say, "Don't let me interrupt," and proceeded to the file cabinet. Several books were stacked on top. He slid them into the top drawer and locked it.

"A little excitement at school today."

Not certain what he meant, "No."

"With Kerelsky."

"That. Yes." Alex looked up from the keyboard.

"What exactly happened?"

"They took him off." Cautiously, "I think he must have looned out."

"Yes. What went on in class?"

"He just seemed a little strange. And he read three poems."

"Yes," he offered as a prompt.

"Well, they were on the board. That was a little strange. And he read them. And then we did."

"What kind of discussion did that lead to?"

"None?"

"Oh?"

"We just recited them, while he sat there."

"Did that strike you as odd?"

"Yes. They weren't what we had been assigned. That was unusual. But we often . . ."

"Recite."

"Yes."

"And there was no discussion?"

"No." After searching for a moment, "He did mention that the last poem was by a Lithuanian?"

"A Lithuanian?"

"Yes." With an awkward laugh, "'A little-known Lithuanian poet who shall remain anonymous.'"

"Yes." To himself, "I suppose he's right there."

"'Permanently,'" Alex added.

"Yes." Thoughtfully, "It is episodes like that that point out how important it is that the DAL system be implemented."

In an attempt to deflect Nurov's inquisitiveness, "I thought I would begin with mechanics. Level five. Level five is a postsecondary summary. That does sound right, doesn't it?"

Nurov sat on the edge of the desk. "Yes." Looking directly at Alex in that way that always made him uneasy, "Preventing episodes like this business with Kerelsky. That is what the DAL system is really for. That will put an end to the circulation of these unauthorized works."

Cautiously, "Then the poems were," he stammered, "unauthorized."

Nurov's eyes probed him. He tried to convince himself that that was of no special importance. That Nurov's eyes always did that.

162

"Is that the opinion at your school?"

"I don't know," he squirmed. "Perhaps."

"Then there was talk?"

"Well, yes, I suppose. But," proudly, "I avoided getting involved."

"Good. The gossip generated in cases like this is as destructive as the works themselves."

Obliquely, "What will happen to him?" He focused his eyes on the terminal. "Can he be rehabilitated?"

"Kerelsky? I'm sure he can be." Walking behind Alex so that he could peer into the screen, "I take it he wasn't too bad a fellow."

Evasively, "He seemed all right. Until today."

"That is often the case. These unauthorized works are a virus. They invade silently, doing their damage without symptom. Insidiously. But finally their destructive influence manifests itself," he reached over Alex's shoulder toward the keyboard, "in aberrant behavior."

Alex shuddered.

"But soon we will be able to save people like poor Kerelsky."

VERY GOOD, COMRADE NUROV!

"Save them?"

"Save them from influences like that. That is something that the DAL system, under the Party's guidance, can, in fact is obligated to, do. The right environment quite naturally produces the right behavior."

2. A SHIP IS SAILING SOUTHWEST AT 12 KPH.
A JACKKNIFE IS DROPPED 1 METER AFT OF A 13-METER MAST.
HOW FAR AFT OF THE MAST WILL THE KNIFE STRIKE THE DECK?

"And the wrong environment produces wrong behavior. That is why it is the Party's duty to ensure that lies and distortions are not permitted to fly about like cold germs."

163

Chapter

7

"Don't we look outdoorsy," his mother had remarked as Martina Antipova approached the breakfast table, her long, hard legs (now they were chapped red from the morning air; a narrow blackberry-barb trickle of blood had dried on the back of her calf) showing under rough khaki shorts.

"I'm ravenous," she had said in Russian.

His mother had smiled unconvincingly. She called these excursions to Saluda their "American weekends." "The rest of the year," she said, "we are Russian. But on these weekends, in the red and yellow of the year, we are Americans."

His father never commented. He would merely smile in a haughty, forbearing way that indicated that while he did not completely concur, a few days couldn't matter enough to squabble about.

"Yes, very," his father had reiterated.

Like a little girl about to depart for school, she had stood at the foot of the table for a moment, giving everyone a chance to look her over.

"Perfect for hiking," he had continued.

His mother chimed, "Yes," with artificial warmth.

Alex couldn't wait to escape.

"Damn, I've got to fix these again," she said with mild irritation before resting against a granite boulder.

The old rock, which jutted up magnificently from the rim of a huge, fog-filled ravine, marked what he used to call "the edge of the world." When he was smaller he had been under instructions not to go beyond that point. Corinne would say, "Better mind, or you'll fall in there. And that'll be that!"

164

"We're in no hurry," he soothed.

"Yes, but," she pulled the thick, blood-red sock up over her heel and smoothed it against her calf, "I don't want to miss anything. Besides, it is important to maintain a sustained pace." Relacing the boot, "For the heart."

While repeating the procedure on her other foot, "Uhhh."

"A blackberry bramble," he explained.

"I don't remember seeing any berries."

"The birds have eaten them all by now."

In Russian, after dipping her fingertip into a drop of saliva, "Greedy little bastards." She rubbed away the trickle of blood with her wet fingertip. "Wounded. And not even a berry to munch on."

"There may be a few left somewhere around here. Of course, if you're hungry we can have some of our lunch." He slid one arm from the small pack he carried.

"No," she protested. "Let's climb down there," pointing into the ravine, "first."

"See that?" he said as she was getting under way. There was a small waterfall on the other side.

"Very nice." Stepping around the boulder, "They have much larger ones in the Urals, you know."

Piqued, "And in Colorado too."

"Really?" she responded genuinely.

"But that's rather a long walk."

"Yes." She continued in a way that made it hard for him to decide if she was joking or just absurdly literal, "That would be too far to walk."

"Come." He laughed. "I'll show you the path. There's a stream at the bottom."

"From the fall."

"Yes. And pool."

"Oh. Then we can swim," she said simply.

On the way down, along the craggy, laurel-engulfed path, which at this place and that dropped two meters straight down so that you had to lower yourself grasping the exposed roots of stunted trees, he pointed out interesting features of the landscape, all the while thinking of swimming with her in the freezing pool at the bottom.

"Isn't it odd how the fog looks so thick from above, but," he reached up around her waist to ease her onto a root-woven earth

165

ledge, "you never seem to actually reach it. It's," he kept his hand on her hip, "always just below you."

"Yes." Pushing on, although he could hear her breathing from exertion, "That's because you are looking through a few hundred meters of it all at once."

"I know, but isn't it mysterious? The way it looks thick enough to reach out and touch, just beyond your fingertips. But really isn't there at all."

With matter-of-fact clarity, "That's because there is really very little of it. In any one place."

He said nothing else until they reached the bottom.

Cautiously, "We'll probably freeze swimming."

"Nonsense." Picking her way from rock to rock across the stream, "But there is no need to stop yet. Let's climb a little more first."

The slippery smooth granite embankment melted into thick mountain laurel where the ground smelled of moist decay.

"This is marvelous," she exclaimed in one large breath. "So alive, and," still exhaling, "rotten. All at once."

They walked right past the place where he had found The Book. He looked straight ahead as they passed by, as if just looking in the direction of the place might arouse her interest.

"I say we climb right up to there," she proclaimed, pointing toward the top of the ravine, "and back. And then," she seemed almost giddy from excitement, "we can swim." Facing him, "How does that sound?"

"Fine," he replied lamely, his mind racing back and forth between her and the spot where he had discovered The Book.

She stopped. Holding the hem of her sweater in her fist, "Does anyone come here?"

"No, not really."

"Good. I'm hot." She pulled the sweater over her head and tied the arms tightly around her waist. "Come on. Let's keep it up. All the way to the top."

By the time they reached the top the sun had burned off the haze and the narrow, deep ravine was as sharply defined as a furrow in a cornfield. The stream glistened like a shattered icicle.

From atop a small granite lookout, shivering from the breeze as it blew across her sweaty back, "Hello! Hello!"

166

"Hello! Hello!" he mimicked.

Disappointed, "I thought it might answer."

"You didn't hear it?"

"That was you," she accused soberly.

Nodding, "No."

"Yes." As if the unconversational ravine was no longer of any interest, "What's that? Up there?"

"I don't know. Just an old building." She stepped off the back of the lookout. "Most of it burned down. A long time ago."

"Oh." She shaded her eyes from the sun as she looked up at the pieces of red brick and masonry that stuck through the explosion of green that gushed up from the hillside.

"It's not," he followed after her, "especially interesting. Unless you like old burned-down buildings."

"Let's look."

"You can't see much. There's a fence around it," he explained.

But a whole section of the fence had collapsed. Perhaps the place had been completely forgotten. The vine-laced cyclone fence rattled out an ugly protest as they walked across it.

"This must have been quite a fire," she remarked, looking up at the gutted second floor, which now resembled an abandoned black-strutted beehive. "What do you suppose it was?" she asked as she entered.

"No telling."

She untied the sweater from around her waist and pulled it over her shoulders. "It was very large. And full of tiny rooms."

"Which might just fall on our heads."

Earnestly, "Do you think it is unsafe?"

"Maybe," he offered coolly.

She waited for him to catch up with her.

"It's certainly old enough to," he continued, while inching so close that his chest brushed against the knotted arms of her rough wool sweater when he inhaled.

"If it's been here this long then there is no reason to think it will fall now," she asserted confidently.

He closed his hand around one of the sweater's lifeless arms.

"Do you know what I wish? I wish," she persisted while he tugged gently on the limp arm, "I wish we had discovered some berries.

167

Don't you?" He slid his hand inside the loosely wrapped sweater onto her breast. "Some wild blackberries. Isn't that what you called them? Blackberries?"

"Yes," he confirmed.

Stepping away, but only after his hand had rested there for a few seconds, "Perhaps we can still find some. Where should we look?"

Finding it hard to maintain his equilibrium, "I'm sure there's some fruit here." He reached up to the pack.

"But not blackberries?"

"I don't know," he replied. "Should we look?"

"No," she reprimanded. "Let's find some."

With disappointment, "That could take half the day."

"And then we can take a swim. And eat our lunch."

The idea of the swim sent a bolt of anticipation through him.

"Okay?" she inquired, the word sounding not at all American the way she said it.

He shrugged.

"Where should we look?"

"I don't know. Maybe the stream. Isn't that the kind of place that berries grow?" he offered analytically.

"Yes," she agreed before bolting down the long valley that had once been the backbone of the old building. She waited at what must have been the front entrance. The masonry that had overhung the doorway lay splattered across the porch in eight or nine knee-high chunks. With a grunt she turned one over. And then another. Turning to him, "Why do I feel so strong today?"

Before he could reply she flipped over another masonry segment. And another. And then she ran down the cracked, uprooted concrete sidewalk until her progress was terminated by the fence.

"I think we'll have to go back around to where the fence has collapsed to get out."

"Yes," she replied. Her face and throat were warm red. As if she had suddenly become embarrassed.

"Look at that." More than anything as a distraction, "There are letters cut in them. Like they were big alphabet blocks."

Awkwardly, "Yes." She cautiously returned to the concrete porch. "What do you suppose it says?"

He flipped over blocks until the letters were all facing upward. "What do you think?"

168

"I'm not especially good at puzzles."

"Forget the letters. All we have to do is fit the fracture lines." Zigzagging one of the blocks toward its neighbor, "Like this."

When they had all been joined into one long rectangle, they read, "Sacred Heart Sanitarium."

Dumbfounded, he sat down on the porch with his arms wrapped around his knees and stared.

"Sacred Heart Sanitarium," she read out as if it were a fifth-grade English lesson. With her hands on her hips, "What is that?"

Mechanically, "A sanitarium is a place where people convalesce."

"Convalesce?"

"Recover from illness."

"So this was a hospital. Yes." She looked at the black honeycomb that showed through the burned-out gaps in the ceiling. "And those are the rooms." As if it were a revelation, "What a strange place for a hospital. In such a remote place." She began to make her way down the hall. Once posed, the question seemed to immediately lose its attraction. "Come on, Alex." Without turning back toward him, "Where do you suppose we should start our search?"

Suspiciously, "What search?"

"For the blackberries, of course," she replied. Glancing back over her shoulder, "You hadn't forgotten them already, had you?"

Relieved, "No." He scrambled to his feet. "Not at all." Without leaving the hallway, or revealing his interest, or even slowing down, he examined each room as he passed by. There were two large ones. A large open area. The rest were small and bare.

Impossible, he thought. The Book was made up. A story.

If it wasn't. If it was real—he couldn't even decide what that meant—it had better be returned to right where he had found it as soon as possible.

After all, he had planned to do that all along. He had even brought it with him, jammed into the bottom of his school bag, with just that in mind.

"I may have seen some last year at the base of the waterfall," he offered so that she would not look (how ridiculous! The place was no different from a thousand other places: just a small, rocky gap in the mountain laurel) where he had found it. "But I'm not sure," he appended guiltily.

With determination, "Then we look there."

There were no blackberries, but very soon she tired of that idea and wanted to swim. Standing on a stone a meter above the elliptical pool that had been carved by the persistent attack of the waterfall, she stripped to her underpants. First, posing like a muscular flamingo, she removed her boots and socks, the left, then the right, all the while standing very steady. Second, her khaki shorts. And then, with a snap, the thick white athletic bra.

She looked much less an athlete. Perhaps it was the absence of the bra, which molded her breasts to her pectorals. Or just being nearly naked.

"Are you going to wait all day, Alexander?"

As he pulled off one shoe, "No."

She fell. He thought at first she had jumped in. But it was clear, after a moment's reflection, that she had fallen. There was that touch of awkwardness. Uncertainty. Perhaps, when she realized she was falling, she had cooperated. To smooth away some of the awkwardness.

"Are you okay?"

Annoyed, "I'm fine." She disappeared into the pool for a few seconds. "Are you coming in?" Disapprovingly, "You aren't shy, are you?"

Within half an hour her ankle was as ugly as a purple grapefruit. He felt kind of weak when he looked at it.

"Damn." Sitting, "Damn, damn, damn."

"Is it broken?" he asked.

"No, you idiot. I wouldn't be able to walk." She dangled her foot in the water. "I need to ice this."

"Yes."

"Bring me my clothes, please. I had better sit as long as possible."

"Of course." He obediently scampered around the edge of the pool to the other side. While collecting her clothes, "Does it hurt?"

"It's too numb from the water to tell," she complained while lifting her foot an inch or two above the pool.

As if he were a small boy who had just dropped an antique figurine, or tipped over a glass at the dinner table, "Sorry." Explaining, "There's a kind of moss or something that grows on these rocks. That's why they're so slippery." He knelt behind her. "I've slipped several times myself."

Somewhat consoled, "Really." Maybe her pride was more injured

170

than her ankle? No. It looked even bigger and blacker than before as she held it just above the water for them to admire.

"It looks—"

"Awful," she interrupted.

Wincing, "Did it hit a rock?"

"No." She reached for the sweater. "I twisted it. As I fell."

"Yes."

"Or, actually, trying to," she shivered, "to keep from falling." Staring down at the ankle, "I don't think I wanted you to see me fall. Wasn't that dumb?"

After a moment, "There's a towel in this pack somewhere. That way you won't get your sweater wet."

"That will take two weeks to heal. Just watch."

He touched the towel to her back.

"Damn. Damn. Damn." He pulled the towel back. "That felt good."

Surprised, "Oh."

"But harder. My trainer always rubs very hard." Twisting her head slightly so that she could see him out of the corner of her eye. "It's quite good for the circulation."

Rubbing vigorously, "Better?"

"Yes," she replied, sounding very husky and Russian. "Don't you love to feel the blood rushing through your body? Yes. But harder. A little harder."

Sliding forward on his haunches, his knees under her arms, Alex pushed the towel up around her neck so that his hands guided it across her throat and upper chest. He massaged her in small, downward-tending circles until his hands had pulled the towel tautly around her neck; his fingertips were just touching the soft upper reaches of her breasts.

Pointing, "How am I going to get up that path?"

"I don't know."

"I'm not even sure I can get my boot back on. See how big it is." As she lifted the foot up, he craned over her shoulder so that he could see, pulling his hands down as he did so. "Some of it is quite steep." Continuing, in an even, mechanical way, while he caressed her with both hands, "Especially there. At the midpoint. Is there any other way out? Perhaps down there?"

"No."

Lifting the sweater, which had been draped loosely across her open palm, "Time to go."

Slightly injured, "Now?"

"Yes. Before the damn thing gets any worse."

"You have beautiful breasts."

With conviction, "They're too large."

"No."

"Much. I am an athlete. Not a cow."

He had no idea what to say.

Half whining, "My foot is beginning to ache."

"Is it?"

"Yes. Although it might just be from the water."

"It's awfully cold," he observed.

"That should help, though. Like ice." She placed her right hand over his and pulled it downward from her breast across her belly so that it rested in her lap. Without removing her hand from on top of his, "Which means I won't have to stop training for as long. Which is good." Earnestly, "I become impossible when I can't train. Impossible." She leaned back and, after she had situated herself comfortably against his chest, pushed down on his fingers, pressing them into her wet underpants. Exhaling, "Yes. I will be very grouchy. You can count on that." Before guiding them inside, she curled his fingers in hers so that they were above the elastic band in her panties. "Tomorrow I will have to spend all day with my foot elevated. I'll probably explode."

While she talked, she guided his fingertip in a circle. When he tried to insert his finger, she restrained him with, "No," before continuing to trace out small, relentless circles. In a minute or two she shivered; he could feel goose bumps form on her left breast.

"Now we can eat our lunch. I'm starving. Aren't you?"

Breathless, "Yes. I guess."

"Good," she exclaimed with one last shudder.

She sat with her foot in the water while he unpacked the lunch. There was ham. And chicken. A big jar of sauerkraut. Pumpernickel bread. Butter. Mustard. Two apples. And a thermos of iced tea.

"There's ice in here. Maybe I can fish it out. To make an ice pack. With the towel."

Still facing the water, "No. This is fine."

172

"Ham or chicken?"

"Chicken, I think."

"Mustard?"

"Yes."

Averting her eyes when he leaned around her to deliver the sandwich, "Thank you."

They ate without speaking, passing the thermos back and forth over her shoulder. When she had finished she slipped on her shorts over her legs, leaned back onto her shoulders, and pulled the shorts up over her hips. She then put on her right sock and boot, carefully tugging up the bright red sock, which reached six or eight inches up her calf.

She gently tugged the other sock up to her heel, waited a second or two, and then pulled it the rest of the way up. She next held up the boot, apparently comparing it with her foot, which, surrounded by the fuzzy, blood-red sock, seemed twice the size of the boot. She removed the top laces, opened the boot, and slid it onto her toes.

Tentatively, "Do you want me to help?"

Without answering she shoved her foot into the boot and, tugging on the leather strings very tightly, laced it to the top. "There," she said before standing. "It's done."

"Can you walk?"

She gingerly tested it. "Of course."

"We'll go slow."

Looking down as she zipped up her khaki shorts, "I shouldn't let you do that, you know."

"What?"

Wiping a tear from her cheek, "You know what."

They climbed out of the ravine. Twice he helped her, but other than that she seemed as strong and agile as before. In fact, once they were on the flat part of the path he had to press to keep up. Perhaps she was trying to prove something?

It was twilight when they reached the house. She stopped about a hundred yards away, on the other side of the small pasture that adjoined the house.

"The horses are inside already?" she asked.

"Yes."

She leaned over and kissed him on the mouth. It was a quick,

173

almost formal kiss. A moment later she slipped between the strands of barbed wire.

"I will see you in the house. I want to look in on the horses on the way in."

He watched her cross the pasture as he circled around to the house. She was limping slightly. But only slightly. Even though it must have hurt. After all, it was the size of a grapefruit. Apparently being an athlete had inured her to pain somewhat. Although there had been that tear.

They had dinner on the elbow porch separated from the black mountain night by an invisible screen that rose from the floor to the ceiling like a veil. The center of attention, Martina Antipova sat sideways with her foot propped up in a rocking chair.

Alex's grandfather presided over the head of the table, his red nose and cheeks illuminated by the fire that raged behind them. The brick fireplace had been cut right in the elbow of the wall so that it was convenient to both long segments of porch—for barbecuing, or just warming hands and backs. Grandfather Simpson was something of a problem. Exactly what kind Alex wasn't sure. But a problem. Alex's mother often chided his father for not transferring Grandfather Simpson to the Ministry. He responded by saying that Grandfather Simpson was a drunk. That state of uncertain equilibrium had persisted for several years, although now it was becoming apparent that Nurov was not completely wrong. His mother responded by saying that Nurov, by relegating her father to the middle of nowhere, was responsible if her father did drink too much.

"More turkey, Vice-Minister?" Grandfather Simpson inquired. For some reason he always addressed Alex's father by his title. The tone varied from obsequious to sarcastic, depending on the number of glasses of bourbon the old man had consumed. Tonight Alex had counted three. An easy task, since the bottle rested on a saucer a foot from Grandfather Simpson's plate.

"No. No thank you."

"Miss Antipova?"

"No. Not just yet."

"Well, I'm sure such a picture of Soviet womanhood is not the product of single helpings."

174

"I'll have a little, Grandfather," Alex interjected.

"Good." With a raised brow, "Better keep your strength up, my boy."

"Corinne has made pumpkin pie for dessert, Alex," his mother reminded.

Ambiguously, "He'll probably need both."

Nurov looked over toward Alex's mother.

"Perhaps we should have dessert inside." To Martina Antipova, "There's a nice fire in there too. We'll fix up something very comfortable for you."

"Good." To Alex, "I don't think I've had pumpkin pie before. You did say pumpkin?"

"Yes. Alex can tell you about it on the way in. Come along, Father. We're going into the sitting room."

"As soon as I carve some of this bird for Alexander."

Sternly, "Don't be too long. You don't want to get a chill."

"There's a fire."

"You know what I'm getting at."

"A second or two. No. No. Sit, Alexander."

"Yes. Finish your supper. I shall help Martina," his father offered.

"That's not necessary, Vice-Minister."

"I insist. Here. Just use my shoulder."

Supporting herself with a hand on Nurov's shoulder, Martina Antipova hopped across the porch.

"Gravy?"

"No, Grandfather."

Grandfather Simpson sat after serving his plate. He watched Alex cut into the meat.

"So, you are going to Moscow University."

"Yes."

Grandfather Simpson poured an inch of bourbon into his glass. "Good." He tilted the glass back. "Very good."

"Thank you. I will try to live up to everyone's expectations."

Refilling the glass, "Good." Silently posing a question, he held the bottle toward Alex.

Alex shook his head.

"Perhaps yes. You can tell them in Moscow what bourbon tastes like." Emptying the water from Alex's glass into another. "I think

175

some of them have forgotten, if," he put the bottle down with a thud, "they ever knew to begin with."

The whiskey smelled sweet and strong.

"To your education," his grandfather whispered before emptying his glass.

"Yes—thank you."

He extinguished the fire in his throat with water. The warm bourbon spread through the rest of him like a sleepy breath.

Grandfather Simpson refilled both glasses.

"I'm sure you will do quite well, Alexander. You," he paused reflectively, "you have your mother's ambition."

"Do I?" Ambition? He had always done well in school. But that had been easy. What did that have to do with ambition? "Well, I have been working especially hard recently. Extra preparation in math. And physics. I've been—" He stopped. "—doing this extra work so I'll be on par with the rest."

"Yes."

"I'm afraid the schools here are not as," he searched for a moment, "competitive as they might be."

"No doubt. But what can you expect," his mother appeared, forcing his grandfather to lower his voice to a rasping whisper, "from a conquered people."

Had that been what he said? Yes. Conquered.

"So," picking up the bourbon bottle, "what have you two been up to?"

Smoothly, "Toasting your son's success."

"Oh? Well, let's all have dessert," she said tiredly. To Alex, "Don't be too impressed with yourself. Your grandfather doesn't need much of an excuse these days to have a toast."

Rising, "Why be stingy with congratulations? I toasted your wedding, didn't I?"

"Indeed. And rightfully so." On her way across the porch, "You've dined on it ever since, haven't you?"

"Crumbs, daughter." Wistfully, as he strolled through the double glass doors that led to the sitting room, "Crumbs! From the tables of princes."

They arranged themselves in an irregular circle around Martina Antipova, who had been installed in the large lounge chair usually

176

reserved for Alex's father. The chair was tilted back so that her round, ice-pack-wrapped foot assumed the position of a sixth person.

Corinne rolled out a cart with pumpkin pie. A bowl of whipped cream. And coffee.

"There's milk on the way," she announced offhandedly.

"Doesn't that look marvelous," his mother remarked. "And whipped cream," she added with a forced smile while she rubbed the back of her forefinger with her thumb. "We'll all be big as houses if we aren't careful." As Alex picked up a cup of coffee, "Especially now that it's getting too cold to swim."

"No," Martina Antipova interjected. "Not yet. Not here." The words appeared to be coming from the large, mouthless foot. "In Russia, certainly. But not yet here."

Indulgently, while she watched Alex sip his coffee, "Well, one gets used to a climate. To its rhythms. What was warm later becomes cold." Still rubbing her finger, "At least so I'm told."

"Yes," Alex's father added cooperatively.

Grandfather Simpson contributed a nod before tilting his head permanently to the side.

"Well, it was perfect for swimming today," Martina Antipova announced from behind her foot.

"Yes, I suppose it was."

"It was a great day for swimming," Alex blurted out, feeling very free from the mixture of coffee and bourbon.

"And I thought you had given up swimming until spring."

"I've just started drinking coffee," he answered after a moment. Why had he felt compelled to explain? And at such a ridiculous time. That made no sense at all. Except that she had been staring at him while he drank it. Toward the kitchen, to mask his embarrassment, "No milk for me, Corinne."

"Careful that it doesn't keep you up all night."

"No danger of that," the foot remarked. "We must have walked twenty kilometers today."

While Martina Antipova was eating her second piece of pie his mother excused herself. "I just need to sprinkle a little water on my eyes. Suddenly they've gotten a little tired." On her way past the big chair, "I'll leave another capsule for you on the bedside table. In case your ankle keeps you awake."

"Thank you. It feels fine now."

"Well," tiredly, "just in case."

"You are not coming back down, Daisy?" Nurov inquired disappointedly.

With mild irritation, "I won't be long."

"Good." He smiled into the fire.

She crossed the room, picked up the black medical bag she had carried down to examine Martina Antipova's ankle, and vanished up the stairs behind a trail of blue wisteria.

"This whipped cream is beyond belief."

"Corinne is an artist," his father remarked comfortably.

"Yes." Lifting her head so that it rivaled her foot, "They have many blacks here, don't they?"

"Yes." Realizing he had never given it a thought, "I guess they do." Reclining, "Strange."

His father laughed. "I suppose it is. Yes. But, like the climate, after a while it seems quite," he paused, "natural. If 'natural' is the correct word."

Alex listened to his mother's door shut.

"Yes, I suppose it is. In the right sense of the word. For obvious reasons they have had difficulty making the transition into socialist society. Of course, that is to be anticipated. In fact, was anticipated." Nurov leaned back. "The jump from a precapitalist social order to socialism is unnatural. And attempts to accelerate the historical process have not been totally successful."

"You would think they'd be grateful," Martina Antipova interjected, before adding, in an explanatory way that must have been prompted by the silence, since she could not see his father's face, "for ending slavery."

Nurov was not accustomed to being interrupted once he began a piece of historical analysis. Usually his mother got that glazed-over look; and he just listened.

"Gratitude is, I'm afraid you'll discover, a rare commodity here," Nurov replied with a sigh. "But," he smiled, "you are quite right. Quite right." There was no doubt that his father approved of Martina Antipova. "But at least they aren't sycophantic Russophiles."

"You can thank your Russification schemes for that, Vice-Minister," Grandfather Simpson announced from what had seemed to be a deep sleep.

178

Startled, probably because he had thought the old man was asleep, "That was certainly before my time."

Grandfather Simpson shrugged without opening his eyes.

"I think I can say," Nurov became coolly defensive, "that that is not the current policy."

His eyes still shut, "Good—I can't say Simpsonsky without spitting."

The row of comical little Brownskys lined up in Alex's mind vanished as soon as Nurov hissed, "That idiocy was never policy! It was concocted by some simpleminded," he paused, "local."

Martina Antipova sat up in her chair so that her head was almost level with her foot.

"And spread like a damned virus," his father added disdainfully.

Grandfather Simpson shrugged again before tilting his head to the side. Was he going to go back to sleep after waking up long enough to spoil their discussion?

"I can only say that that is no longer policy."

As if he were in a trance, "With television full of all that glitz from Moscow there's no need for a policy."

"Personally, I doubt if there ever was a policy regarding any of that." Martina Antipova took Nurov's statement as a sign that the matter was settled and put her head back down on the cushion. "No. I seriously doubt there ever was." Nurov smiled, as if a new idea had struck him, "Of course, being black, they were somewhat immune to that idiocy."

Very seriously, "One of the consequences of preeminence is imitation. That seems perfectly natural to me." Martina Antipova spoke directly into the ceiling. "Of course, that means we should set a good example."

Yes, Alex found himself agreeing, while remarking: She's actually much cleverer than you would think on first sight.

"Yes." Toying with the idea as if it were a mechanical device, "They are a special problem. There are some plans afoot for dispersion. So they won't be clustered together. That is a lot of the problem. Yes. That needs to be done. Some of them," he scratched his head, "are completely out of touch."

"That can't be good," Martina Antipova commented gravely.

"No. It can lead to all kinds of antiquated thinking."

What did phrases like that really mean? Instead of actually saying

179

anything concrete, they were more like doors. Antiquated thinking, he found himself repeating to himself.

Nurov continued in a lighter vein, "Problems. Problems. But then, without problems, what would my job be?"

They both took that to mean that that conversation had come to an end.

After a few minutes his father suggested that Martina Antipova tell them about the javelin. She touched on matters of technique. And training. From time to time Nurov asked a question. But for the most part he seemed content to listen to her. Some of the time she spoke in Russian. Some of the time in English. There was something soothing in her voice. It was so round. And confident.

An hour later, when he was helping Martina Antipova mount the stairs, his father, his glassy cat eyes half shut, instructed, "See what is taking your mother so long. Tell her there's enough moon to take a walk."

"Good night, Vice-Minister Nurov," Martina Antipova announced cheerily.

Staring into the remnants of fire, "Good night."

"Good night, Mr. Hunter Simpson."

Nurov laughed, "Yes, good night, Mr. Hunter Simpson." He pronounced the name with satirical care.

Not getting the joke, "That is right, isn't it?"

"Yes," his father answered for him. "You were exactly right."

"Good." Hopping up the stairs, "I am going to need a crutch, I think."

"I'll get you one tomorrow."

"Good." At the landing, "Is that your mother's room?"

"Yes."

"Do you want me to wait here?"

"No. I'll knock on my way back by."

"Oh." Making no attempt to disguise her disappointment, "If you like."

"She's," the image of her in the mirror, quivering, shot across his mind, "probably asleep anyway."

"The light is on," Martina Antipova pointed out.

"I guess it is." He inched over to the door. "Mother? Father is waiting for you." Energetically, "I think he wants to go for a walk."
180

Silence.

"Perhaps she is asleep."

"No." Correcting himself, "I mean, yes."

He was sure she was in there. Reclining against the headboard of the bed, surrounded by fluffy pillows. Wearing that look of utter, magical relaxation he had seen a thousand times.

He could see the syringe beside her, connected to her forearm by a spidery blood umbilical cord.

"Yes, Alexander?"

She was in the doorway.

Startled, not so much by her sudden appearance as by the idea that Martina Antipova might see that same spidery needle he had seen so clearly just a second before, "Father asked me to . . ."

"Yes, I know." Musically, "Tell him that I'm getting something to wrap around my shoulders." Her fingertips restraining his opposing cheek, she kissed the corner of his mouth. "Tell him I won't be a minute."

He stepped back a few inches.

Girlishly, as she released his cheek, "I've been looking out the window. It's a marvelous night for a walk."

He spoke to his father from the railing and, giving her his shoulder as a crutch, escorted Martina Antipova to her room.

"I'll bet I sleep to noon," she said robustly, her naked foot propped up on two pillows. "How about you?"

Looking at her foot, "Yes."

"It's ugly, isn't it?" she remarked, as if it was very hard to go suddenly from being physically perfect to being flawed.

At first he slept. Perhaps he had been so fatigued from hiking that that overcame any resistance to sleep. But while it was still dark—perhaps it was four? or five?—he awoke. And could not go back to sleep.

Maybe some food, he decided. Or milk.

As he crossed the sitting room, "Only old men are supposed to be up this late."

He could just make out Grandfather Simpson. He was sitting in the same chair a foot or two from the fire, which had been reduced to half a dozen wild, orange eyes.

"I didn't mean to wake you."

"You didn't."

"Just getting some milk."

He tiptoed into the kitchen, poured a glass of milk, and gulped it down with a shiver. Perhaps that would do the trick.

Standing, his back to Alex, "Might as well warm yourself before going back to bed."

Several logs had been added to the fire. They were beginning to smoke. He watched them reluctantly ignite.

"Have you always lived here? In this house?"

"No." He poked the fire. "Not always." He banged on a log with the poker, creating a hail of sparks. "In between," he began, "we lived other places."

Casually, "Do you know the old building on the other side of the ravine? It's burned down. At least most of it."

"Cooper's Gulch?"

"Yes. On the other side."

"No."

"It may have been a hospital?"

"That. It's been there forever."

"Really?" Tentatively, "Since before the Great Uprising?"

Out of breath from fiddling with the fire, "I don't know." His face was bright red from the fire. "Shockingly enough, I'm not that old. At that time I was only three."

Disappointed, "Oh."

"So, I recall," he stuck the poker into a hickory log, "nothing. Nothing at all. And in between, I wasn't here."

"In between?"

"In between leaving and your mother's marriage to Vice-Minister Nurov."

"Why did you leave?"

"I don't know." He sat down. "I was too young to remember. I only know I lived here. Before."

He watched the sun come up from his bedroom window. Or what you could see of it through the morning fog. He dressed. Pulled The Book from the bottom of his school bag and slid it under his tucked-in shirt.

Grandfather Simpson was asleep in his chair.

182

He could hear Corinne in the kitchen.

He gently pushed the screen door to and after a few steps exploded into a gallop, which he kept up until he reached the ravine.

He climbed down into the opaque-as-an-ice-cream-sundae mist, which, like the day before, always seemed to be solidly looming just out of reach; crossed the jagged little stream; and, now breathless, scaled the smooth granite bank that separated it from the thick, wet mountain laurel.

The place where he had found it was no different from any of a thousand tiny, canopied nooks. Odd. He could have been in any of the others and he would not have found it.

Leaning against the low-lying granite shelf, he unbuttoned his shirt and removed The Book. There was no other choice. Short of destroying it. He put it in his lap and thumbed through the slick, faint-lined pages, reading a phrase here, a sentence there. Sometimes just a word. Or a name. Father Paul. Dietra Christian. Jesus Christ. A lot of it didn't make much sense. But then, this Piotr Babulieski was some sort of loony. That much was clear. For a moment Kerelsky flashed through his mind: as usual he was twisting that tiny braid of hair. How did they get that way? he wondered. There was no reason to.

Supporting himself on his elbow, he began to slide The Book into the six-inch-high slit in the granite it had come from. At his mid-forearm it struck something. Perhaps some rock had fallen loose? When he reached in to remove it his hand slid across a smooth plastic surface.

Another book? Had it been there all the time? With the other book on top of it?

He pulled it out.

The transparent binding had darkened to light caramel. It was tightly taped around the edges. Just like The Book had been. He held it in profile. It was less than half an inch thick.

MY CAMPAIGNS AGAINST THE RUSSIANS
by Gustavus Roman

stood alone, in type, in the center of the page. He peeled off the tape and opened the folder. The a's were the same. Yes. Slightly askew. Lighter on the left than the right.

183

The paper screamed when he peeled back the first page. On the reverse side in script:

Hello, friend?
I am Gustavus Roman. I have taken that name because a servant of God could never do the things I have done.
Perhaps you are an archaeologist? Or engineer? No matter. Read this.
If you are one of them? Know that when you destroy this you do not destroy me! I have buried the truth in a hundred places. For some stranger to dig up. Someone will always know. No matter what you do. Someone will always know.
Why?
Because God hates a lie. He must.

The facing page was also in script. As were the others. The paper was that same slick paper. But the writing itself was all in a small rectangular portion of the page, surrounded by a three-sided, sooty black border that met its facing companion so that together they framed pairs of pages like pictures.

The script was small. Cramped. Erect. Sometimes, near the center where the pages were stapled together, it was strangely distorted. The way a magnifying glass distorts when it is held at an angle.

JANUARY 23

Today, after morning exercise, Dr. S told me that she was sure we were making progress. I think she is right. I have prayed very hard.

JANUARY 25

Sorry, Dr. S, no entry yesterday. I know I should be scrupulous about that. But yesterday was an especially bad day. Too rainy for a walk. Locked up inside. How I depend on our walks!

JANUARY 26

12:17. It occurred at exactly 12:17. I remember looking at my watch. It said 12:26. Only nine minutes! Jesus Christ, please accept their souls. I cannot pray for them all. Why did you let this happen?

184

JANUARY 27

Over and over. From every angle. The cameras have shown us the nothingness. It looks like Mars. Or how I think Mars looks. Why are they so relentless? They are interviewing the families. In Omaha. In San Bernardino. How could mindless crazies get hold of something like that? Almost a year after all nuclear weapons have been dismantled? What can they expect to extort from the world?

JANUARY 28

Finally we have been told. It leaked out, slowly, relentlessly, like the news of fatal cancer in a family. And finally the President appeared. Yes. It was an SS-30. With twelve warheads. Yes. They have made a proposal. Yes. We would study it. Yes. There was every reason to believe they had others. Dozens. Perhaps more. Save us, God. If You will.

FEBRUARY 5

Dr. S says that for us things must go on as they were. But how can they?

FEBRUARY 6

I have made up my mind to record the truth of what is going on. It is impossible to figure out exactly what that is. Something grotesque.
   There was a presidential press conference today—

SAM DONALDSON: *Is there any truth to the assertion, Mr. President, that the United States has been violating the Nuclear Weapons Accord?*
THE PRESIDENT: *No, Sam, there is not.*
SD: *Is there any truth to the assertion that a second Soviet thermonuclear device struck Martinsville, Nevada:*
P: *No. There is not.*
SD: *Is there a U.S. nuclear weapons stockpile at Martinsville, Mr. President?*
P: *Sam, as you know that would be a violation of the Nuclear Weapons Accord. We have scrupulously abided by that accord.*
(The President points to Nancy Ross.)

NANCY ROSS: *Are we going to allow an immediate Soviet on-site inspection?*

P: *We will comply with that request. As you know, the Nuclear Weapons Accord specifies that requests for immediate on-site inspections must be granted.*

Rumors abound: there are secret nuclear weapons. Underground. In the West. In Martinsville, Nevada. Or Idaho. And the U.S. is certain to retaliate. The dayroom is divided. Some say we should retaliate. Most say we should not. What is the sane response?

The Soviet ambassador is interviewed after the press conference. He is content to read a statement: The Soviet government has been aware for some time that the United States has been preparing a preemptive attack against the people of the Soviet Union. We have acted in self-defense.

The President has denied that the United States has violated the Nuclear Weapons Accord. What is your response to that?

The Soviet government has been aware for some time that the United States has been preparing a preemptive attack against the people of the Soviet Union. We have acted in self-defense.

Then why only New York City?

FEBRUARY 7

The first Russian troops arrived today. Just a few thousand. They are "here to perform an on-site inspection to ensure future compliance with the Nuclear Weapons Accord."

FEBRUARY 8

No television today. No one knew how to react. For two weeks we have been living in the dayroom. Feeding from the screen. It was our lifeline. Even the very disturbed are worried.

FEBRUARY 10

The President appeared on television today. He appeared drawn. We are to cooperate. The Soviet troops are here only to collect arms. Civil order will be maintained by local police.

186

FEBRUARY 11

One channel operates. It is showing only old movies. No commercials. No news. Just movies.

FEBRUARY 14

The entire evening was devoted to displays of arms. Hidden caches. Tanks. Planes. ICBMs. Dozens of ICBMs. They were in Nevada. Underground. Soviet troops are dismantling them now.

Is it staged? Probably. Almost certainly. Still, we are about equally divided. No one wants to believe the worst. "They will leave now," Sam White says. It is the first thing he has said since I have been here. He eats baby food. And watches television. That he has chosen to speak after so long has made a big impression on everyone.

FEBRUARY 15

The President again. And several senators. An army general. Two movie stars. A football player. A Soviet general. The Soviet Foreign Minister. Father Paul.

Am I responsible for this? He looks exactly the same. Very relaxed.

Perhaps that too was staged? An elaborate production? With me the unwitting but predictable star?

MARCH 12

I have not been well. Dr. S says, "Do not blame yourself." Would it have mattered if the bullet had been six inches to the left? I rack my brain. What was the purpose behind it all? I ask. If I had killed him, the same result. It was foolproof. And I was the fool.

No point in going on about this with Dr. S. Her training disposes her to believe that all conspiracies are paranoia. "There are real plots," I say. But to her the mind is more powerful than events.

But I know the man in the hat was KGB.

MARCH 14

Sooner or later they will come for me. They always keep tabs. The hunchback priest will not be forgotten forever.

What do we know? Here! Facts drift in, like light through a prism. Bent. Broken down into tiny fragments that must be reassembled.

Television is useless. Half the day is devoted to Nicolas Podgorny. He was from Kansas City. Or claims he was. Before defecting to the Soviet Union. Now he educates us. As if we were schoolchildren.

Listen to me; I sound like an American! But why not? They have already stolen my country.

MARCH 16

Nicolas Podgorny is being patient. He is very good at that. Although a few minutes ago he was scolding.

"Socialism is so simple. So natural. Rather than organizing life on the principle of greed, socialism organizes life by function and need. It is the inherently good system. Like small mountain streams everyone's labor empties into a great, common river of productivity. A river that everyone—poor, weak, crippled—is free to drink from."

Yes, I think angrily. Yes. Why won't you let it be like that? It is so beautiful. So perfect. It could be the incarnation of Christ on earth.

"Heretic," I screamed.

Sam White looked up from his jar of banana pudding.

"God damned heretic," I repeated.

I marched to the television and wrenched the dials and buttons, tearing away at it as if it were flesh.

"There are countless ways you can resist," the man said. "Countless ways."

Startled, I stood back.

Below his face, in block letters, it said: AMERICAN FREE TELEVISION.

He was about fifty. Gray. He looked like somebody's father. Not someone I knew. A prototype. Like a father from a television series. Or commercial.

"If you have access to files, destroy them. Any files. Particularly computer files. Particularly personal files. Credit information. Personnel files. Just break the disks into pieces. Or put them in the oven.

"Many of you have done this already. The rest of you must do the same. While you still can."

188

Just as he finished his pudding, Sam White said, "They are not leaving, are they?"

You could feel agitation fill the room. As if it suddenly dawned on them that he was right.

The man on the television vanished into snow. We waited several hours for him to come back, but he didn't.

MARCH 17

I drove into Saluda today with Dr. S. It looks very much the same. The man at the store (he spoke remarkably freely. But that is natural. It takes a while for suspicion to take over. But it would. Soon enough. That's how they worked) said that a Russian officer, along with half a dozen kids, had come by with a truck to collect guns. He laughed when he said, "I wish I had a dollar for every gun left here. Hell. I'm surprised somebody didn't shoot him dead on the spot." He spit into a large peach can. "Course, I'm glad they didn't. Sure as hell nobody around here would have buried the son of a bitch." Grinning, "Woulda been a health hazard. After a month or two." When we were leaving, he said, "They took all the typewriters too. And Xerox machines. Course," he grinned knowingly, "there was only two here to start with."

On the way back I reminded Dr. S what the man on television had said. She replied thoughtfully, "How can I treat my patients without files?" Nevertheless, I am sure she will destroy them.

Tonight I helped her move the Xerox to the basement. It must have been a funny sight for God. She is not as slender as she used to be; and I am, well, less than athletic (although my legs are quite strong!).

"I don't think they realize we are here," she said while we were having coffee.

"Perhaps not," I agreed. "But they will find out. Right now they are a snake trying to swallow a cow. Once the cow passes through the jaws, however, it is only a matter of time before digestion takes place."

"Yes," she replied with a frown. "Until then, perhaps even after, things must go on as usual here. We have work to do that . . ." She trailed off for a second. "The people here are not prepared for anything like this."

I almost said, "Perhaps they are as well prepared as the others," but chose not to. We often have talks like that. Sometimes I wonder if she considers me a patient at all.

189

MARCH 18

We sat in the dayroom waiting for AMERICAN FREE TELEVISION to broadcast again. It did not. Sam White said, "They won't come on again. They're dead." No one seemed convinced. Perhaps now that he was saying something almost every day, they didn't take him as seriously.

MARCH 19

There was a disagreement in the dayroom this morning: should we wait; should we watch Nicolas Podgorny, endless panel discussions, and manufactured news. I had seen all that. "It may seem new to you," I said. "But it's not. I've seen it before."

Sister Grace had to adjudicate. "As always, in the dayroom democracy rules," she announced, before returning to her needlepoint.

The vote was nine to seven in favor of Nicolas Podgorny. It's hard to hold it against them. After all, something is better than nothing. Especially when all you can do is sit and wait.

MARCH 23

On our walk today we discussed sex. Dr. S is very curious about my experiences in Gdansk. About Ivan. Several times she asked me to describe Paul Creticos to her. (She did the same thing last year. It got us nowhere.) She seems to have some theories there, but I suspect she is wrong. Still, to humor her, I played along, letting her excavate my mind. When I noticed she was taping the session, I asked about the files. "Certainly no one will bother to listen to these. That would be absurd."

"Yes," I replied. "You can be sure someone will once they are discovered."

Since that was beyond her experience she gave me one of those peculiar, disbelieving looks.

MARCH 30

Talk of sex continues. Circuitously. Tangentially. But that is nevertheless the subject. Why is Dr. S so absorbed with sex?

190

A Russian officer arrived today, startling everyone. I could tell they didn't know whether to try to act normal, more insane than they really were, or what. In the end they compromised by first affecting normality and then, afraid that that would produce some unexpected result, acting like children pretending to be insane. If Dr. S was embarrassed by all that, she disguised it very well.

After inspecting the facility and counting heads he departed. They collectively breathed a sigh of relief. But I knew better. He, or some-one like him, would be back.

JANUARY 12

Hello, old friend. I have been unable to be with you for fear that you might fall into the wrong hands. A name here or there? Something they could piece together? Once I made up my mind to resist them we had to be apart.

If this is difficult to read it is because the heat is off, so I must wear a sock on my hand.

Everything must be compressed into one night's writing. At dawn we leave. Permanently. We won't be able to take the Xerox machine with us. Which is the end of our little newspaper. At least for now. But I will make as many copies of this as paper allows. Not for to-morrow's news. Or the next day's. But so that someone, as God de-cides, will from time to time discover this and know what happened:

In the summer John Boy arrived. Until then everything had been for the most part unchanged. Which was the way Dr. S wanted it.

He was called John Boy after the television character. Because he was young and quite innocent-looking. And because he introduced himself as John Stiglitz. "I am the political officer of this institution," he announced to us.

It was a very hot day. Most of us were on the porch searching out any hint of afternoon breeze. He made the announcement in the style of a conquering general—one foot on the step leading up to the porch. Behind him were four other boys. Even younger and uni-formed, each carried a carbine.

"Is this all of you?" he asked with unmistakable disappointment.

We all stared blankly. At the floor. Or sky. Or him. No one wanted

191

to take on the responsibility of sanity at a dangerous moment like that.

"Where is Dr. Sullivan?" he asked after unfolding a sheet of paper he had pulled from his pocket.

When no one answered he beckoned for two of the boys to stay behind, and, the other two on his heels, entered the front door.

Later we learned there were many of them. Six-month socialist wonders. They were told, and believed, that they were the salvation of the nation. As always, "education" was proceeding at a feverish pace.

When we were all assembled, John Boy announced, "I will be in charge of your political education. We will begin now." He spoke for three hours. I had heard it all before. But the others had only heard it on television. For the most part from Nicolas Podgorny.

Twice Sam White raised his hand to ask, "Can we watch television?"

The first time John Boy replied, "No. Your education takes precedence over television."

The second time Sam White added, "Democracy always rules in the dayroom."

"The dayroom?" John Boy repeated with irritation.

"Yes. Dr. S always says, 'Democracy rules in the dayroom.' It's one of her rules."

Sam White was escorted from the dayroom by two of the boys. We could hear him being beaten while John Boy finished lecturing us on the virtues of socialism.

The next day a sign was posted at the front door: KARL MARX PSYCHIATRIC HOSPITAL.

Afterward, out of the side of his mouth so that his stitches wouldn't tear, Sam White asked, "Does that mean we can't call it Sacred Heart any longer?"

John Boy can claim responsibility for my conversion to violence. Such a good-looking boy. But with the character of an open sore. Yes. That is precisely what he was. What they were. Open, fresh sores. The portals of disease through which infection was to be passed from generation to generation.

If it hadn't been for him I might never have become angry.

Not that it started that way. In the beginning (I guess this had been

192

*growing since the day the bomb had dropped) I simply became weak.
Despondent. Questioning. I lay in bed most of the day, psychoana-
lyzing God. (Dr. S had manufactured a file for me: schizophrenic—
imagines himself a Polish priest. Clever. That allowed for any kind of
behavior. And, of course, my accent. When I chose to speak.) God, I
inquired, there must be some reason. Was this the final test? The
vicarage of the Antichrist? Should all those who believe proclaim it
now? And accept martyrdom? Or would that just be fruitless sacrifice?*

*During all this I couldn't help but feel that I shared in the blame.
After all, I had helped it happen. Oh, my heart had been in the right
place. But was that any excuse?*

*One morning, after several months of this, I became angry. It
began during one of John Boy's interminable lectures.*

*"You are ill," he announced while sitting on the edge of a large
wooden table, "because the culture you were brought up in is full of
contradictions. In the socialist state all contradictions have been resolved. There is no need for illness."*

*My first thought was to kill him. Perhaps that night? While he
recited I worked out the details of several plans. But in the end I
decided that would be foolish. At least so soon. But we could strike at
them. Disrupt them. Rob them of their sleep.*

*Odd, the scale on which resistance begins. It was on that day that I
took the name Gustavus Roman. After all, I decided, I was no longer
a priest. That had ended on that day in Central Park (gone! In a
flicker. God must have been awakened by the twelve million
screams. If they had time to scream) when I decided I could usurp
God's power. Since then my collar had remained in the drawer. Buried under socks.*

*We slipped out at night. At first we merely broke things. Police-car
windows. We set a fire or two. One behind the police station. Cut
wires. Small, insignificant things that made us feel more like men.*

*Dr. S: You ejaculated?
GR: Yes. (I had never admitted this before.)
Dr. S: And that disturbed you?
GR: No. Humiliated me.
Dr. S: Still?*

193

GR: Yes.

DR. S: But why? It means nothing. Torture elicits all kinds of responses.

GR: You know, of course, they laughed. Always.

We decided to kill the Russian officer in Saluda. We worked out all
the details of the assassination.

DR. S: Father Paul Creticos. Describe him to me.

GR: He was, is, the most beautiful creature I have ever seen.

DR. S: Physically beautiful?

GR: Yes.

DR. S: And how do you feel about him now?

GR: I think he is one of them.

DR. S: But you have no proof of that?

GR: No.

DR. S: Are there any other feelings you would like to express about
Father Paul?

GR: What kind of feelings?

DR. S: Well, any kind. (When I was silent) I think I recall that he
appeared in your dreams? When you couldn't sleep.

GR: Yes. (I knew what she was getting at.) But, in no special way. (If
I had been corrupted, they had done it to me. There had never
been any feelings like that. Not until Gdansk. God will damn
them for that. Not me.)

We bungled it. I suppose because we didn't know what we were
doing. But it served one purpose: I returned to my vocation.

"Am I going to die?" Sam White asked.

"No. You will be fine."

But before we had gotten halfway down the mountain it was apparent that he would die. It took so long off-road.

We sat him against a tree. The inside of his jacket was soaked with
blood.

Without thinking I found myself asking, "Is there anything you
feel you need to confess?"

"Then I am going to die?"

"Yes. In this life. But we all know that is only the beginning."

194

"I have been hiding puddings. I know I shouldn't have. With food so low. But." He paused. "They were the only thing I really enjoyed."

"All-Merciful Christ will forgive you for that."

"There is one left, banana, I believe, under my bed."

After I gave him extreme unction, we carried him down the mountain and slid him down the coal chute. We changed his clothes, stretched him out in his bed, and slit his wrists.

In the morning, when John Boy saw him, he said, "There is no reason in a socialist state for anyone to commit suicide." He instructed Dr. S, "You will report that he was killed in an accident."

Later, in the basement, behind the coal bin, I conducted a mass. They all seemed to find great comfort in it. As did I.

"Thank you, Jesus Christ, for returning my precious faith to me," I prayed that night.

Since then I have been a priest. Nothing more. Nothing less. Clandestinely. For the most part at night, after climbing up the coal chute and walking over the mountain to Saluda or one of the other towns that daisy-chain along the river as it descends to the piedmont. I have been performing the pleasant duties of a parish priest: marriages, christenings, taking confession, preaching. And the darker ones, when called upon. Clandestinely. As churchmen did in the perilous days of early Christendom, I've slipped through the anonymous night like fish through a familiar pond.

Periodically, when Dr. S can concoct a reason, I have accompanied her to Columbia or Charleston to assist my brothers. There is need for us everywhere now, but we are fewer and fewer, since each week or month one of us vanishes.

It is in the cities where the most profound changes have occurred.

Churches have been razed. Or the steeples torn off, leaving purposeless, emasculated blocks that reach upward to the sky like handless beggars.

Thousands (millions? No one knows. Odd, how the precision one becomes accustomed to vanishes along with the faces) are in reeducation centers, both the young, on whom the future depends, and the old, out of whom the past has to be excised.

Without a word, machines, equipment, entire manufacturing centers have been uprooted and carted off to Russia and Eastern Europe, leaving behind only scars . . . and Russians.

There is no way to tell how many there are. Party functionaries. Bureaucrats. Soldiers. Men on the way up, carving out careers. Thousands? Millions. They multiply like lice.

On television there are none. Save the few who have been invited by the General Secretary of the Communist Party, United Soviet States of America, to render assistance to their socialist brothers.

At first they seemed hesitant, but already they affect the certain, arrogant manner of conquerors. I have seen it before.

What I can find out, atrocities, facts, truths, simple occurrences, I cram into our little newspaper, which, thanks to the rare and wonderful Xerox machine we have sequestered in the basement, circulates with me. Each time just a few copies that can be passed around so that a man can touch palpable truth. Strangely, for the most part it is devoted to reporting the ordinary, Christian progression of life: John and Mary were united in holy matrimony under God; Matthew was christened two days after Good Friday; Paul departed us last Wednesday, God accept his soul.

And of course each edition contains a lesson from scripture, as well a few words of consolation from Gustavus Roman, priest.

And, of course, I provide consolation for those who are resisting:

MAN: May I confess now, Father?
FATHER PIOTR: Please do, my son.
M: Just in case?
FP: I understand.
M: Can Christ forgive murder?
FP: Christ forgives all to those who ask in good faith.
M: I know, Father. But, they, we, will gut her.
FP: I know.
M: She deserves it, Father. She has been sleeping with one of them.
  She's just a fucking whore, Father. She deserves it, doesn't she?
FP: Do what you must.
M: We can't let them corrupt our women, can we?
FP: May Christ forgive you your sins.
M: They don't die slowly, you know?

The ones they can catch, under cover of night, they shave, and gut through the vagina, as in old, since that is the orifice through which
196

the devil enters woman. Because, after all, they are just whores sleeping with Russians.

God forgive this weary traveler. Dawn is here.

He crept across the porch, trying not to waken its old, complaining boards.

"Martina Antipova has been asking where you are," his mother informed him from within one of the huge porch rockers.

To the back of the wicker rocking chair, after regaining his composure, "I felt like walking."

"It's a gorgeous day, don't you think?"

"Yes."

"I had to walk with Father. I would have preferred to walk with you. Don't you miss our talks."

Awkwardly, "I thought you were asleep."

"No. He complained the entire time." Philosophically, "Why are the old never satisfied?"

The chair stopped. He stood there for a moment, transfixed like a bug in a garden spider's web, afraid that if she turned to face him, he might explode through the door.

"Corinne has your breakfast," she sang out in a way that let him know she was on top of the world. The chair again began to rock listlessly back and forth.

"Good," he replied with a mixture of relief and sudden exhaustion, before escaping across the porch.

He was halfway up the stairs before Martina Antipova came to mind. The door to her room was open. She would be lying there, bored.

"Were you not even going to stop, Alexander?"

"Oh. I thought you might be napping."

"At this hour?"

Standing in the center of the hallway directly in front of the door, "How's the ankle?"

She shrugged.

"I wanted to get some of the morning air."

"Yes. Well," pouting, "it's difficult to be fun with this ugly ankle."

He couldn't think of anything to say.

With fascination, "See how purple it is."

197

Realizing that he was required to step over and examine it, he stalled with, "It will be fine in no time."

She pushed herself up on one elbow and craned her neck so that her injury was more accessible. Thoughtfully, "I don't know."

She was waiting for him to come over and look at it.

"What do you think?" she persisted.

The thick, exposed leg, resting on a stack of white pillows like a hunk of cow displayed in a butcher's window, awaited his inspection. He inched his way into the room.

Without genuine concern, "You don't suppose anything is broken, do you?" She answered her own question: "Your mother assures me it is only a severe sprain."

Numbly, "I'm sure she's right."

She leaned back against another stack of pillows, pulling the sheet up on both sides of her leg as she did so. Caught in her crotch as tightly as a bathing-suit bottom, the sheet snapped out of her hand at her wrist. "What a mess." In the form of a request, "I am all tangled up."

"Yes." He found himself smiling. It produced a mild tingle of relaxation. He could breathe a little.

"Such a mess."

He took the sheet where it had popped out of her hand and, while she lifted up, slipped it back under her thigh and buttock. She was wearing snug, light blue underpants; a tuft of curly black hair was trapped in the elastic.

In Russian, "You're very sweet, Alexander Mikhailovich. I'm happy that I've gotten to know you."

"Thank you." The Russian seemed awkward and out of place. Embarrassed, he repeated in English, "Thank you."

She bent her leg at the knee, letting her thigh tilt open slightly, so that it was supported by the taut guitar-string tendon that raced up the inside of her thigh.

"I have been restless," she drew up her other leg, creating a fleshy, protruding blue vee, "all morning."

Numbly, as if he were making conversation with a stranger on the bus, "You're not accustomed to lying about all day."

"No. And," pointing listlessly to a crumpled copy of *Soviet Sports,* "I've read that twice already."

198

Addressing the blue vee, "Perhaps I can get you something else. There's a little shop in Saluda."

"That would be nice." Drawing the leg up, tightening the vee, "Are your parents downstairs?"

"I'm not sure. My father might be in his room across the hall."

"Oh." She glanced down between her legs. "If I had a crutch we could go for a short walk later."

"Yes." He draped the sheet over her leg so that it formed a long narrow tent. Suddenly he was very tired. "I have to take a shower first."

Full of anticipation, "Well, don't be all morning."

In his room, he drew himself into a ball in the center of the bed, his arms wrapped around his knees, and lay there wide awake until Corinne insisted that he come to lunch.

Chapter

8

On Monday he feigned illness. It wasn't difficult. His mother was convinced he had some kind of bug.

Knowingly, "You haven't felt right all weekend, have you?"

Looking down, "I guess not."

"A day in bed can do wonders. I think that's," smiling, "what the doctor ordered."

```
MONDAY NOVEMBER 15, 143
PLEASE ENTER YOUR AUTHORIZATION CODE: _ _ _ _ _
```

The characters a-n-0-0-1 beeped into the blanks as he entered them from the keyboard.

```
PASSWORD?
```

He entered m-y-s-o-n, but nothing appeared on the screen. The DAL always supposed someone was looking over your shoulder. He struck the blue key.

```
GOOD MORNING, ALEXANDER.
WHAT CAN I DO FOR YOU?
bibliographical search
SUBJECT/AUTHOR/TITLE?
subject
DO YOU WISH TO BE PROMPTED?
no
```

ENTER SUBJECT.
new york city

He waited.

THERE ARE 0 TITLES ON THE SUBJECT NEW YORK CITY.

After a moment:

bibliographical search
SUBJECT/AUTHOR/TITLE?
subject
DO YOU WISH TO BE PROMPTED?

Impatiently:

no
ENTER SUBJECT
new york

He waited:

THERE ARE 5270 TITLES ON THE SUBJECT NEW YORK. DO YOU
    WISH TO LIST THEM ALL?

After thinking for a moment:

no/classify
LEVEL 1: NEW YORK
    STATISTICAL SUMMARIES
    HISTORY
    GEOGRAPHY
geography
THERE ARE 107 TITLES ON THE SUBJECT NEW YORK/
    GEOGRAPHY. DO YOU WISH TO LIST THEM ALL?
no/classify
LEVEL 1: NEW YORK
    LEVEL 2: GEOGRAPHY
        MINERALS

201

CROPS
ECONOMIC ACTIVITIES
CITIES
DEPARTMENTS
MAPS
WEATHER

He walked over to the bookcase and extracted the *CCCP USSA Atlas*. New York. New York. He examined the map carefully. There was no New York City. He returned to the computer and placed the open atlas in his lap.

maps
THERE ARE 12 TITLES ON THE SUBJECT NEW YORK/GEOGRAPHY/ MAPS. DO YOU WISH TO LIST THEM ALL?

There were hundreds of maps. Maps of cities. Departments. Elevation maps, full of interesting multicolored concentric shapes. Demographic maps, in which each district grew in proportion to its population. But there was no New York City.

bibliographical search
SUBJECT/AUTHOR/TITLE?
subject
DO YOU WISH TO BE PROMPTED?
no
ENTER SUBJECT.
piotr babulieski
THERE ARE 0 TITLES ON THE SUBJECT PIOTR BABULIESKI.
bibliographical search
SUBJECT/AUTHOR TITLE?
subject
DO YOU WISH TO BE PROMPTED?
no
ENTER SUBJECT.
gustavus roman
THERE ARE 0 TITLES ON THE SUBJECT GUSTAVUS ROMAN.
bibliographical search
SUBJECT/AUTHOR/TITLE?

```
subject
DO YOU WISH TO BE PROMPTED?
no
ENTER SUBJECT.
paul creticos
THERE ARE 2 TITLES ON THE SUBJECT PAUL CRETICOS. DO YOU
    WISH TO LIST THEM ALL?
yes
_ CCCP USSA Encyclopedia, 4th Ed., vol. 3, p. 605.
_ Biographical History of Socialist Thought in America, vol. 2,
    The Dialectics of Change: Precursors of the Great Uprising,
    p. 312.
```

Alex placed a d in the blank preceding the first title. It was the same *CCCP USSA Encyclopedia* entry he had read before. Posthumously awarded the Lenin Peace Prize.

He returned the citations to the screen by striking the blue key and placed a d before the second entry.

It was exactly the same. Word for word. Twenty-seven of them in all.

```
bibliographical search
SUBJECT/AUTHOR/TITLE?
subject
DO YOU WISH TO BE PROMPTED?
no
ENTER SUBJECT.
dietra christian
THERE ARE 0 ENTRIES ON THE SUBJECT DIETRA CHRISTIAN.
logoff
CONNECT TIME 1 HOURS 21 MINUTES
```

He sat for a second or two in front of the blank, pale blue screen, feeling, all in all, a little better. That sense of dread associated with finding out something terrible had been paralyzing him since he woke up. He could feel it slowly releasing its grip on his throat.

He switched off the computer.

That left the rest of the day. Perhaps it was sunny. He could go to the dune. Reread one of his mysteries. No. He would take his physics book. He could spend the entire afternoon doing physics problems. That would be productive. All this daydreaming about mysteries was going to be his ruination. What he needed was a little more discipline. That would rid him of all these silly thoughts, anyway. Just being there, alone in the dune, would be just what the doctor ordered. Of course, that would involve dodging Corinne, who was sure to be puttering around waiting for opportunities to "make sure he was all right." She would certainly oppose any attempt to leave the house, if for no other reason than that it would remove him from her care.

He crept to the kitchen door. Just an apple. And some bread. And cheese. That would last the afternoon.

What a friend we have in Jesus,
All our sins and griefs to bear.

In a thick-as-diesel-oil whisper that straddled the line between humming and singing:

What a privilege to carry
Everything to God in prayer.

The words seemed to cling to the back of her throat in the way a small child clings to her mother's hand:

What a friend we have in Jesus,
All our sins and griefs to bear.

The sound was oddly soothing. Almost pretty.

What a privilege to carry.

Silence.

He must have made a noise; or perhaps she just sensed he was there.

Uncomfortably, "I'm getting some juice."

Her eyes narrowed into chocolate-pudding slits. "Aren't you supposed to be in bed, Alexander?"

With a familiar, but false, fatigue, "Oh, Corinne. I'm not dying, you know." His voice seemed to echo across the kitchen.

"Well," she offered slowly, examining him through those chocolate

204

slits, "your mama's counting on me to look after you while she's at clinic." Was she trying to see if he had heard her? "Knowing her, she'll be back early to check on you." Those were just the kinds of things Corinne always said; just the way she said them. But something was off. Slightly. "When did you change out of your pajamas?"

Repeating the song in his head while looking blankly into the refrigerator:

What a friend we have in Jesus,
All our sins and griefs to bear.

He carefully poured half a glass of orange juice and forced it down while she occupied herself with the dishes.

Unconvincingly, "Your mama will expect you to be in bed when she gets back."

He slid the glass into the murky dishwater. "I'm on my way."

She vigorously scrubbed away at the leftover eggs that were clinging to the serving plate, feigning that scolding silence she had used for years to show her disapproval. This morning was completely different. Not just because he was older and no longer afraid of her. It was because, for the first time in his recollection, she was afraid of him.

He went directly to the study and flipped the computer on.

bibliographical search

How had he forgotten that?

SUBJECT/AUTHOR/TITLE?
surject
INVALID COMMAND/REENTER
subject
DO YOU WISH TO BE PROMPTED?
no

He could feel the excitement in his fingertips. Without that sense of dread that had been hanging over him earlier.

    ENTER SUBJECT.
    jesus

He waited impatiently.

    THERE ARE 0 TITLES ON THE SUBJECT JESUS.

He stared at the screen for a second, before quickly entering:

    bibliographical search
    SUBJECT/AUTHOR/TITLE?
    subject
    DO YOU WISH TO BE PROMPTED?

With annoyance:

    no
    ENTER SUBJECT
    jesus christ

After a second or two:

    THERE ARE 0 TITLES ON THE SUBJECT JESUS CHRIST.

He put his forehead down on the cool wood that extended three or four inches from the keyboard to the edge of the desk. The words flashed by while he reproduced the melody:

What a friend we have in Jesus,
All our sins and griefs to bear.

Certainly Corinne had never read The Book. That didn't make any sense at all. "I have buried the truth in a hundred places," it said. But he was just a damned loony! Who didn't exist. And the song wasn't in The Book. Only the name. Jesus Christ.

For a second he wished it were there. Maybe just by reading it one more time it would make some sense. No. It belonged right where it was. It was just the ravings of some damned loony.

What a friend we have in Jesus,
All our sins and griefs to bear.

His voice cracked a little on the last word.

All our sins and griefs to bear.

Better.
He was reaching under the keyboard for the off/on switch when it came to him.

```
bibliographical search
SUBJECT/AUTHOR/TITLE?
title
ENTER TITLE.
the quest of the historical jesus
```

When it came to him he could almost see it there, even with his eyes open. Sitting on the desk with a strip of paper jutting out of it.

```
THE TITLE THE QUEST OF THE HISTORICAL JESUS DOES NOT
EXIST. WOULD YOU LIKE HELP?
yes
IT IS OFTEN DIFFICULT TO LOCATE VOLUMES BY TITLE. ARE
YOU SURE YOU HAVE ENTERED THE CORRECT TITLE?
yes
REPEAT THE SEARCH USING AUTHOR.
```

He could see the book, lying there. *The Quest of the Historical Jesus.* Yes, that was the title. But the author was a complete blank.

He repeated the search by title, carefully entering each letter and checking it.

THE TITLE THE QUEST OF THE HISTORICAL JESUS DOES NOT
EXIST.

How could that be? He had seen the book right in this room.
Within arm's reach of where he was sitting.

His father had come in, picked up the stack of books, and locked
them in the filing cabinet. Could they still be there? No. Probably
not. His father was always locking books in there. And taking them
out.

He jumped when the vacuum cleaner roared into operation on the
other side of the study door.

His fingertips still tingling:

logoff
CONNECT TIME 22 MINUTES

Her head down, her hips and buttocks raised up like an ox or water
buffalo, she inched her way down the hall, dragging the vacuum
cleaner behind her. Without even a why-aren't-you-in-bed look.
That was not like her at all.

Where had she learned that song? he wondered.

She disappeared around the corner.

Alex spent the afternoon at the tip of the island, in and around the
old dune, his pants rolled up to his knees. A couple of times he
leaned against the base of the gnarled water oak and attempted physics, but he couldn't think clearly enough to get anywhere. He even
dug up one of his old mysteries, but it couldn't hold his attention.

Before he could tear himself away from the old dune, the sun had
sunk into Mt. Pleasant, transforming the ocean into a cool, orange
ice cream soda. He ran along the edge just out of reach of the en-
croaching hands the ocean sent out to touch him. He glanced down
just in time to dodge this attempt or that, but for the most part he
kept his eyes straight ahead, the cool off-the-huge-soda air tearing his
eyes slightly, so that when the woman appeared, he could not be sure
from vision alone that it was his mother: she let her robe slide off her
shoulder onto the sand and as freely as some hoofed African animal
gliding across a television special, she tore into placid, shallow, orange water, splashing it up around her like rapids before vanishing.

208

He stopped.

Now only a braided blond head, she bobbed her way across the first line of breakers. And then the second. Why did she always insist on going out so far?

He began to run again. Not, as he always had in the past, to join her, but to get by before the ocean coughed her up.

The blond head vanished. Reappeared. Vanished. Reappeared. Then began bobbing its way back.

Alex curved up toward the far, irregular edge of the beach, away from the water, where the dry, choppy sand abutted the line of stodgy little dunes that protected the island.

Sloshing ankle-deep, water still dripping off her, she waved. "Alex." The voice almost evaporated before reaching him. Perhaps he could just pretend he hadn't heard it? "The water's marvelous."

He stopped and, hidden from the waist down by a thin, rustling skirt of sea oats, waited for her.

She picked up the robe from the sand and, its collar hooked onto the back of her fingertips, draped it over one shoulder. She walked slowly, swaying, her head down.

Purple-lipped, shivering a little, "You should have come in. But then," mischievously, "that might not have been a good idea." Drying her neck with the terry-cloth robe, "Your being ill and all?"

"I started feeling better."

With uncluttered simplicity, "Good."

He turned toward the house.

"There's still a little sunlight left." He turned. "We can go back in." Her skin was blotched with purple. And goose bumps. Several small streams of water were still running down her. "Or we can just sit for a while." Her hand was ice-cold. "We can sit over here. Down low in the dunes. Out of the wind." Each word seemed to be separated by gaps of time. "Yes. That's better, isn't it?"

Reluctantly, "Yes, I guess."

"It is. That's the pleasure in being cold, isn't it? That first rush of warmth." He could smell the residue of the afternoon scent she wore beneath the coat of salt. Leaning forward, so that her wet shoulder touched him, "So, you're feeling better." Her lips were trembling.

"Yes."

Resting her fingertips against his temple, she ran her thumb across

209

his forehead, letting it slide upward until it touched the birthmark. Looking into the winestain, running her thumb over and around it so that the cold thumb began to feel hot, "When you were a baby, I would spend hours staring at that. I know every twist and turn. The way a navigator knows a map."

"I know."

"And that is precisely what this is." Still looking into the birthmark, as if it were a puzzle or cipher, "A map. And, as a map is to a lost sailor, this will be our salvation." The thumb was beginning to feel like a piece of charcoal. "And for that we must each be willing to sacrifice."

He pulled his head to the side in an attempt to evade the thumb.

"You do understand that, don't you, Alexander?"

"Yes, I think."

"You do. I know you do. You are," he could feel her breath, "of each of us. Each. Do you know what that means?"

"I—"

Interrupting, "You look so Russian. So damned Russian." She released him, keeping her face right up against his. "Always remember. You are both. And what role you must play." Rising up, without using her hands, her bathing suit sliding just past him, "You must know that you are the reason." She bent at the waist, her face again very near his, "That I have done all this. The only reason."

At dinner she was very relaxed and treated him in that special way that implied that there was some secret between them. He had seen her do that a thousand times. It was so effortless. Almost second nature.

The cold, salty surf had left her face ruddy. Very alive. Her eyes were like distant, green dreams.

"I think I shall rest awhile, Nurov."

Her gown vanished into the hallway, leaving him at the table with his father.

"She seems in good spirits." Examining Alex carefully, "That's good. Yesterday, and even in her beloved mountains," he looked up sarcastically, "she seemed distracted." Gently probing with his eyes, "I suspect it has had something to do with you. But that seems to have been taken care of."

"I guess." Fixing his eyes on a piece of bread, "She seems fine to me."

"Well," soliciting Alex's help, "this is a delicate period in life for a woman. Hard for a young man to understand." He took a swallow from his glass. "When a son grows up. Is about to go away. Even to school. It can produce something of a crisis." He emptied the glass. "Do you follow me?"

"Yes. I think so."

"So. How have your studies been progressing?" Pointedly, before Alex could answer, "You will make us very proud of you, I am sure." He rose and, with a small gesture emanating from his index finger, bade Alex to follow him down the hallway. "Engineers get things done. You can't imagine what it is like to look around you and see nothing but bodies slowly sinking into quicksand. These damned Americans."

It happened quite by accident:

TUESDAY, NOVEMBER 16, 143
PLEASE ENTER YOUR AUTHORIZATION CODE: _ _ _ _ _

As if he had done it a thousand times:

m n 0 0 1
PASSWORD?

Alex watched his fingers:

e-x-i-l-e

He was struck, first by the word itself. The choice. And, almost simultaneously, before he could digest its meaning, by the sense of possibility that came with it.

He tried to listen, pay attention, but all he could do, in a distracted, confused way, was wonder: could it make any difference? Later, in bed, comfortably surrounded by blackness, he continued to wonder.

211

PLEASE ENTER YOUR AUTHORIZATION CODE: _ _ _ _ _

Quickly, as if someone were watching:

m n 0 0 1
PASSWORD?
e-x-i-l-e
GOOD AFTERNOON, VICE-MINISTER NUROV.
WHAT CAN I DO FOR YOU?
bibliographical search
SUBJECT/AUTHOR/TITLE?
title
ENTER TITLE.
the quest of the historical jesus

He could feel his mouth becoming dry.

_ The Quest of the Historical Jesus, Author unknown, In archival
abstract only.

He placed a d in the blank, but, without pressing down, rested his
finger on the blue key. It had been here all along, in plain view to
the right eyes, as if there were one world for this person, and another for that. Strange. What if the world itself were like that? he
wondered just as he struck the blue key.

The Quest of the Historical Jesus: A feeble attempt to
employ scientific methods to justify a religion. Perversions
of the scientific method were commonly used in presocialist times to justify religion. Of course, the result is thinly
disguised propaganda used by the criminal ruling class
to control the proletarian masses. Correct Marxist-Leninist
methods have made ruses of this type obsolete. Since
the text is only a curiosity of interest to backsliders and
criminal lunatics it is kept only in abstract.

Alex pressed down on the space bar. Nothing happened. He
pressed down again.

212

Was this all there was left? He measured the book in his mind. It was an inch thick! This was all that was left?

He struck the blue key.

WHAT CAN I DO FOR YOU?
bibliographical search
SUBJECT/AUTHOR/TITLE?
subject
DO YOU WISH TO BE PROMPTED?
no
ENTER SUBJECT.
jesus christ
THERE ARE 19 TITLES ON THE SUBJECT JESUS CHRIST. DO YOU
  WISH TO SEE THEM ALL?
yes
_ Annals of Socialist Inquiry, Abstracts of Reports to the
    CCCP/USSA, vol. 4, The Role of Myths in Lunatic Cults, p.
    26.
_ Annals of Socialist Inquiry, Abstracts of Reports to the
    CCCP/USSA, vol. 9, Cults and Criminal Deviance: Selected
    Case Histories, p. 1056.
_ Annals of Socialist Inquiry, Abstracts of Reports to the
    CCCP/USSA, vol. 12, Christian Nonconformists: Are They a
    Threat to the State?, p. 540.
_ Annals of Socialist Inquiry, Abstracts of Reports to the
    CCCP/USSA, vol. 13, Psychiatric Methods in Criminal Social
    Deviance, A Treatment Methodology, p. 1028.

When he pressed the space bar the screen filled with another page of citations. And then another. He placed a d before the last one and pressed the blue key.

The Role of the Myth of Jesus Christ in Lunatic Cults: A Historical Perspective, by C. A. Lermontov, Vice-Minister of Information, North-Central Region, CCCP/USSA. [This report was abstracted from the proceedings of the 23rd Plenary Session of the CCCP/USSA.]

Marxism-Leninism shows us the proper methodology for analyzing "religious" phenomena. We are all familiar with the narcotic role of religion in prerevolutionary eras. We know that its sole purpose was to distract (by subtle chicanery and lies) the proletarian masses from their revolutionary purpose. In a socialist state there is no need for narcotics! Marxist-Leninist historical truth unerringly shows us the way.

Unfortunately, religious cults have not been relegated to the status of mere historical curiosities. They have become the vehicle through which dangerous criminal lunatic groups are spreading their antisocialist lies. The most pernicious of these cults, the so-called Christians (after their namesake, the mythical Jesus Christ), have been systematically attempting (fortunately without real success) to undermine the efforts of our honest and loyal comrades in the Party who have been working to make certain that the inevitable triumph of correct Marxist-Leninist thought is quickly achieved. In spite of these heroic efforts, poisonous lies are being spread by underground fanatics. Their priests, contrary to the correct teachings of Marxism-Leninism, are attempting to create a parasitic shadow that feeds off of and mocks socialist society. Moreover, these priests, who abstain from women in favor of men, are spreading the worst kind of diseased perversion to our young men.

While there is no doubt that this perversion will be speedily stamped out, in the meanwhile we must be continuously vigilant for evidence of knowledge of or participation in cult crimes.

Without indicating what they are used for, police and other officials should be alerted regarding certain Christian paraphernalia, such as crosses, rosaries, candles, and hymnals and other religious texts. Perhaps a special KGB group could be created to infiltrate and root out these fanatics.

He entered another d before pressing the blue key.

Psychiatric Methods in Criminal Social Deviance, a Treatment Methodology, by Boris Brown, M.D., Director, Mir Psychiatric Institute. [This report was abstracted from the proceedings of the 40th Plenary Session of the CCCP/ USSA.]

The treatment and normalization of criminal social deviants, in particular those patients who have fallen under the spell of dangerous criminal cults such as Christianity, is of great importance to the effective growth of correct Marxist-Leninist thought.

It should be recognized from the outset that cult criminals are not very different from patients suffering from standard psychiatric disorders. An inventory of typical cult beliefs points out that they are essentially delusional paranoids:

1. The universe was created by a god (primitive cults always suppose that some homomorphic god has created the world) and Jesus Christ is his son (and also a god!).

2. Individual acts of conscience take precedence over decisions regarding the collective good. (A perverse obsession with antisocialist individualism is a classic cult symptom.)

3. God controls history. Moreover, this "god" will assist you if you pray to him, that is, beg him for favors. (This clearly conflicts with the correct Marxist-Leninist view of history and is inimical to the proper development of socialist society.)

4. Believers in this god will live forever. (That this is a scientific absurdity is obvious.)

5. Jesus Christ came to earth as a man and was sacrificed so that those who believe in him might live forever. (More fanatical believers drink blood in celebration of this "sacrifice.")

Notice the conformity with classical paranoia! This observation makes it clear that the preferred clinical treatment plan will be identical with that prescribed for standard paranoid schizophrenics: psychotropic drugs, shock therapy (good results have been achieved here!), and surgery. The last procedure is 100 percent effective but has obvious drawbacks. Hence it should be reserved for only the most severe cases.

What a friend we have in Jesus,
All our sins and griefs to bear.
What a privilege to carry
Everything to God in prayer.

No wonder Corinne was acting so strangely. She must be one of them. These Christians. Amazing. Why had he never heard of them before. And Piotr Babulieski. And Father Paul. All Christians. And lunatics. Yes. That explained The Book. And the rest of it.

bibliographical search
SUBJECT/AUTHOR/TITLE
subject
DO YOU WISH TO BE PROMPTED?
no
ENTER SUBJECT.
new york city
THERE ARE 0 TITLES ON THE SUBJECT NEW YORK CITY.

"Are you home so soon, Nurov?"
He hadn't heard her come in.
"Oh, Alex. At work already on your preparation."
He froze at the keyboard.
"There's a little sun," crossing the threshold, "what do you think of a swim?"
Stumbling, "That would be great."

logoff

"Don't be long." At the desk, "There's just a smidgen of sun today."

CONNECT TIME 1 HOURS 19 MINUTES

"I'm," he flicked the off/on switch, "finished."
The panic escaped like air from a balloon. He got up and very coolly went to his room and changed.

216

"Will we be going back to the mountains again soon?" he asked casually.

"Do you want to?" She was wearing her emerald-green suit; it clung to her like two swatches of fresh seaweed. Not waiting for him to answer, "Your friend may not have enjoyed herself. Did she say?"

"I didn't see her today. She must have gone in by Zlotny." Annoyed with himself for explaining pointlessly, "Being on crutches and all."

With a knowing air, "Just as well. I suspect she tells her father everything anyway."

"I suppose," he replied with an unpleasant sense of realization.

"But," she began to jog, "if you want, we can."

Tentatively, "I enjoyed talking to Grandfather Simpson."

Breathing hard, "Oh?"

"Well, he remembers a lot of things."

Slowing, "What kind of things?"

"Nothing in particular." With a burst, "See you there."

"Will you, now?"

The water, electric-cold, seemed to explode from within, radiating toward his skin and escaping into the ocean.

Panting as she treaded water, "So, what kind of stories has he been telling you?"

"Nothing really."

"Well, he's an old man. It's not wise to pay too much attention to him. And," with melancholy turn of the mouth, "he drinks too much."

Alex dove under the water; he could feel thousands of tiny explosions going off in his head: boom, boom, pow! Air. And then again. Boom, boom, pow! Treading water, feeling as if he was going to faint, "Yes, I know. But," carefully, "there is still something interesting about him."

Her lips had turned purple and were trembling. It was clearly consuming every bit of her energy just to tread water.

With a sudden attack of bravery, "What was it like," he slowed down, "before?"

"Before what?" she prompted, bobbing up over a ground swell as it rolled past them.

217

"Before you got married," he scrambled, altering the course of the question to something old and familiar.

"I was a typist." She adjusted one of the long blond braids that snaked around her head, causing her to sink a little. "At the Ministry." She typed mindlessly on the curving surface of the water. "But you know that."

He waited.

"I met your father there. And he," she smiled like a young girl, "rescued me."

"From what?" he asked. Even though he had heard her say that a dozen times he had never gone beyond that simple metaphorical statement, which seemed to close off the subject the way a low ivy wall separates passersby from a flower bed.

"From finger exhaustion," she replied before vanishing into the ocean. When she came back up she pointed to the shore and, with the help of a strong, low wave, breast-stroked her way toward land.

Persisting, while she rubbed a dry, what felt like hot, but wasn't, towel across his back and shoulders, "And before that?" She rubbed even harder, bringing the blood to the surface. "Before you were at the Ministry," pulling his back away, "exhausting your fingers."

"I was at school," drying herself with the same towel, "where I studied very hard." She sounded absurdly grave. "And learned," she looked up, bent at the waist, the towel covering her shin, "not to ask silly questions."

"I'm just curious." Tentatively, "You were an American then." That sounded so silly. "You are now, I guess. You know what I mean."

"Yes." She extended the towel toward his chest and began mopping him off. "That was a long time ago. And," he looked down at the towel, which she had gripped in both hands as if she were scrubbing a huge floor, "being young is being young." In the elbow crease of her arm there was a small, blue bruise, which appeared and disappeared, like a winking, mischievous child, as she moved the towel across him. "Which is what you are now. And should," he stepped back the instant he realized what the bruise was, "be enjoying."

First there was a rush of anger, almost jealousy. "Before," she went on, not noticing a thing, "you are forced to take on more serious responsibilities." Then embarrassment: it was as if she were standing

218

there bare-breasted (her nipples had jutted out, quivered, as she expelled that long, screaming sigh), right in front of him. Beginning to sense something was amiss, but persisting, "I know it doesn't seem fair. But you are one of the generation that must do it. If it's going to," he had already backed up three or four feet, so that the towel, still tightly in the grip of her two hands, was pressed, absurdly, motionlessly, against only the air, "be done at all. And, more than anything," her voice took on a pleading tone, "you are of the right blood." Elongating her neck, "I have seen to that."

Without another word he began to run. At first just slowly, but gradually faster and faster until he was galloping. By the time he reached the row of small, sea-oats-topped dunes which skirted the high-tide line like kids frightened of the surf, that sense of paralyzing embarrassment had vanished. He stopped and, astride one of the five-or-six-foot-tall dunes, hollered out, "I don't understand why you have to be so damned sad." She was walking toward him, slowly, gracefully, apparently totally composed, her head cast slightly downward as if she were interested in the sand. "I don't see why. You have everything." The wind had picked up. Perhaps she couldn't even hear him? There was no sign she had. She just walked toward him, in that same comfortable, swaying gait.

When she reached him she said, "It's my fault," as she slipped her cool arm around his shoulder. "I forget you are still a boy." As they walked arm in arm, "And my son. I spend too much time treating you like a little brother instead of a son."

"No," he replied, suddenly feeling responsible for her happiness.

"It's not fair to you. I forget how hard," she tightened her fingers around his shoulder, "it can be to grow up."

He consoled her with, "I guess," masking from her the fact that that had had nothing to do with anything. "Was that hard for you?" he asked, continuing the deception.

"Oh, yes. Agonizingly." Laughing lightly, "But it came to me later, much later, what had to be done."

They meandered, arm in arm, like a funny four-legged crab, astride the too-narrow footpath, so that twice they had to stop to remove stickers, laughing, cheerfully lying.

Why did she have to be so sad? It was always there. Hiding in the recesses of her eyes. Or in the corners. In a line or two.

Always. Except. There was no point in thinking about that. No.

He hated it that the walk from the dunes to the house was so short. Inside everything would go back to the way it was.

During dinner, he found himself watching Corinne. As always she carried out the food in serving dishes and vanished to the other side of the kitchen door.

"Looks delightful, Corinne," his mother remarked.

"Yes," Nurov agreed.

If she was some sort of loony it was beyond him to see it. Kerelsky had been a surprise. Yes. But only beforehand. The minute you heard it, especially after that last day, it made perfectly good sense. But Corinne?

Her big, chocolate hands delivered extra lemon for the grouper. Filled the tea pitcher. Everything was done with the same slow, steady regularity that inspired complete confidence: tick, stop, tick. With three cups of banana pudding on a small tray: tick, stop, tick; tick, stop, tick.

But they were dangerous. There had been attacks. Not often. But they had happened. And the police were always on the alert for them. He avoided her eyes so that she would have no idea he was watching.

How ridiculous. Certainly she couldn't be a threat. After all, she had had a thousand opportunities to poison them. He found himself laughing out loud:

"Poisoned grouper?"

"Yes," the policeman replied.

"Another lunatic?"

They were sprawled out across the table, perversely contorted, their hands at their throats.

"Yes. She had been with them for fifteen years."

The Case of the Lunatic Maid!

"You seem to be enjoying your pudding, Alexander."

"Yes, Father."

Perhaps she had just heard the song. No. That didn't really make sense. But neither did anything else.

Chapter 9

He had spent the week, after school each day, using his father's authorization code and password, searching the DAL system for any clue about New York City. That, more than any of the other questions that had arisen, had plagued him. Had it existed, or was it a delusional creation of Piotr Babulieski? One hour he was convinced of one thing; the next, another.

And now he knew no more than when he had begun. Not really. What did he want to find out, anyway? Had The Book, with all its anti-Soviet propaganda, and antisocialist lies, warped his mind so much that he was now thinking like some lunatic himself?

In the beginning, he had been merely trying to confirm that it was all, a lie. After all, it had to be. But in moments of weakness, he wondered. And then he wondered if even wondering was all wrong. And then half an hour later he would search maps of the state of New York again, figuring that maybe that one would have it.

Of course, if The Book was right, there would be no such place. Not any longer. But there would be some mention of it. Before. If twelve million people had lived here.

He shuddered. Hiroshima flashed across his mind as brightly as a fireball. That, and the other one, at Nagasaki, had been the only ones.

And the capitalists had done that. To one another. That was, after all, the kind of inevitable contradiction that arose from capitalist exploitation.

There was nothing there because there was nothing to be there.

The huge mushroom cloud engulfed the sky; within it, those who were not vaporized had their skins peeled off. And the ground was poisoned by radiation. Forever? No. Maybe not. But for a long time.

There were only three possibilities: the J-Corps Military District, the Patrice Lumumba Bird Preserve, and a third, triangular area, marked in red—Restricted Area. The rest was covered with people or towns or cities or something. They were the only places where something that large could be hidden.

Hidden? Could something that monstrous be hidden? Perhaps. If it had to be. Of course, even if it had happened there must have been a reason.

At lunch on Wednesday he had raised that question with Myslov. Hypothetically.

"If something awful, really awful, has to be done—I mean this only hypothetically, of course—in order for the truth to prevail. Do you think that's all right?"

Myslov had tugged thoughtfully at his scarf for a second or two before replying: "What is right, if that is what you mean by the truth, will prevail as a consequence of inexorable historical processes. What individuals feel about that is of no real consequence." Smiling, "We are all participants in history. We do our part. But the river flows. With or without us."

"But someone has to . . ." he had begun before stopping himself. Yes. That had been the right thing to do. There was no point in pressing things like that. Myslov might get the wrong idea. "Yes. That's true. I suppose the question was a silly question," he had said.

"Well, perhaps," Myslov had agreed, with self-satisfaction. Confidently, "Have I showed you this new variation of the Queen's Indian I've been working on?" He was not accustomed to being right, and even though he did not linger on the point, it was apparent that he enjoyed the experience.

Today there was no hope of continuing the search. Not with his father asleep right down the hall. No. And the dune was no solace: the backyard was buried in thick, misting fog that was sure to hang over the island until noon. Or later.

He meandered into the kitchen. Poked around in the refrigerator. Took out an apple. And then quickly walked across the room to the counter, where he emptied two cups of ground coffee into a plastic bag, sealed it shut, and inserted it into the breast pocket of his jumpsuit. With a rush of excitement he crept down the hallway, fetched his slicker, and, with that same controlled but about to explode stride, slipped back up the hallway and out the door into the glowing, bright-as-a-lightbulb mist.

You couldn't see fifty meters.

It was not until he was on the bus that he admitted where he was going. Until then, in that funny way that self-deception works, he was able to collect the coffee, and his jacket, without allowing the thought of what he was doing to completely form in his mind. The actions themselves each occurred, step by step, purposefully, but in a totally disconnected way that allowed him to walk guiltlessly through each step without admitting what it all added up to.

And why? There was nothing really wrong with what he was doing. Nothing at all. Apart perhaps from the coffee. And what was a small bag of coffee? Nothing.

But he was sure that he didn't want them to find out. In fact, the idea alone produced a kind of sick embarrassment which haunted him in successive, abating waves as the electric bus hummed its way through the cocoonlike mist to the mainland.

At the apex of the first hump of the big bridge they burst through the fog into a rainstorm of blue-skied sunlight. He pressed his face to the window. Below, the river had been replaced by white, glowing fog, which looked as solid as earth. And behind him the same. The island itself, six or seven kilometers away, its view obscured even on a crystal-blue day, seemed to be lurking right there, just out of sight, beneath the mist. But instead of a long, narrow strip of real sand, with wooden stick-legged houses, and people, with three-day-old Russian newspapers spread out across the kitchen table, he saw abstract, concentric ellipses of alternating red, green, and white, labeled with elevations and temperatures and rock formations.

Bayshore, West Sayville, Bayport. Westhampton. Southampton, East Hampton.

The bus descended into the mist. They were in the dead center of the river, which could have been touching the bus's wheels, or been a million miles below—or above. The little bus strained, its electric voice changing from a purr to a tomcat's screech.

Don't break. Dammit. Not today.

But it did. The driver propped his feet up on the dashboard before picking up the radio receiver.

What luck!

223

Leaning comfortably back into the seat, his feet still on the dashboard, "I wouldn't go out there. You might get hit." His duty discharged, the driver pushed his cap over his eyes.

"I'll stay on the sidewalk," Alex replied for no real reason. The driver had that American talent for instant sleep.

He climbed upward, dancing his finger along the wet metal railing, looking back from time to time at the red flashing bus, whose signal, as he rose, became weaker and weaker until only a fuzzy, intermittent warning glow remained. A Zlotny zipped by. And another. Their windshield wipers sounded like hard, short breaths. Gradually as he climbed, the mist thinned, until at the crest of the ancient metal bridge he could see the city. Untouched by the mist, as if it were a slightly tawdry, cellophane-wrapped present, Charleston stretched along the river, consisting first only of piers and docks and two large, flat ships stacked with containers. Farther upriver buildings appeared. Even the horse-drawn carriages were clearly visible. It was, he decided while trying to make out the building she lived in, like looking into a telescope that peered into time. So much of it was old. Even, as Martina Antipova pointed out, run-down and shoddy. But there was something about it that appealed to him. And that he would miss, like an old shirt or sweater.

His arm wrapped around one of the huge, cold joists, he traced his way, street by street, to her apartment. He could see the metal stairs. The funny, square, chopped-off room she lived in. What an odd room. It made no sense at all, sitting there astride the roof like an oversized fireless chimney or a child's misplaced block. Why was it there at all?

And then it came to him: they pulled down the steeples from the churches; ripped out the bells from the towers.

Yes. That was it. He framed the tiny apartment in the notch between his thumb and forefinger. Yes. That was exactly what it was: a church. Suddenly he felt quite pleased with himself. The way he sometimes did when he had solved one of his mysteries.

He descended the long, curving bridge at a near gallop and then headed down the peninsula to her apartment. The whole time he was barely able to contain his excitement. Yes, that's exactly what it was, he repeated to himself half a dozen times.

But before he turned onto her street the submariner came to mind.

224

He stopped. Then started up again—but just walking. If he was there he would . . . well, he wasn't sure what he'd do. In any case there was no point in worrying about that.

When he turned into the driveway he first checked to see if the Zlotny was there, and when it was not he locked his eyes on what he was sure had been a steeple, and breathlessly clanked his way up the stairs.

He rapped on the glass.

After a minute or two her face appeared. She frowned sleepily and then opened the door.

"Hi," he announced excitedly.

Retreating into semidarkness, "Come in." She crumpled onto the mattress before complaining, "Don't you ever sleep in?"

Distracted by the room, which he quickly measured with his eye, "Yes. Well, not often."

"Saturdays are for sleeping in. Especially," she narrowed her eyes into half almonds, "when there's not a drop of coffee."

"There's coffee."

He unzipped his jumpsuit, extracted the coffee, and tossed it to her.

Bobbling the package for a second, "Damn."

It was not until he was sitting in the rocker that he noticed that she was wearing the navy shirt.

She held the clear plastic package in her palm and bounced it up and down. "This is half a kilo of coffee," she announced with a waking amazement.

"Were you asleep? Till just now," he found himself asking. His attention seemed to be ricocheting from the black navy blouse to the room.

Stretching back onto the mattress and placing the coffee on her chest, "I'm not even sure I'm not dreaming now."

Alex puzzled for an instant: certainly she wouldn't invite him in if her friend was just out for a second. And besides, he wouldn't go out without his shirt.

"Why are you all the way over there?" she asked with a catlike yawn.

He shrugged.

"The early morning like this is a good time to cuddle."

225

With mild annoyance, "Is it?"

"You are a strange one, Alex."

He shrugged.

"Well, what you need," she kept him in suspense for a heartbeat, "is . . . something . . . sweet." She immediately sprang up. "Doesn't that sound irresistible?"

"That's an odd shirt to be wearing. For a girl."

"Oh, this. It's great, isn't it?" With that she unbuttoned two buttons and, squeezing her shoulders together, let it drop to the ground. Shivering, "The inside of me must still be asleep."

Persisting, "I didn't know they issued Soviet navy blouses to," he paused, "American girls."

She wrinkled her nose. And then shrugged before picking up her yellow jumpsuit from the floor and slipping it on.

When it was apparent he expected an answer, "What are you, the police?"

A little surprised, "No."

"Look, my brother found it. And he gave it to me." Her palms turned up nonchalantly, "Turn me in for not being a perfect citizen."

Maybe that was where it came from. It was just that for some reason it seemed very important that she tell him the truth.

Impatiently, "Do you want to go get something sweet?"

"Yes," he replied without thinking about it.

She smiled with that same wrinkle of her nose. "Then let's go." She slipped the coffee into her pocket.

After they were on the landing, she reopened the door. "Damn. That breeze is like a can opener. I won't be but a minute."

He followed her back in with his eyes. And then resurveyed the apartment. Yes. He could feel the excitement he had felt earlier racing back in like the tide. It had been a steeple. Or a place where they hung bells.

Pulling a purple sweatshirt over her head, "I don't know how you kept from freezing."

"I walked fast," he replied, before noticing, between his legs, that the Zlotny was there. Right at the foot of the landing.

"Well, come on."

It would serve her right to be caught like this. At least she wasn't wearing that shirt. The man might, in a fit of rage, tear it right off her.

226

She blithely skipped down the stairs.

From the first landing he peered directly into the windshield. It was empty. He felt his chest relax. Still, as they passed by the vacant, shiny old car he kept his distance.

"Nice, isn't it?" she commented, mistaking his caution for admiration.

Wondering, while he regained his composure, how she could be so cool, "Yes. It's in very good shape."

"She washes it twice a week," she observed critically.

"She?"

"The block commander." In a half-whisper, "I think it's only an excuse to watch the doors. As if there were something," more loudly, "to see around here."

He stood for a moment, looking at the old Zlotny, feeling like a complete fool, while she hurried him with, "Let's get going. I'm weak for something sweet." With a laugh, "After that I might have the energy to surprise you."

"I don't remember there being a food distribution center along here," he questioned.

She turned to give him a disbelieving look, but kept his hand in tow until they got to a small alleyway. As soon as they turned in he recognized the shoulder-width brick path as the one the carriage driver had gone into for carrots. After about twenty meters it made a ninety-degree turn to the right. Three or four men were milling about just past the turn.

"Hi, Celly," one acknowledged as they passed.

She responded with a casual wave.

"They have," he paused awkwardly, "sweets here?"

Replicating the disbelieving look, "We'll never know if we don't stop being silly."

The path opened into a rectangular courtyard about the size of a very large room. There were several dozen tables on which were scattered mostly vegetables. On one were seven or eight chickens. Another had a radio with earphones and two very old television sets. One man gestured at a stack of broccoli as they passed. The woman behind the table with the radio said, "It's stereo. Want to try it?" As Celeste walked by she offered confidentially, "Fifteen rubles," but Celeste zipped by as if the woman weren't there.

227

Making a point not to appear shocked, he nonchalantly followed at her heels until she stopped at the last table. As soon as she picked up one of the dozen or so jars that were scattered across the table, a man, who up until that time had been leaning against the brick wall, said, "Buying, Celly? Or just waking up your tastebuds?"

"Swapping."

Suspiciously, "Swapping what?"

"Coffee," she replied confidently.

It took fifteen minutes of haggling to get one jar of marmalade, and another ten to get half a pound cake. Several times she looked at him and said, "Let's go. I don't have time to listen to this shit." But when he did take a step or two she tugged surreptitiously on his sleeve.

"After what you said about that cake I'm not sure I can eat it," he remarked with a laugh as soon as they got back onto the street.

"You've got to talk down the goods," she replied slyly. "But then, you know that. You're the one. Always acting like you don't know what's going on. And then showing up with half a kilo of coffee!" She spun around in the street before grabbing his hand. "And now let's eat till we're sick."

Later, with her feet propped up on the first rung of the rocker, "Soon, when I get my new job, I'm going to eat jam or jelly every day."

He almost burst out into laughter but stopped himself after arousing only a "What's so funny about that?" A second or two later, "You'll see. It's a sure thing." She snapped her finger. "So don't jinx me by laughing."

When they had stuffed themselves with pound cake smeared with marmalade she put some aside with, "I'll save this for Sasha. He's a bit of a loon, but he loves sweets almost as much as I do."

He waited for her to say more, but instead she pushed herself up onto the counter and beckoned him with her finger. When he was close enough she pulled his face up to her and kissed him on the lips. "Right now, now that I've got something to fight back with, I'd like to go back out—maybe over to the river—and let the wind blow in my face." Wrinkling her nose, "Okay?"

"Sure," he shrugged, wishing that they could just stay there.

228

As if she could read his mind, "And then, when we get back, it'll be time for your surprise." She opened her eyes very wide for a second and then jumped down onto the floor.

She checked the seal on the coffee bag, which was still four-fifths full, before sliding it into the cabinet. He couldn't help but be amazed by how much completely trivial things like coffee and sweets meant to her. He was sure she almost caressed the coffee before withdrawing her hand.

They half ran down the block to Battery Park, slicing through the stern, windswept heroes of the revolution as if they were trees or shrubs.

"Well, comrade. Ready for another tour?"

She turned before he did.

"My special, for young lovers, afternoon price, is—"

Interrupting, "Why don't you go out and hustle up a nice fat Bulgarian tourist, Sasha? Then you could pay me the ten rubles you owe me."

Totally relaxed, reclining, just as he had been that morning, against the man-sized leg of the General Secretary, "And leave all the Russians to you, I suppose."

"You're hopeless, Sasha."

"I can't help it if I've become bitter. And dissolute." He pushed the black stovepipe hat back with his thumb. "They've turned," he paused, as if he were testing Alex's eyes, "all our women into whores."

Why was he looking at him when he said that? Alex wondered.

"But can we blame them? Big strong," he paused, "men."

"Big, strong," he paused again, "cunts." In an absurdly philosophical vein, "Ah, now that's historical necessity! Or would that be just plain dialectical materialism?"

"You're drunk again, Sasha."

Aggressively, "So?"

"Come on, Alex." With a shrug, "Pay no attention to him."

"How cozy."

Like a schoolteacher, "If the SP see you it's back to the center. Or worse."

Sasha, looking up into the sky, raised his palm in a show of complete nonchalance.

"Forget him," she said with disgust, her hand extended to Alex. "I've given up worrying about him."

With surprise, "My, what huge nose hairs you have, beloved General Secretary. And a cock to match, I'm sure."

With Alex in tow, "He's harmless. He just becomes a whining baby when he's drunk."

"Perhaps you should pose with your pants down, beloved General Secretary. As an example!"

After they were out of earshot, "He sounds much worse than he is, really. It's when he's drinking that he gets out of hand. Sometimes I wonder if another stay at the reeducation center wouldn't be best." With a pained sigh that seemed to be aimed directly at him, "Before it's too late."

As if it were a trapeze bar, she swung under the lower rung of the railing, and, using it for an armrest, she dangled her feet over the edge of the concrete retaining wall a meter above the river. "You don't suppose it's too late already, do you? He's not really that bad." Catching his eye, "So long as no one gets the wrong idea."

Taking note of what she was saying, "Perhaps not. But," recalling his experience from the carriage tour, "someone is sure to notice." Firmly, but in a philosophical tone, "He routinely makes very thinly disguised antisocialist and anti-Soviet remarks."

Satisfied that he had summed up the problem completely, he rested his head against the railing so that their eyes were only two shoulder widths apart.

"Well, there's no point in letting him get me in trouble." She rubbed her nose with the back of her hand. "Brother or not."

"No," he agreed before realizing what she had said.

"No point at all."

The eyes were the same. And the nose.

"But it's so difficult when someone is your brother." When he did not respond she continued, "You know how one fuck-up can ruin an entire family. They mark it down against you. I know they do." Bluntly, "Maybe I should do it myself. Before someone else does."

"No," he protested spontaneously. "I mean, there must be another way."

With determination, "I don't know how to deal with it myself. I'm up against the wall."

230

He stared out across the river. It was packed with small, frothy whitecaps, each, it seemed, fighting for breathing space. Choking one another to death.

"Doing nothing is risky." As if she were talking to herself, so that he was sharing her secret thoughts, "Very risky. And probably wrong. After all, they might be able to do something for him."

Did she always weigh everything so carefully? He pictured her, with her hand extended, saying, "My hand is a scale." Yes, that is exactly what she had said about the coffee. That first day.

Cautiously, averting her eyes from his before she spoke, "Do you really think it's fair? To hold what your family does against you?" Persisting, "What would you think, if someone in your family was a little loony, and you knew they were going to hold it against you?"

He could feel the excitement, which, along with the coffee, had given his skin a warm, tingling aliveness, evaporate into fear. Not just because of her. Or even Sasha. Not just because they were dangerous to be around, but because he found himself wanting to know more and more about them.

"I'd better be heading back," he announced awkwardly. "I have a lot of studying to do."

But by the time he was halfway across the bridge that black naval blouse had slid off her shoulders a dozen times—leaving him in complete confusion.

At dinner he was so knotted with guilt that the food would barely slide down his throat. He couldn't look at his mother at all.

The topic for Sunday's Young Pioneers meeting, haughtily presided over by Block Commander Gregorov (he must have shined his lapel button for the entire morning; it looked as if it had been chipped off a solar flare), was Vigilance and Self-Discipline. Gregorov summed it up by saying, "Vigilance with regard to others; vigilance with regard to yourself. Insidious wrong thinking grows silently, invisibly. Like fungus on a loaf of bread, which seems one morning to have engulfed the entire loaf in a single night, wrong thinking incubates, multiplies, grows microscopically, long before obvious symptoms appear." How long had it taken him to memorize that? Alex wondered. Not that it wasn't true. It was just that it was disgusting to have to listen to Gregorov pretend to think.

Tuesday they were shown a film on the dangers of sexual promiscuity. Martina Antipova watched from across the small auditorium, surrounded by a gaggle of her friends, including Fat Fede, but when she saw him she slowed down to wait for him.

"Hello, Alexander."

"Hi," he returned uncomfortably.

"I just wanted to say that," she paused, "I enjoyed the weekend in the mountains immensely."

"Yes, me too," he struggled.

"And," tilting her ankle out toward him, "that, even though it still looks disgusting, is completely healed."

"Good."

"So maybe we can go hiking again. And I'll promise to," her chest flushed, perhaps from talking to him in such close proximity to the film, or perhaps from the thought that she had done something as unathletic as fall while diving, "be less trouble."

With a shrug, "I'm just glad you're recovered."

"Thank you." Drifting toward the door, "I'd better not be late."

He smiled.

Melting into a clump of students, "I guess you've been studying a lot."

He nodded.

When she turned, he could see her head, above the other girls, bobbing slightly—left to right; left to right. Perhaps the sprain wasn't completely healed, he decided before heading toward the door.

Wednesday, right after school, on the first day of basketball practice, he went to Celeste's apartment. She wasn't there. He left three oranges neatly stacked inside the screen door and raced back for the last half of practice. Coach Williams was looking right at him when he said, "This year, if we are going to win games, it will come through dedication and self-discipline."

Practice meant he got home too late Thursday and Friday to even think about entering the DAL system. That was just as well. He was feeling a lot better just pushing that out of his mind. And tomorrow would be Saturday.

He took some cookies, a mayonnaise jar of milk, coffee, and two apples, caught the first bus to the mainland, and was at her apartment at eight-thirty. After waiting ten minutes he climbed the stairs, quietly, wondering at each landing which door was the block commander's.

She made him lie there, very still, for an hour while she slept. He studied the ceiling of the room. Measured it, wondering what had gone on in it years ago, when it was a bell tower or steeple. Obviously they rang bells. But why?

In the course of the day, they had sex three times. Each time in a different position. So that, when they finished, he would be "totally experienced."

Around three, while they had coffee, this time with milk, he asked, "Have you ever been in the rest of this building? Downstairs."

"No."

Explaining, "I was just curious. It's a very nice building."

Before he left she said, "I'm not going to be working next week. If you want to you can come by." Without waiting for him to respond, "I'm not laying out or anything. I don't want you to think I'm some kind of parasite." Proudly, "I have a new job."

"Great."

"At the navy base," she continued, before adding with obvious self-satisfaction, "Just the job I wanted."

"I'm sure that's a step up."

"Yes." Stretched out on her small mattress, as he was pulling the door to, "Do you have any more of those cookies? The ones with chocolate. I don't know how you get things like that." Thoughtfully, "You must be the best swapper I've ever met. Better than me. Or even Sasha. Funny, you don't look like it." Smiling, so that the tiny gaps between her teeth showed, "But you're cute."

Half a dozen times over the weekend he wondered if her friend had gotten her the job. Not that he was jealous. Not really. It was just that he didn't like the idea that he, this blank, who perhaps (assuming that had been his shirt? Of course, Sasha may have found it in the carriage) was large, but about whom he knew nothing else, could do something so important for her. And he could not.

Monday, the second time down the court, he sprained his ankle. He had seen Griminsky's foot, waiting there to ambush him; nevertheless, for reasons he couldn't be sure of himself, he did nothing to avoid coming down on it.

"Ice that, Nurov," Coach Williams ordered. "And keep that laced until you get the ice ready."

Halfway down the stairs he unlaced the shoe.

Without giving the ice a second thought he showered and went to Celeste's. By the time he arrived the ankle was the size of a small fist.

She was concerned enough to play nurse while he lounged about the room, drinking coffee. Before he left she had sex with him, insisting that, as part of his treatment, he be completely still. Sitting astride him, her only observable movement was to rub her freshly licked fingertips in tiny circles over her nipples; the rest occurred invisibly and without any apparent expenditure of energy. She tilted her head to the side and smiled when he came. The smile seemed to say, "See how easy that was." That she could do something like that left him amazed. And mystified.

The room felt very warm. But only in a comfortable, friendly way.

Alex sipped the vodka—which had been acquired for six perfect grapefruit. It was a good thing that yesterday was his last day for crutches or he would never have been able to manage getting them out of the house. He looked up at his still slightly swollen ankle and laughed to himself. Too bad he didn't have a huge chair to lean back in. Like Martina Antipova.

He could still see that huge foot looming over the conversation like a satellite. That was the last time things had been . . . what? Normal? Yes. But the next day, up popped Gustavus Roman. And after that, nothing was the same. Yesterday morning, comparing injuries on the bus (trying to act as if everything was fine: although he could tell she was aware of the strain too—and had no idea what it was all about), she seemed a complete stranger. She might as well have been Chinese, he said to himself, which led to the shuddering thought that next year he would be surrounded by Martina Antipovas. And Gregorovs. Or worse.

"More, Alex." Sasha extended his glass without getting up. "Just slide the bottle over."

When Alex attempted to slide the half-full bottle across the room with his toe it tipped over.

234

"Damn." Sasha quickly righted the bottle.

"You've had enough anyway, Sasha."

"Enough. Did you see how I scooped that up? Why, I could be an athlete. If I didn't have to spend all my time working."

"Working?" She was stretched out perpendicular to Alex, her head resting on his thigh.

"Alex, I ask you. Were those the reflexes of a drunk?"

"No," he replied with a laugh, thinking as he did how comfortable he was listening to them argue like children. Yes. That—and the vodka—was totally relaxing. And in a way vastly more productive than plowing through documents in the DAL system. And what had he learned there? Nothing really. Nothing as concrete as what he had learned just being there. In that little room. That had been a steeple. Or a place where they hung bells. Now why they did that was . . .

"I rest my case."

"At least you've used the right word," she sniped, before musing out loud, "I'd love to see your attendance record."

"Mine? Is yours any better? How many days have you missed this week playing nursemaid? And how many others imagining that some white knight is going to rescue you?"

"I'm going to hear about my new job any day now," she replied angrily.

"Of course. I suspect you'll get a personal call from General Secretary Ouspensky," he taunted. Grinning, "If there was a phone in this damned matchbox."

The grin seemed especially aimed at Alex—or was he just imagining?

"You'll see," she replied, snuggling into his thigh.

"See? The only thing I see is that navy blouse. That's not much to show for being a slut."

Chapter 10

"Why, why, why?" Nurov exclaimed, using the word as if it were a battering ram. "Are they blind?"

"Does that even require comment?" she soothed.

"Blind idiots!"

Sincerely, "You are a man of vision, Nurov." She lifted her soup spoon to her mouth and tasted. "Very good."

"Soup? Is that all that concerns you?"

"No. I am not taking you lightly." Confidently, but in a way that suggested further discussion was irrelevant, "On the contrary, I am sure you will find a way to persuade them."

"Politics!" To Alexander, "Be happy you are going to be an engineer. The headaches there are manageable. In my work I am surrounded by knuckleheads."

His mother looked from over her soup patiently.

"They act as if five billion rubles were all the money in the world."

Lightly, "It's not?"

"Certainly not the way some of us spend."

"I thought," haughtily, "you took pleasure in the few things you have given me."

Dismissing her with a tired wave, "I have. I have."

"The table is not the place for discussion of this type anyway."

"This is where we always discuss things like this!"

"I know. And it's terrible for our digestion."

"Americans." Tapping the side of his head with his fist, "That's all they seem to care about. In the planning session with the Governor

236

this morning, all he could talk about was red snapper." Looking up at the ceiling disgustedly, "With shrimp sauce."

"Sounds delightful."

"How are we to come up with ideas to instill enthusiasm for the next regional five-year plan when all the damned Governor thinks about is red snapper," raising his voice, "with shrimp sauce?"

Tartly, "As Vice-Minister of Information it is your job to inspire him to think of other things."

"I will tell you, until the Party is willing to implement the DAL system, things will not change. Not one iota." Lecturing, "It is wrong thinking, this damned wrong thinking, that stops us at every turn. There is no other explanation. With the DAL system the party will be able to control and nurture in a completely unified and systematic way. And all this wrong thinking will just fade away. Not," he snapped his fingers, "like that. But, ultimately, it will vanish, because people will learn the right things. Without contamination. Or subversion."

His mother carefully placed her spoon on the plate beneath her bowl and, using the tips of her fingers on her palm, lightly applauded. "Now, use that on the General Secretary."

Completing his speech as if she had said nothing, "Now, what we have is: garbage in, garbage out!"

"Aptly put." Picking her spoon back up, "Especially for the dinner table."

Almost pleading, "I am right? There can't be another explanation, can there?" Narrowing his eyes, "It can't all just be genetic, can it?"

"What's that?"

"This damned criminal laziness. And carelessness. You don't think it's naturally rooted in the American psyche, do you?"

Refusing to be baited, "Are you enjoying your soup, Alexander?"

"It's fine," he replied reluctantly.

"You prove my point for me. Food? This? That? I am a man surrounded by quicksand, and all the victims do as they slide down into it is talk about food. Or the sun. Or whether it will rain. And all they think about is pilferage. Or laying out sick." Despairingly, "It makes no sense at all. Sixty-six years of revolution, and what do we have? Talk of red snapper. And soup. And petty conspiracies to cheat the state out of an afternoon's work. Don't they know that it merely

237

comes full circle? In the end, they pay. The lazy. And the industrious."

"Have you ever talked to any of them?" Amazed that he had said anything, "I wonder if you know them at all?"

"Do you?" Probing with his eyes, "What an odd question."

"It just," Alex stammered, "occurred to me."

"Did it? Well, I see the reports every day. The results. They are malingerers. And cheats. And petty thieves."

"Nurov." Indicating with her hand that he should lower his voice, "Corinne is in the kitchen."

"And why should that matter? You yourself said she has been stealing from us. They are all the same."

Whispering, "Corinne has always been marvelous."

"No. We have been marvelous to her. And she repays us with petty thievery." Shrilly, "Corinne!"

"I will handle this, Nurov."

"Corinne!"

She squeezed through the door, and, drying her big chocolate hands on her apron, approached the table.

"Corinne."

"Yes, sir."

"Why have you been stealing from us?"

Her round, brown face registered almost no reaction. After a second or two she looked over to his mother.

"There has been a mistake, Corinne. We can discuss it later."

"No. Now."

Her face began to look like a huge bowl of puzzled chocolate pudding.

"It has been brought to my attention that you have been stealing things from the kitchen."

"No, sir."

"Yes. It will be a lot easier for all of us if you just confess. Now."

Her eyes narrowed to slits, "What things?"

"Things like," he paused.

His mother rose. "I am going to my room."

"Things from the kitchen." Looking to Alex's mother for help, "What did you say was missing?"

Corinne stood there, helplessly, as his mother circled around the

238

table and escaped into the hallway. For a second she seemed a little shaken, but she then turned to Nurov, and, looking not directly at him but at the center of the table, in the neighborhood of the soup tureen, she repeated, "What things?"

"I suggest you list them for me."

Corinne stared blankly at the soup tureen.

"You will be better off if you do." Prying, "There are probably extenuating circumstances. I will take them into consideration. But first," he soothed, "you must confess. That will give us a place to start from."

He sat there impassively while his father asked her the same question in half a dozen different ways. Sometimes gently. Sometimes angrily.

Corinne denied everything. Each time. Alex found himself observing her. She was, after all, a member of some lunatic cult. But she did nothing to reveal herself. Nothing at all. In fact, the only strange thing was that she didn't seem especially afraid. Oh, her lip trembled once. And several times she seemed a little confused. But, considering what a powerful man his father was, she didn't seem very afraid. But then, neither did Piotr Babulieski.

What a friend we have in Jesus,
All our sins and griefs to bear.

He repeated the lines several times, in his head, loudly, drowning out the questions, wondering the whole time if she was doing that, or something like that.

"Out of my sight. Now." With exasperation, "And do not come back tomorrow. I will replace you with someone who doesn't steal. And lie—if there is such a person."

Alex was dumbfounded. Corinne had always been there.

Without replying, she turned and walked slowly back to the kitchen. With each pivot of her huge hips he expected his father to say something. To reconsider. To at least give her another chance to confess.

That's all she would have to do. He would be satisfied with that. Perhaps she didn't understand. Just confess, he repeated to himself. Just confess. It doesn't matter if it's true. Just confess.

As soon as she vanished into the kitchen, while he stacked the remnants of his dinner into a pile in the center of his plate, "You know why they don't trust me in Moscow? Why they think that I'm some sort of crackpot?" He shoved a spoonful of food into his mouth. "Because I'm here. In this forsaken place where nobody gives a damn." Touching his fingertips to the birthmark on his forehead, "In spite of this."

Alex stood.

"Don't," he latched his hand around Alex's wrist, "leave just yet." After gripping his wrist very tightly for a second or two he suddenly released it. "On second thought, go ahead."

Alex stepped toward the hallway, not certain whether to stay or leave.

"You didn't eat much," his father remarked. "How do you expect to grow if you don't eat? Corinne. Come put Alexander's plate in the refrigerator. His appetite might return later."

While she was crossing the room, Nurov stacked two rolls and a slice of pork on the plate.

"You can put some more beans on there too."

She silently spooned out a serving of beans and carried the plate into the kitchen.

From the far end of the dining room, near the hallway, "What will happen to her?"

"That is a problem for the Employment Commission." Looking directly into Alex's eyes, "Engineering is the career for you. Perhaps building bridges. Or roads. All the choices are neat and tidy."

He escaped to the bathroom, where he washed his face with ice-cold water. Should he have said anything? He stared at himself in the mirror. If they knew what she was really up to, things would have gone a lot worse for her. Yes. And if they knew about him? What would they do?

He walked down the hall to his mother's room. And knocked.

"Not now, Nurov." Without a hint of irritation, "I need to rest."

"It's me."

"Oh." Musically, "Just a moment." The door clicked and, apparently of its own accord, slowly opened, revealing the back of her emerald-green housecoat. She sat on the edge of the bed, pulled several large pillows around herself, leaned back, and, with a pat on the bedspread, indicated where he was to sit.

240

In disbelief, "Father has told Corinne she must leave."

"Oh." In the bored way a sleepy child might react, "Well, it would serve her right, wouldn't it?"

The look was unmistakable. Too distant. Too serene.

Looking down at the sleeve of her housecoat, "But what if she didn't do it? She said she didn't."

"Of course she said that."

Spiderwebs of gold and black stitching traversed the green silk like tangled, circular roads. He could remember sitting between her legs and running his small fingers along them until, always, he landed up right where he had started.

"There's no real proof. Is there?"

"Things are missing from the kitchen."

He sat there for a moment, waiting.

"I will," she smiled a very relaxed smile, "talk to Nurov."

Gloomily, "Will that do any good?"

Placing her hand on his shoulder, "He'll," smoothing the wrinkles from the fabric, "relent."

"You seem so sure."

As if it didn't matter at all, "He always does. He's," laughing, "not half the bear he makes himself out to be."

She pulled his head down onto her chest. She smelled of jasmine. Stroking his head, "You'll see."

Except her hands. Which smelled of the clinic. Or what she used to wash away the smell of the clinic. He could never decide.

He lay there, very still, but after a while he began to feel queasy. Perhaps it was the jasmine. He couldn't decide.

She barely seemed to notice when he slipped his head from under her hand and left.

He ran up the staircase just ahead of the deafening metallic roar. Rapped on the glass. Waited. Rapped again.

"Celeste," he hissed through the crack between the door and frame. And waited.

He bent his hands into goggles before pressing his face to the glass: the room was empty. The chair was gone. The part of the counter visible when he craned his neck was smoothly vacant. Even the hot plate was gone.

He collapsed onto the metal grate landing with his knees drawn up against his chest. Damn. He even had coffee, from the shiny, multi-aisled distribution center on the island. He could still feel the rush of fear that had hit when the clerk insisted on seeing his identification card. There, even though he was obviously entitled to be there—entitled, in fact, to buy anything there he wanted—he had been much more nervous than when he was with Celeste swapping. Of course, just some casual remark one of the clerks made and Corinne—no. Not to her. But, of course, she would be back. After a day or two.

He pushed himself up the wall, letting the boards click against his back one by one as he rose.

His forehead pressed to the windowpane, he searched the room again, but there was nothing to see. Not a hint that she had ever been there remained. He covered every square centimeter of the floor looking for a crumb, or a spoon, or a sock. Anything.

The Saturday before had been so great. At least up until the time Sasha mentioned that damned blouse. So what if she had lied about it? It was almost as if they couldn't help lying. After what had been done to them. And why was it so important that she tell the truth about that anyway?

Why did he have to be so ridiculous?

Just staring into the window created a swirl of recollections of sex with her. Of what she called "surprises."

He adjusted himself in his pants and descended.

By the time he reached the bottom landing he recalled asking, "Do you know what a church is?"

Why had he done such a stupid thing? It had been so easy, lying there close together.

She had just said, "No," and when he went on to say, "That's what this building was," she didn't seem particularly interested. No. She wouldn't remember that at all.

A woman of about forty stepped out from the azaleas as soon as his foot shuffled in the gravel. She held a spouting garden hose in her hand. She must be the block commander, he decided when she began squirting the hose at the stately Zlotny that occupied the yard's sole parking place.

"Good morning, comrade," she offered grimly, not seeming to take her eyes off a small spot on the Zlotny's hood. "Damned birds."

242

Firing at the spot from three or four inches, "You would think they'd have something better to do."

Nervously, "Than what?"

"Than shit on my car," she replied meanly. After replying she faced him.

"Yes, that must be," he searched blankly, "inconvenient."

Why was she looking at him so intently? Was he still erect? Poking against his pants?

"Inconvenient? Yes. And hard work. It's," she continued to size him up, "quite a responsibility to have an auto. It's clear to me now why the Party is quite careful about bestowing that responsibility."

"Yes." He inched his way around the car. "But you seem to take the responsibility seriously."

Returning her attention to the spot on the hood, "I do, comrade. One must be on guard here. Against rust." To herself, "The salt air corrodes everything. And these damned birds."

He wandered around the Battery, hoping that Sasha would appear. When he finally saw him, standing theatrically, his top hat pushed back, lecturing to what turned out to be a Ukrainian couple here for a Party symposium on shrimp harvesting, Alex walked along beside the carriage, waiting, keeping stride with Daisy, who apparently had had too few or too many carrots to do more than plod, uninspired, down East Bay Street.

"Well, good morning, comrade," Sasha said as soon as the couple stepped down onto the pavement. "Can I give you a lift?"

"Where has Celeste gone?" he demanded.

He shrugged.

"Her apartment is empty."

"Oh?"

Impatiently, "You must know that."

"No, sir, that is a complete surprise." Hawkishly surveying the sidewalk that skirted the river, "I haven't seen her, comrade, since I saw you. Last Saturday, wasn't it?"

His voice seemed distant. No. Just formal. As if he were being careful around someone important.

"Surely, Sasha, you have seen her since then?"

"No, comrade. Ah," unconvincingly, "that officer looks ready for a tour of this historic wonder. And with that belly, he won't be doing it

243

on foot." With a sly wink, "Apparently sixty-some years of peace have taken a toll on the officer corps."

That certainly sounded more like the old Sasha. He found himself wondering if he hadn't been groundlessly suspicious. Perhaps. But even the wink seemed contrived.

"If you don't mind, comrade, I'll snatch him up. They've raised our quota again, so it's work, work, work."

With a jiggle of the reins he prompted Daisy down the street.

Still walking beside him, "If you see her, would you tell her..." He stopped. Lamely, "Tell her I came by."

"Certainly, comrade. I'm sure she'll turn up." With that same unconvincing wink, "She always does."

He watched the carriage meander up to the officer; he watched Sasha's lips; his hands. It was the same. Always the same. Perhaps even the same flip remarks that seemed slightly unpatriotic. They were probably all part of the act. Or if they weren't, it didn't matter, because he was, he could tell, no longer in Sasha's confidence. If he had ever been.

He spent the rest of the day wandering about, grieving. Wondering why she hadn't said something. Perhaps he should have asked the block commander. No. That wouldn't have been wise.

Maybe she was with that anonymous, large Russian? Wearing his shirt?

The Zlotny hummed along, the driver looking straight ahead on the other side of the glass, his mother, beside him, her legs crossed, lost in thought.

"The leaves are just about gone," he offered, just to say something.

"Yes." She patted his hand.

"I think I like it better that way. With them all over the ground. I'm not sure why."

"Don't be surprised if he seems strange," she remarked, as if that were what they had been talking about all along. "A stroke can have odd effects. Just try to remember him the way he was. There will be something there. Some hint, that will remind you."

He squirmed uncertainly.

"If you keep that in mind, then he will seem more himself. Does that make sense?"

244

"Yes," he replied in as adult a way as he could.

She took his hand in hers and placed it in her lap. The hand was cool and dry. It was the kind of hand that never sweated, he decided, while peering absently at the edge of the road. Snowdrift after snowdrift of lazy red and yellow leaves decorated their path like funeral bouquets. There seemed to be an endless supply of them.

From time to time he tried to remind himself what Grandfather Simpson was like. So that he could follow her advice. But all he could see, when he tried to imagine him, was his nose, which, enlarged, crisscrossed with countless exploded capillaries, resembled a confusing, curved earth road map.

He uttered a nearly audible sigh of relief when he saw him. He looked just the same! Pale, almost gray. And there was a tube in his nose, like some plastic shortcut that had been tacked onto the map. But the man lying in the bed was unmistakably Grandfather Simpson.

It was only after they had settled in, and the nurse had left them, that he realized that something was different. He was if anything too alert. In fact, his eyes were disturbingly energetic, the way they flitted from him to his mother and back.

"Hello," he said, in a parched, raspy voice which sounded a hundred years old.

They responded.

"I was awarded a red star today." After a moment, "That's excellent, you know." His eyes were the eyes of a child expecting congratulations.

"How nice," his mother replied, her leg crossed so that the pale silk jumpsuit draped softly across her calf.

"There were only two awarded."

"That's especially nice." There was a small tear in the corner of her eye.

Proudly, "I know."

His mother fidgeted for a moment with the crease in her pants.

"I don't know why the others won't study. Everyone knows they should. It's our duty."

She rose, crossed the room, and left.

Alex sat there for a moment, trying to decide what to do.

Earnestly, "They took them off, you know." He tried to lean for-

245

ward but could not. "Because they didn't study."

"Oh?" Alex replied deferentially.

"They should have studied. And then," his eyes brightened, "they wouldn't have been backsliders. They were, you know. The worst kind."

Absently, "Who?"

"My parents," he confessed anxiously. "But," his voice vanished for an instant, "I am not. I have studied hard."

With interest, "Where did they take them?"

"To a reeducation center, of course." Suspiciously, "You must not study." He examined Alex carefully, as if he could, just by application of eyesight, detect a backslider. In the fashion of a schoolboy impersonating his teacher, "Marxism-Leninism can only be mastered through diligent study."

"How long were they there?"

"They aren't back yet." Grimly, "They won't come back until they are fixed."

"Fixed?"

"Yes. And they aren't fixed yet. But then, it's difficult to fix people. After they have been backsliders for so long."

Sympathetically, while looking through the small rectangular window in the door, "Yes. I guess that must be so."

"It is." Lowering his eyelids, "I'm getting a little sleepy, you know."

"Yes."

With his eyes closed, Grandfather Simpson reclaimed his sixty-some years.

Alex sat there. His mother's head appeared at the window. And then another man's. Perhaps the doctor's. And then hers, as they circled, discussing the case. In the hall, on the other side of the glass, she seemed a quite different person: she looked no different from the doctor she was talking to.

He bumped into the bed on his way by.

"Hello."

"Hello," Alex replied in a way calculated not to really wake him up.

"You were here before?" the youthful eyes said in a bone-dry, dead voice.

"Yes."

246

Seriously, "When do you suppose they'll be fixed?"

"Soon, I guess."

"Yes. I'm sure they are studying now that they've learned their lesson."

Alex nodded and turned toward the door. After half a step he pivoted and, after walking very near the bed, bending over, asked, "Have you ever heard of New York City?"

"I have to tee-tee," Grandfather Simpson responded with a mild note of urgency.

Concealing his embarrassment, "Should I call someone?"

"I have to tee-tee."

On the way to the house his mother explained, in a remote, clinical way, how the stroke had blocked off portions of Grandfather Simpson's brain. The net effect was that he couldn't remember anything at all after the age of about six.

"But what he is saying, and thinking, is so?"

"Yes. In a way. In fact," she seemed to be toying with the idea for a second, "what he is experiencing may be quite vivid. That is, he may remember things he had long ago forgotten. It's sort of like clearing out a closet. Suddenly all kinds of things you'd forgotten completely are right there on the floor."

Puzzled, "You mean like an old tennis racket. Or pair of shoes."

"Yes."

Odd. She didn't seem bothered at all. At least when he was not right there in front of them. Perhaps because she was a doctor? And while they talked, and he was out of sight, Grandfather Simpson was merely another case.

"It seems that if something is there, all along, you'd just remember it."

"Yes, it seems that way. But that isn't the way it works."

He shut his eyes and, feigning sleepiness, tried to imagine what was going on in Grandfather Simpson's six-year-old brain.

When they arrived at the Saluda house, even though there were only the two of them, he put on his sweats and, pretending to be training for basketball, left. Two hours later, just after the sky had turned crisp, mountain black, he crept up the stairs with The Book tucked in his elastic waistband and slid it under his pillow. Perhaps, he reasoned, reading it one more time would make it all understandable.

And later, after she was asleep, and the house was dead quiet, he reread both volumes. In the order he had found them. Without benefit of the *CCCP Dictionary*. Or anything else.

He awoke with it under his cheek, stuck to him like a slick, dry pillow. He bolted upright, startled by its being there in plain view and the vivid imagination that Corinne was at the door: "Alexander! We're gonna have to put your breakfast in the microwave if . . ."

No. She wasn't there. Not at all.

In a sleepy panic he shoved it under the real pillow, creating a deafening crackle and shuffle that roared as loudly as a phonebook in the wind.

Silence.

He sat there for a second or two, panting, wondering if even the fact of reading it was a dream. He convinced himself it was not and got up, shakily, to splash half a dozen cupped handfuls of freezing spring water on his face, which tinglingly evaporated from his cheeks on his way to the breakfast table.

"I couldn't sleep last night. At least not until very late. Even with the fire."

Preoccupied with the numbness in his cheeks, wondering why it was lingering so long, "Oh, mmm."

Smiling, "You should have kept me company."

"Sorry."

"Well, tonight we'll talk for hours."

She didn't seem especially bothered by the prospect of spending the day attending to her father. Although she did look a little tired. Perhaps in the corners of the eyes, at the edge of the pale green makeup that underscored the eyes themselves. When he had gone to bed those same eyes had been serenely hypnotizing the fire.

He forced himself to reply, "That will be nice."

She gave him a peculiar look and then finished off her grapefruit. He could hear her chewing each small section with relish. Followed by her crisp, dry toast.

After waiting for her to finish, he asked, "Will Grandfather die?"

"No." With a hint of sadness, "But he won't be quite the same."

"No, I suppose not," he replied, thinking, the whole time, in a

248

cold, rather distant way that began to disturb him even while he was doing it: No. But he was there. And to him it will be just like yesterday.

Grandfather Simpson spent most of the morning, between having tubes connected and disconnected, talking about how nice it would be to have Whiskers back. After a while Alex decided that Whiskers was a dog. He had Grandfather Simpson describe Whiskers to him. As if he were diverting a child, Alex asked the old man this question and that, all the while making sure that his mother, who sat, paced, consulted, and then sat again, would hear nothing that would cause her to wonder.

About three she said, "I'm going to look at the results of the CAT scan." Appreciatively, "Keep him talking. I think it's good for him."

As soon as he was sure she was far enough down the hall, he pulled his chair right up to the bed. "Grandfather?"

The boyish eyes were puzzled.

"Hunter?"

The eyes smiled.

"Before your parents went away—"

Interrupting, "To be fixed. Yes." Thoughtfully, "Do you suppose I can have Whiskers back after they're fixed?"

"Yes, I think so."

"Good." Impersonating an adult, "I've been studying very hard, you know."

"Yes." Impatiently, his eyes bouncing back and forth between the head-size window and Grandfather Simpson, "Before they went away, was there a," he paused, "bomb? A nuclear explosion?"

The eyes seemed mystified.

"Do you remember seeing something on television? It would be on television. It would have been three years ago." In a flash of insight, "You would have been three."

Alex leaned back dejectedly. How could he remember that? At three?

He picked up the copy of *Soviet Sports Digest* his mother had bought for him and, touching it (the glistening stainless-steel table was probably covered with invisible microbes waiting to seep through his skin) only with his two forefingers, thumbed through that month's heroes. There was a foldout of Svetlana Posner. Martina Antipova's

249

model. With those same powerful thighs. And chest. But Svetlana's was flat and muscular. He could see Martina Antipova's breasts explode as she slipped her thick elastic bra over her shoulders. The same shoulders. But underneath, through the nylon athletic shirt it was clear there was only muscle. Not big round breasts waiting to explode.

"So," his mother winked at him, "have you two been having fun?"

He nodded without looking up from his magazine.

"It was on television, you know?"

Alex nearly dropped the magazine when Grandfather Simpson's voice sliced through the air.

As if he were very impressed, "Over and over again. Everybody watched it." Grimly, "Mother and Father were quite worried."

Patiently, as she adjusted the sheet, "Really."

"Oh, yes." A tear formed in his eye. "It was horrible."

"Yes, I'll bet it was," she replied absently.

Alex looked directly into Grandfather Simpson's eyes. They were the eyes of a boy. What was around them was dead gray old. But the eyes themselves were as clear as a television screen.

Philosophically, "But that's what happens to backsliders."

"Is it?" she queried in a way that suggested a flicker of interest.

Before Grandfather Simpson could say anything, "We've been talking about television."

"Television?"

"Yes."

Thoughtfully, "Odd the things that stick."

"Yes," he agreed, wondering for an instant if she had any idea what Grandfather Simpson had just said.

No.

She smoothed the sheet. Patted Grandfather Simpson's forehead. In that mechanically professional way that she had acquired by working morning after morning in the clinic.

The tear which had accumulated in the corner of his left eye rolled across his temple.

"Is there something in your eye, Father?"

That same puzzled look reappeared.

"There are some interesting articles in this issue," Alex interjected, with a shuffle of the open, shiny magazine.

250

Preoccupied, "Good."

He watched her examine the eye, peering into it, while she checked for some random piece of debris. After a moment she said, "It must have washed away."

No. It was debris in the mind that caused the tear, he reflected. Floating to the top after the sixty years of other debris obscuring it had been blown away by the little explosion in Grandfather Simpson's head.

"Okay?"

Grandfather Simpson nodded.

Had it been just sitting there, that fact? Like facts that sat in the corners of the DAL system waiting for the right password and authorization code? Or had it been there, all this time, accessible, but consciously hidden? The eyes shed no light on that.

That evening, right in front of the fire, shoulder to shoulder, eating frozen spaghetti, he thought about The Book, noticing, perhaps for the first time, how each time she wanted him to listen she touched the back of his hand with her fingertip, and caught his eye, or leaned toward him so that jasmine or burnt orange (tonight it was burnt orange) invaded his nostrils, snatching his attention away from The Book to her.

Just tricks.

And sadness. He kept examining her eyes.

"You will meet the General Secretary, you know. He has, I think, written Nurov. If he has," she stretched, "I will find out. But to meet him yourself? Exciting. And," she stroked the back of his hand "a little frightening. But he will be impressed."

He slipped his hand away.

"And you must show the right kind of interest. In the Party. Particularly that." Turning the hair over his ear into small ringlets, "It is too bad that you have shown so little interest so far. I know it might seem a little dull. But connections in the Party are essential. Oh, up till now, it didn't really matter. But at university it will be important. And it will be lost on no one that you are the great-grandson of Sonia Ouspenskaya."

The burnt orange, and a hint of her, perhaps the crease in her neck, or underarm, was as thick as smoke.

"That is blood. And blood means trust. That will not be lost on the General Secretary." Tilting her head to the side, "The prospects of a great future do not seem to excite you very much."

Saving him from responding, "Don't you realize there," her face was very close, "are no limits? Not really. You can go as," pulling back, "far as your imagination carries you."

"I . . ."

"Your father has paid the price." With a shake of the head that seemed to indicate that whether he had or not was of no real concern, "For me. And you." Without regret, "His future is behind him. Oh, he has hopes. But you," holding his face in her hands, "are our real hope."

Her cool, dry fingers still on his cheeks, "You have the spark. I have seen it. You will take the chances. I know you will."

Great hunks of The Book had been flashing by, competing with her for his imagination.

She kissed him on the mouth.

Gutting whores, was what they called it. He tried to push the picture out of his mind, but it reappeared.

Each word a warm breath, "You will be the one." That familiar, pinpoint dreamy-eyed look was there; perhaps it had been there the whole time. "You merely have to reach out and take it."

He stood.

"You needn't be too concerned with what Nurov says. He's," watching him, "cautious. Always, he's been cautious." Pulling a pin from the braid that circled above her ear, letting it fall, "Except once. And," releasing the other pin, "sometimes he regrets even that one attack of bravery."

"There is the DAL system."

"Oh, he's," slipping the barrette from the end of one braid, "quite clever. But that," she glanced at the emerald-studded barrette while the braid unwound of its own accord, fanning out into a cloud of thick, blond curls, "is no substitute for reaching out for what you want."

She dropped the barrette on the floor beside her and removed its companion.

"It's more than just clever."

Disinterestedly, "I'm sure it is. For people who are intrigued by

252

things like that. For engineers who are preoccupied with this nut and that bolt."

Clearly she had no idea what it was all about.

"But you, Alexander, will be one of those who take large steps." She shook her head, creating a violent rainstorm of blond curls. "One of those who bend the path of history."

He sat on the hearth, as far away from her as he could.

Dreamily, "Does that frighten you?"

"No."

He tried to imagine how she would feel if she read The Book. And believed it.

"Good," she said, extending her hand to him. It reached out, the fingers unfolded like the thin blades of a fan, her arm bent just so.

"Have you ever thought about what it was like before? Even before the Great Uprising?"

"No." Beckoning with her fingertips, "Of course not. The only thing that interests me is the future." Impatiently, as if she were discarding a boring toy, "That stuff's dead as a doornail."

"Yes," suppressing the temptation to just tell her, right then, "I guess so."

"I would prefer you to be excited by the future."

"Yes." After standing and fidgeting in front of the fire for a minute or two, "I think I'm tired."

Rebuffed, "Oh?" Looking up at him from the floor, one leg tucked neatly under the other, leaning on a single arm, she resembled, as much as anything else, a finely carved piece of furniture. Each leg and arm perfectly proportioned; perfectly balanced.

"Yes." He circled over to the stairs and, feeling much more confident with twenty feet of floor between them, smiled at her as he climbed. "Good night." It was not her fault, he decided. It was the only way she knew how to be.

Without saying good night she turned her attention to the fire.

Later, after he had nearly fallen asleep, she sat on the edge of his bed, silently, for what seemed a long time: he lay very still, barely breathing, his heart pounding in the way your heart pounds in a dream, not opening his eyes, smelling her burnt orange scent, and hickory smoke.

Perhaps she stayed until dawn. It was hard to tell.

253

On the way back to Charleston, with the window separating them from the driver rolled up very tight, "You should know that Nurov has discovered your new friend."

He attempted to appear composed.

Tiredly, "That is not the kind of thing he will approve of." When she smiled, a tiny ripple of crow's-feet swept down from her eyes. "I, on the other hand, wonder: perhaps the experience has done you good. So long as you keep it in perspective."

He made up his mind not to respond. At all.

"Her brother," she adjusted the crease in her pantsuit, "apparently felt compelled, no doubt patriotically, to inform Nurov. Feeling, I'm sure, that patriotism is its own reward." Absently, after a long pause, "Sometimes I wonder if Nurov isn't right about Americans after all."

Chapter

11

He had never been with her in the dark. Only in the bell tower with the windows wide open. He tried to imagine what it would be like. To touch her in the dark. Invisibly. He ran his hand across the pillow imagining it was her breast. Which woke him up— not from sleep, but from being able to imagine her. After that one time his mind just dried up.

Not that he couldn't see her. But instead of being there, within reach, she was far away, in an anonymous, gray room. Just standing.

Why did he have to do that? After all, she hadn't really done anything.

Propped stiffly against the backboard, in his mind, carefully picking each word, he repeated: "It's not fair. Not at all. She hasn't done anything. Not really. Other than miss a few days' work."

But afterward he just slid back down under the sheet, and tried to imagine what it would be like if she were there. He even ran his hand across the pillow again. But it was just smooth flat cotton, that felt nice, but nothing more.

Why that room? he wondered. There was no way to know. Or even guess. But, in his mind, there she was. In that room. Alone. Absurdly skinny. Waiting to be fixed.

At breakfast he no longer looked at his father. Not because he was afraid. Or because of what he had done to her. Not really. He just couldn't bring himself to look.

Which didn't matter. Nurov just read the paper. And ate. As if nothing had happened at all.

• • •

When he quit the basketball team, Nurov said, "Don't overdo it with the DAL system. Study. But don't exhaust yourself."

One morning, out of the blue, from the other side of "New Quotas for Tractor Production," he asked, "What's been going on with your friend?" The paper crackled as he lowered it. "Martina Antipova."

Alex felt himself turn red. As always it began on his forehead, as if the red splash at his hairline were a warm spring.

Perhaps just the thought of Martina Antipova had made Nurov smile? But only for a second. He looked at Alex quite carefully, as if, for the first time, he realized something was wrong.

He went back to searching the DAL system, in a quiet frenzy, masquerading as Nurov:

The DAL System and the Development of Correct Marxist-Leninist Thought, by M.N. Nurov, Vice-Minister of Information, South-Central Region, CCCP/USSA. [This report was abstracted from the proceedings of the 61st Plenary Session of the CCCP/USSA.]

THE CURRENT SYSTEM

Currently, printed information is stored and distributed in hard-copy form, i.e., books, magazines, newspapers, manuscripts, etc. This system is expensive (thousands, even millions, of copies have to be printed, distributed, and maintained), difficult to control (everyone is aware of the problems posed by unauthorized works!), and subject to security breaches. In fact, this author finds it hard to call the current situation a system at all.

THE DAL SYSTEM

The *Direct Access Library* (or DAL) system is a computer-based library system that will make the maintenance of hard-copy libraries obsolete. The DAL system consists of four parts: the library, in which electromagnetic files are stored (the books!); the index, which lists all files

256

and maintains addresses for them (the card catalogue); the cross-reference, which is the electronic brain of the DAL system (the cross-reference allows users to interactively retrieve bibliographical lists based on an assortment of logical keys, such as author, subject, date, and so on); and, lastly, geographically distributed terminals from which users can retrieve stored material for display on personal viewing screens.

THE ADVANTAGES OF THE DAL SYSTEM

The DAL system has a number of advantages over hard-copy systems:

1. It will be unnecessary to maintain expensive and redundant hard-copy libraries. A single, centrally stored electronic copy of each document will be sufficient for everyone's needs.

2. There will be complete control over what books and documents exist. Literally. Since there will be no other books, the problem of unauthorized materials will be eliminated. At present, unauthorized works swim by like small fish in a huge sea of books. Each with the potential for damaging minds—at who knows what costs.

3. Through the unique password system, data and knowledge security problems will be all but eliminated. Each user's unique password will offer that user a "view" of the library. That "view" will be determined by the user's role and function, so that the system offers a "view" consistent with the needs of the user. Presently, physical segregation of classified materials is required. This method is expensive, inefficient, and flawed. Once implemented, the system will include audio or visual password confirmation to ensure proper system security.

4. The Party can control history. This is more than a metaphor. It is a fact. By establishing, through the DAL system, what has happened (by purging the system of extraneous or false information), this untainted "view" of the past will ensure the proper development of correct Marxist-Leninist thought.

257

Alex discovered the minutes of meetings. Apparently everything was recorded and stored. It seemed very odd to read the ones in which his father was a participant.

Minutes of Special Planning Subcommittee Four, Ministry of Information, South-Central Region, CCCP/USSA, October 17, 143 AR. [Agenda: The DAL System]

The meeting was brought to order by the subcommittee chairman, M. N. Nurov.

NUROV: No one is suggesting otherwise, comrade.
ZAROTKIN: Planned Technological Development has worked quite well.
N: No one has suggested it hasn't. I am not suggesting the wholesale introduction of computers. Only a library system which will allow the Party to decide what books there will be. The books have been entered into the system through a unified clearinghouse.
Z: I still see no reason to change something that has worked so well.
N: It hasn't. That is, in one respect we have failed. We have not been able to instill that vision of the socialist ideal that will truly transform the world.
Z: I see no evidence we haven't, comrade.
N: You, Comrade Minister, seem to see only what you wish.
Z: The next order of business is our new campaign to promote factory morale. I know—factory morale will not really change one iota until the DAL system is implemented.
N: I could not have said it better myself.
Z: I believe, Comrade Simms, you have a few recommendations?

The Role of Computers and Other Forms of Technology in the Underground Resistance, A Confidential Report to the Central Committee of the Communist Party, United Soviet States of America. [This report was abstracted from the proceedings of the 6th Plenary Session of the CCCP/USSA.]

There is no doubt that computer technology (as well as several other forms of communications technology, such as word processors, photocopying devices, and intelligent typewriters) is interfering with the transition from presocialist thinking to proper Marxist-Leninist thought. These devices are being used by criminal gangsters and backsliders in two ways:

1. As a support system for radical underground communications.

2. For the dissemination of treasonous lies intended to undermine socialist order and development.

There are not at the moment nearly enough trained, reliable personnel to operate and/or monitor these systems. They are clearly a threat to the Party. It is the recommendation of this committee that all such devices be collected and either destroyed or centrally warehoused until such time as they can properly serve socialism.

After two weeks he could take it no longer. Perhaps it was making him wacky? he decided. There really was no other explanation. But, crazy or not, he couldn't keep it to himself any longer.

He chose Myslov because there was no other choice. He was a Russamsky. And certainly not a hook. At least that seemed very unlikely.

Alex merely took him to the dune, dug up The Book—where it had been buried since they had returned from Saluda— and handed it to him, one volume stacked on top of the other.

"I don't understand," he said with a shiver, looking down at the cold sand, rather than the unopened Book in his lap.

"Neither do I," Alex replied.

"You know, Alexander, you have been behaving quite strangely. I think people are beginning to notice."

"Aren't you curious?"

"About what?"

"About that," he said, pointing at the two thin, plastic-covered folders. "I call it The Book."

Uncertainly, "Oh?"

"Don't be so damned afraid. Open it."

Stiffly, "I'm not afraid."

"Then open it."

He adjusted his scarf, settled against the trunk of the tree, and peeled back the cover.

After a moment, "Who is Ahab?"

"I don't know. It doesn't matter."

"No need to be short."

"Sorry." Pleading, "Just read awhile. I'll go for a walk."

"No. I'd prefer you stay."

"Okay." Why was Myslov like that? What a waste to even let him see it. He wouldn't understand it. Or if he did, he'd just fall apart. Yes. He was certainly no hook. But what if he just fell apart? He was so nervous to start with.

While Myslov read, Alex watched, trying to detect what was passing through his brain, wondering at one moment if Myslov thought he was crazy for even having it, the next if Myslov himself could take the strain of knowing what was in there.

"What an odd story," he said after finishing the first volume.

"It's not a story."

Tilting his head to the side, "What else would you call it?"

"History."

Myslov frowned, put The Book down at his side, and pushed himself up with his hands.

Over the sound of Myslov dusting the sand off his hands, "A little different kind of history than we are used to?"

"It's damp in here this time of year."

"Is that all you have to say?"

"Well, I've never been particularly taken with stories."

Threateningly, "That is not a story."

"I read it, didn't I?"

"You turned the pages, but," angrily, "I don't think there's any room left in your head for something that doesn't," stammering, "fit!"

Myslov pulled back, his hands wrapped tightly around his scarf.

"Things don't always fit. They just don't!"

Myslov began inching away, backward, up the soft interior of the dune.

"Can you understand that?"

Pliantly, "Yes."

"No. I don't think you can."

"Actually, it's rather cold in here. So little sun gets in."

"Get used to it. You're not going anywhere until you finish."

"We can come back tomorrow," Myslov replied with a tinge of concern. "I'll read it then."

260

"No. Now. Right now."

When Myslov turned to run, his ankles sank into the sand, so that the more he pumped his skinny legs the closer he was. After a second Alex threw him to the ground and sat on him, pinning his knotty little elbows to the ground with his knees.

Panting, "That hurts."

Alex looked down at him. There was sand on the side of his face, stuck to the corner of his mouth.

"If you let me up, right now, I won't tell anybody about this," Myslov promised, in a slow, rational voice which revealed only a hint of fear. "You have my word."

"You're going to read the rest of it. Now."

"I can't."

"Now."

"I . . ."

Alex began slapping at his face and head, letting his hand carom off the side of his head or the sand. After the first quick blow it was easy; in fact, after that it felt good, almost relaxing.

"Are you going to read it?"

Crying, "I can't."

Alex pulled back his fist.

"My glasses are broken," he whimpered just as Alex was about to let his fist come crashing down.

Breathing more easily, "I'll read it to you."

Keeping one arm pinned with his knee, Alex retrieved The Book. Shaking away the loose sand, "I think a man died to write this. That must mean something."

Alex read out loud, clearly, carefully, remaining astride Myslov's narrow chest, the open Book half-obscuring his face, which still comically supported those bent, metal-framed glasses.

After a few minutes Myslov said, matter-of-factly, "My arm has fallen asleep."

Without pausing, he slid his knees off Myslov's arms.

"Thank you."

While he read, he listened to it himself, picking up this or that detail, and wondered, from time to time, what he was going to do when he finished—if he couldn't trust Myslov. He had gotten himself into this. What if Myslov went straight to the authorities? Or just Gregorov? He could see beady-eyed Gregorov scratching his head with glee at the idea of something so juicy: a real criminal to latch on to.

When he finished, he let Myslov up.

Refraining from asking, "What do you think?" he merely sat, cross-legged, waiting, watching. What would he do if . . .

Myslov leaned to his side, and without even trying to stand, threw up. He smiled, turning the corners of his mouth pasty gray, and peered at Alex. Absurdly warped, his metal glasses, instead of resting on his ear, now jutted meaninglessly into nowhere just above his temple. It was an odd, uninspired little smile.

"Are you all right?"

"Yes." Sitting, "I think so."

After that it seemed impossible to say anything. Or ask anything. They walked back quietly to Myslov's walkway. He stood there, still looking a little stupid, and absurd, the cold inland breeze blowing from behind him, pushing his hair out into a crazy, tangled fan, and waved, slowly, while Alex walked on the remaining three hundred meters.

Why doesn't he just go inside? he asked himself two or three times, punctuating the question with a wave, hoping that would satisfy Myslov. But it didn't. He was there, the size of a little stick man, when Alex turned down the bleached wood walkway. He waved one last time himself.

At supper he was ravenous. Perhaps from being outside in the cold?

His father nodded approvingly. He always seemed quite satisfied when Alex ate a lot.

Perhaps from just letting someone else see it? Yes. That was it. Already he felt better. Saner. Just from the fact that someone else confirmed it was real. Not that he didn't know that. He wasn't that far gone. At least he hoped not. No. But seeing it there, in someone else's hands, took it squarely from that private world, dominated by uncertainty, to the world of facts.

Even though he had said nothing.

Later, in bed, he began to wonder. All kinds of horrible things came to mind. Especially in that zone between sleep and wakefulness, where ideas seem to be able to wrestle facts to the ground and hold them there, suspended, while they have their way.

262

At dawn he asked himself: Why had he done it?

By midmorning, on his way to the Young Pioneers, he was sick from fear himself. Perhaps Myslov wouldn't be there at all. That would be the best thing. Then he wouldn't have to sit there waiting for him to fall apart.

Gregorov was waiting at the door.

Extending his hand, "Good morning, Nurov."

Gregorov's eyes, as always, were searching for anything to latch hold of.

"Yes." Casually, "It's a little breezy out."

Expressing concern, "Yes. I hope that doesn't keep anyone away."

When Myslov arrived, looking deadly pale, his glasses more or less repaired, he sat in one of the last seats near the back corner.

That morning they had a panel discussion on the role of youth in promoting correct socialist thought: Gregorov acted as moderator; Planov and Grichenko, behind a narrow wooden table, fielded questions.

"Vigilance," Gregorov began, wasting no time in getting to his favorite theme, "that is the key. Vigilance," he said the word in a funny, kind of private way that suggested it was his own personal word, "with respect to yourself, with respect to others."

"Studying," Myslov offered unsteadily. "How else can one know correct Marxist-Leninist thought when one sees it?"

"Of course, comrade," Gregorov agreed perfunctorily.

"Then vigilance." In a quivering, reedy voice, "That has its place." Continuing, while unbuttoning the huge gray coat that engulfed everything but his face, "But only after a thorough study of Marxist-Leninist thought."

Irritably, "Yes, comrade."

Myslov swayed back and forth uncertainly.

"Are you all right, comrade?"

"Yes. I'm fine."

"Good," Gregorov replied, more in the spirit of proceeding than concern.

"That includes both a thorough study of doctrine, and," he made everyone wait, "history."

Alex panicked.

"Of course," Gregorov replied with affected boredom.

A little nervously, "I just wanted to make that point."

Alex was able to breathe again.

After that he felt quite good about Myslov's being there. Without looking directly at him, or even thinking about it, he knew he was there, thinking the same thoughts he was, drawing the same conclusions.

As they walked around the schoolyard, their hands stuffed into their pockets, "I think you should destroy it."

"I can't."

As if he were delivering a weather report, "If you are caught with it, the authorities will get a very wrong idea of what's going on. I'm sure they will think you are some kind of loony." Grimly, "And you know what that means."

Alex shrugged.

"It's just bullshit, anyway."

"Is that what you believe?"

"Basically that's what it is. Just reading what lunatics like that have written is serious. Very serious."

"So you don't think it's true?" Alex persisted.

"No." Looking back at the school building, "Besides, we'll be in Moscow next fall."

Annoyed, "What does that have to do with anything?"

Rather than answer, Myslov slid down into his coat, letting the collar ride up over his red-tipped ears.

"There's more to it than The Book, you know? Something that will surprise you."

Occupying himself with the ground as he walked, "I'm surprised Martina Antipova isn't out here today. It's not like her to miss a day of training. I can remember when you were content to spend lunch ogling her."

"I've made up my mind I'm going to find out where it was."

"Where what was?"

"New York City," Alex replied. "I'm going to find it. Or where it was."

Refusing to look up from the ground, "You mean, go there?"

"No." Laughing a dry-throated laugh that seemed to carry across the cool air, "No. I have another way. Something kind of amazing."

264

Myslov didn't display a hint of interest.

"It's like traveling, but you don't have to go anywhere."

"It's one-ten," Myslov announced.

"Aren't you curious, at all?"

"No," he replied with a swallow. Alex could smell Myslov's sandwich churning in his stomach.

"I've narrowed it down to three places."

Later that afternoon, while the new maid was scrubbing the back porch, he showed Myslov the DAL system.

"The best bet is this," he said pointing at the screen.

"The Patrice Lumumba Bird Preserve," Myslov read incredulously.

"Yes. Odd," whispering, "it's on an island. Just like this one."

Thursday, when he arrived home from school, before Myslov could get there, his father was waiting, along with a very Russian-looking man. There was a medical bag resting on the floor beside his chair.

"This is Dr. Vinkov," his father said tiredly.

He knew immediately who the man was. Before he heard his name. Before his father even spoke.

"So," feeling kind of giddy, "me now."

Dr. Vinkov rose.

"Will I be in the same place she is?" he found himself asking. "Or have you finished with her?"

"She?" his father puzzled.

"There's no longer any point in hiding it from me. I figured it out. The minute she was gone."

Apparently realizing who he meant, "Has she got something to do with this?" Alex could see him considering. Evaluating.

"I don't understand what she had done," he continued, even though, abruptly, the question didn't seem right. "Or does that really matter at all?"

"Nothing," his father replied, as if after a long, tiring search he had stumbled across something valuable.

"I don't see how things like that can happen. And be called justice." He could hear the words ringing in his head as he spoke. "When it's just another lie."

Dr. Vinkov interjected soothingly, "There is no reason to excite yourself. Exhaustion can play tricks on you."

Stepping back from Dr. Vinkov's grasping, reassuring hand, "I just don't see why you did it. It's pointless."

Restraining the doctor with a raised hand, his father agreed, "You're quite right. What you're suggesting would have been pointless." Wryly, "Certainly ambition is no crime. Although you might suspect so while strolling through a Zlotny factory."

Alex's legs were as weak as dandelion stems.

Firmly, "Come with me. We'll be right back, Doctor."

With his back turned, Alex following giddily after him, "So we have young love to thank for this. I should have known." More to himself, "I would have thought you had learned from my example."

GOOD EVENING, VICE-MINISTER NUROV.
WHAT CAN I DO FOR YOU?
personnel search
DO YOU WISH TO BE PROMPTED?
yes
ENTER KEY: NAME/EMPL NUMBER/DEPT/JOB TITLE
            /SECTION/LOCATION/AGE/EDUCATION
department: ministry of information
ENTER KEY/COMMAND
section: vital records
ENTER KEY/COMMAND
job title: clerk
ENTER KEY/COMMAND
location: columbia, s.c.
ENTER KEY/COMMAND
list
BALL, GEORGE C.
HUFF, RAVEN K.
MICHEVITZ, CELESTE O.
WARREN, NANCY T.
ENTER KEY/COMMAND
name: michevitz, celeste o.
JOB TITLE: CLERK
GRADE: 6
LOCATION: COLUMBIA, S.C.
SECTION: VITAL RECORDS
BEGINNING DATE: 12/13/143
PREVIOUS JOB TITLE: CLERK

PREVIOUS GRADE: 4
PREVIOUS LOCATION: CHARLESTON, S.C.
PREVIOUS DEPARTMENT: MINISTRY OF AQUACULTURE
PREVIOUS SECTION: PERSONNEL
FOR ADDITIONAL INFORMATION ENTER KEY/COMMAND/HELP

"Does that answer any questions you might have?" his father asked as he reached over to the switch under the terminal. "About your friend?"

It had been there. All along. Right in front of him. He shook his head weakly while looking into the blank-faced terminal.

Disdainfully, as Alex stumbled into the corner of the desk, "Love."

He rubbed his thigh.

"Is that what led you into this idiocy?"

No, he almost replied, struck, as he stood there, with the oddness of the idea. No. He hadn't loved her at all. She was just a girl who fucked Russians.

"Did you learn nothing at all from me?" his father said with a mixture of puzzlement and exhaustion, before turning into the hallway.

By the time they returned, Dr. Vinkov had extracted a syringe from his bag. He neatly rolled up Alex's sleeve and injected it into his forearm.

It never crossed Alex's mind to resist. Or even speak out. He wondered himself, as the needle slid under the skin, why. Perhaps it was Dr. Vinkov's quiet, very professional manner. Or just fatigue.

Dr. Vinkov sat upright, his chest jammed right up to the steering wheel.

"Your father was quite right to call me," he offered, without taking his thick-glassed eyes from the road. "And of course, he can count on my discretion." Gravely, "In matters like this that is of the utmost importance."

Grade six, he said to himself. Better than just a pay step. What a stupid thing to be thinking about! he warned himself.

"Yes. It's a very good thing that we are old friends."

Why couldn't she have just said goodbye? "Don't you think she

267

should have said goodbye? Even though it was a two-grade jump?" Why had he just blurted that out? "Of course, it's the way they live that makes them that way. So damned hard."

Dr. Vinkov nodded approvingly, his eyes still locked on the head-lighted road.

With a stroke of insight, "If it weren't for me she would never have had a chance for a promotion like that. If she'd realized that . . ." He restarted, "If she'd just thought about it that way, she'd have said goodbye."

Alex began to laugh. Very hard. All the time wondering why he was doing it. And why he couldn't stop. After wiping a tear from his eye, and catching his breath, he continued, "Of course, merit must mean something. And hard work?"

Dr. Vinkov noncommittally bounced his head left to right.

"Except that that's just another lie." There was no point in saying things like that. No point at all. "Isn't it?" He wasn't angry. Or any-thing. "Just another lie." Dr. Vinkov was going to think he was a complete loony if he didn't shut up. "Of course, things like lies don't bother Vice-Minister Nurov at all."

"Oh, they do." Softly clicking his lip with the tip of his tongue, "A great deal."

"Then why did he do it?"

Philosophically, "Fathers do all kinds of things."

"And he knows all the other lies." It wasn't that he felt like talking. Or even comfortable. It was as if his head were one of those round bubble-gum machines that dispense a gum marble for a coin. Except here you didn't have to put a coin in. The gum just fell out the second it got near the slot.

Dr. Vinkov smiled benignly.

"I know he does." It was a very uncomfortable feeling, having each of his thoughts pop out like that. Unchecked. Trying to make amends, "I guess it's his job."

"He certainly has a demanding job."

"But he shouldn't lie. I mean, isn't it wrong to tell huge lies?" After a moment, "All the while pretending they're the truth."

He bit down on his lip, but then continued: "This isn't really me talking, you know. I'm not like this at all. I'm usually very much one to keep my thoughts to myself."

Chapter 12

Toward the end of the hallway the regularly spaced bare light bulbs, which ticked by like pulses from a mute clock, collapsed into the white line of an inverted highway. He had been down this road before. Yes. But how many times? He should be able to remember. He searched for the number, which hid, like a teasing child, just around some corner in his mind. He could almost hear the number breathing. Teasing him.

The guards were slowing down. Almost imperceptibly. Yes. This was the door.

When they stopped he could smell their wool uniforms. The smell was thick, almost suffocating.

"Is this it?" he almost asked.

There was no point. They never answered.

Dr. Vinkov was standing. His back to him. But still he knew exactly who it was. And what he was doing.

"No," he wanted to say, but couldn't.

The needle was as bright as a diamond-tipped drill.

"No." He could hear himself saying it, but there was no sound.

It stung. Like a yellow jacket. Or small bee. That was all. Why had he been so worried? If it was only going to be such a small, burning sting?

Janovich arrived. Always, he arrived right after the injection. Where did he know him from? He smoked a cigarette. And watched.

"You have been quite an embarrassment, Alex." Dr. Vinkov seemed always to be speaking with his back turned, so that the sound appeared out of nowhere. But there was no doubt it was his voice.

Alex noticed the guards had taken out their sticks. They were tapping them menacingly in their palms.

"What are we going to do with you, Alex?" Dr. Vinkov wondered out loud, while he reached into his bag. "That is our problem. You have been quite an embarrassment."

As if he were tightening a huge bolt, the guard on his right began twisting the stick in his closed hand.

"And a disappointment."

He wanted to say he was sorry, but couldn't.

"Yes. A disappointment."

They draped him across the table, one guard holding each arm. He could feel his heart begin to pound. In his throat.

"I didn't really do anything," his mind said, but the words stuck in his throat like a fishhook.

"Yes, you did. You know you did."

"It's not my fault," he tried to say.

"Perhaps you're right."

He could feel himself melting with relief.

"Yes. That's why we aren't angry with you, Alex." He could breathe again. "We know you will get better."

"Yes," he wanted to assure him.

"You probably wouldn't have been sick at all," the hands tightened their grip on his arms, forcing his chin to turn up as it jammed into the table, "under the right circumstances."

The light in the far end of the room clicked on. They pressed down very hard, driving his shoulders and chin farther into the table, forcing him to look, as the elliptical disk of light slowly moved back and forth, in smaller and smaller circuits.

She was there, again, her wrist chained to a small table so that she was slightly bent forward. Her eyes were sunken, drawn. If she recognized him she gave no indication of it.

It was not his fault.

Her attention was fixed on the syringe that glistened in Dr. Vinkov's hand.

"It is a mother's job to educate her son," Dr. Vinkov observed dryly.

She longingly surveyed the needle. It was clear she wanted it more than anything in the world.

270

"When she fails, we must educate her."

A tall, uniformed guard stepped over to her and, in one abrupt motion, tore the silk jumpsuit from her shoulder. The fabric created a deafening scream.

"Mustn't we?"

No, he thought, unable to end the paralysis in his throat.

"I'm glad you agree."

The green fabric let out another scream. Her arms and ribs were layered with bruises. Some were faint, dying blue; some were as bright as fresh raspberries.

The guard slapped the nightstick against her upper arm, almost playfully, eliciting a quiver of the lip. Nothing more. She stared at the needle.

The guard hit her again. And again. Much harder. He could hear a thud, as the wooden stick met flesh, and then a gasp. The guard mechanically repeated the blows, creating a dead, monotonous rhythm. Thud. Gasp. Thud. Gasp. Thud. Gasp. The thuds were perfectly and neatly paced. Thud. Thud. Thud. But the gasps grew longer, attenuated. Meaningful. Soon, almost imperceptibly, they were accompanied by motion. Until, finally, each gasp danced with her hips, as they swayed, painfully slowly, with a slight up-and-down motion, while she leaned against the small wooden table.

Always her eyes remained on the syringe.

"Give it to her," he heard himself scream.

The guard stopped and looked at him. He was young. Alex had never noticed that before. At least he didn't think he had. His eyes were pale, childlike blue. And a little sad.

He ripped off the rest of the jumpsuit, leaving the green silk legs dead on the floor at her feet.

"Give it to her. Can't you see she needs it?"

She stared at the needle longingly, still bent over the table, her hips and buttocks swaying.

"Yes, you are right," Dr. Vinkov replied with a nod. The guard rammed the stick into her, splitting her underpants as he forced it in.

"No. Not that."

"Oh?" Dr. Vinkov had that puzzled, slightly evaluative expression Alex had seen before. "Perhaps you're right."

The guard agitated the stick, in and out, while she stared at the needle, swaying, offering herself, gorging on the stick.

271

"Give it to her!"

Dr. Vinkov swabbed her arm, skillfully putting off the moment.

"Can't you see she needs it?"

When the needle slid into her arm, he came.

Laughter.

First Janovich. Yes. He recognized him. And then Dr. Vinkov.

He collapsed into a pile on the floor, his hands cupped around his crotch, hiding the wet spot on his pants.

When he came to, in his cell, Piotr Babulieski was there.

"I couldn't help it. I came," he explained frantically.

"Oh, we all do. You are forgiven."

"You did?"

"Oh, yes. Don't you remember?"

"Yes." After a moment, "How can you be here?"

"We are cellmates."

Suspiciously, "That's impossible. They killed you."

"No."

"Even if they didn't, that was seventy years ago," he said. "You'd be dead."

With a round, deep laugh, "No. Those who believe in Jesus Christ live forever."

"How can that be?"

Smiling, adjusting his huge hunched back against the wall, "No one knows."

He awoke. Soaking wet.

"Good morning, Alexander Mikhailovich."

"Good morning, Doctor."

He smiled and, with a wave of the hand, offered Alex a seat on the other side of his desk.

"Do you feel we are making progress? With your treatment."

Hesitantly, "Yes."

"You are not saying that just to please me." Knowingly, "I can tell sincerity when I hear it. After all, where would I be in my profession if I could be deceived that easily?"

Alex fidgeted with his hands.

"Yes. I'm inclined to agree. But we still have a long way to go."

Agreeably, "I know."

"Yes. Well, I have promised your parents that," he paused to brush away something from his nose, "you will be just fine." Firmly, "But I have warned them we must be thorough."

Alex nodded.

"Now." He opened a spiral-bound notebook and lifted a pencil from a red coffee cup. "Back to business." Holding the pencil up to his temple, twisting it, "It is most important that you tell me about anyone who has come into contact with this." He tapped his fingers on The Book.

It had been there, right from the beginning. Dr. Vinkov never opened it. At least while Alex was present. But it was kept there, apparently as a reminder of what had gone wrong.

"There are two reasons why that is important." He raised a finger. "One. How can you become well if you are holding anything back from me?" After a moment, he raised another finger. "Two. Anyone who has come into contact with this requires help. You do understand that, Alexander Mikhailovich?"

"Yes," he replied.

Right away he had told him about Myslov, figuring that that was really telling him nothing at all. Disguising his anger, he pretended to be informing, when in fact there was no doubt that it had been Myslov who had informed on him. He knew that from the start.

That was easy to do. Back when they were still playing games. But later, when he wanted to tell everything, in one of those moments of profound, exhilarating openness, which Dr. Vinkov, in spite of his exterior, was able to elicit, he admitted that he had known that they knew about Myslov already.

Dr. Vinkov had thanked him for his candor, and, while not coming right out and saying that Myslov had informed on him, asked, sympathetically, "You feel he betrayed you?"

After some cajoling he had admitted, "Yes."

"That is just another indication of your illness."

Was each step forward just another trick? he had wondered. When would he finally be right?

"You confided in him."

"Yes."

"Gave him your trust?"

"Yes."

"And he was disloyal?"

Reluctantly, "Yes."

Dr. Vinkov tapped his fingers lightly on the desktop. That was a signal he had seen before.

Searching for some way out, "You said I was to be candid."

"And I appreciate that." Smiling, "But you are wrong. What you perceive, in your illness, as disloyalty, is loyalty. Speaking hypothetically, let us say, in an apparent conflict between personal loyalty and loyalty to the Party there can be no contest. It is important that you understand that."

"I do," he pleaded.

"No. You are only saying that to please me, but eventually, after a lot of work, you will understand."

He stared at the floor.

"You recall," he leaned forward and smiled, "I said hypothetically. It is amazing how infrequently conflicts of the type we have been speaking of actually arise. I sometimes think never." He paused for a second to appreciate the profundity of what he had said. "In your case, for instance. Someone informs on you. Are you worse off for it? Really? Or are you, through what is actually an act of friendship, better off?"

"Better off," he had replied. "I am better off now."

"You must stop trying to please me."

"Really. I am."

But that was in the beginning. He saw things much more clearly now.

"There was no one else. Except Myslov."

Sharing his obvious satisfaction, "Good."

Dr. Vinkov stopped to scribble in the notebook. When he looked up, he inquired, "Has anything been troubling you?"

"No," he almost replied before correcting himself: "Yes. A little. The dreams."

"They will go away soon."

"I," he stammered, "wonder if it isn't the medicine."

"No." Sympathetically, "But I can tell you that they will go away."

Alex nodded.

When the session ended he felt especially relaxed. He buttoned up

274

his jacket and walked briskly along the gravel path to his barracks, barely slowing to note the sound of the wind as it blew through the long twin row of pines that bisected the courtyard.

He was pleased to discover they were showing a film. Just for those in his barracks. That made him happy. There was a kind of comradery since they were getting better together.

Afterward, in group, they discussed the importance of vigilance and dedication.

The cell was small. And wet. And even though it was dark he could sense that he was there, leaning against the wall.

"I don't believe a word you say," he said vindictively. "You are a liar. And a lunatic."

Tiredly, "So they have convinced you?"

"The truth has convinced me."

"Oh." He could see him now. Wild-eyed. And hairy. The great hump on his back making it impossible for him to actually rest against the wall. "And I thought I had convinced you."

"No. I just pretended. So I could inform on you later." He didn't seem to be concerned at all. "And I will."

"What about New York City?"

"What about it?"

"That's the question that keeps bothering you, isn't it?"

"No. That's a lie. Like the rest."

"Yes." Folding his hands in his lap and dozing off. "That's true."

He awoke soaking wet again. Panting.

"What do you really know?" Dr. Vinkov asked with his finger raised.

Alex felt himself tense up.

Pointing at The Book, "Beyond this."

What did he want him to say? he wondered.

"Think about it carefully. Beyond this, what facts—notice I am not talking about flights of imagination here—what facts have you encountered?"

What did he know? he asked himself. He knew he must say something. After a moment's thought, "There were things in the DAL system."

With mild impatience, "Things? What concrete reference was

275

there to anything in here?" His fingers descended onto The Book.

"It . . . nothing. But."

"But what?"

"It seemed," he struggled.

Dr. Vinkov waited. Ultimately he had to admit: there was nothing. Nothing you could really sink your teeth into.

"So everything—our whole little mystery—hinges on this." He tapped on The Book with his fingertip. "So the question is: what really is this?" He leaned back in his chair so that his eyes were directed at the ceiling. "The way I look at it, there are four possibilities." Dr. Vinkov reached for his pencil. "First, it could be authentic."

Alex found himself leaning forward.

"That is, it could be just what it claims to be. A revelation of something hideous." He paused. "Let's leave that possibility dangling."

He tried to show no reaction.

"Second, it could be a clever forgery. I guess it would be clever. What do you think?" Before Alex could respond, "Does that seem possible?"

"Yes, I guess."

Dr. Vinkov reprimanded, "I was hoping you had given this more thought than that," but quickly continued, "Or, it could be art."

Alex found himself looking puzzled.

"A story," Dr. Vinkov explained. "It could just be a story. An invention."

"That's what I thought it was," he blurted out. "In the beginning I thought it was," he hesitated, "a mystery story."

"Yes. That's certainly a possibility."

Alex found himself feeling better.

"Where do we stand?"

"I . . ." Alex stammered.

The pencil in the air, "We're counting."

Apologetically, "Oh."

Dr. Vinkov was clearly waiting.

"That's three." When it became apparent that Dr. Vinkov wanted more, he ventured, "A forgery. It could be a forgery. A story." After a moment he forced out, "It could be real."

276

"And that leaves," after convincing himself that Alex had nothing to contribute, "number four." He leaned forward, propping his elbows on the desk. "Any ideas?"

Tentatively, "He was in a sanitarium."

"Yes." Dr. Vinkov smiled. "Perhaps."

Alex prevented himself from saying, "Yes, I remember. Sacred Heart Sanitarium."

"See how many possibilities there are?"

"Yes."

"What bothers me," Dr. Vinkov's lip twisted up gravely, "is that all these possibilities did not occur to you before. Why do you suppose you found it so easy to assume the worst?"

Alex sat there hoping he would not have to answer.

"I know." Soothingly, "That's a difficult question. A very difficult question. But when we are finished," he put his pencil down, "we will know the answer. Both of us."

"I have something for you today," Dr. Vinkov said at the end of their session.

"Thank you," he replied blankly.

"I think you will find it interesting."

He looked down at the thin book. There was a large beautiful picture of a duck on the cover. The bird was just taking off. There were hundreds of tiny, iridescent drops of water surrounding it. "Patrice Lumumba Bird Preserve" was printed in bold, black letters right below the photograph.

"We can talk about this tomorrow."

When he got back to his barracks he showed it to everybody. Without explanation, since they were forbidden to talk about the particulars of their cases. They circled around his cot, excitedly, while he thumbed through each page.

It was important to share your feelings with your comrades.

"Can we see the first picture again?" Ben asked.

"Yes."

"I think it's the best of the lot, don't you?"

"Yes," they all agreed.

That night, after group, and instruction, and supper, he read it:

The Patrice Lumumba Bird Preserve was established by the Central Committee of the Communist Party, United Soviet States of America, in commemoration of the natural bond between socialist man and nature. History has shown us that presocialist man lived in conflict with nature: exploiter versus exploited. Socialist man is one with nature, each serving the needs of the other, in harmony.

The Patrice Lumumba Bird Preserve is located on the southern tip of New York State. The preserve includes a small portion of eastern New Jersey and the western half of Long Island, as well as adjacent waterways. The preserve abounds in waterfowl, including up to three hundred species peculiar to North America.

Due to the delicate balance of nature maintained in the preserve, admission is reserved to trained professionals, for whom the preserve has become a great natural laboratory.

The photographs were beautiful.

That night he dreamed; but not afterward. The dreams just stopped.

Much later, he asked Dr. Vinkov, "Did you know all along? That it was a fraud?" By then he felt very comfortable asking questions like that. "You seemed to be wondering yourself."

"No. But sometimes it is my job to wonder along with those who are lost. So that I can lead them back."

"You deceive them?"

"No. I merely suspend belief for a moment or two. So we can touch."

"Then you have never had any doubt?"

"No. How else could I do what I do? The only way to wade into uncertainty, day after day, is to be absolutely certain yourself."

There was no doubt that Dr. Vinkov was a great man.

"Of course, in this case," he stood, "there was something." His voice trailed off. With his finger pressed to his chin, as if he were deciding whether to do something or not, he approached a file cabinet and pulled out a drawer. "Perhaps you should see this," he commented absently while extracting a manila folder.

Inside were two sheets of paper held together with a paper clip. The one on top was a form. It was crumpled on one edge. And slightly discolored from age.

278

NAME: PIOTR BABULIESKI
ADMISSION DATE: MARCH 15, 120
DATE OF BIRTH: APRIL 2, 101

"He was here?"

"No. Not here. Another hospital."

"Today is his forty-third birthday?" Alex announced.

"Yes," Dr. Vinkov laughed in that somewhat awkward way that people do at funerals or in hospital rooms, "I suppose that would be true. Unfortunately, he's dead."

"Dead?"

"Yes. With people this ill it's hard to protect them from themselves."

He examined the form. And the one accompanying it.

"He murdered three women, you know." Dr. Vinkov paused a moment before adding, "In a very peculiar way."

"The man who wrote it?"

"Yes. When he was in a hospital near where you found it."

He felt a surge of hate for Piotr Babulieski.

"I suppose you're wondering why I didn't show you this earlier?"

"No." After reminding himself how important it was to be truthful, "Yes."

"That does seem as though it would have been easier, doesn't it? Just say," he sat back down in his chair with such great force that it rolled back half a meter, "'This man has been ill. See, these are his records. Therefore, don't pay any attention to him.' How does that sound?"

"Fine, I guess."

"No. There's," he waited for Alex to catch up with him, "a problem there."

Alex felt a little stupid.

With his pencil held up like a baton, "Is it likely that some book, like this book, is going to have stamped on it: 'The man who wrote this book is a dangerous lunatic'?" He laughed raucously. "No." Very earnestly, "There's the problem."

"Yes," he nodded.

"This," he shook Piotr Babulieski's file in his hand, "is not what proves the man is ill. This is not the real proof. That lies here." He tapped his finger a few centimeters above The Book. "Right here."

There was no denying that. But that didn't keep him from hating him. Even though it was wrong to hate someone so ill.

Even though that wasn't fair at all. Not really. Anybody should have been able to see that he was a lunatic.

Today would be the day. He was certain. He examined the row of pines. And the clump of full-bloom dogwoods huddled at the apex of the driveway. Yes. Today would be the day. He tucked the book under his arm as he mounted the stairs to Dr. Vinkov's office. He had carried it with him every day since receiving it. As a reminder. As proof. Sometimes he would get the sudden urge to open it. Just to see the beautiful pictures. Of the birds. And swamp. That always made him feel better.

Yes. It was time to go. And he was happy about it.

"Well, Alexander Mikhailovich, today is the day we have all been waiting for."

"Yes."

"You seem pleased enough about it."

"I am. But . . ."

"No buts. We have talked through everything. There will be problems. But they will be manageable."

"I'm confident."

"Good, comrade." Arranging a few papers into a stack. "I have talked to your parents. The fact that your mother is a doctor makes things easier."

"Thank you, Dr. Vinkov. For your efforts."

He nodded, indicating that it was time for Alex to leave. He stacked up several more papers.

Just as Alex reached the door, "Do not imagine that your parents are more disappointed than they are. Or more angry. Or more anything. You will do fine."

"Thank you."

He packed his small duffel bag and waited outside his barracks for the bus. There was a warm dry breeze, filling the air with pine pollen, which cast a soft yellowness on everything. All in all, it was a pretty place. Nothing like he would have thought.

When the bus came he stepped carefully up to the driver, showed him his papers, and, after the driver nodded, claimed a seat.

There was no one else leaving.

The bus hummed its way around the courtyard, passing by each of the seven barracks that encircled it, changed gears, and sped onto the road. He watched the sign through the back window: "Camp 3."

Camp 3. And that was all it said. The little bus groaned up a hill, took a slow turn through a cluster of pines, and then began to descend.

"Camp 4" was written on a rectangular sign. The sign was nearly hidden in the trees. Camp 4? It had never occurred to him that such a thing existed. Or, for that matter, that he was at Camp 3. As the road flattened out, and they entered, he could see it was almost exactly like his camp: a two-story building at the base of a circular drive; seven or eight narrow wooden barracks.

A man of about forty, carrying a tightly packed duffel bag, got on. He looked a little tired, but at ease. After the driver okayed his papers the man sat down, nodded, and then occupied himself with the open window.

Saying goodbye, Alex decided. Yes. Odd, unless you looked really carefully the two camps were mirror images. The administration building had been painted, actually touched up, just on the right corner. The one in his camp had not.

The little bus hummed.

Camp 4. I guess that must mean there are two others, he speculated, just to pass the time as they crept around the courtyard.

As they made the right turn back onto the road, he saw him. At least it looked like him. He mashed his face to the glass, trying to get one last look before they began accelerating. Yes. It was Myslov. His coat was buttoned up to his chin—in spite of the fact that it was shirtsleeve weather!

What was he doing there? That made no sense at all. He rubbed his temples. Just thinking about Myslov's being there made him feel warm. And a little queasy.

He refused to ask himself any more questions. It was just that propensity for asking questions that had gotten him in trouble before.

After all, Myslov had read The Book. Perhaps that was enough?

Stop!

Perhaps Myslov hadn't informed at all? Perhaps he had?

Stop!

In either case, it was all for the better.

He counted the pine trees. And then the water oaks. And the bridges. Keeping track of each total. There were a lot more pine trees. And very few bridges. Of course, that made it more interesting when one appeared.

The Zlotny was waiting for him at a service station. The driver opened the door for him. While his bag was being put in the trunk, his father nodded hello.

On the way back to the island his father explained what he was to say. That took only about ten minutes.

The rest of the way he occupied himself with the newspaper, while Alex went back to counting trees and bridges.

Alex was already seated when his mother came in to dinner. Uncertain what to expect, he had been absently fidgeting with his napkin, so he didn't realize she had arrived until she was at her chair.

Just the sight of her engulfed him with embarrassment. It was completely unexpected. Almost shocking. And physically overwhelming: he could feel himself shrivel into a pinpoint where the center of his stomach had been.

"You look well, Alexander," she offered serenely.

"Thank you, Mother," he managed to stammer.

She had that faraway look. As if it were not really her getting ready to eat dinner with them, but someone else who had been paid to sit in for her.

"Yes." Nurov sipped from his water glass. "He does, doesn't he."

He sat there, like a small insect that had stumbled into a spider-web, unable to move, until, with a kind of strained conviviality, his father called out, "Rebecca, I'm sure that Alex is starving. He's had a very long drive."

"Yes. I'm starving," he agreed before suddenly wondering if he could remember what he was supposed to say. "Driving always makes me famished."

The maid entered with several serving dishes and placed them on the table.

Alex stared at the serving dishes, letting the shiny, smooth edges of

282

each one catch his eye so that he wouldn't have to look up.

"Well, you'd never know he's been sick at all," she observed, her large brown fingers confidently guiding the food to the table.

"Thank you, Rebecca," his mother replied.

Nurov served the plates from the head of the table: first his mother's, then his.

He wasn't hungry at all. But he was able to get his supper down. He just stuck spoonful after spoonful into his mouth. And chewed until there was room for another.

"Well, a good appetite," his father remarked approvingly, while extending his hand for Alex's plate.

Alex obediently picked up the plate and offered it to him.

"Good food. One of the pleasures of home life."

Alex emptied the plate, just as he had its predecessor: one spoonful at a time.

"I have to look at this month's DAL utilization reports," Nurov said after the maid had served the chocolate ice cream.

Terrified that he was going to be left alone, and have to look up, Alex ticked the seconds off as his father rose, pushed his chair in with an exhausted grunt, and circled the table. He listened for some sound that she might get up herself. But he could feel her sitting there, immobile, as his father tromped past her.

"So, Nurov," she offered without raising her voice, just as his father's footsteps were choked off by the hallway carpet, "are you quite satisfied with yourself?"

The study door clicked shut.

She stood. "Here. Go ahead and finish this." The plate made a neat click when she deposited the ice cream at his elbow. "Apparently you haven't forgotten how to eat."

Without raising his eyes, but knowing nevertheless that she was disappearing into the hallway, he picked up his spoon and slowly consumed the ice cream.

"You finished?"

He nodded to the maid.

"Well, there's lots more. You'll need all your strength after being in the hospital so long. And being so sick." It was only then that it struck him that she was not Corinne, but somebody entirely different. "My sister's been in the hospital lately. It takes a lot out of you."

283

No. This was not Corinne. That would have been enough talking to last her a week.

He looked at the woman for a minute before getting up to escape to his room. She was as skinny as a wooden-handled mop. And as hard. In spite of all the talking.

"But she's a lot better now. Like you. Thanks to the dedication and hard work of the hospital staff."

"Yes, I'm very grateful to them myself," he replied.

On the way to his bedroom he found himself wondering why he liked Corinne so much better. But made himself stop. There was no point in wondering about things like that. No point at all.

Everything in his room was his. There was no doubt about that. He recognized each and every piece of furniture and snapshot. But he took inventory just the same, reminding himself along the way when this item had appeared. And that. Not to erase any doubt. No. That wasn't necessary. It was just that the act of touching each item's past made him feel a little more sure.

He moved down to the floor at the foot of his chest and took out each article of clothing and sat there for a while with his clothes neatly stacked around him like wagons waiting for an Indian attack. Again he reviewed each item's unique history: when, where, what he'd done. When he had convinced himself that each of those times, and places, and events was irrevocably defined and locked in place, he began to undress, first by removing one shoe and then the other. In each case he listened to the shoe hit the floor. Funny, at Camp 3 (why had he decided to call it that? he wondered. He had only discovered the sign that day. On the way out) that sound had been drowned out by two dozen other pairs of shoes making that same sound. Now he could hear himself breathe. He missed those sounds, he decided as he carefully zipped his jumpsuit on a hanger and slid it into the closet. Yes. There was something kind of comforting about them.

He took the red pill that was on the bedside table to the bathroom and washed it down with water from the plastic glass that was always on the back of the sink. It was pleasing to see that he had remembered just where that glass was. Without a moment's hesitation.

He slept instantly.

When he woke, after first staring at the wall for a moment to make

284

sure that he was actually in his room, and it was actually the next morning and not ten minutes or twenty minutes later, it occurred to him how empty his sleep had been: it was as if a surgeon had cut out the eight or nine hours with a scalpel and sewn the morning to the night before.

He cracked the blinds. It was misting, but the grass was still desert-brown. But that never changed. Even in summer it would be dead brown. With all the rain. And a billion gallons of water just on the other side of the dunes. The water just poured through the sandy ground like a sieve.

He slipped on his robe and ambled to the kitchen. On his way he heard them talking in the study.

He poured himself a glass of orange juice and turned on the television. "The weather today will be cool and wet. High in the mid-sixties. A one hundred percent chance of rain." At the bottom of the screen it said Sunday, May 3.

Did that mean he would be going to Young Pioneers? His father hadn't said anything about that. To be on the safe side he showered and put on a freshly pressed jumpsuit.

Perhaps his father would be out of the study now, he decided after brushing his hair. If he just walked out there and made himself available his father might say something like "Don't forget your Young Pioneers meeting." No. He never said things like that. But perhaps now, considering the circumstances, he would let him know one way or the other what he should do.

Nurov was slouched at the kitchen table.

"Good morning," Alex ventured into the tangled mass of gray-and-black curls obscuring his father's head.

"You shouldn't leave the television on. It's a criminal waste of electricity."

"Sorry. I forgot."

"A few kilowatts here. A few kilowatts there. Multiply that by millions of I forgots and what do you have?"

Was he supposed to respond?

"Millions of kilowatts," his father answered tersely.

Alex left the kitchen for the porch without finding out whether he was going to the Young Pioneers meeting.

The screens were drenched with water. Not from the rain crashing

285

against them but from condensation. That happened every time it was foggy or misty. You couldn't see a thing. Nevertheless he sat there, at the picnic table, with his back to the kitchen, looking directly into the featureless, opaque screens, wondering about the meeting. After a few minutes he got up and thumped the screen with his finger, sending a rainstorm of droplets out onto the yard. There was no point in not asking.

After sliding open the glass door, "Should I go to Young Pioneers this morning?" He said it very quickly, but without stumbling.

"No." His mother was standing there in a wisteria gown, munching on a carrot. The word had been fired out like a pistol shot. Clearly. Decisively.

He was attacked by that same overwhelming embarrassment.

"He's not ready yet."

"Did I say anything?" his father replied.

Alex stood there feeling ill. Panting.

"Eat breakfast," his mother recommended as she strolled out of the kitchen. He could hear her chewing on the carrot.

As soon as she disappeared he felt okay and ate a bowl of cereal, standing, with his back against the refrigerator, while Nurov rotated a cup of coffee with his thumb and forefinger. Strange, he didn't feel that way around his father. And he had been just as much of a disappointment to each of them. That didn't make any sense at all.

As soon as he had finished he put down the cereal bowl and raced back to his room, dreading the whole way that he might run into her again—and be faced with that feeling.

With his door pushed to, he lay in bed the remainder of the day, his picture book opened up in front of him so that from time to time he could examine one of the beautiful birds as it flew up from the water.

There was really no way to avoid her. Not completely. During the week he could have breakfast after she had gone to clinic. And lunch would be no problem. And he could avoid the television room. And unplanned trips to the kitchen. And on Saturdays and Sundays he could go out on the beach early. But in the end there would be dinner. That was unavoidable. He lay there the rest of the day trying to think of some solution, knowing all the time there wasn't one. And knowing he would do anything to avoid that feeling.

· · ·

"I kept this warm for you," Rebecca announced as she extracted his breakfast from the oven.

Alex smiled approvingly.

"I guess you need all the sleep you can get?"

When it was apparent she expected an answer he nodded.

"Sure you do," she agreed.

Her small, calculating eyes flitted back and forth between Alex and the plate. "And all the food you can eat."

"I guess," he replied energetically. His stomach had been eating itself for the last hour.

"They still hurt?" she asked as if his teeth were departed relatives, while pointing through her cheeks at her molars.

"No." In a distracted way that made it easier to begin the lie, "They're completely healed."

"That's good." After a few seconds, which he ticked off in the certain anticipation that she would persist, "Many stitches?"

"What was that?" he replied, in the hope that immersing himself in the food would prevent her from making further inquiries.

She tilted her head toward him without raising it so that her ear was only a centimeter or two above the sponge she had been pushing down the counter.

"A few," he forced out, while directing his eyes through the glass doors, across the porch toward the dunes. There was no point in getting on her wrong side. Not if he was going to eat at odd times.

"I've never had to have stitches," she announced as if stitches were a form of punishment.

"They weren't that bad."

"Oh?"

"There were stitches. Where each tooth had been," he embellished, playing up to her apparent interest in the macabre, before adding, "I was asleep through it all, of course." Explaining it that way, that he had been asleep, seemed to make it less of a lie. "But I could feel them the next day."

"They don't have to take those out, do they?"

"No," he agreed. "They dissolve."

"Yeah." He listened to her rinse the sponge. "I guess that's a lot better than having 'em pulled out?"

There was no doubt that she was completely absorbed with the details of his illness, that the whole of it was being accepted without

287

hesitation. Yes, he decided while emptying his glass of orange juice, there was no reason for her not to accept it as the truth. But in the beginning he hadn't even been able to look at her when he answered.

Out of the blue, "It's hard to believe somebody could get so sick from wisdom teeth."

Well, it hadn't gone down as smoothly as he had thought. Not at all. Or was she only expressing a kind of amazement? He stammered for a second before replying, in as close an approximation of Nurov's words as he could manage, "Well, my wisdom teeth weren't really the problem. At least not the surgery. It was the infection. That was the real problem."

She squinched up her face in disbelief.

"Peritonitis."

"Peritonitis?" she questioned, but in a way that let him know that it was only the word that bothered her.

"That's an inflammation of the peritoneal sac. That's the sac that holds all your organs. It's like a big plastic bag. But of course it's not plastic."

"Oh." As she pushed her fingertip into each cabinet door to make sure it was securely shut, "And that's what almost killed you? Peritonitis?"

"Yes," he replied, feeling like a little boy, who, up until that instant, imagined that adults could see through lies as easily as a tissue, but now knew that they could only see and hear just what he could see and hear—and hence were as susceptible to lies as he was. "It can be quite dangerous. But I'm completely recovered now."

He first saw Myslov on a Friday. He had been sunning himself on the steps of the walkway to the beach. Just as he had been doing every day that was nice enough. That day he had decided, after some hesitation, that it was warm enough, but he had had to build a barricade against the wind out of an overturned chair and a blanket. And even then the gusts burned his cheeks.

Myslov just walked by. Head down. Apparently lost in thought. Right then, just by looking at him, he could tell it was Myslov he had seen the afternoon he was discharged. Not because he could see the person that clearly. On that day. But he could tell nevertheless.

How was he supposed to react? he puzzled.

● ● ●

"How did you feel? Seeing him."

"Okay." Too noncommittal. Why did he always have to answer like that?

"Just okay?" It was his fault. Why didn't he just answer?

"We didn't talk or anything."

"Why was that?"

"He was too far away. In fact, I'm sure he didn't see me at all."

"Surely you must have felt some way or other. Considering." Yes. Dr. Vinkov made a habit of dangling provocative words like "considering" at the end of questions.

"Oh, I don't hold anything against him." Yes, that was just the kind of thing he would blurt out. Was that what he was really thinking? No. He just wasn't thinking.

After an answer like that, Dr. Vinkov would twist a pencil between his thumb and forefinger, and wait.

"There's nothing to hold against him. He was only doing his duty. And I'm better off for it anyway. I really am."

Seeing things clearly like that always seemed to please Dr. Vinkov. Alex could see him smile contentedly.

Talking things over with Dr. Vinkov always seemed to help. Even in Camp 3, lying in his bunk, he had had imaginary conversations like that. Even though Dr. Vinkov was there, right across the quadrangle.

After that he saw Myslov every few days. Around lunch. Just passing by. Finally he waved.

On his way back by, Myslov stopped about ten meters away. He didn't seem to know whether to keep going or wait.

"Hi, how are you?" Alex offered.

"Fine," Myslov replied, in a reedy voice that was nearly swallowed by a gust of wind.

"Good."

"And you?" Myslov was crouching into his coat so that the wind would have a smaller target.

"Fine."

Myslov nodded and then, after a quick wave, was on his way.

From then on Myslov made a point of waving, sometimes with a "Hello." But he didn't stop to chat, which suited Alex fine. Dr.

Vinkov was right. Myslov had only done his duty. But there was really nothing for them to say beyond "Hello" or "How are you?"

The weekdays were a problem. Mornings he watched television: a lot of it was very informative. After lunch, weather permitting, he sunned himself. That was all very relaxed and cozy. But by midafternoon he was hiding out in his room. With a magazine. Or newspaper. Or nothing. Even boredom was preferable to the anguished embarrassment triggered by her presence. Later, he would count the seconds to supper, and when he was finally forced to the table, he would occupy himself with the place settings or anything else he could invent to divert his eyes.

They didn't talk at the table beyond the essentials. And there was never laughter. There or in the study. And of course they could thank him for that.

But, from time to time, he could hear them in the study. Talking. In the beginning he raced by the closed door to make sure he heard nothing. But later he began to inch his way by so that a stray word or two would creep under the door. The tone was that of discussion, not conversation, each word measured out and delivered like the ingredients in a recipe.

The first day he actually stopped to listen they were talking about Nurov's grandmother:

"You can be sure she knows."

"No," his father assured her.

"Sonia Ouspenskaya makes it a point to know everything."

Alex visualized his great-grandmother sitting there contentedly knowing everything. In his mind she was as old as a mummy. Even though the photograph on his mother's chest was of a much younger woman.

"Vinkov was chosen because I can trust him completely."

His mother laughed. "Trust. You've been a simpleton throughout this whole business."

When his father's chair creaked, Alex bolted down the hallway to the kitchen and posed in front of the open refrigerator door.

If they would just talk he wouldn't be forced to eavesdrop like that, he decided, staring blankly at the frothy surface of a pitcher of orange juice. It wasn't fair to treat him like some sort of idiot.

290

But instantly he realized that he couldn't speak to her anyway. Or even listen. Unless she was on the other side of the door.

"Peritonitis?"

"Yes."

Screwing up her face, "It sounds awful, doesn't it?"

He mixed his cereal.

"An infection." She scrubbed down the counter. Whenever she brought it up she began cleaning. As though the germs were all around them.

"Yes." He would describe it to her as graphically as he could, watching her face screw up tighter and tighter until it looked like dried brown leather. He could almost feel his insides rotting from the disease when he talked about it. Even though it had never been there. At least not in his body cavity where he felt it.

No. But it felt good for what had been wrong with him to have some concrete expression. Something that could be the object of his disgust. Something that he could tell was gone. And had left not the slightest taint.

Something he could describe completely. Because it was so clearly comprehensible. And unfrightening.

In the just-before-breakfast semidarkness the horizon slammed down on the water so tightly that the light leaked out like the light under a door.

He was rubbing his hands together to fight off the chill when Myslov said, "Good morning." He hadn't been expecting him. Or thinking about him. But right away Alex recognized the blend of stilted formality and desperate friendliness that gave a "good morning" from Myslov a special flavor.

"How are you?" Alex replied.

"Fine. It's a beautiful sunrise, isn't it?"

"Yes."

With surprised interest, "Are you often up this early?"

"Well, sometimes on Saturdays," he answered, as if the question were invasive.

Tentatively, after taking a step up the beach, "You did know that I've been ill."

291

Alex nodded.

"Appendicitis." Myslov cast his eyes out over the breakers in a way that Alex recognized right away. "With complications. But I'm much improved now."

"That's good."

"It was a," he began before blurting out, in a surprised whisper, "I'm sorry, I've lost control of my bladder." A dark blue wet spot began racing down Myslov's jumpsuit.

"Are you all right?" Alex asked reflexively.

Myslov stood there for a second, smiling stoically, and then with a shrug, turned up the beach.

"I'm not angry, you know," Alex hollered after he had gone about fifty meters. Correcting himself, "If anything, I should be grateful." Myslov turned a quizzical face to him before continuing toward home.

The next few days Alex took his sun on the deck.

"At least this is the last we will hear from that slimy little man."

"Yes," his father replied, packing what sounded like years of fatigue into one word.

"I feel like I should take a bath. But I know it won't do any good."

"It's over."

"The idea of that slimy little man knowing all about us. Question after question after question." She clicked out the word like a metronome. "I can hear them right now."

"You've never even seen the man. He's not some kind of monster."

"Little men like that are all the same. You don't have to see them."

With finality, "It was necessary."

"It makes me ill. Just the idea. That he can know all about me. Everything that goes on here."

"That did not interest him at all. He did his duty."

Screaming, "It makes me ill!"

"It may not have been like that at all."

"You have the report right in front of you. Are you blind as well as a fool?" Before he could respond, "Just the idea. That he's been over us inch by inch."

"You make it sound like he has been poking through your underwear."

"Hasn't he?" she hissed.

292

It was right then that it struck him. Yes. That was it. That was the reason he couldn't even look at her.

He crumpled down the wall onto the floor.

That she was there, in all those dreams. That was the reason. Yes, he nearly screamed out, while images of her, there, with Vinkov, and Janovich, slashed through his mind.

He could hear the study door open.

"What are you doing?" His father was standing at the doorway looking down at him.

"Nothing."

She was there, on the other side of him.

"Just sitting."

Nurov looked at his wife and then back at Alex. "Just sitting?"

With mild disgust, "Perhaps you should try a chair." She stepped around his father, and then him, before turning down the hallway toward her room.

He had been able to look right at her without feeling like he was shriveling up. He leaned over onto his side so that he could watch her disappear into her room.

That night there was no red pill on his bedside table.

The next day the sand was really hot. The dry grass stuck the tender parts of his feet again.

It was low tide. So the breakers were a football field away. But he could still see her, bobbing like a blond cork just on the other side of the sandbar.

When she dove, and was down for what seemed like eternity, he could feel his stomach tighten against the sand. And then, when she reappeared, he would exhale with relief.

Just as the sun set, so that all you could see was the tops of the breakers, she trudged out, clearly unhappy to return to the dry land.

Alex slid down the small dune on his belly and crept back to the walkway so that he would get there before her.

"How was your swim, ma'am?"

"Wonderful, Rebecca. Just wonderful."

• • •

He anchored down one edge of the workbook with his soda can and the other with his knee, and read the problem while eating a tuna sandwich. A ship leaves port sailing due east at 12 kph. The Gulf Stream is moving northward at 3 kph. Determine the velocity of the ship.

He read the problem again. It looked cool and soft through sunglasses.

"Hello." Myslov sounded like he was hollering into a well.

"Hi." When Myslov didn't immediately restart his walk, Alex added, "I'm getting a little studying in."

"I'm sure that's a good idea."

"Yes." He tried to smile enthusiastically enough to keep Myslov from wetting his pants again, but not enough to lure him over. What did he think I was going to do? he wondered while saying, "Physics. It fades if you don't look out."

"Yes. It always pays to work hard." Myslov continued his walk down the beach after a quick wave.

"Yes," Alex repeated to himself, before returning to his physics notes.

He stayed with it the rest of the day, stopping only to spread sunscreen on his shoulders from time to time. Or chase down a page when the wind ripped it away from him.

Just before sunset he went out into the surf. Beyond the breakers. And waited for her. But she didn't come.

At dinner he could see why. Right after sitting down she rapped the side of her glass with a spoon while calling out, "An ice cube, Rebecca."

"Yes, ma'am, it's on its way."

She rubbed the ice cube into her temple until it was only a damp spot on her fingertip.

"I think it is time for Alex to resume his Young Pioneers," his father announced, in a way that bordered on a question.

When she replied, "Whatever you think, Nurov," he had to fight off the urge to wince.

"I think yes."

With a shrug, "Rebecca, more ice. That last piece was the size of a snowflake."

Nurov emptied his vodka glass and with what sounded like mild disappointment announced, "I have to go over some DAL system utilization reports."

That was it. That was it exactly.

He watched his father rise, push his chair in, and, after leaning over, empty his water glass. "Is this tap water, Rebecca?"

"No, Vice-Minister Nurov. That's bottle water."

Yes. The DAL system kept track of everything. Every inquiry. Every word you read.

"It tastes like tap water," he frowned.

When Rebecca appeared at the door to shrug, Nurov dismissed her with a gesture and plowed down the hall to his study.

It was so obvious. A schoolboy should have seen it. Yes. He found himself smiling. Yes. I ought to run down Myslov. And tell him. When Myslov came to mind it was with that big, lake-shaped wet spot spreading from his crotch. Poor Myslov. They must have scared the piss out of him.

"You must be feeling a lot better, sir," Rebecca offered.

"Yes."

"Well, it takes a pretty long time to recover from an operation like that."

"Ah, yes," he replied absently, as it occurred to him that they hadn't known a thing about Myslov until he had told them. Yes. He had gotten them both caught. He laughed. And was Myslov better off for it?

And Dr. Vinkov knew that. He must have. All along.

His mother had been looking directly at him. Her face was puffy. And tired. But still quite beautiful, in that composed, distant way.

"I," he began, but she got up and turned away before he could finish saying that he had been swimming that day.

And he probably knew about the dreams. Was responsible for them. That would be the end of his conversations with him, he decided.

The small meeting room was crisply cool even though at least twenty-five of them had been packed in there.

He made up his mind to appear completely composed. He crossed his leg. And smiled.

"Good morning, Young Pioneers. As you know, one of our

295

comrades has been ill. Let us all welcome him back."

With Gregorov leading them with his upturned hand, "Welcome back, Comrade Nurov."

Alex nodded. And then smiled.

They showed a videotape. Which was nice.

As they were filing out, several of them came over to congratulate him on his recovery. Which was very kind of them, he decided.

"I hope you haven't fallen too far behind in school?" Gregorov asked discreetly, pausing in his characteristic way before the last word of the sentence.

"I'm scrambling to catch up now."

Gregorov formed a concerned "oh" with his mouth and nodded. Of course, he was curious about Moscow University. But with Gregorov everything had to be done obliquely.

Affecting confidentiality, "We'll just have to see whether I can catch up."

Gregorov nodded approvingly.

When he got home his mother was standing in the kitchen. Rubbing the back of her neck with a monstrous yellow beach towel that nearly engulfed her head, "How'd it go?"

"Fine," he replied with as nonchalant a shrug as he could manage.

"Only fine?"

"We saw a video."

Impatiently, "You know I don't give a damn about that."

"Everything went fine."

She stood there for a moment, observing him, her head still capped by that absurdly large yellow towel, which she pulled methodically back and forth across her neck as if it were part of some nonsensical machine.

"Just fine," he repeated.

"Good."

After walking through the sliding glass door onto the porch she turned and, after starting to say something else, said, "If Nurov asks, tell him I've gone for a swim."

He changed into shorts, picked up his notebook, and went out to the end of the walkway. From there he could watch her swim while he studied.

He had no trouble picking her out, even though it was a Sunday afternoon. She was the only one out beyond the breakers.

At 22:30 a ship leaves port heading due east at 15 kph. Another ship leaves 2 hours later in the same direction at 20 kph. When will the second ship overtake the first?

The area beyond the breakers was smooth and empty. He waited for her to come back up, counting by thousand-and-ones. She surfaced at thirty-two thousand and one. And then vanished again.

In ten hours the first ship would travel 150 kilometers; the second, after eight hours, would travel 160 kilometers. So the answer was less than ten hours after the first ship leaves.

She was underwater again.

He tried eight hours. The first ship would have gone 120 kilometers. The second 120 kilometers.

He jotted down "6:30." Now, how do you do it? he wondered. Obviously you use the derivative. $s' = 15$. Also $s' = 20$. So $s = 15t$. And $s = 20t$. But $15t = 20t$ was nonsense.

She was back underwater. When he got to fifty-thousand-and-one he saw her step out of a breaker.

There must be some trick. $15t = 20t$ was clearly wrong. And then he saw it! The ships started at different times. So $s(O) = 30$. Bang. $15t + 30 = 20t$ and so $t = 6$. And 8 hours was right.

"You can study that crap anywhere, you know." Her remark was followed by a shower of salty drops as she stepped across him onto the walkway.

"I guess."

"Of course, you'll be lucky if they let you study sewage control in Moscow after what you've done," she said as if she were posing a question to herself.

She lowered herself cross-legged so that her knees were flush with his notebook and sat there for a second. "What possessed you to do that?" Her lip was trembling. "Why would you try to ruin us?" He could hear the water dripping from her hair onto his notebook.

"I thought I had discovered something important. About what had happened."

"Really?" With a raised eyebrow, "What had happened."

"Well, it turned out not to be true. The man was a lunatic."

"A lunatic?"

"Yes. He's dead now. But he was a lunatic."

She struck him just below the ear with her fist. He saw it coming, in fact watched it glide along a lazy, circular path until it disappeared behind his ear. But he made no effort to duck.

She put her wrist to her mouth, where his head must have bruised it; then withdrew it before standing. "It wouldn't make any difference to me if the man was another Lenin. He's dead. And we're not." With her back to him, "Only a fool would risk everything for," she stammered, "a dead man."

His ear was ringing. And hot. But he didn't touch it. He wanted it to keep hurting as long as it could.

As soon as she was out of sight he packed up his notes and began to run. Even though he hadn't run in months. And in fact had been content to watch television and lounge on the fringes of the beach.

He immediately broke into a sweat. And his legs began to ache.

He skirted the edge of two long wooden chairs. General and Mrs. Grichenko frowned. Not because he had come close enough to spatter sand on them. Just because he had invaded the borders of their little empire of two chairs, a cooler, and an umbrella. Alex shook his head apologetically, but the general, who looked more like a shaved bulldog than a man, only snarled, while his wife said in very loud Russian, "The boys these days. They have no respect. No respect at all."

Alex raised his hands in a "What can I say?" gesture before speeding back up.

As it raced by, the island splintered into a succession of disconnected details: a pair of legs, a pail, a shell, breasts, an umbrella, a bobbing head, breasts dense enough to form a suffocating cloud.

Finally there was only open beach. Stretching three or four hundred meters. And exhaustion.

He collapsed onto the sand. Panting. Feeling horrible and blank and wonderful all at once.

There it was. The old dune. Not a hundred meters away. Lording over him like an ancient volcano.

He rolled over onto his elbow. It was so quiet this far north. Past the houses. There was a time when he would have been in there. Reading one of his mysteries. That seemed a million years ago. And distinctly something you would do when you were a boy.

Not that he felt too bad about it. At least not the mysteries. The rest? Well, his mother was right about that: he had been a fool.

He lay there for half an hour. Never once feeling tempted to climb the old dune. To go back inside. Not that he couldn't. There was nothing in there. Certainly not The Book. (Just the word produced a shudder.) And the old mysteries had certainly been dug up too. Well, that was just as well. They were a waste of time anyway.

When he could stand again, Alex wandered into the sandy rift where the old dune met the row of low-lying, sea-oats-topped dunes that guarded the beach. And sat. From that perspective the steep white dune was immense. He could almost feel that sense of awe and familiarity it had evoked when he was a boy. Long before the mysteries. Or anything else.

Just as he was about to get up, he noticed that there were footprints leading up to the rim. They rose in a long, lazy semicircle that began near his feet and then swooped off to the right. Before he could decide whether they were old or new, he heard laughter. At first just a murmur that could have been confused with the wind blowing through the water oaks, it exploded as soon as the voices reached the crest.

Martina Antipova's hand was clasped to another hand whose body was still half a stride behind her. She stood there for a moment, alone on the soft edge of the dune, looking, in her blue swim suit that fit as tightly as a fish's skin, like some island princess from an island where everyone was perfect and she was the most perfect of the perfect.

"Don't be so slow," she reprimanded teasingly.

"Slow?" The hand yanked her back into the dune. As the young man who belonged to the hand burst over the top he announced, "You shouldn't cheat."

"Me?" She pounced on him from behind. "Who started it?" They tumbled down the dune in a tangle of arms and legs. Laughing.

When they came to rest, just a few meters from his feet, he jumped up.

"Alex," she announced with surprise. Regaining her composure, but making no effort to get up out of the sand, "This is my friend, actually my second cousin—by marriage—Leo Vasilief." She got up and began carefully to dust the sand off her arms and shoulders.

"He's here on a visit." She didn't seem the slightest bit unsettled to run into him. There at the dune.

The young man extended his hand.

"This is Alex Nurov."

"Hello," he said in English.

"Hi, I was just cooling off. After a run." Explaining, awkwardly, "I haven't been here in a while."

"You've been quite ill," she said with concern.

"Yes. An infection. But I'm much better now."

"Yes. I can see you are."

"Shall we go for a swim? And get this sand off," the young man asked, before adding unconvincingly, "Why don't you join us?"

"No. I'm out running," he explained with a smile.

"Alex is a basketball player," she announced. "For the school team." She could have said he hadn't played that year, but she didn't. That was generous of her, he decided.

"A good game. Basketball," Leo Vasilief said accommodatingly, after taking one step toward the beach.

Alex nodded.

"Leo is a coach. In Leningrad." When she smiled her teeth glistened. "Nice to see you."

"Right. And nice to meet you." So that they wouldn't feel he was tagging along he jogged off parallel to the water along the rift separating the two rows of sand dunes. In the dry, ankle-deep sand the best he could manage was an exhausted, lunging stride that made him resemble a wounded bird more than an athlete.

Damn! The fellow's going to think I'm some kind of invalid, he screamed silently to himself. They're probably chuckling to themselves right now.

But when he turned to cut between a pair of small dunes they were already halfway to the water, his arm comfortably draped along her shoulder. Odd. She hadn't seemed the slightest bit unsettled by bumping into him. Even though it was right at that dune. Of course, after all this time, she probably thought of Leo Vasilief when she thought of the dune. And not him at all. Even though he had been the first one to take her there.

After he had traveled a respectable distance he slowed to a walk. Just out of reach of the surf.

300

There had been a time when she was the most beautiful thing in the world. An ideal. And for a moment, when she was standing there, she was again. And although now he wasn't sure of that at all, it did seem amazing that there had been a time when he was almost repelled by her. He must have been in an amazing frame of mind for that ever to be the case, he decided.

The problems in section b were always the hardest. By severalfold. But then, they were preparation for advanced placement.

Gasoline flows into a tank at a rate of 200 lps. The tank is in the shape of a triangular beaker 1 meter in diameter at the neck and 5 meters in diameter at the base. The tank is 8 meters high. At what rate is the gasoline rising after 60 seconds?

He drew a sketch of the tank and labeled it. And then an arrow into the top with "200 lps" along it. And then let the gasoline pour in while he dug his feet into the cool sand under the steps.

"Aren't you being diligent, though," she said, looking down from the end of the walkway. The late-afternoon sun was directly behind her.

With a noncommittal shrug while he squinted up at her, "I guess." He pushed his notebook to the side so she could pass by the make-shift desk he had created out of the stairs.

Sitting, "More mathematics?"

He nodded.

"Well, perhaps that isn't a complete waste. For now."

She sat there quietly for a while with her legs drawn up to her chest while he puzzled over the problem.

All he could do with her sitting there was watch the gasoline flow relentlessly into the tank, liter after liter after liter. But he did manage to convince himself that the level would rise faster and faster as the tank filled.

"You'll ruin your eyes in this light," she announced matter-of-factly before standing. "Come go for a swim with me."

The breeze that blew across the island in the afternoons had died down. The water was as soft and warm as soda pop as they sliced through the breakers.

Out where the water was still she said in a whisper, "Don't throw away what I've done for you."

When he tried to reply she pressed her hand to his mouth. Perhaps she didn't want to hear an explanation, or anything that might spoil the moment. So they just floated there for a while. Quietly.

Four or five times during the day he went back to the sketch of the gasoline tank. He even looked up the formula for the volume of a beaker. But he couldn't really make any progress.

When the sun was parallel to the bottom of the porch, and he had decided that she wasn't really going to come, she appeared. She walked slowly. Her head down the way it sometimes was.

He listened to wooden shoes clank down the walkway while he finished computing the depth of the gasoline after 59 seconds. If he did the same thing for 60 seconds he could make a guess about the rate.

As he was sliding the sketch of the gasoline tank into his notebook she said, "Still fiddling with that stuff? I don't know why you waste your time. Don't you know they're not going to let you in?"

"I haven't heard," he blurted out.

"What do you expect? To be welcomed by a band?" she asked derisively, as her shoes clanked down the four steps to the sand.

He could feel the hope escaping like air from a punctured balloon. Not that he hadn't known. It was just that there was no point in thinking about it. Not really.

"So you've heard?"

"No. They," she kicked off her shoes and began to run toward the water, "prefer to torture me."

He stood there for a moment, knowing he shouldn't follow after her. What was the point? When she was like that, being with her was worse than being alone.

The footprints were still there. Or at least it looked like them. After hesitating for moment he went right up the side of the dune, which, with a running start, could be scaled in twenty or so giant steps.

He stopped at the crest and peered down through the foliage: it was empty. No point in stumbling across them doing it right there. Of course, they might not be. In fact, he had a hard time picturing her actually having sex. He could picture her breasts. And thighs. And her crotch, even though he had never actually seen it. But those were all images of her. And only her.

302

He looked up at the edge of the dune where she had said, "I'm not some American whore." He could almost hear it. But it didn't sound convincing. She hadn't done it because she was afraid. All that talk about dedication was probably just talk.

Why think about something like that anyway? In fact, what was the point in poking around there at all? he asked himself as he crept under the branches of the water oak.

Why did he feel like that? Like an intruder. After all, it had been his place long before it was theirs. And for all he knew they had been there only that one time.

There was the place where they'd been sitting, he decided. Yes. They'd had lunch. You'd think they'd take their junk with them when they left. Instead of leaving it there to rot.

"Damn," he said with a kick at the place. You could see where they'd stretched out. The sand was a mess.

"Another great throw?" he questioned, before expelling a deep, guttural roar that made the old dune sound like an erupting volcano. "That kind of a throw, eh?" After roaring again, he laughed, and sat down.

"Mind if I watch?" he said to the indentations in the sand. "Oh, don't be shy. Just be dedicated."

After sitting there for a moment, he felt funny. Not because of them. Or any of that. But because they had been lying right where The Book had been. Just the thought of it produced a weakening nausea.

Well, that was not the reason he had come there, he said to himself. If there had been any reason at all.

But when he left he found himself looking to see if anyone was around. And when there wasn't he burst into a run.

When he got back his mother was on the back porch drying herself. "Where were you?" she asked.

"Running," he replied with a rush of embarrassment, in spite of the fact that the question had not been an accusation at all.

"You missed a marvelous swim," she announced as if the afternoon before had been erased from the calendar.

He turned to go in.

"So, how did the work go today?"

"I," he stammered, before deciding to lie. "Fine. In spots."

303

"Oh?" She smiled a relaxed smile. "Well, sometimes you have to make things happen."

As if it didn't matter too much, "Yes."

"And not give in to moments of blackness." She tossed the towel over her shoulder. "I make it a rule not to give in to that myself."

He stood there dumbfounded while she strolled across the kitchen. On her way by she picked up a string bean from the colander and snapped it off with her teeth.

"Shut the door, please."

Alex reluctantly pushed it to.

"Of course, that's no guarantee of our privacy," his father commented dryly.

Alex had not been in the study since the day Dr. Vinkov arrived. On the surface it was exactly the same: the cabinets were tightly locked, official books filled the shelves, and the long-necked computer terminal mutely surveyed the room from atop the desk—but, of course, being in there was different now. Completely different.

After a moment he noticed there was a letter on the desk. Seeing it knocked the breath out of him.

"You've been gone all afternoon?" his father inquired.

Apologetically, "Yes." He stared at the letter. "Just walking. I guess the time got away from me."

His father gave him an evaluative glance, before announcing, "This is for you." The chair squeaked when he leaned to push the letter across the desktop.

"The official news," his mother sighed disgustedly.

After the letter had been sitting there for a few seconds his father inquired, "Aren't you going to read it?"

Alex extracted the letter. The two-line-long message was dwarfed by an imposing letterhead:

> We regret to inform you that your admission to the Polytechnic
> Division of Moscow University has been canceled.

"Well?" his mother insisted.

Alex nodded stupidly. It was exactly the result that they all knew was inescapable. In fact, there seemed no point at all in doing more

304

than opening the letter, verifying that it said what it had to say, and disposing of it.

She sat there for a moment. Her arm quietly draped over the back of the chair. And then said, "You must write Sonia Ouspenskaya."

"No," Nurov replied.

"You," she enunciated the pronoun carefully, "must write the letter, Alexander. She is your great-grandmother. Tell her that you are sorry. Tell her that you are better. Tell her any damned thing that will move her."

"No," Nurov repeated in a way that made it impossible for him to respond.

"Sonia Ouspenskaya is the General Secretary's sister. More than his sister. She is—"

He restrained her with a look of bored disgust.

Skeptically, "You are still his father?"

Nurov waved her off disgustedly.

"You must write her tonight," his mother insisted. With unmistakable agitation, "If you have any hopes left."

"It is foolish to get carried away over this," his father responded, before adding, as if he were a railway conductor ticking off the next stop, "It was inevitable."

With resignation, "Yes. I suppose it was." She looked directly at Alex. "But that is no reason to accept it."

"We will do exactly that. Besides, it's not the end of the world."

She gave Nurov a long, uncomprehending look. "This is what you have wanted, all along, isn't it?"

"No."

"I wonder," she announced distractedly.

He frowned.

"Well, then, do something about it."

"He has not finished the school year."

As if she were talking to a child, "You don't believe that has anything to do with this?"

"Of course it does," Nurov replied.

Looking at Alex, "He can be tutored."

"No."

"Sonia Ouspenskaya could take care of this like that." When she snapped her finger it fired across the table like a pistol shot.

Alex could hear Celeste punctuate the snap with, "You must be some kind of loony if you don't know that." The day he met her. Standing in that tiny room. She had snapped her finger just that way after saying, "They can do things for you. Just like that." Snap.

"Can you deny that?" his mother persisted.

Nurov refused to answer.

"She can do anything she wants. Anything."

Yes, Alex agreed. Sonia Ouspenskaya could do anything she wanted. Probably with just a snap of the fingers.

"There is more to it than that." His father paused, in the way you pause before saying something delicate. "What has happened is serious. Very serious." Before she could respond, "Not just nothing. You seem to take this lightly."

"You have overreacted from the start."

"No. In a communist society we each have our duty. That comes first."

With exasperation, "Have I ever denied that? No. Never. But it has been taken care of. Just the way you wanted it. Now we're dealing with the consequences."

Nurov stood.

"If you told her he has his heart set on Moscow University. Just that. And nothing else. That would do it. Unless—" She stopped. "Damn it all, Nurov. She probably knows anyway. Is there anything she doesn't know?"

During the long silence, while they stood there, Alex peered into the blank, stupid terminal, which seemed to be taking in everything they said, word by word, without emotion or consequence. Just looking at it made him ill.

"Why did you do it, Nurov? Why?" she moaned finally.

Exhaustedly, "We've been over it a dozen times."

"I still don't see."

As if it were a long sigh, "We are not all opportunist, Daisy."

"We've not all had everything handed to us on a silver platter," she hissed at his back as he opened the door. "And then spilled it on the way to the table."

With deadly certitude, "Alexander, you will not write your great-grandmother."

Alex nodded.

His mother raised herself from the chair and walked past Nurov before turning. "Are you mute? Your future is being destroyed right in front of you."

He couldn't respond. It was almost as if he were mute. Not just from fear—but because what he had done was not something that ought to be passed over lightly. It was almost as if he were seeing that for the first time.

"I understand Myslov will be here this morning," Gregorov announced in the manner of a question. His tone suggested that another, less obvious question was being asked.

Alex shrugged.

Answering himself, "Yes. He will. He hasn't been," he paused to add a touch of confidentiality, "well, you know?"

"I've heard that."

"Actually, and I'm not one for rumor-mongering, I've heard that, well, he has suffered something of a breakdown." Alex let Gregorov's sentence dangle there. "I believe it had something to do with unauthorized works." Gravely, "There's no doubt that things like that are a menace."

Alex nodded gravely.

"You don't suppose he got involved with Kerelsky, do you?" Gregorov speculated.

Without completely excluding the possibility, "That doesn't seem very likely."

"Could you see Myslov doing anything like that on his own?" With a mixture of shock and anger he added, "You wouldn't think that they'd let people like that in the schools!" before carefully correcting his harsh judgment with, "but I guess no one can predict with certainty who's going to go loony."

"No."

With a tut-tut of the lips, "Well, I can see why his family is choosing to avoid embarrassment. Episodes like that can be tragic for a family. Of course, they are innocent, I'm sure, so there is no point in our not going along with," he gestured with his hands to finish the thought.

Alex attempted a half-step toward his chair.

"Our role, as I see it, is to be as helpful as possible," Gregorov ruminated with what seemed heartfelt concern. "Of course, we must be vigilant. Not that I am expecting any kind of relapse, mind you. But we must be on the alert—for his sake."

Myslov walked into the room.

"In some ways he's the last one you would expect to get involved with anything like that," Gregorov whispered disdainfully, before adding, just as Alex was about to claim his seat, "But what is one to expect from a Russamsky?"

Alex must have appeared startled.

Genuinely, "Don't take offense, Nurov. You are a special case. Yes. I would say exactly that. A very special case." He nodded before circling around the block of chairs to the small table reserved for the chapter secretary.

"Good morning, Young Pioneers. I hope everyone is ready for an energetic discussion. We have a very busy agenda. Before we get started I'd like to welcome back Comrade Myslov, who has just finished convalescing from a bout of appendicitis."

Alex turned, with the other Young Pioneers, to give Myslov an encouraging smile.

"I would like to announce that the details for our tour of the Ministry of Information have been finalized. Thanks to the kind offices of Comrade Nurov's father," Gregorov paused, "Vice-Minister of Information M. N. Nurov."

Alex acknowledged the smiles with a nod.

"The bus will leave from here at fourteen-thirty Wednesday. Please be prompt."

The subject for the panel discussion was the university student as a model for socialist youth. The discussion was quite lively, since almost half of them were entering university in the fall. Alex contributed one question.

As soon as Gregorov said, "Have a good day, comrades—and remember, the bus will be leaving at fourteen-thirty sharp," Alex began inching his way toward the door.

"Alex?"

Myslov was trapped in his row by a small bottleneck.

After dodging his head to each side of the bottleneck, "I've been trying to get back to chess."

"Good," Alex replied with an accommodating smile.

"Perhaps we could get together for a game or two one afternoon." When Myslov attempted to raise his voice it developed holes—like a stretched rubber band.

"Maybe." Gregorov was stacking papers into his briefcase. "But I'm pretty busy studying."

With a patient smile, "Yes."

As if the letter from Moscow University had never arrived, "With school only a few months away."

After Alex had waved and turned toward the door, he heard Myslov say, "Good luck with your studies." There were too many bodies jammed in the doorway for him to let him know that he had heard him. But that was just as well. There was no point in being overly intimate. Considering the circumstances.

"We ought to have him show us that appendectomy scar," Planov said with a knowing grin.

Alex smiled noncommittally.

"Hey, Myslov," Planov called out as he turned to push back into the meeting room, "how many stitches did you get?"

"There's no point in that," Alex began, but after a second, when he saw Planov was halfway there, he turned back toward the exit.

The half orange and coffee sat there throughout breakfast, loudly announcing that she wasn't there. That was just as well, Alex decided. He didn't think he could face her if she was still disgusted with him.

With a rustle of *The Spark*, "Don't plan to be loafing about all day. You will attend university here. That will still take preparation."

"It's not like Mother to miss clinic," he tried obliquely.

"No," he lowered the paper to eye level, "it isn't."

The thing you noticed right away was the doors, which faced one another from opposite sides of the lobby like faceless, blind sentries. And the floors. The slick, hard marble was filled with thousands of convoluted pink cracks.

"Good afternoon, comrades," his father offered with a raised palm. "Welcome to the Ministry of Information."

After a moment he was able to just listen. What was there to feel awkward about, anyway? In fact, there was no reason not to feel proud. After all, his father was an important man. With grave responsibilities.

He tried to listen as if he were just one of twenty-eight Young Pioneers being greeted by an important official. That was surprisingly easy to do, for twenty or thirty seconds, and then he would be struck by the familiarity of a particular phrase or idea. And that would make him aware again that it was his father speaking.

"I will now put you in the competent hands of our tour guide, Comrade Sasha Michevitz." Making it clear that he was joking, "If we haven't heard from you by dark we'll tell your parents not to wait dinner."

There was polite laughter. And then applause as Vice-Minister Nurov exited through a set of double doors.

"As you can tell from Vice-Minister Nurov's remarks, I haven't been with the Ministry very long. But I do promise I won't get you so lost you miss supper."

When Alex heard the voice he pushed his way up until only one row of shoulders separated him from the tour guide.

Why wasn't he more shocked? he puzzled. There was Sasha. Disrespectful, joking Sasha. His period hat and jacket replaced by a crisp gray jumpsuit with "Ministry of Information" stitched in a semicircle above "Tour Guide." And certainly without his not-such-a-good-socialist horse which required carrots in advance to move—unless you threatened it with a visit to a reeducation center. Perhaps that's where it is at this very moment, Alex laughed to himself, as an absurd picture of Dr. Vinkov interrogating Sasha's recalcitrant horse popped into his head.

"If you would bunch up a little. But not too much. We can begin."

Alex stepped back the depth of one shoulder.

Sasha seemed no less at home leading the Young Pioneers down the halls of the Ministry of Information than he did standing with his foot propped up on the carriage seat pointing at the exterior of the Bureau of Wetlands Management while Alex and Celeste nestled deliciously beneath a blanket in the backseat.

The thought of Celeste caused him to fall back another few shoulders.

"Don't straggle, comrades," Sasha cautioned.

There was none of that undertone—that hadn't just been his

imagination?—that had given everything Sasha said a double meaning. No. That wasn't there at all. And it had been there. Even through all the confusion, Alex could clearly remember that taunting, double-edged tone that said "This is what I am saying and this is what I am thinking" in such a way that when you wrote down the words, to make some accusation or demonstration, there would be nothing left but that first innocent, literal meaning. Now when Sasha's voice identified the offices of *The Charleston Spark* or the Subministry of Television Production you had no reason to suspect that they were anything other than what they seemed.

When they arrived at the DAL computer center—they stood on the other side of a fifteen-meter piece of glass that separated them from a series of perforated tan boxes that might as well have held dry cereal for giants—Sasha announced: "This is the Direct Access Library system main computer. It presently contains over three million books."

Sasha waited for a reaction.

"Yes," Markov remarked. "We have had terminals in our school since March." Proudly, "We have been issued authorization codes and passwords."

Several others nodded their heads in agreement.

Smiling, "Now it is as if our school library had three million volumes."

Apparently this part of the tour usually evoked ooohs and aaahs rather than words. After registering mild surprise, Sasha continued, evidently not ready to deviate from the planned itinerary, "Vice-Minister of Information Nurov, whom you met earlier, is responsible for the operation of the DAL system."

Alex received several smiles for his father.

He couldn't help but be impressed as he peered at the Zlotny-size boxes. That they could do any of the things they did was a mystery. And they were so innocuously unrevealing! Compared to those boxes, the terminal on his father's desk seemed profoundly human. He then realized why his father's talk had seemed so familiar. Yes. He had read so many of them from the DAL system. Now it was hard to tell that from actually hearing them.

With the DAL system they had gone full circle. The tour had been, as his father promised, competent. So Sasha's new position wasn't solely the result of passing on a little information. The irony of that phrase, "a little information," produced an uncomfortable chuckle. Certainly that was the kind of double meaning that suited the old Sasha.

Sasha stood by the door as they filed out. When Alex passed by, Sasha tilted his head imperceptibly, as if to say, "Ah, Alex. What do you think of my new position?"

Well, what other way was there to be? he remarked to himself once he had reached his seat on the bus. And weren't they both better off for it? Sasha, with his new jumpsuit and badge. And Celeste. Now a grade six. Or that's what she had been seven months ago. By now there was no telling how far she had gotten.

At least now they weren't examples of criminal laziness. If they ever were.

It was the third time he had come to the door. Each time he had stood for a minute or two, listening, trying to force himself to knock, before retreating to his room.

"Mother, it's me, Alex," he announced softly, not sure what he was going to say. Or if he could say anything. He just knew he couldn't sit there, in his room, knowing she was revolted by the sight of him.

He listened.

"Are you okay?" he whispered while pushing the door open.

The air was close. And unpleasantly sweet—as though someone had vomited licorice. "Are you here?" He peered at the mountain of covers and pillows that stretched diagonally across the bed. The only light hovered around the edges of the drawn shades. "Are you asleep?" he asked uncertainly, examining the covers for movement as he advanced. Yes, she must just be asleep, he decided, after convincing himself that there was a body under the contorted mass of bed things.

"Good morning, Alexander."

He stared at the covers for a second. The voice didn't sound muffled at all. Just distant. And kind of musical.

"Any special reason for this visit?"

"No," he stammered. "I was just wondering how you were." The voice was coming from the other side of the bed.

"Me? I'm doing marvelously," she offered lightly.

312

When he walked around the bed she was there, sitting on the carpet, her back resting against the side of the mattress so that she was facing the bank of eerie rectangles of light that would have been windows if the shades had been lifted.

"Beautiful morning, isn't it?" she announced with a laugh.

"I guess." After a moment, "Aren't you afraid they'll miss you at clinic?"

"No."

Her unpinned hair was a mass of grotesque tangles that reached out like tentacles.

"You can leave now."

"I," he began.

With complete indifference, "Then stay." Without standing she reached up to the bedside table and opened the drawer. Her hand began searching the drawer, the way the hand of a child searches a drawer that is just out of reach. She smiled after a second or two, making it clear that her hand had located what it was searching for.

At first all he could make out was the surgical tubing, which, doubled over in her fist, dangled like the legs of a captured spider. But then he could see the syringe. And bottle.

"Getting your illusions shattered?" she asked as the rubber tubing escaped from her grasp and bounced across her lap onto the carpet. Leaning to pick it up with her left hand, "This is how I create mine —my illusions."

She deposited the contents of her hands into her lap.

Odd. He hadn't thought about that at all. That night in the mirror had receded into those horrible dreams. And even though it had been real, he had let it rest there with the others, as if it had just been part of those dreams.

While sliding her arm up out of her sleeve, "That is my greatest talent. The talent of illusion." The nightgown stretched up from her armpit to her opposite shoulder, leaving the shoulder and arm near him bare. She picked up the tubing and tied it tightly around her biceps. Over the crinkle of cellophane as she tore open a package and extracted a needle, "It's a talent that everyone loves." She slid the syringe into the bottle, extracted the contents, and transferred it to her right hand.

"And the place I practice it best is," she reached up over her head

313

with her left hand and patted the mattress, "right here." Holding that pose, the syringe in her right hand, her left resting above her head on the mattress, "Losing your illusions?"

He just stared.

"Well?" she shrugged, before transferring the syringe back to her left hand. "This is what I have to do." She slipped the needle under the skin very gently and then pushed it in. "You do what you have to do."

She shuddered for an instant. And then carefully untied the surgical tubing. Before he turned to leave, her eyes had that faraway serenity that he had always supposed was the result of some inner strength that mesmerized those around her through its sheer perfection.

He noticed him when he was still half a kilometer away. Right away you could tell it was Myslov. Just the sight of him produced a blend of anger and disgust.

He waved from near the water. And Alex waved back. In a way that indicated that he was busy working. He even put his notebook in his lap and picked up his pencil. But Myslov wandered his way toward the walkway in a circuitous but inevitable route that Alex knew would lead right to the steps. He even considered packing up, but it was too late.

"Nice day for a stroll," Myslov ventured. He was pale. And tired. Even though he walked in the sun every day. How could anyone walk in the sun every day and still be so white?

"I've got too much work for that," Alex replied.

"Yes. I guess I ought to be working too. I just can't seem to be able to."

Uncomfortably, "That doesn't sound like you, Myslov."

"It doesn't? Not being well, I guess." He dangled his arms over the railing while his chest rested against it. He leaned down so that his face was only a foot above Alex's. "I haven't really been sick. But then you know that." Myslov let the sentence lie there for a second, so that Alex could pick it up if he wished.

"You look a lot better," Alex replied, breathing Myslov's sour breath.

With disappointment, "Yes. I guess I must."

314

Repeating the lie so that the pretense would be even harder to dissolve, "There's no doubt about it."

As soon as Myslov smiled, his eyes lost that pleading look. In fact, he looked fine. Although you would think by looking that he was just getting over a long illness.

When Myslov was out of sight he tucked his notebook under the steps and went for a walk.

The sun was scorching hot. He let it bake into his shoulders. And when he got to the tip of the island he stretched out in the dunes.

"This is what I have to do," he repeated with mild revulsion. "Do what you have to do." What did that even mean? It had been tacked on. With a matter-of-fact shrug. As if everyone had to do something.

She sat erect, her housecoat cinched tightly at her waist. There was a touch of fatigue in her face, but beyond that she looked fine.

"This orange is dreadful."

"Complain to Rebecca, not me," Nurov responded from the other side of *The Spark*.

She shrugged before putting it into her mouth.

Over the sound of the juice being sucked from the orange, his father exclaimed, "How awful." After a moment he announced earnestly, "Your friend Myslov has died. Complications ensuing from an appendectomy." His father lowered the paper, "Yesterday afternoon. How strange."

"I wonder who will get his specimens," his mother inquired. The residue from the orange, in the form of a few flecks of pulp, still clung to her upper lip. "Perhaps you should offer to take them over for him, Alex."

He poked at his cereal.

"No point in being glum over something like this." She bit into her toast. "That's all I meant by that."

His father lifted the paper back up.

Nothing else was said about it. As if not mentioning it would sever any connection between them.

When he arrived at Young Pioneers, Gregorov was at the door. There was no doubt he would say something about Myslov. Why did he feel compelled to do that? To act as if Myslov were a special concern of

315

theirs? "Too bad about Myslov." After a heartbeat or two, he commented remorsefully, "We certainly failed in our duty."

Alex furrowed his brows.

"Miserably," Gregorov reiterated.

"What are we, doctors?" Alex responded reflexively. It was the first time the absurdity of Myslov's death had hit him. It was as if he had just come to accept the patently false notion that Myslov had indeed had appendicitis.

"Then you haven't heard?"

Until then he hadn't allowed himself to think about it at all, preferring instead to let his mind go along with the idea that miraculously, in spite of the fact that there had been no appendectomy, it explained his death.

Gregorov leaned toward his ear. "He hanged himself." After leaning back to make sure that Alex had received the message. "In the outdoor shower. Their maid found him."

"There is no reason in a socialist state for anyone to commit suicide," rang through his head. He tried to picture John Boy—but all he could see was Gregorov.

"It must have been too much for him. With everyone knowing." He brushed a little sweat into his hair with the palm of his hand. "As block commander I should have been able to see what was going on. Of course, we all should have," he reiterated with a shrug before heading up to the front of the room.

During the meeting the line from The Book fired through his head a dozen times; but when it did, he stopped it right away.

As for blame? Well, it hadn't been his fault. Not beyond what Gregorov had said: it had been their duty to see that something was wrong.

The Young Pioneers all appeared at the funeral. Gregorov had selected half a dozen to act as pallbearers, with himself and Alex among them. They were all quite solemn.

It was partly just the occasion. And partly, he suspected, because they were sorry that he was gone. Not that they had liked him very much. But no one really had wished him any harm.

But more than anything it was because they knew exactly what had happened. Not that anyone mentioned it. It might as well have been

316

a state secret. But the thought of it was there, hanging like a cloud that almost had the same sick sweetness as Myslov's breath.

Not that any of them could really become involved in something like that. That was out of the question. But you could see in their faces that they could comprehend the consequences of that kind of mistake. And that, once it had occurred, what he had done was the kind of thing that any of them might have been driven to. Because, even though they couldn't imagine doing something like reading The Book, and certainly could not comprehend believing any of it, they were perfectly capable of feeling the crushing embarrassment that would follow being caught doing something like that.

They were right enough feeling that way, he decided. Yes. And, of course, like them he felt derelict in not seeing what was happening in time to prevent it. Not that he hadn't wanted, like the rest of them, to do his duty. It was nothing like that. It was just a mistake.

A few times he suspected that the whole thing was slightly hypocritical, but he managed to drive that out of his mind. Even the short statement Gregorov made on behalf of the Young Pioneers seemed, in the end, quite genuine.

After all, it wasn't anyone's fault that Myslov had fallen apart like that.

He watched her for a while before going in after her. She was out so far. And with the surf so big, she seemed frail and overmatched. The last line of breakers had tossed her back like a shuttlecock until she finally fought through.

"It's going to storm," he announced protectively when he got to her.

"Were you invited out here?"

He just treaded water.

Sarcastically, "So how was your friend's funeral?"

"All right," he struggled out.

"Everyone grim enough to fill you to the brim with self-pity?" She laughed, "Don't look so offended. Self-pity is oozing out of you like pus from a boil."

He was having trouble treading water.

"I lance boils every day. That's what doctors do. Nasty, slimy things that nobody else can bear to look at."

317

Breathing hard from propelling herself over a large ground swell, "Glorifying cowardice. It makes me sick." Her leg collided with his. "I could vomit." After a moment, "I know what you're thinking. Well, my sins are all private. Now, get out of my sight. I want this part of the ocean to myself. That's the way I've always liked it." Looking at his forehead, as if she had just discovered the birthmark, "And that, it makes me want to vomit too." She wrapped her hand around the side of his face and pressed her thumb to the birthmark. He could feel her nail slicing into it. "I'm embarrassed to see it wasted."

He could feel warm blood running down the bridge of his nose.

"Leave, dammit!"

It began to rain. Very hard. She looked up at the sky. In anger. And then disgusted disbelief, before screaming, over the rain, which was exploding around them like firecrackers, "I don't want you feeling sorry for me. That wasn't the point."

"I know," he answered.

She pushed off toward shore and then vanished in a huge white breaker.

He bobbed up and down there for a while, letting the rain hammer down on his head until it was numb. Staring into just rain. But he could see her. Anytime he wanted. Sitting there against the bed. And when he did he was still filled with that same revulsion. And disgust. But that must have been what she wanted him to feel. Or why else would she have done it? Up until then, when he knew but she didn't know that he did, it didn't seem completely real.

He tried to picture her the thousand other times. When she was laughing. Or angry. Or anything else. But he couldn't.

And then what it meant came to him: to get what she wanted—to get him to think the way she wanted him to think—she was willing to destroy every feeling except disgust. And revulsion.

He let the surf wash him in, the way it might the corpse of a drowned sailor, or a big hunk of seaweed that had been torn up from the bottom.

And when he stood up he could see her there. Waiting. She looked so sad. Her hair was stringing down her shoulders.

It didn't surprise him at all that she was there. Or when she walked up to him and, after a moment or two, draped her arm along his shoulder and began to walk toward the wooden steps.

"All that matters is tomorrow. And the day after," she said softly.

Which had to be right. And if nobody else cared, why should he?

"And perhaps now is not the time to write Sonia Ouspenskaya. But when the time comes I know you will do what you have to do."

Stopping, chest to chest with him, touching the birthmark with her fingertips, "Our time will come. Later. They'll forget. You'll see." She pressed her lips to it. They were as cool as rain.

He had never felt farther from her than he did at that moment. Never.

But he smiled. And let her drape her arm over his shoulder while they walked back to the house.

Chapter

13

INTERRUPT: YOU HAVE ONE MINUTE OF RESERVED
TIME LEFT. PLEASE LOGOFF.

Alex could feel the sigh of relief from over his shoulder. He copied
"t = 2.78 seconds" into his notebook.

LOGOFF OR BE TERMINATED.

Just as well, he decided. She'd be coming by just after twelve anyway.

YOUR ACCESS HAS BEEN TERMINATED.
CONNECT TIME 1 HOUR.

Before he was really out of the chair, Mulliner was squeezing
around the other side. At least he thought it was Mulliner. Or Mul-
hany. Or something like that. Not that it really mattered. They were
all the same. Just blanks. Polite blanks. Even after a semester and a
half of seeing them every day.

He half tripped over the feet that jutted out from the waiting chair.
Even that had been filled instantly.

"You okay?" Alex muttered.

"Yes." Circumspectly, "Didn't mean to be blocking the way."

Why did they have to be so damned polite? he almost complained
out loud as he forced his way past yet another waiting body. You'd
think they'd be used to him by now.

He skipped down the stairs, checked his watch as it bounced up and down a foot from his nose, and slipped out the library door. It would only take a minute or two to get to the gymnasium, so he slowed down. The trick would be to arrive just as she did.

When he got there she was nowhere in sight. Perhaps she had arrived already? No. Always—even that first time, when he had seen her quite by accident—she arrived right after twelve. Which meant that she was coming over from school during lunchtime.

If she was coming. But that was, he decided, a certainty. She was not the kind of person that would be coming over helter-skelter. No. With her, coming, once begun, would be as certain as the swing of a pendulum.

He walked past the gymnasium door, sat on a bench, and opened his notebook. Every few seconds he surveyed the sidewalk until he caught sight of her.

A small canvas gym bag was tossed over her shoulder. And she walked with that completely confident stride that was Martina Antipova's and no one else's.

He stood and began absently drifting toward her, the notebook open, and very much the subject of his attention. As they passed he allowed his shoulder to collide with hers.

"Excuse me."

She stood there for a moment, evidently surprised to see him, and then said, "Alex?"

Attempting lightness, "Has it been that long?"

"No. I just wasn't . . ." She stopped herself before continuing with obvious enthusiasm, "When did you get back?"

It hadn't occurred to him that she would think he had been gone.

"There's not illness in your family? Or something like that?" She examined him quickly, as if it had crossed her mind that he might be ill again.

"No." He tried to smile a convincingly healthy smile. "I've been in school here." She cocked her head to the side. "Just for this year."

"Oh."

"I was too far behind," he stammered for a second, "in my studies." Smiling, "Things aren't quite so competitive here."

She fidgeted with her bag. "No, I guess not."

"But I'll be ready next fall. For," looking at a crack in the sidewalk, "Moscow University."

"That's great," she replied. "I'll be there in the fall. They have," she seemed to hesitate, as if she were thinking about something else while she spoke, "an excellent physical education program there."

"Yes." Improvising, "I've heard that. So you've been accepted."

"Yes. I only just heard."

"Congratulations, then."

With a half-step toward the gymnasium door, "Thank you. We'll have to get together there."

"Yes."

Before he could continue, "I'm here for a workout. They have more equipment here at the university."

"That doesn't surprise me. Actually, the facilities here are excellent."

Preventing her from escaping, "So you don't throw the javelin at lunch any longer?"

"No. Now I do weight training during lunch. And throw in the afternoon."

He nodded.

Smiling, "It was nice to see you."

"Yes. I'm glad I bumped into you." As she turned, he added, "Have a good workout."

"Thank you."

"Maybe," she half turned when he left the word dangling there, "we could go to a film sometime."

"That would be nice, but, I'm . . ." She stopped. "I'm very busy preparing for this summer's competition." She smiled noncommittally. "That doesn't leave me much time for a social life."

"No. I guess not."

He waved as she stepped through the door.

Maybe she was still involved with her cousin from Leningrad. No. Or she wouldn't have been so pleased to see him. It was only after she heard that he was stuck here that she seemed so uncomfortable.

He should have said, "Would you like to go to a film tonight?" No. That wouldn't have made any difference. He was dead the minute she found out he was going to school there.

He would just spend the afternoon downtown. Like he had for the last few weeks. Yes. For some reason he found that relaxing.

Odd. He didn't really feel too bad about her. It was only an idea. After all, she had been somebody he knew.

322

Yes. He would go downtown. That would be dull. But he would still do it. Just because that was what he had been doing.

First he would have lunch. And drop off his notebook. And then walk down to the Battery. It was a sunny day, and that would be nice.

On the way to the cafeteria he decided he would just skip lunch. It was such a dreary place. And would be full of all those blank, polite faces.

And he wasn't really hungry anyway, he said to himself. Which meant that he would land up getting something from "the place." Which was what he called it—to himself—since he didn't know what else to call it. Not that there was anything wrong with going there. Not really. Certainly the authorities must know it was there. How could they not? It was something that was just winked at. For some reason.

Still, he always felt a little odd going there. And not at all free and easy the way he had when Celeste first took him there. To swap for sweets. And coffee. No. Now he felt odd. But he went anyway. Because, he convinced himself, it was much easier. After all, there were no lines at all. And there were all kinds of things there.

He got a large block of cheese and ate it at the Battery. With his feet dangling over the edge. A meter above the river.

And then he began listlessly meandering back toward the college. He picked his way through the Friday-afternoon lines that criss-crossed the street like broken, windblown fences. Each encounter was marked with a frown, a kind of sullen resistance to moving, followed by the giving of only enough space for him to squeeze by. Just before he was about to turn down a side street, so that he could miss the last of the lines, he saw her. That silent, chocolate grimness he had seen so many times set her face apart from the fifty or so faces around her. She was looking straight ahead, oblivious to, and certainly unaffected by, the five-meter billboard photograph of the General Secretary that floated over her head like a thundercloud. Odd, unlike the rest of the faces, which seemed to cower beneath the photograph's imposing sternness, she was quite able to hold her own.

When she saw him there was that spontaneous flicker of recognition that hits when you see someone you haven't seen in a while, followed by a blank, over-his-shoulder stare that slowly dropped to the ground. She had been happy to see him, at least for that instant, before it all came back to her. If it hadn't been for that he would probably never have walked up to her.

"Hello, Corinne," he offered as naturally as he could.

Uncertainly, "Hello."

To the brim of her hat, "How have you been?"

The faces, at least those around them, seemed to awake from the trance induced by mindless waiting. Not that they actually looked at them. No. But from the moment he arrived they seemed slightly more aware.

She shrugged. That was Corinne. Never one to waste words.

He stood there, inventing things to say, as they inched their way forward.

The whole time she was watching him. Discreetly. As if she were trying to ferret out something hidden behind his eyes. Perhaps she knew that he had been in a reeducation center? No. How could she? Perhaps she was wondering why he had not left already?

"I'm going to unversity here for a year," he explained.

"Oh?" she replied with a cautious smile. Evidently there was something about that that pleased her.

"Just to get my feet wet."

She nodded her head, still observing him. Perhaps she knew, had figured out, that he had been the one responsible for the missing coffee, and fruit, and sweets? Perhaps she had known all along? With Corinne it was impossible to tell: she just stood there, behind that opaque chocolate mask that no one, not even his father that night he had questioned her for an hour, could penetrate.

Suddenly he wanted to tell her, to let her know, that he had done it. Not so much to confess, but to let her know that he knew she had had nothing to do with the missing things. "Mother wanted you back, you know," he said quietly. Embarrassingly aware of the faces in the line, "And so did I. But," he paused, "before we could convince Father, something came up." He ran out of words.

"What you need," she announced suddenly, her head tilted back, almost haughtily, "is some of my cooking. You look a little peaked." When she said that, her hat blotting out the sun, she seemed even more enormous. "If I can ever get to the end of this line." Authoritatively, "Can't very well eat dinner on Friday without meat."

The line recoiled slightly, almost imperceptibly, in both directions,

324

leaving them separated from the rest, like the center of a snake after it has been run over by a lawnmower.

"After the cafeteria," loudly, in the same spirit she had spoken out in, "that would be great."

For a moment she seemed uncertain, as if the invitation had not been real, but only rhetorical, but then she nodded, more to herself than to him, and said, "Won't be nothing fancy."

The house was near the end of a meandering black dirt road, which itself commenced at the last bus stop of the run that crept northward on the other side of Mt. Pleasant. The thick palmettos that sprang up from between the mixture of oaks and pines gave the roadside a schizophrenically tropical look that was absent from the Charleston peninsula. And certainly from the desert-dry island that had only patches of oak and oleander eking out lives in the dunes. Here the green exploded onto the road. Scattered every few hundred meters were tiny concrete block houses. In the front yard, or at the side, of each a small plot had been carved. Alex had no idea that such places even existed.

As she abandoned the road for a grassless, sliver-wide path, she exclaimed, in a way that did not minimize the effort required to get them there, "See? We made it. Bet you thought I was lost." Fanning herself with her hat as she mounted the two steps to the porch, "Hard to believe it's only April."

In spite of the hat, several beads of afternoon sweat had formed just below her hairline and were filling the chocolate creases in her fore-head as if they were irrigation ditches.

Exaggerating, "Yes. I'm about to drop myself."

"Well, sit down. And I'll get you a tall glass of tea." Pointing with the hat, "Be careful with that rocker. The arm likes to hop off." She opened the screen door and stepped into the little house.

"Irene? Jacob? Where are you?" He could feel each step as she crossed the floor. She began, "I . . ." but didn't finish. He didn't know whether she was beginning the name again or what. She just stopped, perhaps realizing suddenly where they were, or why they weren't there. He listened to her tromp around, wondering, as he looked at the decaying block wall, if the entire structure was about to collapse.

325

Even before the screen door whined open he knew she was back. "This ought to fix you up." The ice crackled loudly against the sweaty glass.

"Thank you."

"It looks like I'm going to be picking greens myself," she said with mild annoyance.

Genuinely, "This is great."

"Nothing like iced tea," she observed matter-of-factly, while descending from the porch to the yard.

He rocked back and forth, sipping the iced tea, while she worked her way up and down a row of the plot, her head down, her huge black hands searching for just the right leaves before dropping them into a basket. Just before she finished, the breeze began to pick up. He could hear it rustling through the large oaks that protected the far side of the house. Odd. It almost sounded like voices. In the distance.

"It won't take me but a minute to put these on simmer," she remarked while turning sideways so that she and the basket could squeeze through the door. Her voice deepened as she receded into the house: "There's more tea on the kitchen table. One glass of tea is just a tease on a day like this."

He followed her in, circling the last of the ice under his tongue as he walked. The five-meter-square room was full of foreign, thick smells that offered palpable, undeniable evidence that people sat on the sofa, and the chair, and perhaps the floor. Instead of salt air, and space, and perhaps the vague hint of perfume, there was that density that made it impossible to forget that people used the place.

Without looking up she nodded to the pitcher on the corner of the table. A huge, wide-bladed knife, under pinpoint control, danced up the calf of what must have once been a pig, scaling back its thick, rubbery skin. The shiny, narrow point slipped under the skin and then in a single quick motion inflicted a hand-length incision.

"That sofa's a little sprung, but relaxing."

"I'm fine," he replied. Funny. Here in her little house she was almost talkative.

As she amputated the foot with a single sharp chop, "Looks like we left the breeze behind us."

"This is all I need," he replied with a shake of the glass.

326

He watched her reduce the leg to small, trimmed chunks, wondering, while she chopped, if he could actually eat something so real. He knew he shouldn't be watching each tendon be sliced. And bone split. But he found it impossible to stop watching.

"If you push that door open, a little breeze might sneak in," she remarked. "If you don't mind shooing away flies."

When he propped the door open with the brick that had been strategically left nearby a faint breeze ambled in.

"That's more a hope than a breeze," she observed without stopping or even slowing down her relentless assault on the pile of scraps that had been a leg.

The air seemed to be transporting fragile, inaudible voices that, like the sound of playing, up-late children, vanished when he really tried to listen.

"Course, that's better than suffocating," she added.

After inching his way back to the door, "What's that?"

Still chopping, "They're praising the Lord."

"The lord?"

"The Lord God Almighty." She stopped chopping and, balancing the knife loosely in her hand, looked directly at him. "Today is the day that Jesus died for our sins."

What a friend we have in Jesus,
All our sins and griefs to bear.

"So that we could be saved," she continued, wiping the knife on her apron. The thin coat of pork fat glistened on the blade as she rounded the table.

"I won't tell," he blurted out.

Without responding, she carefully hung the knife on a nail and walked over to the sink, where she began retrieving the freshly picked greens. While extracting the leaves from the water one by one, "There's nothing to be afraid of when you're witnessing for Jesus Christ."

He stood there for a moment. Watching her. First tingling. And then feeling foolish. And finally, perhaps because she was doing something so simple and ordinary, he began to feel at ease. After a minute or two he asked, uncertainly, "Have you ever read The

327

Book?" As soon as he asked he realized that that was a private name that would mean nothing to anyone but him.

Shaking a dark green leaf over the sink, "Oh, yes. How else are you going to know what the Lord has to say to you?"

Mystified, he waited for her to empty the sink. After wiping her hands on her apron she crossed the floor to the living room, pushed back the edge of the sofa, and pressed on one of the floorboards, causing the other end to rise up like the light end of a foot-long teeter-totter. After extracting something from the space under the floor she pushed herself back up with a groan.

The cover was black, faded, frayed at the corners; in the center was written: THE BOOK.

Holding it up to him, "I used to sing psalms to you. When you were a tiny baby. But in my heart I was afraid you'd never get to know the Lord."

He touched it with his fingers. Without making any effort to actually take it in his hand.

"That day you heard me singing."

Afraid to actually wrap his hand around it, "Yes."

"I . . ." She opened THE BOOK and after a brief search read, her blunt chocolate finger underlining each word: "'The maid who kept the door said to Peter, "Are you not one of this man's disciples?" He said, "I am not." Now the servants and officers had made a charcoal fire, because it was cold, and they were standing and warming themselves; Peter was also with them, standing and warming himself.'" Sadly, "I should have been willing to spread the news. But I was afraid." Closing THE BOOK, "Course, Jesus understands that. But I wasn't going to make the same mistake twice." Absorbing the import of what she was saying, "But you knew. Already. Ain't that amazing?"

"Yes," he struggled out.

"Read me your favorite passage. I'd like to hear that." Offering THE BOOK to him. "To think how I've fretted over you."

Hidden in cool, sherbet greenery, it was still as hot as an oven. The rough log walls had been chinked with plaster so that not a breath of air was admitted—except through the low wooden door, which had been propped open so that they wouldn't suffocate. The air, alive with sweat and after-shave lotion and cologne, was thick enough to

328

row with a boat paddle. The little building must have been, in its former use, a smokehouse. For tobacco. Or meat.

The plain wooden benches were loaded hip to hip. Children were stacked on laps like pocketbooks.

So this was a church?

"Brothers, sisters. Little children," Corinne's brother Lester intoned roundly from in front of them, handkerchief in hand, already prepared to mop his brow. "Mt. Zion has a visitor to welcome." Handkerchiefing his forehead, "A young man."

A sea of black faces, of every shade from weak milk chocolate to midnight black, turned to look.

"Who is ready?"

"Amen," a voice proclaimed.

"Yes, ready."

A woman, from behind him, sang out, "Halleluiah." Her voice was beautifully exotic and sounded far, far away.

"To be snatched from the breast of Satan."

Three or four voices: "Amen." And one more, an instant later, "Take him, Jesus."

The faces were hot. And smiling. And awestruck.

"Welcome him," Lester nearly whispered, extinguishing even the sound of breathing.

Curious. Mean. Afraid.

"Welcome, brother," a lone voice offered.

"Jesus loves you," another proclaimed.

"Amen."

"Welcome, brother," they chimed, each voice operating independently, but overlapping, like waves on a point after a boat has passed by.

And then they turned back to Lester.

"Preach, brother," the beautiful voice instructed.

His mind operated in parallel. Neatly sliced in two. One half listened to every word; locked onto every strange response, or sneeze, or fidget. The other half was a thousand miles away, near that distant voice, peering down at them through a telescope, wondering: Are these really lunatics? How can they be dangerous? Wouldn't they, all of them, be better off if they were given a chance to be reeducated?

"He was crucified. Buried."

"Yes," they responded.

Mopping his brow, "Rose again."

"Amen."

"To sit on the right hand of God Almighty. To save us."

"Amen."

"And later to judge us." Lester looked at him threateningly. "Are you ready to be judged?"

"I'm trying, Lord," an old man answered for him.

"Are you ready to be saved?"

"Oh, yes," several answered in unison, including the beautiful voice which seemed to hold the others together like glue.

Firmly, "Well, only you can let it happen. Your mama can't do it for you."

"No."

"Your daddy can't do it for you," Lester continued.

"No."

"That's right. You've got to do it yourself. You." Lester stopped to sponge the sweat from his eyelids. "Satan'll try to talk you out of it. And you know who I mean."

"Amen, brother," the old man responded.

"Yes, Satan. Evil, hoary, deathless Satan will try to talk you out of it. He'll try to lull you into evil. He'll try to bribe you into evil."

"Amen."

"He'll try to scare you into evil." Lester walked slowly across the room, his head down, letting the familiar idea of fear sink in. "But," he raised his head, "we're here today to talk about salvation." Looking right at him, "Life everlasting. Paradise. Bought and paid for with the blood of Jesus Christ. Or," Lester took a long, deep breath, "eternal death. It's you who must decide. One man. One heart. One God. You must let it happen. Jesus is waiting to enter your heart. To free you from hate. And envy. And jealousy. And fear. He's waiting to replace Satan. And you know what I mean when I say Satan."

"Amen."

"But you've got to unlock your heart. No one else has that key. Only you can let Jesus in. And love out. That's what Easter's all about. Love. God's love for you. Every one of you. And how God's love can shine through you."

"Praise the Lord," the beautiful voice replied.

330

They sang. Their voices exploding against the walls of the tiny, chink-walled church, that had been a smokehouse, or something like that.

Afterward, when Lester asked them, "Are you ready to go down to the River Jordan?" they replied, "Yes. Right now, Lord. Yes," and then left in two ragged lines, singing, almost to themselves, so that no one else could hear, descending, slowly, along the ragtag path that proceeded in wide, flat steps to the water. He could feel the sweat racing from his body into the open air. Suddenly he was wide awake. Almost giddy.

"Cynthia, are you ready to be saved?" Lester's voice was deep and full, but spent around the edges from preaching.

The girl nodded.

"Then let Jesus wash your sins away," Lester replied before pushing her down into the slow, slick-as-paper river.

He could almost feel the water himself. Or at least that part of him that was there, in the midst of it, could. While that other part of him, that was just watching, was far away. And completely dry.

"Are you saved?"

Before she could respond, Lester immersed her again. Alex could feel the excitement building—as if he were watching a magician. Or circus act. No. It was more like watching a baby being born, he decided. That thought produced a mild rush of embarrassment. But when he looked, self-consciously out of the corners of his eyes, he saw that they were all looking on in just the way you might imagine they would be watching a baby be born.

"Are you saved?" greeted her again, and she nodded; but Lester was not satisfied—and pressed her head down into the water again.

The curious faces all seemed to lean forward toward the river, in anticipation, waiting for her to reappear.

"Are you saved?"

"Yes," she exclaimed. "Yes." The water streaming down her face looked almost like tears. And when, half strangling, she cried "Yes" again, it almost sounded like tears.

But all the faces along the bank were smiling.

After Lester had drawn her to him, and, with one mightly wallop of his chocolate hand, knocked the water from her lungs, she slowly climbed out of the river up onto the bank with the others.

She was smiling.

Even though she was only ten or eleven, and still looked almost as if she had been crying, it was self-evident that she was, at least for that moment, totally and mysteriously happy.

Watching her, he felt very far away. And almost hurt. Not just because he had never been that happy; but because, even though he had seen the whole thing, the source of her joy was completely incomprehensible to him—and therefore unattainable.

He watched her embrace her family. And then disappear up the path into the greenery.

That sense of anguish and mystification stayed with him even while they drank iced tea—under the observing eyes of her son Jacob, who kept him under surveillance from the other side of a low tree limb as he chewed on a sprig of grass. Even while he was asking her whether she had ever heard of New York City. Which she had not. But when he considered telling her about The Book—she evidently knew nothing about it—he was filled with that same embarrassed disgust that any thought of the hunchbacked priest aroused.

After that, walking alone on the road to the bus stop, he tried to figure out what it was about the episode in the river that had filled him with that sense of longing. But he really couldn't. In fact, even that feeling seemed removed. Almost imaginary. The way a feeling aroused by a movie—or even a dream—can be remembered but not rekindled once the lights in the theater come on, or the sun comes up.

Now, all he could really feel was that old uncertainty. And the periodic waves of "Didn't you learn anything the last time?" which were crashing against his head every few steps.

"You going to tell on us," rifled across the road.

Jacob was buried to the waist in undergrowth. He was panting. From anger. Or fear. Or just running.

"Why should I do that?"

"Because you ain't no Christian." There was a large piece of concrete in his hand, hiding, just in the tops of the weeds.

"What makes you think that?"

"'Cause you ain't black."

"So."

332

Derisively, "There ain't no white Christians."

Piotr Babulieski immediately popped to mind. Followed by an attack of dread: was that all going to start up again? After he had kept it out of his mind all these months?

"Tell me you ain't considered it," he asked slyly, as he stepped onto the road.

"No." Weakly, "Not really. It's just that, well, it's hard to explain."

As if his judgment had been vindicated, "Then you've been thinking about it."

"No," Alex objected. "It's just that," he stopped, "you can't control every thought that pops into your head."

Suspiciously, "That so?"

"You know that." More comfortably, "But I have been wondering why they think you're so dangerous."

"Dangerous? Hell." Brandishing the piece of concrete, "They don't know about us at all."

Soothingly, "Sure they do."

"I go to school. I'm not just rottin' away in these backwoods. Like some old man. They don't know about us at all."

Alex shrugged. "Just because they don't say anything doesn't mean they don't know. They may not know about you in particular, but—"

"Hell. They don't even know there's such a thing as Christians." The hum of the approaching bus grazed over the weeds. "At least not yet." He stood there, the rough, dirt-studded piece of concrete angrily swaying back and forth in his hand. "I been watching you. You're going to tell. You will."

An image of Babulieski aiming the gun across the stage snapped into Alex's mind: why was he so violent? If he was a Christian?

"Aren't you?" Jacob insisted.

Around the bend the bus whined its way through a three-point turn.

"That's the bus," Alex said in the form of a request.

Jacob disgustedly tossed the piece of concrete toward the side of the road.

"I won't," Alex began to promise, but Jacob turned toward home, apparently not able to listen any longer. Clearly not really believing, but not able to bring himself to stop him.

After a second Alex chased after the bus, hollering as he went, hoping the driver would hear him over the whine of the electric motor, but before he reached the road he slowed down. Old men, he thought. How old? Perhaps someone older than Grandfather Simpson? Someone who was there? Who would know. The bus halted at the stop for a heartbeat or two before escaping.

By the time he reached Jacob his mouth was coated with fine black dust. Circling his tongue around his mouth in search of moisture, panting, "Who are these men? These old men?"

"You must be some kind of fool. I've been cussing the fact that I let you go the first time."

"How old are they?" Alex persisted.

With a mixture of anger and amazement, "Are you listening to me?"

Evenly, "I'd like to talk to one. If they're really old."

"Why?" Jacob rifled.

"They might know things. About," he paused for a second, "history."

With disgust, "History?"

Ignoring Jacob's reaction, "You could take me there, couldn't you?"

"Yeah. But," bending to snap off a weed, "to get there we might have to go by boat. What do you think of that?" He inserted the sprig in his mouth and began to suck on it.

"So, we go by boat."

"Boats have been known to flip over."

Alex snapped off a weed himself. "So. I can swim."

Chewing, "You sure are thick."

"If the boat capsizes," Alex inserted the sprig in his mouth, "then I guess you'll have to save me."

"Now you're dreaming," Jacob replied disdainfully.

"No. You're a Christian."

"Huh. My mama is. And maybe I am. But I wouldn't count on it. Specially when it comes to some Russian who's going to get us re-educated. Or worse."

With a hint of a laugh, "You'll live through it."

"I don't plan to live through nothin' like that," Jacob replied, his eyes narrowed to blood-red slits.

"I did." It was the first time the thought of it didn't produce a warm, prickly embarrassment.

334

As if he had just been told the world was flat, "Shit."

For an instant Alex wished that it showed. Like a tattoo. Or something. But it was all inside. Right between his ears.

Spitting out the sprig of grass, "They don't do that to Russians."

Alex watched Jacob's face, which, like a strange mirror, began to reflect what he was seeing. And realizing. Yes. There was something you could see. Once you knew to look for it.

"Do they?" Screwing his face up, "To Russians too?" Jacob seemed lost for a second. As if some article of faith had been contradicted.

"What makes you think I'm Russian?" The words just popped out. Like flakes from an early-morning cereal box.

The vague unease he felt on Wednesdays was absent. Even though his father would not be there. Instead, he felt excited. He had kept expecting it to vanish. On the bus back. Or after a day or two of school. But it didn't.

She had let Rebecca go and cooked for him herself. And then served coffee and brandy on the porch—while they reclined in juxtaposed cushioned lounges. Which should have been cozy. But wasn't. That familiar unease began to insinuate itself. Not because she was being moody. Or difficult. Far from it.

"Isn't that a fabulous breeze."

It smelled of salt. And sea oats. Sometimes he'd lie in his dormitory room—which smelled of socks—and try to imagine that smell.

"I hope that," he could tell, from the way she was balancing her cup on the rim of the saucer, that she was going to head off in an entirely new direction, "you've been giving some thought to your future."

He shrugged while removing his eyes to the surf, which was being lazily patrolled by an elliptical disk of light.

"It's time for this silliness to end." As if she were announcing breakfast, "You must write Sonia Ouspenskaya." When he did not reply she persisted, "Nurov is not infallible, you know. Far from it." She whispered, "He may order you not to write, but he can't very well order Sonia Ouspenskaya to send the letter back, can he?" Laughing lightly, "Not likely."

She said the name with that same mixture of awe and admiration that any mention of her provoked. Odd, nothing else ever produced that effect.

Pouring half an inch of brandy into her glass, "Certainly you don't want to vegetate here the rest of your life." She picked up his glass and refilled it. "Up until now you have not called on her." She leaned across the little table that separated them. "Now," her breath smelled of liquor, "you must." When he thought of her smell, nothing but exotic perfume came to mind. "You do see that, don't you?"

"I was the one who took those things, you know," he announced, still watching the searchlight cruise up the beach. "The coffee." His voice was surprisingly calm. "And other things. Corinne didn't take them."

When he turned, all he could see in her face was mild displeasure.

"I was the one who took those things," he repeated.

Lifting her glass, "We can't very well take her back now, can we?"

"I know that, but . . ."

"Then don't confess your petty sins to me." Disgustedly, "And expect some kind of absolution. All it does is make me think less of you—and to what purpose?"

"Certainly it must," he began before starting over, "Don't you believe in anything?"

"I believe in what I can sink my teeth into."

Yes. And before she replied he knew that. Not that she didn't care about Corinne. In her own way. It was that all that was on a different scale from what mattered to her.

Emptying the glass, "But what I believe is of no significance. The important question is: how far you are willing to go? I have already done what I had to do."

"I don't think I want to be a Russian anyway."

She laughed. A raw, hard laugh that drove home how absurd the sentence had sounded. Not the idea, he decided. Just the words. And he immediately recalled what he had said—in the road Sunday—to Jacob.

"No." Still laughing, "There are too damned many of them already."

That wasn't the kind of thing he expected her to say at all, but before he could respond, or say any more about the coffee, and what that meant, she lifted the neck of the brandy bottle between her forefinger and index finger and said, "It's suffocating in here." As she pushed open the screen door, "Don't you think it's suffocating in here?"

The walkway was just visible in the half-moon light—and seemed to vanish right into the beam of light that jumped down from the moon onto the ocean. It was not until they reached the end of the walkway, and were descending the three wooden stairs to the sand, that you could even tell there was a beach at all.

After a few meters the searchlight passed by.

"Yes," to the accompaniment of that same laugh, "there really are too many Russians here already." She lifted the brandy bottle to her lips. "So why would I waste you on that?" With a broad wave of the bottle, "Poor Alexander, I don't think you understand at all."

She stepped up to him, so that her face was nearly touching his. "No. I don't think you do." The brandy smelled coarse, and too sweet, mixed with the smell of the ocean. Again he found himself recalling that she always smelled of perfume. Light and distant, but still perfume. "And that's why you've been such a damned fool." Hissing, "Instead of reaching out for what is yours for the taking."

He stood there, paralyzed with that same disgust that had been with him since that day in her bedroom. Knowing that she expected him to say something. To say, "Yes."

The light inched back by.

"I'm going for a swim." She planted the brandy bottle in the sand and then pulled her gown over her head. "The question is, Alexander, how far," she balled the gown up in her fist, "are you willing to go?"

"All that," he stammered, "with Corinne, means something."

"No," she tossed the balled-up gown into the middle of his chest, "it means nothing."

"There's more to it than that."

Receding into the water, "It means nothing. All I want to know is how far you are willing to go." Taunting, "Well, stay there then. I'm going out to the breakers. Where the sharks feed."

As soon as she dove in she vanished.

He picked up the bottle and sat with it resting on his knee for a second before drinking from it.

There was no point in fighting it, he decided. He wouldn't be able to keep himself from swimming out to her. So there was no point in pretending he could fight it.

By the time he reached her his teeth were chattering. Uncontrollably. He treaded water a moment, watching her.

"So. An attack of courage. I hope it isn't temporary."

His teeth still chattering, "If I'm not to be Russian, then what?"

"You are both. You should never forget that. That will be the key to your success. But from time to time you will have to take chances. And always, you must be willing to make sacrifices."

He kept thinking of how they smiled after Corinne's brother Lester held them under the water. Even from the bank he had been able to feel the warm excitement as it rushed through them.

Now he was just cold.

"There is more to that business with Corinne," her leg collided with his, "than you think."

"It is you—and people like you—who will be able to change things," she whispered as if he had said nothing. "And, you'll see," she began stroking the birthmark on his forehead, "after you write Sonia Ouspenskaya things will be right back where they were."

He wondered how she could have such complete faith in someone she had never seen—except for an old photograph. Someone she had never so much as spoken to. That seemed odd. And childlike.

And certainly it seemed it would take more than a letter to put things back where they were.

Chapter

14

"What do you expect to find here, anyway?"

"Someone who was around a long time ago."

"So?" Jacob replied as he pushed the boat pole into the water.

"Then I'll know for sure. About something that I've got to know."

"Got to know," Jacob repeated disdainfully.

"It's something that's been bothering me. For a long time."

Turning, so that he was a dark shadow against a backdrop of silver marsh grass, "Is that what got you reeducated?"

No. This was different. Even though several times that old feeling of exhilaration—and strangeness—had come back. No. This was different. Because once he was able to convince himself that it had all been an invention the whole thing would go away.

"You sure didn't learn much," Jacob persisted, before turning back.

They pushed their way past hours of windless marsh-grass islands. After they stopped to eat biscuits—which they washed down with tea from a pickle jar—Jacob said, as he was slipping the pole from under the seat, "I don't see why a damned Russian would get himself reeducated."

Without waiting for Alex to reply he stepped up onto the bow of the boat and pushed off.

In half an hour a light rain began. Which at first felt nice, but then grew harder.

"Can you see where you're going?" Alex hollered out.

"I ain't lost, if that's what you mean," he replied. But a minute or two later he could hear them slithering into the marsh grass. And then slamming to a stop.

Without saying anything, Jacob pulled a canvas tarpaulin across them.

"Might as well get some sleep," he announced.

Alex lay there for a while, listening to the rain pop against the canvas. Well, in the morning, he would probably find out. One way or the other. And then he could relax.

Soon the rain stopped. Or maybe he was dreaming that, he thought, when he heard Jacob demand, "You going to sleep all day?"

The canvas had been rolled back, exposing the sky—which was pale blue.

"No." Sitting, "I wasn't even sure I was asleep."

Jacob shrugged, snapped off a piece of marsh grass to chew on, and started walking.

The boat was resting a meter or two beyond the waterline. Apparently Jacob had known right where he was.

"When did the rain stop?" he asked, mostly to himself, as he stood.

Jacob was already up on the bank.

The land was sandy. And covered with small, dry bushes. And pines. Sprinkled here and there were a few oaks. Gray moss dangled from the branches, eating up the sunlight, so that everything seemed to be in a cool, relaxing shade.

They followed what appeared to be a path. That is, where there was enough grass for one to be worn. And after a kilometer or so Alex saw chimney smoke. And then a small wooden house. It was bleached gray. The porch was bowed so far that a concrete block was holding up its center.

As they crossed the yard, an old black man came out. Alex thought, There's somebody old enough for sure. Around the edges his eyes were red as blood.

"Do you know where Ezekiel Greeley is?" Jacob asked. "He's my great-uncle."

The old man looked at Alex. And then at Jacob.

"I'm Corinne Watson's boy," he said. "Jacob Watson."

Without taking his eyes off them, the old man lifted a rectangular piece of cornbread and bit into it.

"This here's a friend of my mama's."

He chewed for a moment before pointing between a pair of water oaks.

340

Jacob thanked him and headed across the yard.

"Thank you," Alex added uncertainly. The man's red eyes were glued to him as he turned to follow Jacob.

"White people don't just wander in every day?" Alex ventured.

"Nope. Or anybody else," he added with an evident sense of accomplishment.

Past the oaks the undergrowth closed in on the path. And then opened again into a tiny clearing.

Jacob stopped and then expelled, "Jesus."

Beside the path were scattered several rough wooden crosses. Alex crouched to look at one. The name "Frank" was barely decipherable. The one next to it had "O'Neil" carved in it. Insects and water had made them nearly unreadable.

"What you boys lookin' for?" a voice cracked.

After regaining his composure Jacob replied, "Ezekiel Greeley."

"Why's that?" the voice inquired menacingly. A second or two later a man stood up from behind a clump of bushes. His gray hair was swept back into the air, giving him the appearance of a big gray owl.

"He's my great-uncle," Jacob announced confidently enough for Alex to take a breath.

"Well," the man knelt down to pull a few weeds from the ground, "he ain't here, if that's what you're worried about." He extracted a few more weeds, each time with a kind of snap of the wrist that produced a small sound as the weed was severed in two. "You boys had breakfast?"

"Nope."

"Well, if you wait for me on the porch," he pointed to a house that they could just make out through the undergrowth, "I'll get us a little somethin'." The man went back to weeding.

"Was that him?" Alex asked after they were out of earshot.

Jacob chose not to answer.

The little house was that same bleached gray. And the porch floor was so shriveled up you could see the ground. A piece of screen, rusted out at the bottom, dangled down in front of two rockers—in the manner of a shade. The rest of the screen had apparently rusted away.

Referring to the voices they could hear from inside, Alex ventured, "Maybe that's him?"

The chatter stopped.

Alex shrugged in an attempt to communicate, "Why do you suppose they stopped?"

A black, creased face craned around the edge of the door. Then disappeared long enough for Alex to give Jacob another questioning look before reappearing. "You boys looking for something?"

After Jacob explained who they had come to see, she replied, "I'm Sister Kate."

"Oh."

"That don't mean anything to you?" she inquired while tightening her scarf.

"Yeah."

"I'm your great-aunt. By marriage."

"I know."

The head disappeared back into the house.

Alex noticed that two men were smoking pipes on the far edge of the yard near a garden. Their heads were close together, and he could see their lips moving. But they were too far away to be heard.

"This cornbread's still warm," Sister Kate announced after pushing the door open with her hip. A cloth-covered plate was in one hand. A pitcher was in the crook of her other arm. And two cups were strung on her index finger.

"So, what you boys," she paused long enough to give a meaningful glance toward Alex, "here to see Reverend Zeke about?"

"Well, it's not exactly him we came to see," Jacob meandered.

"You boys here to be baptized?" she inquired in a way that let you know she was sure she was right.

"Nope," Jacob replied indifferently.

Narrowing her eyes, "You been baptized?"

Jacob nodded.

"Good." She smiled approvingly, while keeping a watchful eye on Alex.

They stood there for a moment, uncertain how to proceed.

"Well, sit down over here on the stoop and I'll pour you some buttermilk."

After she put the plate down they sat on either side of it and watched while she poured the buttermilk. It poured into the cups in gushes that accumulated around pearl-white lumps.

342

When Alex washed down a mouthful of cornbread with it he had to fight off the urge to gag.

"That'll fix you up." She walked to the door with both of them watching her. "He's just out cleanin' up the cemetery. He won't be long."

Alex pushed the buttermilk to the side, uncertain whether he could drink any more of it. But after chewing another hunk of cornbread he used some more to wash it down.

Before they finished, Reverend Zeke began crossing the clearing.

"Now, how's your mama doin'," he asked at the porch.

"Okay," Jacob replied.

"That's good."

The two men who had been on the other side of the yard were now only a few meters away.

"This is my sister's grandson. Jacob."

They smiled, but without much enthusiasm. Their eyes were that same blood red.

"Baptized your mother myself," he said with obvious satisfaction. "A long time ago." He pulled a pipe from his breast pocket and held a match to it while he puffed. The pipe crackled when he inhaled, and then, as the smoke drifted slowly out of his mouth and nostrils, the air became thick and sweet. "So, you boys want to be baptized," he said with a smile. "That's a big step. But," he looked up from the pipe, "one you ought to take."

Jacob shuffled his feet in the mixture of sand and grass inhabiting the side of the stoop.

"You been readin' the Bible?"

Jacob nodded. Alex could see he was trying to figure out how to explain that he had already been baptized.

"That's good." Reverend Zeke held his thumb over the pipe until it was out and then slipped it back into his pocket. Getting up, "Well, right now we got to do a little work."

The two men nodded solemnly.

"But a little work never hurt anybody." As he shuffled across the yard, "So long as it's just a little."

The men chuckled while nodding their heads.

They followed after the three of them. They first went to the shed behind the house and got four buckets, which they hung from a pair of side-by-side poles that stretched across the two men's shoulders. The rusty buckets clanged together as they marched along an irregular path that emerged fifteen minutes later at the water. As far as Alex could see to both the left and the right there was nothing but silver-brown marsh grass. Straight across was the mainland, skirting the marsh like a green fence.

When the men lowered the poles to the ground the buckets issued one last complaint.

With the same deliberateness that had characterized the trip there they divided the poles and buckets between two crusty boats that sunned themselves in the grass like alligators.

"You come with me, Jacob," Reverend Zeke said as he pushed one of the small green boats into the water. Alex watched uncertainly as the boat groaned off into the marsh with Jacob poling the sitting Reverend Zeke.

After a minute or two one of the men said, "Can't stand here all day." There was a long scar from just below his ear to his Adam's apple. The flesh was as pink as a dog's nose.

"That's for sure," the other replied before climbing unsteadily into the little boat.

They sat in opposite ends of the boat looking at Alex for a second or two. They were of undeterminable age. But clearly old. And not a bit like what he had expected. They seemed more like old zoo animals, the way their red-rimmed eyes drifted from dull suspicion to disinterest and back.

"Sorry," Alex apologized before sloshing around to the side of the boat and stepping in.

When they pushed off, Reverend Zeke and Jacob were just fifty meters or so to their right. Jacob had put the pole down and was leaning forward in rapt conversation with Reverend Zeke. Without hearing a word he could tell they were talking about him.

"What brings you to Greeley's Island, boy," the man with the scar asked as he squinted at Alex.

"Just," he struggled, "curiosity."

Derisively, "Curiosity." He looked at the other man. "Don't you know curiosity done killed the cat?"

Alex tried to smile.

A moment later Reverend Zeke waved. While Alex puzzled over

344

the wave for a second or two—trying to figure out what it meant—
the two men began slowly poling toward one of the narrow veins of
water that crisscrossed the marsh.

He certainly hadn't expected them to go off in opposite directions.

After a few hundred meters the boat stopped. Reverend Zeke and
Jacob were completely obscured by a ridge of grass.

The man with the scar leaned over the side and began pulling up a
chain.

"What you think?"

"One or two."

"You never know," the other man observed.

Alex could feel himself stop breathing.

"Fifty cent," the man with the scar challenged.

With a confident smile, "Fifty cent."

Alex watched the rusty, finger-thick chain loop onto the floor of
the boat. It smelled of oyster silt and decay.

"And to get baptized," he blurted out. "With Jacob. That's why we
came here."

The man yanked on the chain with a long, ugly grunt, as he
struggled out, "Huh."

Apparently that wasn't going to satisfy them, he decided as he
scanned the marsh.

"I'll be damned," the man expelled meanly as water raced out of
the meter-square wire cage that had popped up at the end of the
chain.

He rotated the cage into the boat. Two crabs were locked in com-
bat at the bottom of the cage.

"Where's that bucket, boy?" he grunted raspily. "Or you just along
for the ride?"

Alex picked up the bucket. He could feel the air race into his
lungs. And the muscles in his legs relax.

Tauntingly, "So how much is that?"

"You been keepin' track," the man with the scar replied irritably as
he dumped the crabs into the bucket.

"Well, I make it to be three hundred and eighty-two dollars.
Includin' that fifty cent." He slid down into the boat and, with his
back resting against the bow, took out his pipe.

"You sure that's right?"

Lighting the pipe, "Now why would I try to cheat you?"

"Just bein' sure."

To Alex, "This old man here's the worst gambler ever. Hell, he won't have a bit of his cut left by lunchtime."

"I'll have my cut. And more," the man with the scar replied sulkily.

Alex must have looked mystified.

"His cut o' the bidness," the man explained. Offering the pipe to Alex, "This here's a democracy. You know what that is, boy?"

Alex nodded.

"But, like Reverend Zeke says, 'This here's a democracy, but we ain't a buncha damned communists.'"

"Pretty easy for him to say—he owns the whole damned place," the man with the scar fired back.

"So," to Alex, "everything is done bidnesslike. Down to the letter."

Alex wondered, as the man inhaled from the pipe, if there really was anything he could find out from these two.

"You wanta try some of this?" the man said with the pipe extended.

If there really was anything to find out.

When they returned, the pole suspended from their shoulders in the style of proud hunters, the two buckets dangling from the pole, Sister Kate asked threateningly, "You been filling that boy full of ganja?"

The two men lowered the pole from their shoulders.

"Just look at that boy's eyes. He didn't come here to be smokin' that damned ganja."

The two men escaped around the side of the house with the pole.

Sister Kate squirreled up her mouth disapprovingly before stepping back into the house, leaving Alex standing in the yard alone with the two buckets.

He sat on the step.

His face still hurt from laughing. Odd. As soon as he had smoked that pipe he had started laughing. Especially when one of the crabs had escaped. At least after he had caught it. And the man with the scar had said, "You be ready to jump in after that thing if it goes over the side."

He had said it with the same deadpan meanness that he said everything. And Alex had started laughing. Right after he caught the crab. And so did they.

346

And then he had laughed when he thought: "What would Gregorov think if he knew that people were using Old Names—like dollar. Every time they used the word he laughed harder. Until he was sure his face was going to crack.

Alex began laughing. By himself on the porch. And then, when one of the crabs began climbing out of the bucket, he stepped over and popped it back in. Which made him laugh even harder.

Yes, that's just the thing Gregorov should hear: betting in dollars. Not that he would laugh. At all. Nor would he laugh if he had heard the man say—as he was lounging back in the boat without a care in the world—"This here's a democracy, but we ain't a buncha damned communists."

No, he wouldn't, he said to himself, as he laughed. But after a second or two he stopped and sat back down on the stoop. Maybe it wasn't as funny as all that, he decided, as he got his breath back. No.

"Well, you back already?" Reverend Zeke boomed out heartily, as he crossed the yard.

Alex stood.

"Well, how'd you do?"

"Good, I guess," Alex replied, just as the two men appeared from around the corner. They must have been waiting there, by the shed where the poles were stored.

"Well, the Lord decides the catch. Course, we still have to do the work," Reverend Zeke philosophized.

"Forty-two," the man with the scar announced.

"Not bad, Leonard," Reverend Zeke congratulated, before going into the house.

A few minutes later he came out with a large book, sat on the step, and opened it. "Let's see. Forty-two." He leaned over the book and repeated, as he wrote, "Forty-two."

"This here's the ledger, boys. A good bidnessman always keeps his accounts. So," he smiled, "he'll know where he stands."

Beckoning to Jacob, "Come here, boy. I'll show you something." He opened the ledger to the beginning and then flipped a few pages. "See there. That's where I baptized your mama." After a moment, "Received, one chicken. And that was a good chicken, boy. It laid a mountain o' eggs."

• • •

There were fifteen or twenty of them scattered around a fire, which now was the glowing remnant of a huge blaze that rested in a longitudinally sliced oil drum. A few of them were still roasting potatoes on sticks. Some were standing in the fringes so that when they moved, long, menacing shadows raced along the trees behind them. The crabs had been boiled and eaten.

Alex was sitting on a makeshift bench, leaning forward with his elbows on his knees. He could feel Jacob's hip pressing against his. He could smell Reverend Zeke's pipe.

The coals from the fire cast an orange hue on Sister Kate's brown face. Her eyes shined.

"Armageddon came not once. Or twice. But once every four or five years—like the fever from malaria.

"Some of 'em had names. Some didn't. But the worst was the Shining Path.

"They called themselves the Guardians of the Shining Path. And wore red bandannas around their necks. The year one hundred became the year zero. From then on we could start with a clean slate. But how could we do that? When so many people remembered?

"So they rounded up everybody who was old enough when it happened to realize what was going on. The ones who were left.

"Ten was decided on. As the age you could remember from. I guess that before that it could all pass for dreams. Those violent dreams you have when you're a child. So—they were thirty-three and up. Just the age of Jesus, don't you know."

Someone from the shadows responded, "Amen."

"By then most of them had families. But that didn't matter. They just carted 'em off anyway. Leaving the kids behind.

"And a few came back. When that one ended. But most didn't. And some—didn't go at all."

"Praise the Lord."

"Which is why we're here," she announced with her eyes wide open and the fingers on her hand fanned out.

"That's right," one of the men who had been in the boat with Alex agreed. His pipe was lighting up his eyes.

Reverend Zeke whispered across Jacob, "There're two things about Sister Kate. She never forgets a thing. And can tell it so it's better than what it was—at least more excitin'. Now the second is why I

348

married her. The first," he laughed raucously, "is why I shoulda thought it over."

"What you fillin' those boys full of?"

"I was telling 'em you know how to make what *was* real. And excitin'. Wasn't I?"

"Excitin'? The Shining Path was straight out of the Book of Revelation. And you know it."

"Oh, they were plenty bad all right," Reverend Zeke agreed.

"Bad? They were a buncha lunatics. Mostly just boys. Just your age. In a blood rage."

"I said they were bad."

"Bad? They were bad enough to keep you hidin' back here all this time."

He laughed, "When they found out I was here with you they figured I was worse off than in one of them camps. So they left me alone."

There was a ripple of laughter. But not too much. Apparently no one wanted to get on Sister Kate's bad side.

"And eventually I guess they plain forgot," he added.

She stared at him for a second.

"Just teasin'. You know that."

"Well, I don't want these boys thinkin' I'm exaggeratin'." After a moment, "Course with all this ganja in the air they might think the whole thing's some kind of hallucination."

"Oh, no such thing." Graciously, "Tell 'em more." Reverend Zeke's voice was still big and round. And in some hard-to-identify way different from the others.

"No. Time for these boys to be in bed."

"One more story won't hurt," he cajoled.

Of course, they weren't really stories. Reverend Zeke just called them that. They were history. Alex leaned farther forward on his knees, so that his face was only a meter or so from the coals. Yes, he decided, this was history—from someone who could remember it, just the way it was.

"Is there anything special you'd like to hear?"

"What about New York City?" Alex blurted out.

She tilted her head to the side.

"It was destroyed?" he asked tentatively.

349

"Oh, yes. The new Babylon."

"Babylon," a voice repeated.

"That's the way it was told to me. A sinful place." Looking upward, so the fire illuminated her stringy neck, "Babylon is fallen, is fallen, that great city, because she made all nations drink of the wine of the wrath of her fornication."

Examining Alex's face, "It was removed from the face of the earth. The way God can remove anything, with a sweep of his hand. Because it was an evil place. Full of drinkin'. An' womanizin'. And," she scanned the circle of faces, "and gamblin'—but then, vice is the lot of man. But the worst of it was idolatry. And for that they were destroyed by a wind of fire. And earthquakes that gobbled up entire buildings like they was slices of cornbread."

As she described it he could see the wind of fire. And the awful explosion. Partly because she could, as Reverend Zeke said, make what *was* so real. But mainly, it was that to him, the place she was describing was a real place. That had been inhabited by real people.

Odd. Apart from the tingling produced by Reverend Zeke's pipe, and the sense, way back in the back of his head, that yes, he had been right all along, having it all confirmed produced almost no feeling at all—except a kind of sadness.

Explaining, "But in everything, there's a message from God Almighty. Even in the destruction of a mighty city. In the middle of the night."

Now that she had finished they shuffled around for a moment or two and then began drifting off to their houses.

He and Reverend Zeke and Jacob sat on the bench for a while, looking into the fire—smoking several times from his pipe.

The shadows from the trees grappled on the side of the house like big bears.

Before he went to bed, Reverend Zeke said, "You boys be sure to rattle the door to that privy before you go in so," he paused, "it don't get too crowded in there."

When Jacob leaned over, mystified, he added, "You don't want to shut yourself in there with some 'coon, do you?"

Later, rather than go inside, which was dark, and certainly threatening, they silently urinated in the grass on the far side of the privy. Neither had suggested it. It was just one of those things that occurred without a word.

Afterward, with the bear-sized shadows circling around them they raced back to the living room to the quilt pallet that Sister Kate had made for them on the floor.

"You know," Jacob whispered, after they had warmed themselves under the quilt for a moment, "we may have to get baptized tomorrow. He don't get to do that much anymore."

"I don't mind," Alex replied, still full of awe from Sister Kate's stories—and the huge shadows.

No. That'll be fine, he thought.

Before he went to sleep he let himself think of The Book. And Piotr Babulieski. Which was the first time he had let himself do that in a long time. And it felt good.

But, just as he was dropping off, for some reason, he could see Dr. Vinkov saying, "In a very peculiar way." And in spite of the fact that Dr. Vinkov had never said anything more about it, Alex knew— could even visualize—exactly what he meant. And for an instant, as he was poised on that thin line between sleep and wakefulness, he felt oddly cheated, because he ought to be able to think about it now, after tonight, without his stomach shrinking into that tiny ball.

When he opened his eyes it was barely dawn. But he could hear her in the kitchen lighting the fire.

He lay there for a while, waking up very slowly. Odd, he thought. Everything seemed so normal. Not at all the way it had been the night before when elongated shadows made everything seem absurdly large—and strange. Now the room seemed kind of small. And ordinary.

Without disturbing Jacob, he slid out of bed and went to the kitchen.

"What's a young man like you doin' up this time o' day?" Sister Kate asked as she closed the oven door. "That's just for women with achy bones." Irritably, "Ain't got no coffee. At least no real coffee."

"That's okay." He smiled. "I don't drink coffee. At least not usually."

Unconvinced, "But you could get it if you wanted?"

He nodded.

With a frown, "Well, if the Lord wanted me to have coffee, he'd still be sendin' younguns over to be baptized—or he'd make it grow this far north."

He laughed.

"Course this stuff Reverend Zeke makes is sorta like coffee."

"Really?" he replied distractedly, while he tried to figure out how to get her started.

"Well, it's hot. And that's what counts."

She filled a cup for him and placed it on the table.

"Usually, this time o' day, it's just me and The Good Book." She sat at the table. An open book had been left at her chair. "These damn men want to sleep every day till noon. But that's the way the Lord made man, you know. So it must be part of the plan." With her hand resting on the book, "But it's sure hard to understand how that can be."

Soberly, "Did you know a man. A priest." He could feel his mouth getting chalk-dry. "He had a hunched back."

She cocked her head to one side.

"His name was Babulieski," he forced out. "Piotr Babulieski."

"I don't know no Russians. Except maybe you."

"He was a Pole," he corrected.

With her head tilted like that she looked like an emaciated brown bird.

"At the time of the Great Uprising," he added, unsure what else to call it.

She searched for a moment. "I've never had that name recounted to me."

Hiding his disappointment, "Was it really awful? When they dropped the bomb?"

"Oh, yes. That's what they say."

"With it on television and all."

"I guess it was," she replied as if the idea had never occurred to her.

He could feel his hands begin to tingle—with a kind of numbness.

"I guess it's not something you like to talk about."

"Makes no nevermind to me." Her face was right up against the book as she paged. "I just tell it the way I remember it being told to me."

With surprise, "You weren't there?"

"Lord no, child! The only ones who was here then are up there." She pointed at the ceiling. "With Jesus."

352

"But you made it seem so real."

"Well, sure." She smiled graciously. "You heard me say 'They say,' didn't you? Course with all that damn ganja in the air it's a wonder you could hear anything. Sometimes I tell what I seen; sometimes I tell what I was told. It's all the same to me."

No, it's not, he thought.

"But what's all that matter? Compared to this." She had stopped paging. Alex could see a large upside-down "R" on the page. She began reading about a woman clothed with the sun, and the moon under her feet—with a crown of twelve stars on her head. While she read, he thought: These people really are lunatics. Harmless, but lunatics.

After a while she stood and turned the book toward him. "Maybe you should read, boy. That cornbread may be done. I love to hear The Good Book read out loud." She pushed out of the chair with a groan and went to the oven door. "Go ahead."

He looked down at the book, which was still on the page she had begun on—even though she had been reading far too long for that. He began reading phrases here and there, trying to find where she had left off: the pages were full of beasts, and angels. And Satan, whom he remembered from Lester, was mentioned. "And you know what I mean when I say Satan," Lester had said. Yes, it was clear what he meant. Even then.

"'And I stood upon the sand of the sea,'" she said to identify where she left off. He began reading.

With the hot cornbread held tightly between two potholders, she joined in, "'And he opened his mouth in blasphemy against God, to blaspheme his name, and his tabernacle, and them that dwell in heaven. And it was given unto him to make war with the saints, and to overcome them: the power was given him over all kindreds, and tongues, and nations. And all that dwell upon the earth shall worship him, whose names are not written in the book of life of the Lamb slain from the foundation of the world.'"

She nodded her head and put the cornbread down on the counter.

"No, keep readin', boy," she instructed when he stopped. "I love to hear the words of the Lord while I'm workin'."

Most of the time, as he read, she repeated along with him, unless she was stooping to get something, like a bowl or some eggs. And

353

once when she was getting something from the porch.

"'And there followed another angel saying, "Babylon is fallen, that great city."'" He stopped when he realized that that was exactly what she had said the night before. Yes. That was it, exactly, he decided weakly. Which was something that didn't have a thing to do with New York City. Or anything like that. Of course, to her, there was no real difference.

"No need to stop," she reminded.

"'If any man worship the beast and his image, and receive his mark on his forehead, or in his hand, the same shall drink of the wine of the wrath of god, which is poured out without mixture into the cup of his indignation.'"

"You know what that means, boy?"

The birthmark on his forehead felt as if hot fingers were pressing against it.

She leaned over toward him. "It means that in the end there will be a great uprising—led by Jesus Christ himself. And those who have been persecuting us will pay. Forever."

"Last night was fire and brimstone," Reverend Zeke said from the door, while scratching his head. "Which fits the night. But now the sun's up, woman. And the birds are singin'."

"True enough," she agreed. "But do you know, for a fact, when Jesus comes back whether it'll be morning or night?"

Alex looked at her, out of the corner of his eye, as she sliced the cornbread. Perhaps the passage had nothing to do with him at all.

Shaking his head, "Nope. And it won't matter a bit. Unless, of course, you're plannin' to serve him hot cornbread. In that case he better come in the morning—early."

Reverend Zeke then laughed to himself for a minute before sitting down at the table.

Bowing his head, "Good Lord Jesus, thank you for the food we are about to receive." He lifted a piece of cornbread. "Eat up, boy." To Sister Kate, "Where's that other boy?"

"He's your blood, ain't he?"

"Can't argue that."

"Then I suspect he's still sleepin'."

"Women," he said knowingly. "You think they'd be more respect-ful, wouldn't you?"

354

Alex nodded uncertainly.

"Especially of a man of property," he continued. "But they ain't." With a wink, and a tilt of his head in the direction of the living room, "Course, if that boy knew breakfast was ready, he might get up."

"I'll get him," Alex said as he stood, happy to seize the opportunity to leave the room.

He shook Jacob, and then, after telling him there was hot corn-bread in the kitchen, he wandered out into the yard toward the privy.

No. She hadn't even been looking at it. The way some people did, curiously. No. She didn't have him in mind when she had him read it. But it was an odd coincidence—that made him feel completely out of place.

He opened the door to the privy, circumspectly, and squinted into the interior. Probably Reverend Zeke had just been teasing them, but with him, it was hard to tell.

He stepped inside, and after convincing himself that a dark, solid presence against the wall was only a pile of trash, he urinated.

Instead of leaving, he stepped up on the trash and peered through the small window at the house. It was as weatherbeaten as the privy—which had cracks in the wooden walls wide enough to slide your little finger through.

Why they would chose to stay there, in the middle of nowhere, in these little houses, was a mystery to him. State housing didn't have cracks in the walls like that. Or outdoor bathrooms.

When he got back inside, Reverend Zeke was showing Jacob a map on the wall.

"My papa drew this himself," Reverend Zeke said proudly.

The map was a simple ink drawing, apparently of the island they were on. Below, in block letters, was written "Greeley's Island."

"And, o' course, he left the whole thing to me. Let me show you." He took Jacob over to the ledger book and opened it up. "See? This is the deed." He pulled out a brownish sheet of paper.

Alex looked at the sheet of paper, from four or five feet, wondering, while looking at the back of it, what it really said. But after a minute or two Reverend Zeke took the paper and slid it back into the ledger book.

"You gonna preach this morning?" Sister Kate inquired from the doorway to the kitchen. She asked without so much as glancing at

Alex—which convinced him it had been coincidence. Still, he found himself leaning in the direction of the map, so that the warm, damp birthmark was on the far side of his head.

"In good time. First, me and these boys are going to do a little fishin'."

"Hmmm," she ruminated out loud.

"The Good Book don't have any mention of clocks in it."

"No," turning back toward the kitchen, "but it has plenty to say about laziness."

"Your great-aunt's as religious a woman as you'll ever find," Reverend Zeke explained on their way to the shed to get the fishing poles. "Almost too religious. If there is such a thing."

Alex thought about that as they traveled single-file down the sandy path to the inland waterway. Yes. That was certainly true. She was just as fanatical as the DAL system said. Yes. Or worse.

They fished with plugs, so that all they had to do was sit on the bank and watch for the plug to move, which gave Reverend Zeke plenty of time to talk. Apparently talking was Reverend Zeke's favorite pastime, he decided. And some of it was interesting, but not as much as it had been—when he was sure that they would know exactly what had happened firsthand.

Now it didn't seem the same at all.

After about an hour Zeke said, "You know, I think it's gonna cloud up and rain."

Jacob said, "It might."

"Well, you boys don't want to get caught in a rainstorm," he announced as he began wrapping the line around the cane pole by twisting it in his palm.

"You been baptized, ain't you, boy?" he said to Jacob when he had finished.

Jacob nodded.

"Well, that's good. And you," he turned to Alex, "I suspect you need to think it over. After you done that," he began climbing up the gently sloping bank, "you might want to come back."

"You ever heard of a man named Piotr Babulieski?" he asked when they were back on the path.

"No, can't say that I have."

"He was a priest," he explained, all the while knowing that the

356

name would mean nothing to him. "With a hunchback." Feeling an odd kind of desperation, "Maybe you heard about him. From someone who's dead now."

"Not a very tall man?" Reverend Zeke half questioned.

"No." Exasperated, "I don't think so."

"Could be. But," without much concern, "it's hard to say for sure."

Alex could feel his stomach knot up in anger. If he hadn't heard of him, and it was clear he hadn't—because there was no such person, at least not the real person that The Book pretended to be by—why didn't he just say so?

Chapter

15

He walked just beyond the reach of the outgoing tide, so that his bare feet could feel where the waves had been—without having actually to touch the still-cool water.

"Nurov."

Before he turned he knew it was Gregorov, even though he hadn't heard his voice in nine months. And certainly was not expecting him to come riding up on his bicycle.

"Out hunting for shells again?" Gregorov asked with a cautious smile.

"No." As the occasion Gregorov was referring to came to mind, "Just getting some sun."

"Yes. It is rather intense, isn't it?" Rubbing back his hair with the palm of his hand, "And a little shocking. After Leningrad."

That didn't take long, Alex reflected.

"Not that the cold weather wasn't stimulating."

Alex smiled blankly.

"Sorry to hear you weren't able to make it."

"I've been going to university here," Alex explained.

"Yes. That's what I was told."

Of course, Gregorov would know already.

"I've thought several times what rotten luck it was for you to get ill," Gregorov said with genuine concern. "But you look fit as a fiddle now."

"Yes, I'm fine."

"I've been keeping up with most of our class. You know, just out of

358

curiosity. They all seem to be doing splendidly."

"That's good," Alex replied.

Why was he getting that old feeling? he wondered. It wasn't really fair. When The Book was there, that made sense. But now he shouldn't be feeling that way at all.

"I take it your studies went well?"

"Yes. Very well. I still have exams next week."

"I'm sure you'll do well. You always were a clever student." Putting his foot on the pedal, "Engineering still?"

"Yes."

"Well, there is certainly a great need for engineers. I could never fathom mathematics, you know," he confessed. "Or I might have tried that myself. Of course, the curriculum in Government and Marxist Studies is quite demanding." Confidentially, "It's quite competitive there, you know."

"Yes, I'm sure it is."

"I was able to be in Moscow last week for the May Day celebration," he announced proudly before inching the bike forward. "It was most impressive. A whole contingent of us went by train as soon as the term was over." He paused for a second. "Odd, I thought of you several times when I was there. I suppose I was imagining how much you would have enjoyed it. Which isn't the kind of thing I ought to be bringing up, is it?"

"No. That's fine." Without really being able to stop himself, "I'm sure they'll have it next year."

"Oh," he expelled. "Then you'll be transferring?"

Alex nodded.

"Well, I'll have to write the others and let them know. Most of them are staying in school for the summer. Or traveling."

"No need to do that," Alex replied, already regretting the lie.

"Oh, they'll all be pleased for you. After all, we have something in common, don't we?"

Alex puzzled for a second.

"Our being here, I mean." In a philosophical vein, "I think it creates a kind of bond, don't you? I didn't realize that until I left. But after I had been in Leningrad awhile, it came to me. That's when I began keeping the others posted."

Nodding, "Yes. I'd never thought of it that way."

359

"Well, good luck with your exams. And," as he pedaled off, "congratulations."

"Thank you," Alex replied weakly.

Well, it was very likely that he would be there next fall, he said to himself as he watched Gregorov awkwardly weave his way along the hard sand that bordered the water. Yes. And of course you could see the difference in his attitude right away. Especially since Moscow University was a cut above Leningrad.

Actually he should have said the same thing to Martina Antipova. Perhaps he would the next time he saw her. Which would make more sense than just watching her walk into the gymnasium.

He was in the dunes—just the edge where the high tide had left an irregular line of debris—when Gregorov pedaled back by. Just seeing him produced that same odd feeling. That really wasn't fair, he decided, as he tried to push the feeling out of his mind. But still, even though it was very different, he kept feeling the way he had with The Book. And this was very different, because he wasn't, as he had been then, the slightest bit confused. No. He knew now that the whole business had been a lie. Invented by a lunatic. Which made it all the more strange that seeing Gregorov should produce that same feeling that he was splitting into two people: one who was completely normal, like everyone else; and another person, who was right there with him, but seeing things entirely differently.

Perhaps it was just knowing about them—that they were there, just thirty or forty kilometers up the inland waterway—that made him feel that way. Yes, that was probably it. After all, the others, like Gregorov, saw what everybody else saw, and knew what everybody else knew, so it was quite natural that they felt so at ease about everything.

If it hadn't been for The Book he would be able to see things in that natural, uncomplicated way himself, he decided. Yes. That was quite true. And it had been just luck. Just blind, stupid luck.

Of course, his father seemed to be able to know about things like that. Like The Book. And not be bothered at all. It was odd that he was completely able to know that there was this other, secret view of things that paralleled the regular world that everybody else like Gregorov saw—and not be bothered about it at all.

But then, he was in a position to know exactly what had happened.

360

He could get hold of the facts. So he was not victim to that gnawing uncertainty that hid in the pit of his stomach like a frightened animal.

Dinner, like dinner every Wednesday, was full of questions about school. Sometimes the same question would be asked more than once. Or at least in only a slightly different way. He sometimes wondered if they listened to his responses at all—except in the most general way.

And as soon as the food was finished his father retired to his study, explaining that he had work to do.

That evening his mother had been full of secret glances. Of the type they used to have after they had been for an afternoon swim. They were the kind of glances that said something special was going on. Which meant that she had decided that he would write Sonia Ouspenskaya. Which was the kind of thing she decided not because he had agreed to—in fact, he had said nothing at all the previous week—but simply because, in her mind, it was a certainty. Of course, he would do that. But later, he had decided. When he had something important to say. Something that she could be proud of. Yes. He had more or less made up his mind. And certainly that would show her how far he was willing to go.

"Rebecca, bring Alexander some more ice cream."

"No, I have something I have to ask Father," he replied as he stood.

"But I enjoy our after-dinner chats," she replied with a mixture of mild irritation and curiosity, before adding, "How else am I going to find out what you're up to?"

"I did see Martina Antipova," he answered. "Just recently."

She frowned, but only with her eyes.

"We might go to a film. Or something," he added on his way to the hallway. We might do that, he added to himself. Yes. Next year in Moscow.

When he rapped on the half-open door, his father replied, "Just catching up on some DAL reports."

The only light came from a small rubber-necked lamp that had been bent down so that it created a disk of light a foot in diameter on the desktop. And the terminal—which dressed his father's face in a

361

thin red-and-white mask that flickered eerily as his fingers manipulated the keys.

Alex stayed at the doorway.

Beckoning with his left hand, "Sit down. Pour yourself a vodka."

A decanter was sitting on the desk.

"I've been using the DAL system a lot with my studies," he began tentatively. "Almost every day. In fact, sometimes twice a day."

"That doesn't surprise me." Looking up, "It's good you got a head start."

"Yes," Alex stammered out awkwardly, as ugly pictures of his search of the DAL system flashed through his mind.

"Which shows that something can be learned from any experience," Nurov added philosophically.

"Yes," Alex replied. It was just as well to get that over with. There would be no way to talk about it without that being there. "In fact, there's always a line. It can be a real circus."

His father frowned.

"But if you have reservations, that's no problem," Alex soothed.

He filled a small glass with vodka.

Nurov's face was less than a foot from the screen. Every half minute or so he nodded approvingly, and then pressed on the space bar. Alex could see the page change evidence itself as the mask of light flickered, and then settled back down into a steady blue and red.

"Is everything in there?" Alex asked before quickly lifting the glass to his lips.

"Well, we try to keep the system as up to date as possible," Nurov replied proudly.

"Yes. But what I mean is," he paused, "is everything in there? I mean, are there things that have been left out?"

He could feel his father turning away from the screen toward him. "What purpose would that serve?"

"I don't know." Forcing himself, "I know that what's in there isn't the same for everybody. And—"

"What exactly does that mean?" Nurov interrupted.

"I know—from before—that there are things in the system that are not accessible to everybody."

"There could be reasons for structuring it in that way," Nurov re-

362

plied obliquely. "I suppose that was a conclusion you drew while using my access rights?"

"Yes," Alex admitted.

"Well, I'm sure you can see reasons for that."

"Yes."

"But that's been bothering you?"

"A little."

"Well, see how much better it is when you just ask. Rather than sulking about."

"Yes," Alex acknowledged with a nod.

After a moment, "The dinner was very good tonight, wasn't it? Rebecca has turned out very well."

"Yes," Alex agreed.

Nurov rolled his desk chair to his right so that the decanter was within reach.

"Do you," Alex watched him fill his glass, "have access to everything in the system?"

"I think what you mean," his father corrected as he lifted his glass, "is: did you have access to everything in the system when you were masquerading as me?"

Alex nodded.

With concern, "Is there some special reason you want to know?"

"Not really," he replied vaguely. "I was just curious."

"Well," his face relaxed a little, "I suppose that's natural. To be curious about something like the DAL system." He walked over to the door and gently pushed it shut. "Yes. And there's nothing wrong with curiosity. As long as it's a healthy curiosity."

Alex nodded awkwardly.

"My access rights are unrestricted," he announced. "So," he lifted the decanter, "for a while everything was there—at your fingertips." He sat back down, before adding, with that mixture of disappointment and mild contempt he seemed to be able to conjure up without effort, "Which you chose to fritter away with your little obsession." After leaning back to prop his feet up on the desk, "Perhaps the next time you're given an opportunity like that you'll know better than to waste it."

"Yes, I hope so," Alex responded mechanically.

Well, at least that settled that, he decided. And it hadn't been half

363

as terrible as he had worried. In fact, apart from having to bring it all up again, it hadn't really been that bad.

By and large, he felt pretty good. And certainly relieved, because, in the back of his mind, he had never been able to convince himself that it was all just a sick invention. Not completely. But if it had happened, it would have been in there. Somewhere.

Chapter

16

It was impossible not to feel the surge of excitement as the police launch raced up the waterway. Even though just before they left he had begun to feel ill. And to doubt that he ever should have done it.

But as soon as the boat raced off, the whining motor drove every trace of nausea from his stomach.

The SP sat in two rows of three. Facing one another. It was clear that to them this was just another day on the job—even though two of them were armed with small machine guns. Which was ludicrous —and would seem ludicrous to them the minute they arrived and saw how pathetically harmless Reverend Zeke and the rest were.

"You said it was about forty kilometers," the lieutenant screamed over the motor. It was the first time he had removed his eyes from the waterway in front of them.

"I was only guessing."

The lieutenant narrowed his eyes in way that indicated that he didn't really approve of something as imprecise as guessing.

"It's not much farther," Alex mumbled. Although it was not loud enough, the lieutenant nodded. After leaning over toward him, his hand clamped to the aluminum railing for support, Alex screamed, "You won't need all these weapons." He pointed to one of the machine guns.

Before returning his attention to the waterway, the lieutenant appeared puzzled and then frowned in a way that let it be known that he was more than qualified to make determinations like that.

Well, it would soon be clear that he was right. In fact, he was surprised they had brought them. He had been very careful to explain that they weren't really dangerous at all. In fact, they weren't really a threat to anybody. But there was no point in lingering on that. And besides, if they did think that, at least at the outset, wasn't it for the best? Since that would make his discovering them that much more important.

And even if they weren't a threat, it was clearly antisocial to be isolated like this. And just being there, so far away from everything else, led to a kind of antisocial thinking. And the perpetuation of ridiculous ideas.

The lieutenant tapped him on the shoulder. "Don't forget why you're here, Nurov. This isn't supposed to be a holiday."

He had that same slightly bored look on his face that he had had when Alex first told him. Well, he'd soon see that they were real enough. Everyone would.

He carefully scanned the right side of the waterway from the horizon back toward them. After a minute or two he announced proudly, "It's there. About three or four kilometers."

The lieutenant smiled before leaning over to speak into the driver's ear.

The boat lurched forward, the way a cat might the instant it knows it is close enough to a mouse or lizard to overtake it with certainty. Simultaneously the motor altered its pitch to a screeching animal whine.

The lieutenant looked back over to Alex, his mouth still poised by the driver's ear. Alex traced out their path with his finger; the lieutenant nodded, and then relayed the instructions to the driver.

Yes, they would all see, from the lieutenant all the way up to Sonia Ouspenskaya, he said to himself, as the boat skimmed between two islands of marsh grass toward the bank.

When they skidded to a stop, and the black-uniformed police sprang up, each group of three racing along the narrow gunwale, past the windshield and across the bow so that they could jump directly onto the bank, his legs nearly collapsed under him.

And the wobbliness raced directly to his stomach.

"Let's go," the lieutenant barked. "There's no point in letting them run off."

366

The ground was as soft as jelly.

"You two, fan out along there."

Alex watched them trot off in single file in the direction of the crabbing boats.

"Nurov." He caught Alex's eye. "It's just the boat ride. In a minute or two your head will realize you're on solid ground."

"I'm fine."

Ignoring Alex's denial, he motioned for the remaining four SP to advance up the path.

"The first house is just on the other side of those pines," he offered as proof he wasn't falling apart.

"Then let's get cracking."

The two SP with machine guns led the way.

The act of running seemed to return the strength to his legs. And drive the nausea away. Even though the ground, which was hard-packed sand, still bounced like jelly. It was ridiculous that now, instead of in the boat, he would be seasick. But the lieutenant had said that as if he knew exactly what he was talking about.

As soon as they entered the stand of pines it got dark. Not from the foliage, which he blamed at first, but because the sky had clouded over. And then, just after two SP had been sent toward the house he and Jacob had stumbled across looking for Reverend Zeke, there was a crack of thunder—which he for an instant, in horror, mistook for a shot.

The horror must have been broadcast by his face, because the lieutenant immediately replied with a look of mild contempt and then pointed at the sky.

Alex nodded.

"If you're so worried about these people, why did you report them?" the lieutenant asked suspiciously.

He could hear the door to the house being kicked in.

"It's not that. It's just that—they're not violent. Just," he searched for moment, "out of touch."

The lieutenant shrugged, "Makes no difference to me either way. They're loonies of some kind, right?"

As Alex nodded he could feel the contents of his stomach rising in his throat as if it were a stopped-up drain. He clamped his hand over his mouth and forced himself to run, so that they wouldn't see him vomit.

By the time he got to the other side of the pine stand, to the privy, his hand was wet with saliva, but when he leaned over nothing came up.

He stood there, over the hole in the ground, gagging—hoping he could just get it over with—but nothing came up except warm saliva.

The whole time he listened. But all you could hear was the wind. And even that wasn't loud.

If you didn't know better you would think there was nobody there at all, he realized. Not the SP. Not anybody.

He climbed up onto a stack of debris so that he could reach the privy window, clamping his hands on the lips of the bare wooden opening while he balanced on his toes.

The house was dark. In fact, there wasn't a sign that anyone was there at all. And the same thing had been true at the other house.

Perhaps they had realized the SP was on the way—and disappeared? A sense of relief slowly spread across his body. Yes, that would be perfect. They would be able to see that they had been there. And no one would be hurt. But would that be enough? Well, it would have to be. After all, he had done his part. There would have to be a record of that.

Two SP began approaching the house in a half-crouch. Advancing slowly, like a pair of angry crabs, they were almost there when a light appeared on the porch. Just for an instant. On the side that was still screened. They froze, clearly having seen the light, but uncertain what it meant. How could they know it was only Reverend Zeke lighting his pipe?

One of the SP dropped to one knee and pointed a small machine gun in the direction the light had come from.

"He's just sitting there," Alex blurted out. "Smoking his pipe." But they couldn't hear him, because he hadn't really hollered out; the words had just escaped in a normal, conversational tone—leaving him feeling the way you feel when you cry out in a dream and no one can hear you.

Certainly they're not going to fire, he thought.

"You, on the porch. This is the security police," the lieutenant's voice announced. The amplified voice was strangely soothing. Alex could feel his larynx relax. "Raise your hands over your head."

Yes. That would do it. All they had to do was be sensible.

Another match ignited: you could see him very clearly, sitting in his rocking chair. He didn't seem afraid at all. In fact, there was the usual completely contented smile on his face.

"Raise your hands over your head," the bullhorn repeated threateningly.

The match persisted for a second, and then Reverend Zeke shook it out.

"Put your hands up," Alex whispered.

After a second one of the SP waved, indicating that Reverend Zeke had complied, and the lieutenant began crossing the clearing. The bullhorn was cocked to the side at shoulder height. About halfway across the opening he turned, and, with an expression that said, "Well, we've got a first-class loony on our hands here," he signaled for the other SP to advance.

Before he had time to turn back toward the house a shot rang out. It was a single, thunderous blast, which carried with it several shattered windowpanes that rained down on the porch after the sound of the shot had vanished. They all stood there. For a second or two. Then the machine gun yanked over to the window the blast had come from. Alex turned to the lieutenant, who was standing there, completely still, with a look of utter amazement on his face.

Right away Alex could see that the bullhorn was gone and that his arm had been sheared off at the elbow.

The machine gun issued a long, staccato burst. Then another. And it was silent.

Alex leaned to the right, trying to look down the porch to see where the blast had come from but before he could see anything his feet gave way—sending him sprawling across the privy floor into the wall. As he fell he could hear another blast from the machine gun. And another.

Why did they have to do something that stupid? Leaving his back jammed up against the wall, he pulled his knees up against his chest and buried his face, waiting for the next burst from the machine gun, but there was nothing. Maybe they were all dead. It served them right for doing something that stupid. And for what?

"Where are the others?" he heard one of the SP scream.

369

There was no response. At least not that he could hear.

They really were lunatics. Complete lunatics. To shoot at the SP. "Where are they?"

Alex lifted his head. The open door was right beside him. The field looked completely peaceful, ringed by pines, which were deep bluish-green, from the rain.

There was a burst from the machine gun.

He tried to stand, but slipped. The floor was covered with magazines. And newspapers. Apparently they had given way while he was standing on them and collapsed across the floor like a deck of cards. Pushing them over had released the dead, pungent odor of mold.

There was a black face on the cover of one of the magazines. Across the top it said *Ebony*. Alex shoved it aside, revealing another. He tried to push up from the floor again after kicking several of the magazines aside.

Before he was halfway up he realized he was too weak to stand. Had he hit his head when he fell? Crouching on all fours, he felt his head with his hand. There didn't seem to be anything. At least anything he could feel. As he searched he realized that right in front of him, no more than six inches away, was a man's face. He was blond. And smiling. Alex pulled back, which caused him to see spots for a second, but then he could focus. The man was wearing a black shirt. With a white collar.

His smile was very comforting. Almost hypnotic.

Beneath the photograph it said, "Man of the Year."

Man of the year? Without even opening it he knew exactly who the man was.

The storm had gotten worse the minute the boat left. Even though a black canvas top had been pulled from the windshield to two posts at the rear over the engine, the rain fired in from the sides, forcing them to huddle so near the windshield that the lieutenant's stretcher seemed to be surrounded by black, wet trees.

Reverend Zeke was on the floor between two SP in jump seats. He seemed completely at home cross-legged on the floor, even though an inch of water sloshed across him every time the boat veered. Alex found it hard to take his eyes off him.

"Now, she was a woman who knew her own mind. That's why she

did it," Reverend Zeke explained more to himself than anyone else.

"Well, now her mind is smeared all over the wall," the SP on his right barked. It was only then, from the voice, that Alex realized it was a woman.

"Oh, I don't have to worry about her."

"Why's that, old man?" the woman asked derisively.

Looking at Alex, "Cause now she's with the Lord."

"Well, I hope he likes hamburger."

"There's no point in that," the SP on the other side interjected. He had also been looking at Reverend Zeke. Surreptitiously.

"Well, who's this lord then, old man? The guy who gave the old lady that shotgun?"

"The Lord's the Lord, honey. It's as simple as that."

Poking the machine gun into Reverend Zeke's ribs, "One more 'honey' and you're going to be in the same dog-food can as that old lady."

Innocently, while gesturing with his pipe, "You asked about the Lord, didn't you?"

"Would you shut him up?" the lieutenant hissed, without raising his head from the stretcher.

Teasing Reverend Zeke's shoulder with the gun butt, "You hear that, old man?"

He smiled that he understood and then began slowly to search his breast pocket with his fingers. After a minute he transferred his fingers to his other breast.

"You know, I been wonderin' what's been going on out here," he began philosophically—as if they could just have a perfectly normal conversation.

Raising the gun so that the butt threatened his head, "Didn't I tell you to shut up?"

"Can't you tell he's senile?" the SP on his left complained.

"The lieutenant wants him to shut up."

"The lieutenant's out of it."

"No, Smith." Still looking straight up, his arm, which was now only a nub ending at the elbow, clamped to his chest, "I'm not out of it."

"Well, you ought to be." With concern, as he leaned over from the jump seat, "You want another shot?"

"No." Despairingly, "I just want him to shut up."

"See," the female SP hissed, as she slammed the gun into Reverend Zeke.

After rubbing the spot the gun had struck for a while, Reverend Zeke went back to searching his pockets. Certainly, Alex wondered, he couldn't be looking for a match? That was just the way he looked for matches: kind of absently, while he talked. But if one was in his pants pocket it would be soaking wet. Just as he said that to himself, as if to drive the point home, the boat tilted, sending a small wave sloshing across Reverend Zeke's hips. But even that didn't keep him from turning to his side so that he could dig farther down into his pocket.

Maybe he was senile. Of course, that's what Alex had thought before. In fact, that had been the whole point. But now he wondered.

He pressed his hand against his belly, so that he could feel the magazine through his jumpsuit. Amazing, that it had been there, right in that damned privy, all along. Perhaps that's what Reverend Zeke had meant when he said it could be that he had heard of Piotr Babulieski. At that time Alex had discounted that completely. But maybe he had recalled one of the photographs of Babulieski posing with Father Paul. Maybe there were others. He hadn't had time to look. Perhaps even in other magazines—but they were all ashes by now. Along with the rest of it.

"What you looking for, old man?" the female SP asked suspiciously.

"I told you he's senile," the man on the left said. "Just leave him alone."

"I don't give a damn if he's just had brain surgery." Menacingly, "Whatcha looking for?"

"He's looking for a match," Alex interjected.

"A match?" she laughed, which got several of the others to laugh. "Don't you know that wet matches won't light, old man? Or are you just too," she made a face like a teasing child might, "senile to know that?"

He could see that they were comfortable with that idea. Because that explained why he had been so unshakable. Every time they had asked where the others were, and he had not answered, they had fired a burst from the machine gun just past his head into the wall. And each time he just stood there: unfazed. Even though the bullets had smashed into the side of the house right over his head. Yes. There was no doubt that that explanation suited them. Just as it had suited him to think—when it had first crossed his mind to report them—that they were just lunatics.

Yes. When the man had said, "He's senile," the others jumped on it. Even though, after the business with the machine gun, when he had been completely unshakable, some of them had been affected. Even later, in the boat, he could see that several of them kept looking at him. Trying to figure it out.

But there was more to it than that. In fact, he had the proof. Right inside his jumpsuit.

Which was also the proof that he was an idiot. But how was he to know? That it had been there all the time.

It didn't seem fair.

And then Sister Kate blasting the lieutenant with a shotgun. How could he know that something like that would happen?

It had all seemed so simple. And if everything had gone the way it was supposed to, everybody would have been better off. Or no worse off.

But now things were entirely different. Somehow, when he was sure it had all been a lie—or some kind of delusion—turning them in seemed so right. Now just the thought of it made him weak with anger and disgust.

Reverend Zeke had shifted over to his right so that he could search his left pocket.

"Do you have a match?" Alex asked the SP beside him.

He shook his head.

"Anybody here got a match?" he asked in a louder voice.

The female SP glared at him.

"Or a lighter?" he persisted, this time questioning them with his eyes, one by one.

After a moment the SP nearest the driver reached inside his jumpsuit and pulled out a pack of matches. Alex stepped over, took them, and, after kneeling, extended the matches to Reverend Zeke.

He took them with a nod and pulled out the small pipe he kept in his breast pocket.

"You been fillin' that boy full of ganja?" fired through his head as he stood. Yes, he thought, they had.

When Reverend Zeke touched the match to the pipe, Alex could see its contents brighten into a small red ball. He took a long puff, held it down, and then smiled contentedly.

The female SP looked at Reverend Zeke and him. Alex wondered what she would think if she knew what was in the pipe. Of course, there was no way for her even to guess. Any more than she could guess what was in the magazine. Or what it meant.

Reverend Zeke held his thumb over the bowl for a minute or so and then stuck it back into his pocket. And sat, with his legs crossed. Everything was so simple for him. Or seemed to be. You would never know, from looking at him, that he was in trouble at all. In fact, as Alex looked around the small boat, not one of them seemed so at ease.

And it wasn't just what was in the pipe. After all, he had tried that. No. There was more to it than that. It was more that something else, something inside, made it possible for Reverend Zeke to just smoke his pipe—and take it for granted that everything would be all right.

The boat flew off a large swell, staying airborne for long enough for the occupants to realize it, and exchange glances, before it slammed jarringly back down—which caused the lieutenant to cry out. It was a sharp, animal-like cry that vanished as soon as the boat skidded on its way.

Alex turned toward the windshield: the sky was smoky black, and violently alive.

The boat slammed again, punctuated by another cry from the lieutenant. This time a gasp.

The SP on the right side of Reverend Zeke leaned forward. "Sorry about that, lieutenant. But," with a kind of equivocal lightness, "we're kind of in a hurry. Morrison over there has got the hots for a guy in the patrol division."

The female SP glared suspiciously.

"After all, it's not every day she gets a chance to get fucked in the ass."

The lieutenant looked up blankly.

"You okay, Lieutenant?"

Rising up from the stretcher, looking directly at Reverend Zeke, "Would you shut him up?"

"The old man?"

"Yeah."

"He ain't said anything, Lieutenant. That was me. Just giving Morrison the raspberry."

Still staring at Reverend Zeke, "I'm telling you to shut him up."

"Didja hear the man?" the female SP hissed at Reverend Zeke, before slamming the gun butt into his ribs.

"Just prayin' for you, Lieutenant. Makin' sure the Lord's on the job."

Directing his stare into the man's face, "Shut him up."

"Sure, Lieutenant," the man answered with resignation.

After letting his head back down so that he was staring into the canvas boat top, "Call someone from the political section as soon as we get in."

"Yes, sir."

"And I don't want to hear another word out of him."

The SP turned to Reverend Zeke. "You hear him, old man?"

Reverend Zeke nodded, but as soon as the man was back in the jump seat, he announced, "The Good Book says: pray for your enemies and your friends."

The female SP popped him behind the ear with the gun butt and then said, by way of explanation, "He's the dumbest thing I've ever seen," while she shook her head in disbelief.

Reverend Zeke put his hand to his head and brought it down with blood on it.

"Well, he asked for it," she continued, but the rest of them just shuffled around uncomfortably.

After a minute or two, the man who had dug out the matches said, "Look at that damned stuff. It's hail."

While the female SP marveled, "Can you believe that," Alex tried to convince Reverend Zeke to be quiet: first by just staring, and then by pressing his fingers to his lips.

"You know, I shoulda baptized you, boy," he announced, and then looked out of the corner of his eye for the response from the female SP, but she had inched her way over to the gunwale.

Alex could feel the lieutenant looking at him. He seemed completely befuddled. From shock. Or the injection they had given him.

"'Cause this is going to be one hell of a storm—if the good Lord don't mind my saying so," Reverend Zeke persisted.

"What's he talking about?" the lieutenant hissed.

"I'm talking about Jesus Christ."

"Shut up," Alex pleaded.

"He should know, boy. Considering, he should know."

Jerking telegraphically on Alex's pants leg, "Would you shut him up?"

Alex stood there, completely at a loss.

"Morrison! Morrison!" the lieutenant pleaded in a thin scream, but all of them were absorbed with the hailstorm.

Reverend Zeke leaned forward so that he was on his haunches— no more than a foot or two from the stretcher. "Jesus Christ is life everlasting," he announced.

"Hush," Alex requested softly.

"You know I can't do that, boy. The lieutenant needs me." With a broad smile, "How else's he going to find out about Jesus?"

"Whatcha doing, you damned scumbag?" the female SP bellowed as she pushed Reverend Zeke over with the sole of her boot. "Don't you hear at all?"

"Stop," Alex screamed. "Just stop." He grabbed at the muzzle of the gun, but she wrenched it away, before looking up at him, the gun butt angrily poised to slam into Reverend Zeke's face.

The lieutenant began tugging on his pants leg.

Looking for permission from the lieutenant, "I been told to shut this old man up."

Alex looked down at the lieutenant, who gestured for him to bend over before saying, "I don't understand." He picked his head up, so that he could see Reverend Zeke. "Why'd you report them? It doesn't make any sense."

Before he could answer they were overwhelmed by a horrendous roar.

It sounded, he decided as it was approaching, like a train. But right away, in that compression that occurs when something is about to happen, and happen very fast, but still seems to be taking forever to actually take place, he said to himself, No, what a ridiculous idea. Before he could dispose of that thought it became apparent that the noise was not merely a noise, but something more palpable—as if a sound could have solid form.

He could feel them being lifted into the air as if the ten-meter boat were as light as a piece of broom straw; he could see, or thought he could see, two of the SP being batted into the canvas top like shuttle-cocks. Each of their faces had that look of utter, comical surprise that made him, even while he was watching them, think: No. This must be a dream. Wake up. But even though everything was happening in that dream slow motion that lets you know, yes this is a dream, not something real—so that you can be horrified, but only the way you are in a dream, as opposed to real horror—he knew it was com-pletely real.

And still he was not really afraid. At least not after a second or two. Not the way he should have been, he repeated to himself, in that same dream slow motion that seemed to have trapped everything.

Perhaps it was the sight of Reverend Zeke, sitting there, looking awestruck. But not in terror, like the others. No, it was more the kind of look a child might have on a roller coaster. Or something more spectacular.

As if he had fully expected it. The way a child, after getting on board knows this is a roller coaster, and the ride is going to be spec-tacular—but, in spite of knowing what it is, and fully expecting it, is nevertheless filled with awe at the power of it all at the moment of its happening.

As Alex reached for him it became dark. Not the way it *becomes* dark at night. Or even the way it gets dark when a cloud passes in front of the sun. No. This was sudden. And absolute. The way the shadow cast by a rock in a child's hand must seem sudden and abso-lute to an ant that is about to be smashed. But here the rock seemed only to be that locomotive roar, which was so nearly palpable that it could blot out the sun.

When it hit it felt as if his eardrums would burst.

And then it was suddenly and mysteriously quiet. Much more sud-denly quiet than was physically possible, he decided, before the elec-tric jolt of cold let him know he was underwater. Odd, it was so jet-black and cold he couldn't seem to remember which way was up, but instead of feeling panicky he found himself just dreading the return to the surface, which, for that instant, seemed to consist of that deafening sound and nothing else.

But when he surfaced there was only rain. And he realized that his fist was wrapped around the vee in the back of Reverend Zeke's overalls. Very quickly, as if what must have surely been a tornado bred by the thunderstorm could be hiding, ready to pounce on them from behind, he corkscrewed his body a full three hundred and sixty degrees—Reverend Zeke still tightly in his grasp. There was nothing. Whatever it was had simply evaporated. Or raced on to smash into something else.

And then he realized the boat was gone. He bounced up and down trying to see over the ground swells, thinking he might catch sight of another bobbing head. Or a piece of debris. But they were surrounded by jagged, foot-high mountains that made it impossible to see what was in the next valley. Or the next.

He almost hollered out. To check if someone was twenty feet away. Or thirty. But he didn't. Instead, with Reverend Zeke in tow, he began swimming toward the shore, which appeared, not as beach, or marsh grass, but as a fuzzy, not too distant mountain of greenery that dwarfed the ground swells.

After a few strokes he could tell they were in one of the countless inlets connecting the waterway to the Atlantic—which appeared simply as a blank spot in the horizon. Instead of resisting the outgoing tide, he merely angled them toward the green spot that he now could tell was treetops.

"Now that was God Almighty," Reverend Zeke announced. He had been lying flat on his back looking straight up into the rain for two or three minutes. And had not said a word.

As soon as he spoke, Alex felt a surge of electricity spread through his body. Along with an uncontrollable urge to laugh.

"Yes, that was the Lord," Reverend Zeke said with finality.

Alex shivered. Not from the cold. But from excitement. And laughed until a mouthful of seawater started him choking.

"You all right, boy?" Reverend Zeke boomed out.

"Yes. I'm fine."

"Well, have you ever seen anything to beat that?" he asked with obvious satisfaction.

"No," Alex choked out.

"You can wait a lifetime and never feel God that close," Reverend Zeke noted philosophically. "A lifetime."

The treetops were getting sharper. And around them there was white, fuzzy sand.

378

"You know the story of Jonah, boy?"

"No," he puzzled, his attention fixed on the beach for a second before returning to the more comfortable position of looking back as he pulled water toward them with his right hand.

"Well, Jonah was swallowed by a whale. A huge whale. Which wasn't good. He was," Reverend Zeke twisted his head back so that they were facing one another, "in a fix. Sorta like we were."

There wasn't a hint of anger in his eyes. Or even disapproval. He must have known that Alex had brought the SP there.

"And of course," he turned back so that he was flat on his back, "Jonah prayed for the Lord to save him. Which is what I was doing. While I was thinking about Jonah."

Yes. But for some reason he was willing to act as if it had never happened at all. That feeling of disgust—which he had tried to rid himself of by vomiting, but which had just stayed there, in the pit of his stomach—was gone.

"What was so special about Jonah that made the Lord save him? I was wondering. And you know what that was?"

Yes. It was completely gone.

Repeating, "You know what that was, boy?"

"Tell me," he replied.

"Why, it was simple. He believed." Reverend Zeke began chuckling. "And he prayed. So I thought, I believe. And," the chuckling turned into laughter, "I prayed. I said, 'God, just make this here storm blow this boat away.' And He sure as hell did!" The deep laughter boomed across the water over the sound of the rain. "And," he turned again, so that he could look at Alex, to gauge his reaction, "and you saw what happened?"

As Alex was about to reply he realized they could stand. In fact, the water was just to their waists.

"Don't ever forget that, boy. It never hurts to pray when you're in trouble."

Distractedly, because it was dawning on him where they were, "I thought you were praying for the lieutenant." He found himself searching the inlet, which, in the light, steady rain, seemed much wider than it was.

"Oh, I was." Reverend Zeke turned toward the inlet. "I was."

Still searching the water, convincing himself as he did that the

379

lieutenant was drowned, "It doesn't make much sense to pray for both."

"Oh, I don't worry about things like that. Me, I do the prayin'. And I leave it to the Lord to sort it all out."

Yes, that seemed simple enough, Alex decided, as he looked first at Reverend Zeke, who still had that awestruck, boylike expression, and then up at the dune—which, fenced in by sea oats, towered thirty or forty feet above them just on the other side of the narrow beach.

No wonder the inlet had seemed so familiar. Even though he hadn't been able to see much of anything in the rain. His house was less than five kilometers away, directly on the other side of the old dune. Which meant that there were Russian SP all over the place— and that they would have to find some way to get Reverend Zeke off the island.

Maybe they could cross the inlet. In a few hours, when the tide was coming back in. But now the deep channel, which had carried them there so effortlessly from the inland waterway, would probably drag them out into the Atlantic. Of course, if they could get hold of a boat, they could... and then he noticed first a head, and then shoulders, rise up out of the inlet.

"Run," Alex blurted out.

The black-clad figure was only ten meters away, shaking off the water while trying to get his bearings.

"Stay down," Alex whispered, "and head into those dunes."

But it was too late. He could tell that the SP saw them.

"Hurry," he hissed, which sent Reverend Zeke stumbling across the narrow strip of sand toward the sea oats.

The SP was trudging through the waist-deep water, looking directly at him. He tried to make out which one it was. If it was the female there was certainly no hope.

"Stop that man," the SP forced out between gasping for air.

It was the one who had given him the matches. The one who had been looking so intently at Reverend Zeke.

"Did you hear me?" He was splashing through ankle-deep water, reaching for his sidearm. When he got abreast of Alex he stopped, looked at him for an instant, and then knelt with his pistol extended.

Reverend Zeke was just at the edge of the sea oats.

"Halt! Halt or I'll fire!"

380

"No," Alex screamed, as he reached down toward the gun. "Wait!"

The gun fired just as he grabbed the man's wrists. He could feel the recoil.

"Are you out of your mind?" the SP struggled out in disbelief as they rolled to the ground. "That man is a dangerous criminal."

"No. He's not. You know he's not." The pistol was wedged between them, pointing up. "I saw the way you were looking at him."

"You're as loony as he is," he replied convincingly. But for an instant there was a flicker of hesitation in his eyes. As if he had at least considered the possibility.

And then the gun went off. The bullet entered right under his throat and blew the top of his head off.

Alex lay there for a second, feeling the rain falling on his back. Odd, in that one moment, while the man was hesitating, he had been able to push the gun into his chest. Now it was resting there. Like an ashtray on a table.

Alex stood, peered down at the man for an instant, and then, after stooping to a half-crouch, scanned the inlet for evidence of the rest of the SP. There was nothing. But the last time there had been nothing either. Until the man just appeared.

Odd, his heart was pounding—he could hear it even in the rain—but he felt very cool. He picked the gun up off the man's chest, put it in his pocket, and, after sliding his hands under the man's armpits, dragged him out into the inlet. By the time it was waist-deep he could feel the channel racing parallel to the shore into the Atlantic. In another step or two the sloping shelf he was on would turn sharply downward. He worked his way around to the man's feet and shoved him out into the channel. In a second or two he had vanished, like the police boat, and the rest of them.

Still looking out into the channel, he began inching his way back toward the shore. After a few steps, without stopping completely, he splashed his face and chest with water. And then dumped several handfuls over his head. But even then he wasn't sure he had gotten off all the blood. The man's face had been just a few inches away when the gun went off. He let himself slide down into the water, which was only up to his waist when he knelt, and carefully washed his face and neck and hair. As soon as he had finished he headed up toward the dune.

Before he was halfway across the beach he could see Reverend Zeke sitting there, a foot or two into the sea oats. He was facing inland. More or less erect. He looked very odd, sitting there, staring up at the old dune, with a few scraggly brown sea oats on either side of him.

"We can't stay out here," he whispered as he broke into a trot. "Some of the others could have come ashore farther down." Breathlessly, after he had come to a stop beside him, "We can hide in there." He pointed at the dune. "At least for a while."

Smiling, "That might be a little too much of a climb for me."

"That?" he puzzled out loud before turning to him.

"That's a great-lookin' old dune, ain't it?"

"Yeah," Alex replied. "It's all hollow inside—like a volcano."

"You know," Reverend Zeke offered philosophically, "a long time ago—when they didn't know no better—they thought volcanoes was gods."

"They did?" Alex replied mechanically, while reaching down for Reverend Zeke's arm.

"Definitely. Of course, in Jamaica there're people who thinks this thing's a god. And that thing." Reproachfully, "Even though they been taught better."

"Here, let me get you up," Alex offered as he lifted the old man's arm so that he could slide it across his shoulder.

"If you say so," Reverend Zeke replied agreeably.

As soon as he began to lift him he saw the blood, which, for a second, he thought had come from him—from the SP's head exploding right next to him. Which produced a shiver of repulsion. But right away he knew that there couldn't still be blood left from that. Not that much.

"Looks like I'm leakin' a little," Reverend Zeke announced matter-of-factly.

"Yes," Alex replied. He pressed his finger to the hole in the bib of the overalls; and then looked in the back, where the bullet must have entered. He could feel himself wanting to cry out—just to scream.

He lifted the old man up, and with him draped across his shoulder, they climbed up the side of the old dune.

"Look's like the weather's breakin'," Reverend Zeke observed as they sat down.

382

"Yes," Alex agreed.

They sat there for a few minutes, at the crest, looking directly out across the inlet, which now, as the rain slowed to a stop, could be seen racing out into the Atlantic. On either side you could see the breakers, which looked as though they had been pushed aside.

"I'm sorry. I," Alex began softly.

"How long you think this old dune's been here?" Reverend Zeke asked as if he hadn't heard Alex at all. "A thousand years? Yep," he said with an authoritative nod, while his hand began searching his breast pocket, which was dark red with blood. "Or more. And you know what?"

"Don't you want to know why I did it?" Alex pleaded.

"You know what?" he repeated.

"What?"

"I'll bet that even this old boy, as old as he is, ain't never seen a real miracle. Until today. Well," he announced with satisfaction, "I have. And if it hadn't been for what you done, how else would I have seen a miracle?"

Alex nodded.

"I mean, most folks go all their lives and never see a real miracle. At least not one they can recognize."

After a moment, rather suddenly, he said, "You know, boy, I shoulda baptized you."

Alex nodded.

When he smiled a trickle of blood inched down the corner of his mouth onto his beard. And he didn't say anything else. After a while Alex knew he was dead, but he left him sitting there for a while— looking out into the Atlantic.

The late-afternoon sun had broken out behind them and was shining through the mixture of water oak and oleander leaves that rimmed the old dune. You could see all the way across the inlet now. And down the beach to his right, the solar reflectors were now the shade of dying embers.

He took Reverend Zeke down to the bottom of the dune and rested him against one of the water oaks, while he scooped out a long place in the sand. Odd, this was just the place where he had kept his mysteries. And The Book.

After he had covered him up he made a small cross from oak branches and stuck it in the ground—just like Reverend Zeke had been doing that first day he saw him.

Then he pulled the magazine from out of his belt. It was wet and soggy, but still in one piece.

There were two pages of pictures to go with the story about Father Paul. Wet, so that the print from the back side of the paper showed through, they seemed out of focus and grainy. But looking at them, especially the ones with Piotr Babulieski, produced a strange feeling of completeness. A kind of certitude, which made all of it seem worthwhile. Even the one of Babulieski at his trial—where he looked so lost.

And he would have it here. So that he could look at it anytime he wanted. So that he would know what happened.

He dug out a place next to Reverend Zeke and placed the magazine there. That would have to do for now, he decided as he started to push the sand over it. He would just leave it there. Like he had The Book. And his mysteries.

But that idea—which had seemed the only thing to do with The Book, and the mysteries—created a feeling of complete emptiness.

If, after all, there was some point in it, could it be right just to bury it here? So that he could look at it from time to time. To convince himself. The way he had looked at the picture book Dr. Vinkov had given him.

He picked it up, slipped it back into the waistband of his jumpsuit, and climbed out of the dune.

Lights were just beginning to appear in the houses. You could see them scattered here and there like fireflies along the edge of a creek. He sat on the crest of the dune and watched them come on, one by one, until the entire eastern side of the island was a glowing, firefly necklace that curled up the beach to the lighthouse before fading into nothing.

Soon the lighthouse beacon would begin scanning the beach. He glanced back down into the old dune, which had been the home of all his secret treasures—and would always be the focus of all his memories of the island—and then descended to the beach.

On his way to the house he let himself think about the dune. All the sumptuous afternoons he had lounged in the cool sand. And read his mysteries. With the pages splotched with shadows of oleander and oak leaves. And about Martina Antipova. And her huge breasts, which now, for some odd reason, seemed very funny.

Too bad there was no way to go back to that, he thought sadly. But that was impossible, apart from just remembering it—in that controlled sort of pretense that allows, just for some fixed span of time, like ten minutes, or half an hour, the suspension of everything that has happened.

He entered through the side door that opened directly into the hallway. His mother's room was shut. And so was his father's study. But a bit of light was leaking out from under the door.

"Alex?" his father questioned from his desk after Alex had pushed the door open. "We weren't expecting you tonight. I'm afraid you've missed dinner." The colored screen of the DAL terminal illuminated his face. "But then, dinner isn't what it used to be here now that you're off to school. We hardly bother."

He rolled his chair a little to his left so that he could reach the decanter that had been left just on the edge of the disk of white light cast by the bent-over desk lamp. "Let me pour you a vodka." Thoughtfully, as he looked up, so that his hand was pouring the drink unaided by his eyes, "You're something of a mess. You must have been caught outdoors in the storm?"

"Yes," Alex agreed.

"Well, this will warm you up." He extended the glass. "So, what," he paused to pick up his glass and then gestured with it in the fashion of a small, discreet toast, "have you been up to in school?"

"Reading."

"Well, in school there's always reading," he replied as he rolled back in front of the screen.

"Did you see the book that I found?"

Without looking up from the keyboard, "What book was that?"

"It's a book by a man called Piotr Babulieski," he forced out over the light clicking of the keyboard. "About the time of," he hesitated, "what's called the Great Uprising." The keyboard stopped clicking. "The last I saw it, Dr. Vinkov had it."

After a long pause, "There may have been some mention of that in the medical report."

"Did you read it?"

"Why should I do that?"

"Is it in there?" He pointed at the terminal.

"Of course not. You can't expect to find the ravings of every lunatic in the DAL system. That would be absurd."

"There are a lot of things that are not in there, aren't there? Things that have been just left out."

"Certainly you can't expect to find scribblings from some person in an institution in there."

Ignoring him, "And some things are just plain lies."

"No." Conclusively, "What's in the DAL system is the truth. That's the whole purpose behind it."

"What if I could prove to you that there are lies in it?"

"Now, of course there are errors. Nothing this large can be free of errors."

Shaking his head, "I don't mean errors. I mean lies."

Humoring him, "What kind of lies?"

"Huge, terrible lies."

"Look, I think," he spoke soothingly, "that perhaps you should take a few days off from school. So that you can rest completely."

"Find New York City in there."

"Really, after a few days' rest, you won't know yourself."

"Find New York City," Alex repeated.

"Fine," he acquiesced with a shrug. "If it's that important to you. That is a city?"

As Alex nodded, he wondered if it was possible that his father just didn't know.

"A question of geography," he said to himself as his face took on the blue-and-red patina of the screen.

"Or history," Alex added softly, as he listened to the keys clicking. And then silence. And then more clicking.

"There is no such place," his father announced when he looked up.

"I know."

Nurov screwed up his face, which was still grotesquely colored by the screen.

"It doesn't exist any longer. But," emphatically, "it used to."

"When was that?" Nurov asked.

"It was there until seventy years ago. And then," he offered quietly, "a year or two later, it was gone."

Nurov leaned back in his chair and rested his interlocked fingers on his chest.

"Destroyed," Alex exhaled.

It was obvious that the time had not been lost on him. But he didn't seem shocked. He must know after all, Alex decided with a mixture of disappointment and resignation.

"And that's why it's not in there," Alex announced with quiet authority.

"Well, then there never was such a place. But," humoring him, "if it will make you feel better, we can look further. Perhaps if we conduct a historical search."

The keys began to click again.

Of course, he wouldn't find it. Alex had looked a dozen times himself.

The most terrible thing about it was not just that they had lied. He could see why they had done that. There probably were things too horrible for everyone to know. Which is certainly what his father would say. And there was something, about hiding that one point, that made a certain sense. But that they could just remove it from existence as if it never happened—that was what was so terrible. Even if it was buried in there, deep in the DAL system, that would be better than removing it altogether.

"There was no such place," his father announced matter-of-factly, after sliding his chair away from the screen.

Alex unzipped his jumpsuit and pulled out the magazine. "There was," Alex began quietly, "such a place." He walked around to his father's side of the desk and spread the magazine out. He opened it carefully so as not to damage the wet pages.

"That," he announced, while pointing at a photograph, "is New York City."

The caption read: "Father Paul Creticos marches down New York City's Fifth Avenue."

"Where did this come from?" his father asked with interest.

"Something I acquired while doing my patriotic duty."

"Really," Nurov replied distractedly, his face a few inches above the open magazine.

"Yes."

"Well, this is something of an artifact. Or at least appears to be one." After a moment he looked up, as if what Alex had said had just dawned on him.

"This means that," Alex leaned over so that his face was directly in

front of his father's, "the whole damned thing's a lie. Just a huge lie."
Disgustedly, "The Great Uprising!—the great lie would be more like
it."

His father raised his brow. Odd, he didn't even seem angry. He just
raised his brow in a way that said: Don't say another word.

Stammering, "Doesn't that bother you? Well, it makes me sick to
my stomach. You can't murder twelve million people, like that," he
snapped his fingers, "and just let them vanish as if it never happened."

"I see nothing in here," he tapped his finger on the photograph,
"about murder. Nothing at all."

"Then why," Alex hissed, "isn't it in there? Or," he moved his
finger from the terminal to the bookshelves, "in any of those?"

"It is apparent that you have not completely recovered from your
breakdown." Firmly, "But you've got to get a grip on yourself. It's one
thing for you to say," he paused, "unwise things in here. After all, we
understand what you've been through."

"There's nothing wrong with me."

"Then you would have no objection to seeing your doctor." Calcu-
latedly, "To confirm that."

Pulling the pistol from his pocket, "I want you to listen. Just listen."

"Where did you get that?" he asked, as if the pistol were a toy—
even though it was quite clear that it was real.

"From a patriotic member of the American SP who died doing his
duty."

"You really have gone over the deep end."

"No."

"No?"

"Actually, I was doing my duty too. At least I had been. Funny, if I
had just left well enough alone, I never would have found out. But
no. I had to do my duty. Helping round up dangerous lunatics is
doing your duty, isn't it?"

Nurov stared at him uncomfortably.

"But then I had to stumble across this." He planted his finger on
the magazine. "And everything changed."

"No. Nothing changed."

"I mean, they weren't dangerous lunatics at all. And they had
trusted me."

388

"Who were these people?"

"Christians."

Gravely, "These cults are very dangerous. You must know that. No, perhaps you don't. I suspect you've been seduced by them. And that they've filled your head full of all kinds of outrageous lies."

"No." Pointing the pistol at the terminal, "That is where the lies are." As he looked into the blank screen, exactly what must be done came to him. "I want you to make an entry in the system."

"Just stop and think for a second."

"No." He motioned with the pistol. "I want to enter a book. The title of the book," he began, "is *The Plot to Kill Paul Creticos*."

Nurov sat there.

"It will explain everything."

"Naturally," he replied with resignation.

Alex recounted it as best he could. In as close to the way Babulieski told it as he could, except that here and there, he added things in brackets for clarity. Things like "Jesus Christ is not a general, as you might think—He is the Son of God."

Even when he described the destruction of New York City, his father said nothing, so that it was impossible to tell whether it was completely new to him or something he was aware of.

When they were finished he poured a glass of vodka for himself. And one for Nurov.

Nurov picked up the vodka glass and sipped from it with his face a few inches above the magazine. "And this interesting artifact you got..." he inquired as he scanned the photographs and captions. Odd, he seemed much more interested in the magazine than The Book. Perhaps he had known all along.

Alex stepped up to the terminal.

logoff
CONNECT TIME 2 HOURS 11 MINUTES

He touched the keyboard.

SATURDAY MAY 10, 145
PLEASE ENTER YOUR AUTHORIZATION CODE: _ _ _ _ _

He entered "an001."

PASSWORD?

As he typed the password the cursor skipped blankly across the screen.

    GOOD MORNING, ALEXANDER.
    WHAT CAN I DO FOR YOU?
    bibliographical search
    SUBJECT/AUTHOR/TITLE?
    author
    DO YOU WISH TO BE PROMPTED?
    no
    ENTER AUTHOR.
    babulieski, piotr
    THERE ARE TWO TITLES BY AUTHOR PIOTR BABULIESKI:
    THE PLOT TO KILL PAUL CRETICOS
    MY CAMPAIGNS AGAINST THE RUSSIANS

He put the cursor by the first title and pressed the blue key.

    [The original text of this book was destroyed by the au-
    thorities in 144 A.R. The following is an attempt to recon-
    struct it.]

He hit the space bar to page; and then hit it again.

Yes. There it was. Accessible to anyone. Waiting. Just the way he would have wanted it. "I have buried the truth in a hundred places," he repeated to himself. Yes. That's just the way he would have wanted it.

"And where did you get this interesting artifact?" Nurov repeated, his face still buried in the old magazine.

"Things were much different then from what I supposed," Alex remarked, hoping that would trigger some reaction.

"How's that?" his father replied.

"Well, look at the people. They don't look like slaves. And..."

Closing the magazine, "Things like this can be very deceiving. This was produced to titillate the rich, so of course it reflects their view of capitalist society. Which accounts for why everyone looks so well fed."

390

"It's more than that. They look happy."

"Those were just models."

"Models?"

"Actors. They were paid to look happy."

"Paid to look happy?"

"Well, after a fashion. They were actually paid to sell products. It was called advertising."

"So, you were aware of what had happened all along?"

"What was that?" Nurov replied obliquely.

"That the Great Uprising never occurred. That the whole thing is a fabrication."

"It occurred just as you were taught."

"No. I know that it didn't."

"You suppose that it didn't."

"Next, you'll tell me there was no New York City. That I'm just hallucinating the entire thing."

"No. But you are not seeing things clearly."

"How can you deny something so obvious?" Alex stammered with frustration.

"In what way would we be better off if your version of what happened were true?"

"That's not the issue."

"But of course it's the issue." Filling his glass, "What purpose does history have if it can't guide us? Does your version of what happened offer anything but—"

"The truth," Alex interrupted. "That's all. It's simply what was."

"That, my son, is a completely amoral view of history."

"Have you known, all along?"

"Known? Actually, there is another completely plausible way to look at this." Alex could feel the pistol in his hand. Rather than being cold or distant it felt sticky—the way something alive feels sticky. "There was a New York City. Of course there was. Which these photographs verify. And books like the one you encountered mention." He recalled Piotr Babulieski, sitting there, on the stage behind Father Paul. With the pistol hidden in his waistband. "In those days nuclear power was a new thing. And, in the absence of our technological expertise, a not completely safe thing. I suspect if we were able to examine all the records—there are raw records, you

391

know, that are so far undigested—we would find that a nuclear power plant exploded and destroyed the entire city. And made it uninhabitable. Even today. Some sixty odd years afterward."

While he listened he was able to see them all. Clearly. On the stage. Now that he had seen the photographs it was easy. Even Dietra Christian.

And at the same time he could hear every word his father was saying. And could understand exactly what he meant.

"And of course, in order not to alarm people unduly—especially the many people who live near nuclear power facilities—it has been necessary to leave the event unreported. Of course, at some future time, reporting it may be the correct thing to do."

Smiling, "Naturally an event of that magnitude would give rise to rumors. And distortions."

When he had shot him, just as he did he had screamed, "Antichrist." Yes. That's exactly what he had screamed. Antichrist. Odd. It wasn't until that moment that Alex had any idea of what that meant. But now he did.

"Now, you see, there is a perfectly sensible explanation. And certainly it is time for us to end this silliness. Before it gets out of hand." He rolled over to the terminal and reached for the keyboard.

Alex fired the pistol before his finger touched the keyboard. The screen exploded—leaving a leering cavity.

Nurov stared into the terminal, which now resembled a shocked, toothless old man, and then, after turning in his chair, tilted his head to the side, as if he were about to ask a question. But after a moment he just stood, looked down at the terminal again, and then pushed the chair aside.

"You are completely out of your mind," he said disgustedly. His face was ash-white.

Now he would have to leave the island to delete it, Alex said to himself. Which could take an hour or two.

"That was a meaningless gesture," Nurov hissed tiredly, as he brushed past him, rounding the corner of the desk. The pistol dragged across his elbow on the way by. "Put that damned thing down before someone gets hurt."

"The thing about the truth," Alex announced, "is that you can't just erase it completely."

"What do you know about the truth?"

392

Alexander?" his mother asked from the door. In a sleepy, relaxed way that was only slightly frayed by annoyance, "Did you hear that awful noise?"

"It was your son demanding a psychiatric evaluation."

Puzzled, "There was an awful noise." Her eyes had that faraway look. But then when she looked down at the pistol, which was still dangling at his side, they narrowed slightly. And then she looked at the terminal.

"I," Nurov shook his head, "am on my way to call Vinkov. Perhaps he can fathom all this."

"Over that?" she questioned, pointing to the terminal. Her voice was dry from having been asleep, but almost musical—like a little girl's music box.

"It's his job to be able to unravel things like this," Nurov mumbled as he disappeared into the hallway.

"What have you done?" she asked. Not in an accusatory way. Just in bafflement. The way you might ask, when you first wake up in the morning, what a dream means.

Alex collapsed into the chair. Odd. He was tired. Almost tired enough to sleep. Except that his hands were trembling. He looked down at the pistol, which was now in his lap, and put it on the desk.

"You look awful," his mother said as she glided over toward him.

"Yes."

She cupped her hand along his temple, so that her thumb was just touching the birthmark. He could smell the hint of gardenia in her hair, which, instead of being fresh and clear, smelled of stale sleep. Gazing into the birthmark, "Perhaps you should just go to bed. I'll handle Nurov. He's not half the bear he makes out to be."

Her eyes had that faraway look he had seen a thousand times. So that it seemed that she was halfway across the universe. In a place where everyone was perfectly composed.

"There's something I have to do," he said quietly.

"At this hour?"

Rising, "This is the last chance I'll get."

"Nurov has just lost his temper. Why, as soon as you write Sonia Ouspenskaya, he will have forgotten completely." As if it didn't really matter at all, while gesturing toward the shattered terminal with her head, "Why did you do that? You know how Nurov is about that damned thing."

"Because," her hand fell from his face, "as Piotr Babulieski says: God hates a lie."

"Babulieski?" she repeated comically.

He nodded. "That's him right there," he replied with his finger pressed to the photograph in the open magazine.

She glanced down, apparently completely puzzled for a second or two, but then, as the words, which could mean nothing to her, worked around in her head, he could see it dawning on her that it was all starting up again. She changed color. As if she might throw up.

"I'm not a complete lunatic, you know," he said from the door. "Even though it looks that way."

"No?" She began laughing. Very loudly. It was that same laugh he remembered from the night they had gone swimming.

As he walked down the hallway, he could still hear her laughing. And then he could hear her ask, "Did you reach Vinkov?"

"No," his father replied tiredly. "I left a message for him to call."

"You see where that got us last time?" The raw edge from the laughter was still there.

"I'm afraid there's no choice."

"Certainly things can't be that serious," he heard her say in a near whisper as he escaped through the door.

Did she really think it could all be smoothed over with a few whispers? Perhaps she did. Because there was no way for her to know.

The night air was cool. And silent, except for the wind, which seemed, when you listened carefully, to be carrying those distant voices he had first heard at Corinne's.

Epilogue

As soon as they left the little church—that had been used to cure tobacco, or as a smokehouse—he could feel the sweat exploding from his body into the air.

And he felt kind of giddy. From being up all night. And from the sudden rush of fresh air.

They descended along the ragtag path down to the river, in a long line: singing.

Yes, it was just like before. But this time, instead of both being there and being far away, there was just himself there—which felt completely different. Even though they were lined up along the bank in the same way. With that same look of expectation. And this time, curiosity.

Lester stood in the water, waist-deep, and waited for him. He was smiling; but serious—the way a man might be serious about work he enjoys.

Taking Alex's head in his hands, "Are you ready to be saved?"

He nodded.

The water was cool. And he could feel it flowing. Very slowly.

"Are you saved?" Lester asked when he came back up. His voice was solid, but didn't seem loud enough to carry up to the bank. But he knew it was. He could remember that from before. With the little girl.

He shook his head, but Lester was unconvinced, and sent him down again.

Yes, he thought, with his eyes wide open under the water. That's just what he would say, the next time up. "Yes," which would be what they all knew he would say. Even though they would be looking down at him as if the result were in suspense. Yes, he thought.

"Are you saved?"

"Yes," he stammered out through the water as it poured off his head back into the stream. "Yes," he repeated, loud enough for Reverend Zeke to hear—if you could still hear in heaven.

And when he went down again, for what he knew would be the last time, Piotr Babulieski came to mind. And he thought, Yes, maybe he can hear too. And, Yes, it's all there for everyone to see. Just the way he would have wanted it. And even if it's only for a week, or a day, or an hour, someone else will see it. And know.

Lester drew him to his chest and slammed his hand against his back.

"Yes."

And they were all smiling. And he thought, Yes, I know exactly what she was feeling when she left the stream. Odd. That day, he couldn't understand. But now it seemed so simple. "Yes."

And he smiled back at them.

Yes, he thought, now I understand: and no matter what they do—later—there is no way they can take away this one moment of sheer bliss.